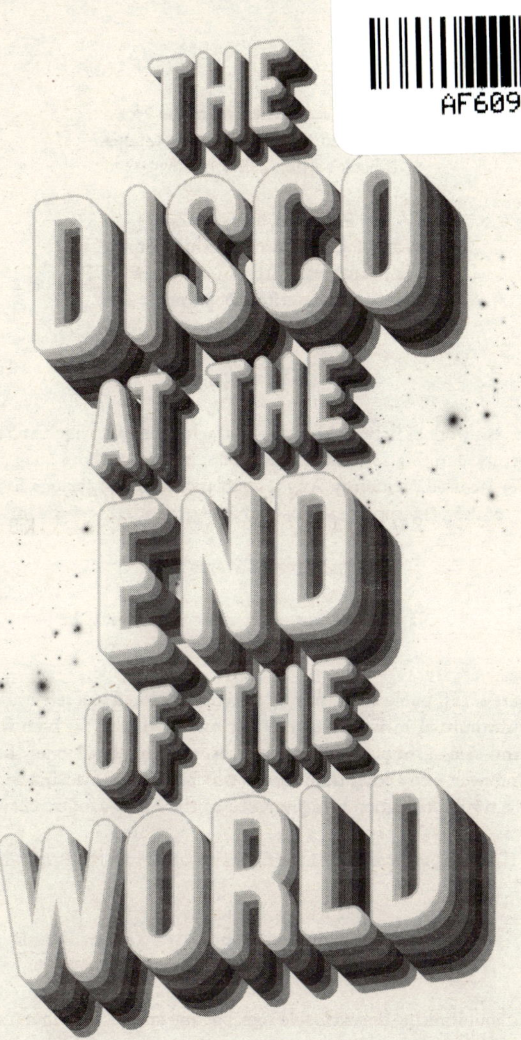

NATHAN TAVARES

TITAN BOOKS

The Disco at the End of the World
Print edition ISBN: 9781835414194
E-book edition ISBN: 9781835414200

Published by Titan Books
A division of Titan Publishing Group Ltd
144 Southwark Street, London SE1 0UP
www.titanbooks.com

First edition: June 2026
10 9 8 7 6 5 4 3 2

A CIP catalogue record for this title is available from the British Library.

EU RP (for authorities only)
eucomply OÜ, Pärnu mnt. 139b-14, 11317 Tallinn, Estonia
hello@eucompliancepartner.com, +33757690241

Designed and typeset in Raritas by Richard Mason.

Printed and bound by CPI (UK) Ltd, Croydon CR0 4YY.

"A rousing cosmic battle cry for people who refuse to bow to petty captains and authoritarian regimes. The novel is also a love story that takes bold gestures and yearning to new heights. I was hooked from the start. His skillful intertwining of creeping political oppression and cultural rebellion creates a riveting portrait of clever misfits remaining true to themselves as the walls around them begin to close in—as queer joy and subversiveness prove vital to queer survival."

RASHEED NEWSON, bestselling author of *My Government Means to Kill Me*, *There's Only One Sin in Hollywood*, and executive producer of the drama series *Bel-Air*.

"Retrofuturistic space, disco dancing, and fighting fascism. This book does it all!"

CALVIN JAMES, author of *Affairs of State*

PRAISE FOR NATHAN TAVARES

"A very beautiful, tender portrait of a romance, its unremarkable mundanity made precious against the backdrop of so many iterations... [A] delightful, spiraling, idiosyncratic book that uses the language and techniques of filmmaking to structure a more interesting reading experience."

The New York Times

"A powerful and touching love story."

The Times

"Populated by some of the best sci-fi has to offer... The multiverse trope offers an easy and entertaining vehicle for very deep philosophical lessons about what it takes to grow up at any age."

New Scientist

ALSO BY NATHAN TAVARES
AND AVAILABLE FROM TITAN BOOKS

Welcome to Forever
A Fractured Infinity

ONE

CONTRABAND

Delivery day for the base always feels like Christmas. Through the window of the airlock door, I eye the guys unloading the steel shipping crates from the rovers. I'm technically off duty, but picking up deliveries is the best use of rec time. In their space suits with their fishbowl helmets, the twenty guys are little tin men in a tin room, against the lead-pencil-sketch backdrop of the moon. The day's haul is thirty crates—supplies to last us the next three months—and the tin men line them up on the floor. The loading dock door rolls shut behind them, sealing the airlock off from the permanent night outside. Drumming my fingers on my hand truck, I watch them crank open each lid with a crowbar. I could help, but staying outta the way saves me from hearing jokes about Mitch the Queer with his delicate hands, who doesn't want to break a nail.

The guys get one joke like that, each. I'm not totally unreasonable. Two jokes and they're cut off. Booted out of the Lodge. Goodbye, booze, mags and cigs. The starmen learn real fast that they don't have to be my friend, but I'm not taking shit from them either.

I learned a lot about how it works to be gay from my Uncles back home in Miami—not Uncles by blood, but something deeper—as I watched them hover around Ma, backstage at the Calypso Room. Pouring her drinks, and cackling, and laughing in that space where they could be themselves. Uncle Javi clocked the swaying way I walked early on, and was the first one to look out for me.

"They'll let you be queer, Mitchy," he told me, trailing cigar smoke backstage. "As long as you're useful to them."

The *Thems* in their space suits weave through the lines of crates, and Webber, the shift commander, opens the inner airlock door. I shuffle out of the way as the starmen clunk in on their magnetic boots and yank off their helmets. I stick to the wall and let them look through me like I'm not even here. The airlock already stinks of sweat. The starmen jostle each other and wriggle out of their space suits, down to the red jumpsuits all two hundred of us on the base wear, and stow their gear. An instant airlock locker room. My turn to look past them, now. Looking would only prove that I'm the leery perv machine some of them think I am. And lusting after straight boys is so boring, anyhow.

Besides, I've got work to do.

Webber tells the starmen to double-check the seals on their suits and clean their helmets before they load everything into storage. Code for *Everyone look the other way and let Ward work*. I bounce my fingers off my head at him in a mock salute. He only rolls his eyes and taps his wrist.

Heard. I roll into the loading bay. The steel walls are painted a deep butch blue and slashed with white block letters: *ADAMS LOADING DOCK* 7. I check the foam-lined crates as I go. Nothing in the first three. The fourth crate—bingo. A red fire extinguisher stares up at me from a pile of shredded newspaper and foam chunks. Something red on the top layer is the signal from the guys in shipping down at the Columbia Space Center in Florida. *Red marks the spot.*

I dig past the fire extinguisher, and boxes of bolts for the base expansion project, and *bam*. Five cartons of Marlboro Reds.

Holy smokes, the whole base will be puffing coins into my pockets.

I drop the cartons in my cart and keep rolling. I find a stash of Old Spice deodorant and a couple of bottles of Jovan Musk in the next crate. The way the Lodge has been stinking up the last week, I'm happy for those. Two crates down, I spot eight twelve-packs of Bud. Then six bottles of Jack Daniels wrapped up in T-shirts, six of Maker's Mark, and eight of Captain Morgan. That one's special. I'll mix it up with Kool-Aid and trade cigs for some extra oranges from the mess hall to whip up some punch for tonight's show.

Under a red tarp, the last crate is loaded up with the real payload: twenty issues of *Playboy*, twenty of *Penthouse*, fifteen of *Heavy Naturals*, ten of *Blonde on Blonde*. The boys will pay primo to buy those—plus I'll let them rent some time in the supply closet of the Lodge to *read* them in private.

My special deliveries are wrapped up in extra jumpsuits in the last crate, like the boys in supply don't even want to look at what I asked for. They bitch about them until, every now and then, I have to threaten to boot them out of the ring. One issue of *Mandate*, one of *Honcho*, one of *Manpower*. *Honcho's* February 1977 issue—a special report on the leather scene according to the cover, with a dark-haired muscle god in a black leather harness scowling at me—is the most recent, even if it's two months old. Finally, wadded up in the April 6, 1977 sports page of the *Cape Canaveral Times*: a tube of Revlon Cadillac Red lipstick.

Webber's dry cough floats over the butch blue of the loading dock. I don't need to look back to see that's his tell. *Move your ass*, I can practically hear his voice in my head.

I slip the lipstick in one of the side leg pockets of my jumpsuit. I'll inspect *Manpower* and the other special deliveries later, when I'm alone. Quality control.

I toss the haul into my crate and wheel out of the supply room.

* * *

Outside the airlock, the hallways are bleeding red against the blue.

My mag boots click over the polished floors as I weave in and out of starmen in their red jumpsuits, on the way down the John Adams artery from the Adams Loading Dock, towards the main drag of the base. The funk of powdered eggs from breakfast hangs over the whole place, the air buzzing because of shift change. Normally I'd whistle for them to clear out of the way or get run over, but the fresh meat is struggling enough already. Easy to spot the newbies by how they clop in their boots like their knees bend the wrong way, hugging the walls so they don't keel over. In a couple of days they'll master the roll-step dance, like we all did. Just another completely useless skill that'll do me squat if I decide not to re-up, and ship out in three months—unless I join a marching band. But horns ain't the things I want to be blowing once I'm done serving my sentence at the Founding Fathers' Monastery for Repressed Urges, thanks.

"You'll wanna lean forward," Rollins with the dump-truck caboose tells a green-faced newbie, elbowing Fratelli.

Fratelli nods solemnly to Sousa at his side, both of them catching the drift. "Really put all the weight in your toes."

I know I shouldn't give a shit and ought to keep rolling by, but I remember the jelly-kneed fresh meat feels. Nearly five years back, I looked out the shuttle window as Fort Founding Fathers zoomed into view like a fat blue star in the middle of a gray sea. Soon enough, I was bobbing through these blue-painted hallways, and trying not to flail in the moon's weaker gravity.

"Stay centered, pal," I sing out, wheeling past them. "Stand up straight. Roll on your heels."

"You always gotta ruin shit," Fratelli grumbles.

"Yeah, fuck you, man," Rollins spits.

I turn back to him and salute. "Rollins, not even with Fratelli's dick and Sousa pushing."

I keep on truckin' around the corner of Adams and down John Jay Ave., with red, white, and blue stars painted everywhere like a Fourth of July jizzfest. Quotes from long-dead presidents and historical schmucks join the stars, covering almost every free inch of the walls. *WE THE PEOPLE* screams at me in block letters between the safety-light-ringed doorways that lead to the west wing and the east wing head that always stinks of piss and powdered soap. I repeated two grades in high school after almost getting kicked out, and even a blockhead like me knows those words are from the Constitution. A whopper of a quote from the inauguration of the first president covers the wall by the doorway to the east barracks. *And since the preservation of the sacred fire of liberty, and the destiny of the Republican model of Government, are justly considered as deeply, perhaps as finally staked, on the experiment entrusted to the hands of the American people.*

Sure, Georgie. I flash a peace sign at the mural of Washington crossing the Delaware, only the river is a band of stars.

I don't cross into east barracks much anymore, since boss-man Rear Admiral Watkins moved me out of there. America is supposed to be in some cold war with Russia—a few klicks away in their Lunogorod research base—and we even patrol the exterior of Founding Fathers for any sign of them Reds snooping around. They keep to themselves. The only hot wars around here happened between me and the others in the bunks when I was fresh meat. I laughed off a lot, at first. A "fag" or a "sissy" tossed here and there, sometimes at me, sometimes the other guys. I was different than the others—I never denied anything, or returned fire. Although the last brawl over poker night at the folding table in the corner of the barracks was part my fault, even if Hernandez had been riding me since basic, and not in the fun way. *Everyone cover your dicks,* he'd holler when I walked into the showers. I didn't want to slug him before my enlistment bonus even cleared. I figured I'd take his money in poker instead.

I kicked his ass in six straight hands before he got in my face and said I must've been cheating. Using some fairy magic to get into his head. And sure, I was cheating. I've just known things, ever since I was a kid. The way he tapped the edges of his cards as he spread them, the way he scratched his nose. Like I could hear a whisper, see a flash in my noggin of what he was thinking—*kings over eights, I got this*—telling me when to hold and fold. I can tell just about everyone's tell.

If Hernandez only gave me the cash I'd won like he was supposed to, I wouldn't have punched him square in the jaw and sent him spinning onto the card table. He didn't even report me to Watkins. I don't think he wanted to let on that a fairy laid him out.

A whistle cuts through the air once I'm almost clear of the east barracks.

"Hey Ward, hold up," Hernandez calls.

Bunk springs creak and he bounces off one of the lower racks from the row by the door. Most of the racks are topped with rumpled piles of sheets, since Watkins isn't the type to holler at us about making our beds with crisp hospital folds. The starmen rotating out of here tomorrow are yakking it up while they shove wadded-up socks in their rucksacks and yank pictures of their girls off the bed frames. The Starman's Oath stabs one wall with white block letters. *Honor, Valor, Integrity, Brotherhood, Strength, and Heart. We find Faith along the stellar road. And trust Courage at the start.* Eight Virtues symbolized by the eight-point star pins we all wear on our lapels, and that some of the others get tattooed on their forearms.

"I got a special delivery of Old Spice," I tell Hernandez, wagging my nose. "Seems like you need it."

He flashes his crooked teeth when he laughs. Somehow, knocking his block off won him over. Like I proved I was a man. He's told the other poker night guys to cram it if he heard them calling me a fag since then. And every now and then I'd even catch his eye and think, *maybe?* Maybe he talks about sissies too much to keep the others off the scent.

He's the one who started calling me "Last Mitch Effort." No one here really remembers that it used to be an insult. Just that if your family doesn't put enough cash in your account to buy something from the commissary—and that's if you want a pocket Constitution, or some rosary beads, or oat bars—you go to Last Mitch Effort. See what he can do about smuggling you something here.

Hernandez slaps a few chits in my hands. The jagged-edged bits of scrap metal stamped with dollar signs are what we trade with each other up here, then bring to the commissary to get the real money added to our accounts. "Here's what I owe you for that last *Penthouse*."

I whistle. "You win the lottery or something?"

"Nah. Gambling's not for me no more." He pretends to sock himself in the jaw. Why did this doughy-faced goof get cool all of a sudden? "I'm paying off what I owe before I ship out next rotation. I want a clean ledger."

I shove the bills in my pocket. "Come to the bar tonight, and your first drink's on me."

"Hoorah."

I round the corner of Washington, past the wide lab where the goggle-eyed space nerds of the research unit stare down at moon rocks, and down the main drag of District of Columbia Ave. Watkins's door is the only thing that has me patting my jumpsuit pockets for my inhaler, just in case.

An open door, and Watkins is Watkins. When he's not poring over screens and survey maps in the White House—the mission control room at the center of the base that's all painted up with white columns—he's usually in his private quarters, whittling wood or huffing on his harmonica. Everyone calls this place Summer Camp because Watkins runs his backwater base filled with screw-ups, three days away from the top brass on Earth, any way he wants. Do your duty, save the goofing off for rec time, and he leaves you alone.

A closed door, and he is Rear Admiral Watkins, commanding officer. DEFCON Level Cut the Shit: we have three days to deep-clean the whole base, and stash every last bit of contraband, and shave, and bleach the Franklin airlock so it don't stink of cigarette smoke, because some Admiral Asshole is dropping in on the next shuttle from Earth to run things for the next three months while Watkins gives his body a break from low-gravity, back on Earth. We'll all have to snap to attention and pretend to be vigilant starmen keeping the black skies from here to the United States of America safe from the Reds—and long may the Republic stand, from sea to shining sea and from star to blazing star, hoorah. His door is a warning. Another way he looks out for us more than most of our folks ever did.

I wheel past the med bay and the gym of the main hub, my heart ticking up a beat. Almost four months since a closed door, the Rear Admiral had to be coming back eventually to kill our cakewalk. And yeah, "Rear Admiral" had me snickering every time, picturing boys from *Mandate* half out of their red jumpsuits and flashing their asses, while I put the "petty" in "petty officer." Ranks don't matter a hell of a lot on this rock. Petty Officer Third Class Mitchell Ward, reporting for booty.

If only. Christ, I miss getting laid.

I find Watkins just past his open door, frowning at his clipboard. His bushy moustache—black and white, same as his close-cropped hair—twitches. He's got twenty years on me, at least, but he's still muscled and straight-backed. His blue epaulets with their white stars cap his shoulders. He shifts on his mag boots when I roll right in. His quarters aren't much bigger than a closet, with a desk, a couple of shelves, and a sink. Tidy, except for the out-of-place shipping crate on the floor by his desk, where a framed picture of a hugging couple who must be his parents rests on a bed of balled-up socks. His duffel is a wide-open mouth on his bed.

Oh, shit. Summer camp is canceled, then.

"How're you living, Ward?" Always his same greeting to everyone. I don't know why it gets me smiling every time.

My hands stumble a quick salute as I tear my eyes from the crate. "Happy to be on the right side of the airlock, sir."

"Glad to hear it."

I bob my chin to the crate. "Doing some housecleaning, sir?"

"I'm rotating down, starman."

I squint. "But there was no—"

"All hands?" He puffs a laugh through his nose. "The order just came this morning with the shuttle. Columbia has decided to reward me with some leave time on account of..." He lifts his eyebrows. There's that laugh without laughing, again. "My service record."

"Well-deserved, sir. And the commanding officer taking over for you?"

His pinched lips scold me enough. "Will fill you in during Reels."

I've got a helluva game of poker ahead of me. Lucky that I just got a fresh shipment in, then, to see if I can gamble. Give Admiral Whoever a couple of bottles of Maker's Mark so he doesn't try to make his mark too hard, and mess with business. We've always survived by snapping to attention until Watkins comes back.

But that was before Gloria started being herself and the starmen made trouble for her in the barracks at night. *Are you good? I'm worried about you* turned into *Check your tank*. She rescued me from suffocating and I was going to do the same for her. I told her, *I'm swapping out your tank*. I went to Watkins so I didn't start busting heads, and he kept an eye on her. Not everyone else would.

Watkins looks away from my cart, his bushy moustache twitching. His moustache is his tell. *Well?* My cue to drop my latest delivery on his desk. A glass bottle clinks against the metal.

"Is that a bottle of Jack which I am not seeing, Ward?"

"Sir. And an extra pack of smokes. Which you are also definitely not seeing."

"Thank you, starman." I see him eyeing the bottle like it's a fuel report on his clipboard until he grabs it by the neck, twists open the cap, and pours a generous glug into his coffee mug. When he takes a pull, my mag boots do their job real good, keeping me bolted to the floor.

He hands the bottle back over. "You pour this out for the boys tonight, on me."

I've never seen the shadows over his face like this. Never heard the sing-song sucked outta his voice. The whisky sloshes in the bottle when I slip it back into the crate.

"Open invite to tonight's Lodge show, as usual, sir."

"Hmm." He pulls from the mug again, and turns back to his clipboard. "Maybe I'll finally take you up on that. You boys oughta enjoy tonight. It'll be the last one for a while."

I nod at him. "Heard, sir."

And then he looks back up at me and down to my cart, finally folding in this game we play of him not seeing it. He jabs his clipboard at my cart. "You take care, Ward."

I roll away, off on my next delivery, dodging stumbling newbie starmen on my way down the painted halls.

TWO

TO THE STARS

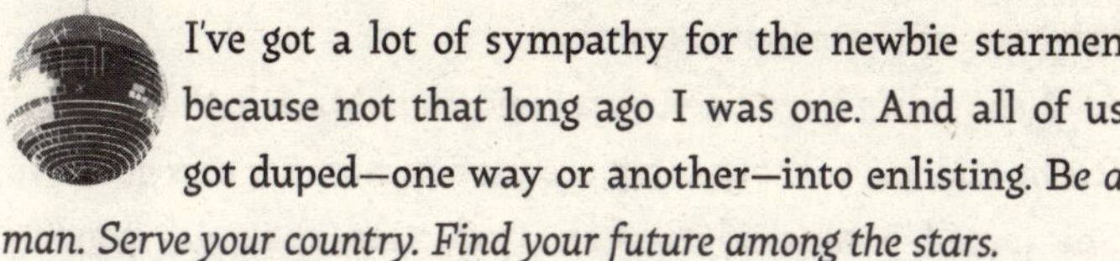

I've got a lot of sympathy for the newbie starmen because not that long ago I was one. And all of us got duped—one way or another—into enlisting. B*e a man. Serve your country. Find your future among the stars.*

Me and Ma used to watch a lot of old Hollywood movies when I was a kid, backstage in her dressing room, and upstairs in our apartment over the Calypso Room. *Casablanca. Sunset Boulevard.* Those were pretty heavy, so we usually stuck to the fun stuff. *How to Marry a Starman, Some Like It Hot,* and *Gentlemen Prefer Blondes* with Marilyn Monroe. *Singin' in the Rain. Guys and Dolls.* Ma and the Uncles and me loved the glamor—the costumes, the stages, the big production numbers—until Ma didn't, anymore. I probably had something to do with it when I told her how it sure seemed like the movies were mostly about broads wanting to give up their lives for men. And weird, how no one on screen looked like any of us. Soon after she decided I was the reason her name was never gonna be in lights someplace other than this shitty little club in this shitty little city. Then she started pouring her pre-show martinis before lunch, saying things like *I was gonna be something. Your father was right, I should've just let him take you.*

That's when I switched to the *God's Guardsmen* flicks about the United States Space Guard that Mayflower Studios pumped out every two years. No music. Big on the action. They're real cheese fests, but at least the boys are something to look at. Starman North, the main character in the series, always turned to camera and delivered speeches about American bravery and destiny, and the evils of Communism. Starman North was like a compass *pointing American men in the Just direction*, and the Guard only took in the best and brightest of those men. *Hoorah.*

I shouldn't have been surprised that Ma left the Calypso Room and me without a big production number of a goodbye. She joined a musical theater production that was touring Europe, and she packed a bag, telling me *nothing's better than that feeling of the spotlight, baby.* I had a month left of high school and nowhere to live, with the club's new headliner moving into our apartment. I stayed with Uncle Javi for a bit. He didn't ask for anything from me—money or otherwise—when I knew others would. I could've gone to Pop for help. He'd moved to a boring California desert town to work construction, and I spent weeks each summer with him. He couldn't be near Ma, he told me more than once. I was the only good thing to come out of the two of them being near each other, and she wasn't even convinced of that. I heard Pop telling her, one Christmas visit before I even started shaving, that it was fine that I was who I was, I just had to learn how to throw a punch to back it up. That got me throwing more than enough punches in school.

I wanted to prove I could go it alone. I was big and strong and didn't need anyone's help, and if Ma left Miami, I'd one-up her. I'd leave Earth. There was a boy I knew who'd joined the Guard, and maybe I'd see him again. Maybe I'd be strong enough for him to dig me. And maybe the *God's Guardsmen* flicks rubbed off on me. I certainly did enough below-the-belt rubbing during those barracks bonding scenes where the characters learned how to watch each other's sixes.

A week after barely graduating high school two years late, I strolled into the recruiting office in Miami. I didn't tell Uncle Javi or Pop. Pop had served in Korea and threatened to drive me to Canada to dodge the draft, and here I was signing up without telling him. I figured I was beating Uncle Sam to the punch, anyhow. Back in '72, Vietnam was still a warzone, with the draft showing no sign of letting up. Not with the huge oil deposits Nixon found. Plus the palladium mines that were keeping the Space Program running had him suddenly all interested in *preserving democracy* and setting up the Camp Puller Space Guard base there just after he turned Vietnam into a US territory. At least the Space Guard was supposed to be easy. No combat, so long as you didn't mind screaming into the sky on one of three shuttles that bounced back and forth between Earth and the moon: the *Saint Christopher*, the *Saint Michael*, the *Saint James*. Starmen shielded by saints' wings.

The too-bright recruiting office in Miami stank of copy machine fumes and government-issue boredom. Rows of flimsy chairs borrowed from a dentist's office, a table with stale donuts and instant coffee by the window, a TV playing footage of a colonel with a giant forehead explaining the *sacred duty of serving your country.* The posters that lined the bad drywall showed starmen of every race in red jumpsuits saluting the American flag. *IN SPACE, WE ARE ALL*

BROTHERS IN ARMS. Meanwhile, the recruiting officer eyed me while he filled out my intake form, his pen hovering over the RACE boxes. What was I, exactly? Ma is Black and Seminole, Pop white as a pale ass. With my dark, curly hair, a guy I'd fooled around with said I could pass for tan Italian, like he'd expected me to say *thanks*. The recruiter didn't care much about my asthma. Didn't blink when I told him I was gay. *Very* gay. They needed whatever living bodies they could get with how enlistment was down after another failed launch had blown a hundred recruits to dust.

The Guard or the frontlines, I knew. The recruiter said it wasn't so bad. Didn't I dig the *God's Guardsmen* movies? Think of the adventure. I'd never get bored. Starmen bounced between different rotations: six months at Fort Founding Fathers on the moon and three months down at the Columbia Space Guard base in Cape Canaveral, Florida for our bodies to get a breather in Earth's gravity. Repeat for one five-year enlistment. I'd be twenty-five by the time my enlistment was up. I could re-up or pop back down to Earth with my whole life ahead of me.

And there was that boy already in the Guard that I knew. I could write a goodbye letter to Pop and say I was going off to serve my country, when more than a little part of me knew I was doing this on the off-chance of seeing that boy again.

White officers in basic training, where me and the other baby starmen yakked our powdered-egg breakfasts MREs in the launch sim for three months, but enough of the other starmen looked like me, hovering between RACE boxes. We touched down on Founding Fathers for the first time—more than one of us had puked in our helmets during landing—wriggled out of our space suits, and lined up in front of Rear Admiral Watkins in the White House. Watkins, dark as Ma, who looked more like most of us than the top brass back on Columbia.

"Whatever happened to you out there"—he stabbed a finger at the blue-painted ceiling, somewhere in the direction of Earth—"is a million miles away. You're starmen, now."

Always the answer: a shouted, bass-heavy *hoorah*.

A big starman family. Not everyone thought of it like that, though.

I knew Gloria was like me the second we met in the mess hall in basic. She was hiding herself in a too-big jumpsuit. Two starmen were hollering at each other about the last bread roll on the table—almost throwing fists—and me and Gloria looked at each other like *can you believe this shit.*

I remember me and Gloria's first patrol together out in the black, not long after we landed here. I was huffing inside my too-tight suit with sweat rolling into my eyes. And being a big man like this was what I wanted, right? The fact that I could trip and crack the visor of my helmet—peace out, lungs—had me spiraling. My oxygen meter was screaming even though I was supposed to have eight hours' worth of air, easy. Swatting my helmet, grappling at the seams, Gloria had to grab my hands before I ripped off my helmet and tried to gasp in air. *Hold your horses, Miami.* She checked the main oxygen tank that was strapped to my back and saw that it was loose. More air was seeping out of my suit than in. I still had my backup tank—and this was why we patrolled in teams—but still. She tightened the tank and the cool air gushed over my face.

Her tank was loose on our next patrol. Then mine the one

after that, then both of ours. Once would've been an accident—the starman before me swapped out the used tank for a new one and didn't screw it in enough—but every time?

Gloria gabbed to me about compassion. *Easy to have compassion,* she said, *for the ones who like you. When you got it for the ones that don't, that's the real Grace stuff.* She tried to talk some Bible verse about forgiveness until I snapped at her—the only time I ever have. I don't know how she let the anger move through her, just because she didn't want it. When I'm fired up she tells me *that hurt doesn't belong to you. It's theirs. Let it blow on past.* Maybe one of these times she reminds me of that, it'll actually click. I punched airlock doors before every patrol, nearly tore my suit with how I yanked it around me so hard. I knocked shoulders in the hallways. Watkins had to pull me aside, tell me how people like us can't make enemies. He said to man up and lock my feelings behind an airlock door before I end up *accidentally* on the wrong side of one. Which sounded a lot like how a boy I barely knew told me how I had to play the game and couldn't get mad, before he joined the Space Guard.

Me and Gloria learned to check each other's air tanks before every patrol. Until our first rotation back to the Columbia Space Center in Florida, when I took a page from Uncle Javi's book. He knew which palms to grease down at the precinct for the vice squad to leave the Calypso Room alone. So, it wasn't that hard for me to figure out which boys in supply, shipping, and security I could tap for the contraband ring. Us starmen are rich in virtue, not so much in actual cash.

Funny how my air tanks all started working normally once I could cut off everyone's supply of smokes and skin mags.

So that's why shuttle day, when the newbies get here, has

me on edge. Check your tank, I wanna tell the fresh meat. Especially the ones that are like me. Every once in a while I see one that looks at me a little too long for them to be on the straight-and-narrow, and I give 'em the same eyes I gave to Gloria. *Can you believe this shit.*

I look too long at the starmen coming off each shuttle, too. Just in case one of them is the boy I half-chased up here, almost ten years gone. They never are.

THREE

GUARDED

The metal plate in my hands is still warm. The smell of cinnamon apples and the scrape of forks fill the mess hall that's packed with long gleaming tables and benches. Most of the base is here for the Reels update, except for the fresh meat getting settled in the barracks, some stragglers, and the squads on patrol.

Watching the Reels isn't mandatory, but most of us are happy to be bribed with pie. Gloria's not so gullible. Without her to keep me company, the other starmen leave a three-foot gap around me on the bench. They jostle each other with sticky hands, laughing with milk-moustached mouths. Fine by me. I'll take some peace with my piece of pie.

There's maybe nothing more American than apple pie in space, warmed up by a nuclear reactor, and served with a cup of rehydrated milk.

But pie comes with a price. Columbia drops bombs covered in buttercream, disaster news delivered in glossy Reels with brass choir backing tracks. Two years back, we got slices of chocolate cake for the Fourth of July while the Reels rattled on about how the Big One finally hit California and leveled half of downtown Los Angeles. *But don't worry, starmen,* the Reel announcer sang out, *the light of the land that shares the holy tales of our Country will never be dimmed. Even now, the City of Angels on a Hill rises again.* Boys around me screamed, begged Watkins to ask Columbia to send them word about their folks. He didn't have any more news to give them that wasn't in the Reels. He's from LA, I know, and he delivered the news without his voice even shaking. We only got word of *how* the city was rebuilding—kicking out most of the original residents from downtown and turning it into something closer to a movie set—from other starmen when the next shuttle rotated up from Earth.

I scrape smears of filling off the plate with my fork. I've been so used to eating powder splashed with hot water out of packets for years that the food coming from the new base kitchen—warmed by a fleet of microwaves—tastes like Ma's home cooking. Well, someone's Ma's home cooking, since I was the one who used to whip up boxed macaroni for dinner. The Guard finally got the Constitution reactor, built on Earth and shuttled here in pieces, up and running six months ago. The nuclear power station is supposed to fuel the base expansion and improvements, and the Plymouth Colony civilian module we were building, supervised by Captain Kern. The top brass had the idea to build a separate base for military families, and eventually a small town with gardens and everything, until we got the order to stop work two weeks back.

I'm about to lick my fork clean when a shadow falling over the table has me jumping outta my skin. Powell hits me with a sloppy grin. An hour ago I delivered him two bottles of gin. From the stink of him, I'd say half his stash is gone already.

He flops onto the bench next to me and I don't know how he doesn't keel over into his pie.

"W-ward," he stumbles, rubbing the buzzed-down shadow of hair on his head. "I'm gonna need. I'm gonna need..."

"You're gonna need some black coffee." I scoot an inch away from his booze fumes. "Christ."

He hoots a high laugh, almost falling over again. I have to drop my pie plate on the table and grab his shoulder just to hold him up before he wriggles my hand away. Guardsmen by his other side shoot him the stink eye and clear out. We all know that some of the starmen like Powell who were stationed at Camp Puller left half their marbles back on Earth. Vietnam changed something behind their eyes. *They got Pulled*, we call it. They're the ones who blow the most on smuggled hooch, and wake up the other starmen in the barracks with screams. The ones who rattle about conspiracy theories. Like how the nuclear reactor is talking to them. Or how construction on Plymouth Colony stopped because Watkins found an alien ship in the quarry. After Powell was so in the bag that he almost drove a lunar schooner off a cliff, Gloria got on me about being careful with who I was selling what to. But if the Thems are going to treat me like just a storefront, I'm gonna treat 'em all just like customers. I'm nobody's ma.

"I'm gon' need." Powell burps. "Ssomethin' stronger next time. Y'know, f'r the pain. My pa busted his back, and the doc got'm on some laudanum that fixed 'im up real nice."

The crinkled corners of his eyes are making the apple pie taste a lot less sweet. "Tylenol's all I got for that pain, Powell."

Whatever he grumbles back at me is lost to the starmen stomping and hooting all around us. I look up as a line of a dozen starmen in their dress blues, led by Captain Kern, glide down the runway between the two columns of mess tables. Mag boots move in sync as they line up in two rows by the mural of Miss Moonie, with Kern standing off to the side. Miss Moonie eyes all of us in the room like she always does, in her black bathing suit, back-arched, with her ass parked on the nose of a rocket. Blonde finger-waved hair, curly lashes, and red lipstick behind her space helmet. Over her, a banner reads *PRO AMERICA, AD ASTRA. For America, to the Stars.* She was modeled on Marilyn Monroe after her visit here in '68 when she sang for the first squad of starmen, back when the whole base wasn't much bigger than the mess hall. I heard stories about her rolling up her sleeves, and slapping on an apron to dish out mashed potatoes. Nine years later, and Marilyn is still the only woman to visit space. Besides Gloria, but not everyone sees it like that.

Kern nods to us. He must love that Watkins pawned Reels duty off on him until new Admiral Whoever gets settled in. The sides of Kern's head, bristled with salt-and-pepper hair, look sharp enough to slice the edges of the service cap I've never seen him without. His tell is how his eyes crinkle. I look him in the eyes and get a flash of him at a podium, running for president in the same dress blues he's wearing now.

"I owe to my beloved country, for the many honors it has conferred upon me," Kern booms in greeting. "Still more for the steadfast confidence with which it has supported me, and for the opportunities I have thence enjoyed."

I keep clear of Kern. He gives me the willies with how he actually believes the shit he quotes. The starmen around me look about as interested in his favorite George Washington quote as Miss Moonie is. The wet smack of Powell's lips as he mashes on pie cuts through the quiet.

Kern turns to the twelve starmen standing straight in two lines. They look snazzier than us jumpsuited grunts, in their dark blue pants with a silver stripe down the side, and cream button-downs under stiff blue jackets with silver buttons. Eight-point star pins glint from red ties. Regulation haircuts hidden by leather-brimmed blue and silver caps with a medallion of an eagle holding a rocket—the Space Guard insignia—in the middle. The whole lot of them ready for a production number. Kern nods and one of them steps out, and turns to face the others. The starman raises his white-gloved hands and the other boys suck in one collective breath and sing. I know the words like they're printed on my heart, same as the flowing script on the wall behind the choir. The Hymn of the United States Space Guard.

As Washington wondered the Delaware
We gazed thus out to the moon
From Sea to Shining Sea—
Once, we
Looked to Luna, vowing, "Soon."
First Liberty sent aloft, its torch
O'er States and Commonwealths, all
Next manned Mayflowers *soared, heavenward—*
Never once fearing the fall
Once footsteps marked Luna's silvered soil
We raised banners
Striped and starred—
Thus when God gazes from his stellar throne

He sees the United States Space Guard
Ho, upward! Ho, moon-ward!
Then Mars and asteroid bound
We American kings soar on rocket wings
And no braver men are found
Starmen, unbound by gravity
Who loose our heavenly lightning hard
Blazing red, white and blue across stars,
Sailing true—
We, the United States Space Guard

My hands float to my heart on their own. Less out of respect, more to protect it from the invasion. Songs slip into me, easy. Music is a wave that wraps me up like I'm falling asleep in the spotlight catwalk over the Calypso Room while the band plays 'Fly Me to the Moon.' The wave starts in my throat and I can't hold it back until the overlapping hymn harmonies pinch my eyes. I don't know who the almost-tears are for. The fresh meat starmen who got duped into being here, and now they're trapped, same as all of us? The choir for sounding so soft and strong at the same time, somehow, in the right parts of the song—with basses hushing low, with tenors belting for the imaginary throne of God in an imaginary heaven, and baritones weaving around them? They get to be soft when I have to push that part down. Almost-tears for me, too, with how coming here was a mistake.

At my side, Powell's chin hits his chest. He shakes with choked tears. I need something stronger for the pain, too, buddy.

The white-gloved hands of the toy soldier in front of the choir pinches the air, killing the notes.

"Thank you, Lieutenant Bomer," Kern rumbles.

"Sir." Bomer turns to him with a heel-click, snapping a salute. "Rear Admiral Kern, sir."

The choir glides away to the back of the mess hall. The cotton whispers of their uniforms harmonize with the mumbles all around. But Bomer fumbled the lyrics of the hymn at the end, didn't he? *Rear Admiral* when Kern is Captain.

"Starmen," Kern says. "Let's begin."

Goddamnit. Another bomb dropped by the Guard. I can feel the vibrations shake the room.

Kern folds his arms behind his back and grandstands to the head of the columns of mess tables, his chin up.

* * *

There's no music in Kern's speech. He rambles about how Watkins forgot we are at war with the Reds, same as if there are boots on the ground. How he treated us like friends and not soldiers in his care. And there are wars at home, too. President Reagan issued declarations, and emergency actions, and Presidential Orders for our great Country to win the war against immorality, and anti-Americanism, and depravity. I get that Reagan's antsy. Presidents have got the shelf life of a gallon of milk, lately. Three of them got sworn in since I've been in the Guard. Ford got a bullet to the head in San Francisco in '75, then his vice president warmed the seat until Reagan won in '76. *Men need a war to make them strong,* I remember Reagan saying in some address, reminding the country how he served in World War II. He talked about his war service and not so much the shitty movies he starred in when I was a kid. Kern yaps about how all of us here can be strong, moral men if we win the war in our hearts between self and service.

I don't hear much after that with how all the air seems to leak out of the room. Starmen around me sit up straighter and flash each other wide eyes. At my side, Powell drags in a wet, jagged breath.

Kern waves his hand and Bomer wheels the projector we use for movie night on over to the front of the mess hall. We swapped the old film projector out with a new one that Mayflower Studios made with tech from the space program. The thing looks like a curved white desk lamp attached to a vacuum cleaner. Six months back, Watkins first wheeled it in here, loaded up a big sequin-looking thing called an Opti-Disc in the back, and fiddled with some dials before *Casablanca* burst on the projector screen. So clear, so bright that I swear Humphrey Bogart's cigarettes stank up the room. The remote-controlled surveyor rovers that the research unit rolls around outside to map the moon already had cameras stuck to the front. Kern said that all the other rovers and the big lunar schooners were getting Opti-Disc cameras to record everything. The hallways, too.

Bomer lowers the projection screen by the Miss Moonie mural. The Opti-Disc glints blue in his white-gloved hand when he loads the thing into side of the projector. Someone cuts the overhead lights and the big eye of the projector lamp blinks on, blasting red, white, and blue stars onto the screen as trumpets blaze the Guard Hymn. When the stars clear, Starman North in a red jumpsuit faces the camera with glinting eyes the color of service-dress blues. His hair is a pomaded blond side-part, his jaw square like old film cameras.

Behind him, buttons at grey control panels blink like stars, with lunar maps glowing on the computer screens.

I know the movie set—the Founding Fathers control room—from the last *God's Guardsmen* flick. Whoever painted Starman North's lips didn't nail the color. His lips are too red, like he's been sucking cherries. Still, I wouldn't kick him out of bed.

"Hwhy, hello there, fellow starmen."

Fellow starmen, my ass. He's an actor named Kit Caber—the third Starman North Mayflower Studios has cast in their *God's Guardsmen* series. I've seen all twelve flicks. Everybody has. They brought in Caber two flicks back when the other guy got too long in the tooth. His voice stinks of that fake Old Hollywood accent that Ma and the Uncles would whip out when they were wasted, with *Casablanca* in the background, stretching out their *ahs*, adding in Hs where they don't belong. *Hwhy, get me a glaahss of hwine, daaaling.* Always old movies on TV at home. Never the news, when all the anchors had to talk about was redrawn congressional district lines, new Supreme Court seats, and other crap we didn't understand.

Starman North snaps out a perfect salute.

"I'm here to share hwith you an important update to Guard protocol." The camera follows him as he strides past other central-casting starmen at control panels. "And introduce you to the STAR System, hwhere you'll find new opportunities for self-betterment as you serve your Country."

"There's sssomethin' Kern's not tellin' us," Powell slurs at me with his pie-crust-flecked mouth. Red creeps up his neck. "And somethin' I t-tried to tell you all about. 'Cept you think all of us are off our rockers."

"Powell." I squirm. "Can it, will ya?"

Of course there's something Kern ain't gabbing about. Everyone from here to Earth is a Washington mouthpiece. I look up and Kern glares our way, while Starman North swaggers to a chalk board with *STAR System* written across the top, over a bullet-point list of words.

"—hwould think. Yes, the STAR System. Now, hwe guardsmen aren't spreading American might off in distant star systems quite yet. Though, soon enough!" He gives his best pomade ad smile. "Raaahther, STAR stands for Service." He taps his pointer at the first block-lettered word in the list. "Trust." Tap. "Allegiance." Tap. "And Respect. Following the grand success of the STAR Citizen System in the Studio Zones of Los Angeles, it's only right that we bring the STAR Soldier System here to our bravest. Thus, hwhen our citizens gaze to the heavens, hwhy, they'll see us as shining stars!"

I need Gloria here to make me feel better with a *can you believe this shit* look.

"Do you Serve your Nation, and your fellow soldiers?" Starman North jabs his finger towards the camera, his eyes crinkling in concern for us, after all our time in the trenches together, decking Communists. "Trust it? Show Allegiance and Respect? The STAR System empowers you all to keep each other on the unhwavering path of American Righteousness, and—"

Powell slams me in the shin with one of his magboots when he wriggles off the bench. Starmen whisper and shuffle. Behind me, mag boots clomp, but my eyes jerk back up to the horror movie on the projection screen.

"—to increase recreational time, commissary privileges, and even pecuniary bonuses." Starman North fans his hands at the three starmen bit players in the fake control room. "You might even get a personalized filmed 'thank you' message from one of Mayflower Studios' biggest stars."

"Hwhy!" one of the others burbles. "That sounds ahhwful swell!"

"All for doing our duty, anyhow?" another adds.

I don't know that I got enough bourbon stashed here to convince Kern to keep me out of whatever the hell this is. I follow Kern's eyes away from the screen and into the runway between the columns of mess tables.

"Take a seat, starman," Kern says over the big trumpet fanfare. On the screen, Starman North and a whole squad of red jumpsuits line up in perfect rows.

"Tell them," Powell yells.

Kern flicks his hand to Bomer, who nods and starts in for Powell.

The red jumpsuits sing the Guard Hymn as an announcer's voice tells us, *"To the STARs, Guardsmen!"*

Jesus Christ. You can't really run with mag boots on. Powell tries, anyhow, and I sink watching him lurching against the low gravity—spitting and jerking his half-dead legs—and fighting against the force that keeps his feet to the floor.

"You tell 'em what really happen'd at Puller," Powell snarls. He launches his pie plate at Kern—unfazed, smiling, almost—and misses by ten feet. "You tell 'em, you goddam'd sonuvabitch."

Maybe Gloria's right and I should've kept a better eye on the goodies I gave him and the other Pulled starmen. I should watch. Like I owe it to him to see the mess I helped make. But my eyes blast on over to the screen where actors march in formation, as real starmen around me snicker. *Pull him on outta here*, someone yells. *Maybe he'll finally shut his yap.*

Trumpets blast over red, white, and blue swirling stars as Bomer and two others drag Powell towards the blue hallways, his mag boot scrapes mashing up with his screams on the way out.

FOUR

REELING

Kern softens after Powell's screams and the Reel trumpets fade. We all quit whispering, but I still have to strain to hear him from the back. He understands this is a change, Kern tells us. He's not unreasonable. He won't cancel tonight's Lodge show since he knows we've been looking forward to it. Rather, it'll be a chance to close one chapter, and tomorrow evening—when the shuttle carries the old ways of this place back to Earth—another chapter begins. He's holding a Rules, Regulation, and Reengagement session here in the mess, after the shuttle launch. Attendance mandatory.

"Let those rockets burn up the past as we blaze into the future," he says.

He must be expecting a *hoorah* from us. We don't give it. He waits a beat in silence before his mag boots click down the runway.

Once he's gone, starmen pat Miss Moonie's jugs for luck when they file out of the mess. What the hell. I do too. Me and Gloria are gonna need all the luck we can get if Kern is turning us into rats against each other. I wonder what kinda *pecuniary bonus* there is for leaving us outside an airlock.

From Miss Moonie, my boots stop at the murals outside of the Lodge. To the left of the double-wide doors, a painted banner reads *America's Destiny to the Stars* over a timeline with bullet points, and diagrams, and quotes from presidents. I know the dates well enough. We have to study them for the yearly Loyalty Exams. July 1950 when President Truman established NASA after World War II, all about safeguarding the heavens now that the world was at peace. May 1951, when America launched its first satellite, *The Spirit of Liberty*. October 1960 when the new Space Guard took over NASA, then June 1961 when *Mayflower V* landed on the moon, and Neil Wallace planted an American flag where Fort Founding Fathers, the first permanent lunar military installation, opened up three years later.

Past the Uncle Sam explosion of the hallways, the interior walls of the Lodge are painted up like the insides of a cabin. Gnarled planks, fake windows overlooking a lake, and a fake fireplace and everything. A rerun of *M*A*S*H* putters on the old domed TV by the stage where Kern reads Bible verses during mandatory Sunday Service. Three starmen push tables and stacks of chairs against one log-cabin-painted wall. Two others unfold green cots and line them up in rows. A popup dormitory for the fifty new arrivals until the shuttle leaves tomorrow with shift change, and there's room in the bunks. Tonight, the cots will see two starmen's asses parked on them, each—everyone else standing around—with the Lodge packed for Gloria's show. Her shows at shift-change are always something special. The starmen will never call her Gloria, but when she's twirling on stage in a bedsheet dress, they'll call her Lady Moondust.

Her last Lodge show. It'll kill her.

I know the shows are enough to keep her going, here. Just like I know how Russo is cruising me hard, between shoving cots around, even if he doesn't know it. I know him by the back of his head and the curve of his shoulders. Hell, I'm better at male anatomy than the starmen in the infirmary. His eyes were on me last night while I was in the corner of the Lodge wiping down the bar—the metal sheet on a couple of shipping crates across from the locked cabinet of booze. I don't know if he's rotating out of here with the shuttle. I hope so. That probably means tonight after the show he'll ask to buy an issue of *Playboy*. Ask if he can read it in my room, and, hey, I don't need to scram. I could hang with him. Let him flip through the issue and show me this girl and that girl. *What do you think of her, Ward?* I know the script. *She's a looker. Look at those knockers.* Not long, then, before he lies back and asks if I can *help him out*. And I tell him *just think of Miss January*.

Nothing like the sound of his breath speeding up to blast the trumpets from the Reel out of my head for a night.

I jangle my keys at the locked door to my room next to the cabinet, just loud enough that Russo knows I'm here. He can knock if he wants.

Queer while you're here, me and Gloria joke about those guys. I never chase after them. But if they ask? We starmen are here to serve.

Metal hits metal when I lock the door behind me, sealing out everyone else.

* * *

Me and Gloria's room is the best goddamned place from here to Earth.

The shallow cave—just wide enough to walk between the two cots pushed against the walls—was a janitor's closet, once. The small metal sink at hip-height above a drain on the floor is supposed to be for filling mop buckets. A locked metal cabinet with a Folgers can full of chits I earned from the ring, and a booze-bottle lined shelf are crammed in the corner by the sink. A battery-powered digital alarm clock sits on the top shelf, far from my bed, so I have to get up and turn it off to make it in time for duty. The room smells like Gloria's rose perfume and the dry soap I sprinkle on between rationed showers. Gloria's legs are curled up under her on her cot, with a white sheet on her lap and spilling onto the floor. Leave it to her to spend days sewing a dress she'll only wear for an hour on stage. She hums to herself, bopping her head along with the Aretha album spinning on the portable record player on the floor, as she sews washers to the sheet. We had to give Bowie's *Ziggy Stardust* album a break. The vinyl is so beat up that he kept stammering *five years* over and over again in the first track.

I can't crush her with Kern and the STAR System bullshit, just yet. We have tonight and we have this room. And each other.

"You blind yet?" I force a laugh into my voice.

She doesn't look up. "*Some* of us have dedication to our craft."

Somehow she's perfected the voice of a middle-aged mom scolding me like I'm her kid sneaking in after curfew, even if she's twenty-six, just a year older than me.

"What do you call this?" I thumb over at my cigarette-and-nude-mag-loaded cart against the door.

"I call that a one-way ticket to Earth in chains."

Jesus. She doesn't even know the half of it.

"Thanks, Ma." I collapse dramatically on my cot and it squeaks below me. She doesn't lift her purple-scarf wrapped head, even when I huff again. "Well, don't leave me hanging. Let's see it."

Gloria's eyes dance. She's brushed blue powder over one eyelid, and gold over the other. White lines around her tea-colored eyes. She must be practicing looks for tonight's show already. Everything about her is small—her shoulders, her lips, her nose that turns up just a little—except for her voice that can rattle walls.

One of the Uncles who played bass in Ma's band tried to explain music to me, once. *Timbre,* he said, *is the way a musical instrument sounds. Like, its flavor.* A bass has got that flavor, a horn another. Gloria's got a timbre like a viola solo drizzled with caramel.

"You have to imagine it under the lights." She presses the sheet to her jumpsuit, the washers jangling. "Yes?"

Sometimes her voice packs a tilty nudge, and it's like for a second I can actually see the dress sparkling in the spotlight. I swiped the washers for her from a supply shed in the now-abandoned quarry for the Plymouth Colony module a couple of days back during patrol. The bulldozers and bucket excavators by the cliff edge looked like giant scarecrows. The furnace that we used to melt rock and pour goop into brick molds was an empty casket. When Kern slammed the brakes on construction, I figured we'd abandon the place. Instead, he added round-the-clock patrols of the quarry, like the Reds were dying to steal all our gray bricks.

Unless he was hiding something else there. Wasn't just Powell and the Camp Puller basket cases who talked like that, neither. Starmen spun yarns in the Lodge, while I eavesdropped and handed over their rationed beers. Kern hit a big vein of gold in the quarry and wasn't looking to share. A couple of starmen got trampled by a bulldozer and Kern was hiding the bodies. Kern uncovered a sex palace filled with aliens with big green knockers—right outta *Star Trek*—and he was keeping them for himself.

Gloria doesn't buy into that stuff. She doesn't have a tell that I can spot, neither, because she says what's in her head. Me and Gloria don't even need to talk half the time, like we can hold whole conversations with just our eyes.

That's more Black than supernatural, sugar, she told me.

I whistle at her dress. "Really something. I take back all the no-good, terrible things I've been yakking to the others about you."

There. That lipstick-ad smile of hers calms me down even more than the first puff from my new pack of Reds. Gloria doesn't scold me anymore about what smoking will do to my asthma if I lay off on what it'll do to her voice. I toss her a pack and my matches.

She started wearing her scarf around her head even off-stage a few months back, and painting her eyelids blue even while on patrol. She told me even if it wasn't the one she was born with, her name was really Gloria—calling her by her last name same as everyone else here never felt right, anyhow—and I couldn't imagine calling her anything else. Except Lady Moondust. She can be Lady Moondust on stage and the starmen will cheer. The same ones who'll give her hell at night in the bunks, without Watkins to bark at them. Our room—the Boom Boom Room—is the only place she's herself when she's off-duty and off-stage. I'd already been living here a while, unofficially, since starting the ring. So Watkins let her move in, and assigned us to the same patrol shifts so we could watch out for each other. A queer bonus pack.

And for the ones who want to meet Lady Moondust up close, the Boom Boom Room is a little rose-scented boudoir where no one ever has to know. Not even me, and me and Gloria usually tell each other everything. I even told her about how I know things. How I dream, sometimes, like waking up screaming that morning the Big One hit down in LA. For a church girl, she's got more than a little woo-woo in her, pouring over months-old newspaper horoscopes, talking about star signs, avoiding stepping on boot prints while we're on patrol outside, so she doesn't *interrupt the energy of their path*.

Gloria touches the cig to her lips like a dame in a detective flick. "You find that boy of yours here yet?"

"No dice." I suck on my cig just to do something with my hands. "No Flynn."

"Even after the dream?"

"It weren't a dream so much as a feeling."

You don't ignore dreams, she told me once, going off about some dudes in the Bible that could see the future in their dreams. I ain't feeling so dreamy, so I point to the six-month-old newspaper on her pillow, where she circled her horoscope.

"What do the stars tell you, Capricorn?"

"They tell me that's a sorry change of subject."

"See, the stars are wrong." I puff smoke. "That was one expert pivot."

"Have your feelings ever been wrong?"

"Boy, howdy."

"Mitchell Abraham Ward." The fake middle name has got me laughing, even if Gloria is loading up the invisible rosary beads for one of her church scoldings. She knows my middle name is Terrence. That doesn't stop her whipping out Biblical middle names for me when I'm sinning against her. "You absolutely ain't pulling the Mitch thing."

I blow smoke. "And that is?"

"Get all blockhead macho and angry and stubborn." She shimmies her sheet, jangling the washers, trying to soften the Mama moment, I know.

"See, that's funny, because I got a feeling..." I trail, blowing out smoke nice and slow. "That my feeling is actually about something in *your* future."

She pinches her lips, raising an eyebrow. "Oh?"

"And your show tonight."

"Well, now you're talking," she says.

Watkins. Kern. I can't be the one to break her heart. She'll find out tomorrow. I have to look away so I don't tip her off with my eyes.

"It oughta be your best yet," I tell her.

If tonight is her last show, let it be the biggest and the best, outshining all the STARs in the whole goddamn system.

I fish into my jumpsuit pocket for the lipstick I got her. The tiny black tube is warm and slick in my hands. She doesn't say thank you. Neither of us have to with each other. All the hassle to get it here—the grunt buying it from the drug store and smuggling it into a crate, all the money and research figuring out how to even launch rockets here. I'd pay all that twice over just to see the overhead lights spark in Gloria's tea-colored eyes as she lays a thick coat of red on her lips. There. The perfect color.

FIVE
BODY COUNT

I haven't seen Flynn in nine years, but I see him, still, in the bodies of others. I looked for pieces of him in all the boys and men I met in the bus station bathroom in Miami, after he left. I see bits of him in the bodies in my magazines, and in other starmen, sometimes. The tilt of a neck here, his honker of a nose there. The shoulders-back way he walks, chin up.

How do you get googly-eyed over the back of someone's head?

And how can you miss someone if you barely know them?

Uncle Javi used to sneak me smokes and old mail-order nudie photo sets and "fitness" mags when Ma wasn't looking—which was often enough, when I wasn't pouring her martinis—and his pencil moustache twitched when he smiled. He told me which bus stations to hit up to find guys like us, after I turned sixteen and summer was staring us down the face. He taught me how to look at someone to let them know you want them, and how you can spot in their eyes if they know what you mean.

I'd already noticed Flynn in class. My sophomore year—well, my first one—he'd moved to town just after Christmas and our first-period history teacher, Mrs. Rawley, had made him stand in front of the class and say where he was from. From the look of him, he was gonna be a goddamned movie star. He even had the name. Flynn like Errol Flynn from the old *Robin Hood* movies, swinging in here on a rope. Window-cleaner blue eyes and a pink sunburn creeping over cheeks as pale as the milk Ma dropped into her coffee. A nose too big for his face. He had a buzz cut when everyone else's hair flopped in their eyes. His chin up, his back straight, he'd told us how he'd grown up in Pensacola and was here because his dad in the Space Guard got stationed in Miami. He'd called teachers *sir* and *ma'am* and snapped to attention so fast every time someone looked at him that I could practically hear his Pop yelling for him to keep his elbows off the dinner table.

Because it's always the Pop.

Mrs. Rawley had told him to sit in the empty seat in front of me. For months, I watched him. He kept away, to himself. So I'd been thinking *Maybe. Maybe?*

I watched the back of his neck and the hair that creeped into the neckline of his t-shirts. I watched him poke at pimples and mosquito bites there. Sometimes I left school late to see him running track practice, a dozen paces ahead of everyone else, jumping over hurdles like he had springs in his heels. My lungs burned just watching him go.

My tell told me a fat load of nothing about him. Still, I could've drawn the back of his neck with my eyes closed and gotten every mole right.

* * *

Fists weren't the way I wanted to feel bodies, but sometimes you gotta do it anyway. After the third time Ma had to snap out of a hangover with black coffee and use her White Lady voice in the principal's office—*misunderstanding, surely, and I'll discipline Mitchell and guarantee he'll behave*—she cut corners too hard when she drove us home, her knuckles white on the wheel. *Disappointed*, she said, blowing smoke against the windshield. *Don't let Too-Tall Timmy call you a half-breed faggot again, of course.* She told me to take a tune outta Queen Aretha's playbook. *You better think. Take it out of the hallways and don't get caught.*

That weekend I cruised the boardwalk until I spotted Timmy. One swing and I broke his nose, the word spreading like his blood on the cracked wood. Bloodhound, the kids at school started calling me, slinking back in the hallways and pretending to shiver.

Shit, I'd take that over "half-breed faggot" any day.

Sometimes people need reminding, and that's their fault, not mine. I would've ignored Buckteeth Keith, that last day of school, if he was just talking about me. Then he had to flap his yap in the gym locker room to his three buddies—loud enough for me to hear, of course—about how he heard my skag of a mom sucked every Johnson she saw down at the club. *Bam*, right in the buckteeth. He tripped backwards over the bench and careened onto the floor, his buddies honking like seagulls around him. Down the row of lockers, Flynn slowly tugged his gym uniform over his pale, lanky body. His turn to watch me.

"He tripped," I told Coach with a shrug when he jangled over with his whistle to see what the commotion was about.

Buckteeth Keith mumbled something that sounded like a yes. Better he tripped than let a half-breed faggot lay him out. Still, Coach sent us all to the principal's office. Flynn said he saw it all, and offered to go, too.

The principal's open windows looked out onto the football field, letting in the smell of just-cut grass. Two hours left in the school year, and what was he gonna do? I was already repeating sophomore year, come September. By the look of his bored face, I could tell his brains were already licking ice cream cones out on the boardwalk like everyone else's. Which must've been why he decided to go along with the lie about Buckteeth biting it because he tripped.

That, and Flynn vouched for me.

Flynn, who I found sitting on the floor of the empty hallway outside the principal's office, legs out like a doll on a shelf. His big blue eyes hit mine and it felt like my heartbeat was punching at the side of my neck.

"You have to play the game," he said, so soft I could barely hear.

"What game?"

"We can't let them see us mad." His eyes darted from mine to some spot on the floor in front of him, his jaw muscles pumping. "Don't let them get to you. That way, they win."

We. Us. I didn't know whether to kiss him or knock his teeth in, too.

"Not all of us can hide, easy as you," I snapped.

His frown closed his window-cleaner eyes. "I reckon it's not the same as hiding."

"Jumpin' hurdles is easy for you." I stabbed a thumb at the track. "You come to the Calypso some time and see what it's like for everyone else."

I had to turn on my heels and book it away from him, sucking on my inhaler so he wouldn't see me crying. The tears forcing outta me hurt even worse than my fist on Buckteeth's teeth.

* * *

I had a summer of dodging drunks at the Calypso Room ahead of me. And at home. Two nights a week, the manager brought in a new singer, swearing to Ma that it wasn't a punishment. It was a reward, for her to rest up, maybe take me on a trip. The only trip she took was over the arm of the couch after a Blue Bomber chased with a couple of glasses of wine, and she passed out. By then, Ma had a habit of getting wasted on stage and forgetting about me up in the catwalk. And I had a habit of falling asleep up there. The first time I did, I ended up having dreams about silver fog and voices, and I could spot the tells not long after that. I told Uncle Javi and he made the sign of the cross. At least with Ma offstage, Uncle Javi let me come down from the catwalk and work as a busboy, and I even scored some tips.

That week after my first stab at sophomore year, rainclouds turned the whole city soggy, drowning out the boardwalk lights. The air in the club stank of wet dust and old cigars. The first clear Saturday night—I was scrubbing lipstick stains off rocks glasses while the band warmed up—Uncle Javi zipped over to me behind the bar. He'd caught some kid circling the club four times and finally had to ask him if he was lost.

"You'll never believe what he asked when I stopped him." His pencil moustache wiggled something wild. "'Pardon me, sir, is Mitchell Ward in?'"

I almost dropped the glass, my hands were shaking so much, same as if I was on lookout for the cops in the bus stop bathroom. Uncle Javi shoved a couple of bucks at me, and told me to go be a kid. Told me he'd tan my hide if I came back here tonight. I didn't need to spot the tell of his moustache twist to know he was just fooling.

One huff on my inhaler for luck, and I found Flynn outside, his back against the side of the club, his shoulders curled forward, his eyes on the ground. In his pressed khaki shorts and blue polo shirt, he stuck out against the miniskirts and bell-bottoms trickling into the front door.

"You're a little early," I called out to him. "The Spalding Trio don't hit the stage 'til ten."

He squinted at me like I was a hurdle on the track he wasn't sure he could clear. He looked around—the couples streaming into the club after dinner, the boys already strolling the boardwalk looking for fun, the street vendors slinging arepas and hotdogs to drunk tourists—and I knew. Too many people for him.

"Is there somewhere we can go?" he asked.

"Sure."

I bought us hotdogs from a cart, with Flynn's hands shaking so hard that he squirted mustard on his shoe. Ma was upstairs, passed out on the couch. I was used to scrambling down the fire escape outside my room to sneak off to the bus stop. We held our hotdogs between our teeth to climb up the rusty ladder of the fire escape, feet clunking in time with the music from the club. Seagulls scrapped over discarded arepas most nights, squawking hell until sunrise. Two of them perched on the fire escape flapped off to the far edge of the rusty railing when we climbed up. Their beady black eyes hit our hot dogs.

Flynn followed my lead and sat down, back against the wall by my window, with him on my left and tucked into the corner. We were close enough that I could've brushed the pink sunburned band on his thighs if I wanted to. I knew I had to go easy. That would've had him hurdling over the railing. This side of the building overlooked the dumpster-clogged alleyway between the next row of apartments. Windows across the alleyway were sleeping eyes, lidded over with curtains. The moon dropped a spotlight over the whole neighborhood.

I bit my hot dog, waiting for him, while he poked the bun. He sucked in a breath to speak then stopped. Then did that twice more, each time stealing some of the air out of my lungs. I should've brought my inhaler.

"How do you be yourself?" he asked, finally looking up.

"Who else am I gonna be?"

He took a long time chewing his first bite. "And when did you know?"

"Mom said she knew I had some music in my hips as soon as I started walking. So..." I shrugged. "Always. You?"

"I'm not sure I do. Know. You know?"

"Then why are you here?"

"My folks are at a church dance."

Maybe I was imagining how his leg moved a little to the right, brushing mine.

"And you didn't feel like dancing?"

He ripped off a piece of his hot dog bun and threw it to the other side of the fire escape at the seagulls. The fat one with a red spot on its beak cawed at the smaller brown-speckled one and swooped to gobble the bread.

"Father—my dad—must've known before I did," he said. "Honest word, I've never walked past without his hollering for me to straighten my shoulders and not float like a gee-dee pansy."

I hid a laugh with another bite. Not because of the shitty things his Pop said, but because of the little twang in his voice and the *honest word*.

"He sounds like he's a real gas."

"He's sending me to some camp for the summer, starting next week."

"Splashing naked in a lake with a bunch of boys seems like a sure-fire way to straighten you out."

Flynn's shoulders caved in with his laugh. No mistaking the way he leaned into me, too.

"I reckon it's not that kind of camp. Some military camp to get us whipped up for the Space Guard."

"Yikes."

"My father's been in the Guard since it started. Never made it out to space, though. He got as far as Camp Puller over in Vietnam, then he was an engineer out in Canaveral before he got stationed here on desk duty." Flynn tossed another chunk of bun that Red Spot caught before Brownie had the chance. "He told me I have military camp ahead of me, then I enlist. Then, captain in no time."

"Sounds like he's got it all planned out for you."

"That's why he's after me to get better at running track. He wants my legs stronger than a Ford Mustang, so the Guard won't ground me, same as him. One of his legs doesn't work the same as everyone else's on account'a he had polio when he was a kid."

"And your ma?"

"She's too busy throwing garden parties with the other Guard wives to pay me much mind."

"I'm sorry."

"From what I've heard about your mother..." He winced. "I mean, she's a musician, so she must be real keen on us... artist types. Must be easy to have a mother who knows who you are."

My turn to laugh, testing the waters by leaning into him.

"Not sure about the easy. I take care of her half the time when she's falling over drunk. Pop's not around. I'm on my own, most of the time, which suits me just fine."

"Lone wolf?"

"Bloodhound."

I tossed a chunk of bread to the birds. Red Spot snatched it up again. We both seemed to know that Brownie was hurting for some bites. I whipped a piece over the fire escape railing, and Red Spot cawed after it. Then Flynn scooted forward on his knees and tossed half his bun to the smaller, brown-spotted bird.

We finished our hot dogs and didn't talk for a while, letting the brass band version of 'Fly Me to the Moon' float from the club. I let my hand fall off my leg to brush the edge of his pinkie on the fire escape between us. Electricity could've surged all out, charging through the metal, and blowing the streetlights over the whole neighborhood.

"You don't strike me as a big mean bloodhound."

I had to lean in close to hear. Had to fight the burn to lean into his lips so he wouldn't flap off like one of the seagulls.

"You don't really know me," I told him.

"I would sure like to know you."

His wide-blinking blue eyes sang music right into me.

I'd had my pants half-down with enough guys by then. Still, that was the first moment I ever felt naked with someone else.

* * *

Flynn stuttered that his father would break out the belt if he wasn't home where they left him, and I had to practically grab him by the shoulders so he wouldn't jump over the railing. I should've kissed him. I missed my chance. He asked if he could write me while he was at camp, and I burst into my room and wrote down my address on a slip of paper. The second it was in his hands he hauled down the railing and jumped over trash cans in the alley. Then he was gone.

A notebook page with his neat, blocky handwriting showed up after the Fourth of July fireworks fizzled over the boardwalk. *I apologize that it's taken this long to write. We sure are busy here. Additionally, we have to wait for the counselors to read all the letters that are mailed in and out of camp.* His words might've sounded like a book report, but I got the tell he showed me. We had to speak in code.

At the end of his letter about all the *ways he was learning to serve his Country*, was a line that poked my chest like a bird beak. *I very much enjoy watching the seagulls here and wanted you to know that.*

I wrote him back about working at the club and boring days at the beach. They by the end, *Will you teach me to run as fast as you?* What I meant was *Can I see you again?*

Uncle Javi was the one who taught me about how he and the older gays used winks and toe-taps and code words—friend of Dorothy, fellow traveler, confirmed bachelor—to wrap up what they really mean. How, before *Blueboy*, they used to buy fitness magazines called *Physical Man* and *Strength & Health* with guys posing in loincloths. They got their rocks off from mail-order photo sets from Bruce of LA and Bob Mizer featuring *artistic male portraiture.* I dug the secret language. Me and Flynn talked in code in our letters—three each, weeks apart.

I am meeting boys from all over the Country, he wrote. *None of them remind me of you, though they are friendly.*

I heard his voice, plain as sitting next to me on the fire escape. *I miss you.*

I heard a song I think you'd like, I wrote. Between my messy handwriting: *I miss you, too.*

We didn't always need code. Like when I wrote *Do you ever feel alone?*

Sometimes, he wrote. *Sometimes it's more like I'm waiting for something big that I'm sure will happen to me. Do you?*

I couldn't write what I wanted to write. *I didn't feel alone until you left, and sometimes that makes me more angry than happy that we were out on the fire escape at all.* Instead I told him *Writing to you like this makes me feel less alone.* That one was tough to wrap in code. Hopefully it sounded innocent enough.

Weeks passed. I burned through a whole inhaler with how I couldn't breathe at night, scared I got him caught, somehow. Until I got his last letter.

Father is sending me to military school outside of Cape Canaveral so I can enroll in Officer's Training Corp and enlist once I graduate. I don't know if I will be able to write to you. If I can't, I hope you know that makes me glad that I will help protect this Country and the people like you I care about from the dangers of Communism.

On the back, he'd sketched the full moon over a fire escape, in pencil lead as gray as seagull wings.

No more letters from him. When I enlisted—if I was going nowhere in life I might as well go somewhere I might run into him—I took his letters with me. I kept them in my jumpsuit inner pocket on my first launch up to the moon, tucked close to my heart.

* * *

I knew it was better for me to stick to boys as bodies from then on, with how mooning over Flynn tore me up. For weeks, my stomach burned so much that whatever I managed to eat shot straight outta me. I couldn't find enough air, laid out in bed, no matter how hard I breathed, so I had to trawl the boardwalk and the bus stop bathrooms, looking for others. Counting streetlights from here to Cape Canaveral as the summer smoldered out into the fall.

Just bodies on boardwalks, on beaches, on pages that I smuggled here, on the moon. Bodies to give and take from, since my heart was already walking around in someone else's chest, anyway. Like once I heard Flynn tell me *I would sure like to know you*, it made me not want to get to know anyone else.

Me and Gloria talked body counts while Bowie blurred in the background, one of our first nights in the Boom Boom Room. Gloria was no angel, either, as much as she blushed and dodged, all *a lady never tells*, and told me not to be crass. Until I told her how cruising for dick made me feel like I was flashing the middle-finger to all the people who wanted to throw us in jail, or be like Flynn's father and bust out the belt. People like me and her grew up not being totally ourselves. So I'd be damned if I was gonna be anyone else, now.

With her sheeny, blue-lidded eyes, I knew she understood.

* * *

Starman North isn't invited to the Lodge show. Webber turns the lights low over the cabin-painted walls of the Lodge while the drummer and the pianist from the church band start warming up on the tiny stage by the far wall. I take chits from bodies in the bar line and ladle them tin cups of a wicked punch of Captain Morgan and Kool-Aid I whipped up in a big metal flour bin. Except Watkins and a handful of starmen on skeleton patrol duty, the whole base crams in for Gloria's shift-change show. Kern's not here, either. Tonight is ours before tomorrow is his. My hand doles out heavy pours—figuring the more punch flows out, the more cash flows back to me—while I nurse a beer. The drummer tap-taps the high-hats, and then a slurring Webber hits the stage to introduce the fresh meat and lay out the rules for the base. We're all brothers here. Hoorah. After some skit about the Starman's Oath that Hernandez and his poker night crew are so wasted they can barely get through, Webber shoves them off stage.

"And th'real reason y'all are here t'night," he slurs. "Fresh offa ssold-out show in th'Mare Serenitatis," Webber says, "please welcome th'nly girl on th'moon. Lady Moondust!"

The second that the driving piano chord of the real Space Guard anthem rolls into the air, the crowd cheers so loud that the booze bottles behind me rattle. The drummer keeps tip-tapping as the piano chords build. Gloria is taking her sweet time with the vamp, strolling halfway between bored and sad in the shadows along the edge of the room towards the stage. And when she hits the spotlight her eyes are already telling a story. *Oh, you're all here? Well, we're in this mess together, ain't that a laugh?*

And goddamnit, she was right about her dress in the lights.

Can lights pointed up at her from the edge of the stage spark off the washers, turning her into one of her star maps. Her hair is wrapped up in a white turban, with gold shimmering around her eyes. She whisper-sings the first lines of 'Five Years,' drawing us in with a campfire story. She hesitates, her eyes lost somewhere in the darkness over all the bodies in the audience, until she builds. Until her eyes fall closed and her voice wraps us all up, swaying from silk to sandpaper. Building to a growl when she waves her hands and cues us all to join in.

Five years. A sentence we all signed up for, pricking our fingers and writing our names in blood. Five years. All of us fuckups and idiots who couldn't cut it on Earth, so we rocketed over to the empty moon. Five years. Toy soldiers pointing rifles at nothing in the darkness. And if one of our stray cigs accidentally sparks the rocket-fume breath in the Lodge and blows up one of the fat star-spokes of the base? Well, we're expendable. We're just bodies. Sandbags to hold back a Red tide that isn't even coming.

So, five years. From my corner, alone in the dark, I watch some of them crumple, soldiers sagging, wiping at their eyes as they sway and sing. Starmen and fresh meat, all.

They must hear us howling all the way down on Earth.

SIX

MAG BOOT BOOGIE

I'm moving a little slower than I'd like on my cot the next morning. Gloria lays the sunshine on thick, calling out *a beautiful day to serve this great nation of ours,* while she gets dressed. Loudly. By the time I mag-boot-clap into the airlock for patrol duty, she's already suited up and snapping her helmet over her blue-scarfed head. She smirks while I flail into my space suit and end up knocking into the wall. Over breakfast, I finally told her about Kern taking over and the STAR System. She already figured something was up. Every starman in the mess around us looked like someone just drowned their puppy, and it wasn't just because they were all hungover.

Mostly, anyway.

Not even my worry could turn the lights offa her after-Lodge show shine. *We'll get through it,* she said. *We always do.* She didn't even need to bust out the tilting voice to make me believe her.

"There some reason breakfast ain't sitting too well with you?" she asks sweetly, crackling through her helmet's speaker.

"I *might* have sampled some of my punch while waiting for

Russo to show." My space suit squeezes just a little too tight, like it always does. "He never did."

"Next time, Romeo."

"N'why are you so chipper?"

"Temperance. Something y'all should give a nice big think to."

"Wasn't Jesus into wine?" I click my helmet in place and it hisses cool air onto my face.

"You turn water into rum punch, then holler at me."

"I'll see what I can do next welcome night."

We're supposed to grab two rifles from the rack by the line of space suits and sling them over our shoulders, though me and Gloria never do. Holding a gun makes us feel too much like cops, and the only thing to shoot outside are boulders, anyway. Somehow, the white plastic air guns that shoot rubber bullets are the Guard's way of getting around a half-assed promise with Russia not to use weapons outside of Founding Fathers. I shove the airlock lever up, and red lights dance around the outer door before it opens up with a hiss. We wobble through the airlock and out onto the black-and-white movie set of the moon.

I stop for a second and look up at the light of a clear black morning. I'll never get used to this view.

The moon is a sea of gray dust and craggy hills capped with a black sky, where a white-swirled blue and green half-Earth watches us. A few paved roads lead out to the abandoned construction zone of the Plymouth Colony civilian module and the Plymouth Rock landing site, both bordered in flashing red lights. Four squat watchtowers are birthday candles poking out of gray cake frosting. Six other teams are circling the base perimeter patrol, same as us, looking for micro-meteorite damage to the walls and the solar panels. Reagan loves to talk about *protecting American ingenuity from outside interest* in the Reels, so another two teams take reactor patrol duty. To me and Gloria's right, six lunar rovers—the two-soldier buggy things that look like toy Jeeps with the doors torn off—are parked in their charging stations by the base airlock. We call the twenty-seat rovers "lunar schooners" on account of them looking like boats on wheels, with satellite dishes for sails. Two are parked in the charging dock and the third must be patrolling the Plymouth Colony construction site. I don't know much about what the round-the-clock patrol out there is like, just that Kern hand-picked two squads of twelve starmen—each led by a lieutenant that kissed his ass—to keep watch. And they never leave their rifles in the airlock.

Me and Gloria start our patrol, bounce-stumbling and launching silver dust inches off the ground with each step. We're supposed to march loops around for our whole eight-hour shift, though me and Gloria usually end up wandering once or twice then taking a few laps with an RV and shooting the shit, same as everyone else.

I'm huffing by the time we make it out to the edge of the Delaware watchtower.

"Either or," Gloria says. One of our favorite games to pass the time. "Your first breakfast once you're back home. Pancakes or eggs."

"Both. I gotta make up for all those powdered egg breakfasts."

"Don't I know it."

"Either or." My turn to ask. "'Hey Jude' or 'Hello Goodbye'?"

"My ma says that the Beatles are the devil's music," Gloria adds with a sigh.

"If that was true, they'd be better." I kick at the gray dirt. "So, which is—"

A crackle in our helmet radios cuts me off. "Delaware, Diaz. You got your specs on?"

I stop in my tracks, bumbling in the low gravity, and Gloria *konks* into my side.

"Delaware, go for Diaz." Another weak voice echoes in my helmet, must be whoever's on duty at the Delaware watchtower nearby. The starman sounds like he's talking out of a paper bag.

"We got a starman MIA from Plymouth patrol," Diaz snaps. He wheezes and swears. Rustling in the background. Static hisses through my ears. "Repeat, MIA."

"MIA, heard," Delaware returns. Someone behind him groans. *Shit, shit.* "How in the hell did you get lights-out on a starman?"

"Bite my ass, Perkins," Diaz grumbles. Sandpaper scrapes away half of what he says next. "—until our radio helmets filled with chatter and noise, and some kind of—of dust storm blew in from nowhere. I called for the squad to hit the schooner." More static. "—hammered down to the Trenton Muster Station until—he must've wandered off."

"Dipshit, there's no atmosphere for weather up here, never mind dust storms," Delaware grumbles.

"Tell that to the twelve of us that saw a goddamned cloud blow around the quarry," Diaz yells. "It's the Russians mounting some kind of invasion, or, or—"

I slam the comms button by my collarbone. "Ward to dumbass Diaz. How the hell did you *not* notice a missing starman?"

"Ward, what was in that goddamned punch?" Diaz bites back.

"Idiots were still drunk on patrol." Gloria sighs at my side.

"Not my fault they're lightweights," I grumble.

"Heading back out now," Diaz continues. "Requesting recon out to Point Philadelphia side of the quarry." He grunts against what must be a blast of dust. "You got eyes on him yet, Delaware?"

"Negative," Perkins says. "Give us a minute to get to the scopes. We got a, uh..."

A wet gurgle floods my radio. I wince at Gloria and her lips curl under her helmet.

I huff. "And why is the goddamned watchtower not watching?"

"Norman to Ward," another voice snaps through the comms. "Perkins and I are puking our brains out. The boys in Delaware watchtower have looked a whole hell of a lot better. Give me a goddamned sec to get to the scope."

"Who's missing?" Gloria asks. "Did Miller stop to collect moon rocks again and trip, or...?"

"It's some lieutenant, Flynn Parker, just rotated in yesterday," Diaz says.

Diaz's words dump rocket fuel into my veins. I can feel my inhaler in my jumpsuit pocket, but it might as well be back on Earth. Flynn, here with me. *Sometimes it's more like I'm waiting for something big that I'm sure will happen to me*, he wrote. I'm sure that *something big* wasn't running out of oxygen, keeled out on the moon.

Gloria's space-suited hand on my shoulder steadies me. Behind her face shield—reflecting the lights of the base behind us—her blue-powdered eyes are steady, telling me *we got this.*

"Specs on," Perkins says. "We're not seeing clouds on the scope. No invading Russians on the radar, either."

"I know what we goddamned saw," Diaz grumbles.

"Freeman to Delaware," Gloria says, knowing I can't speak. "Me and Ward'll hammer to Philly for recon."

"What's your twenty?" Diaz asks.

"Five minutes," Gloria says. "We'll boogie to the base and hop in a rover."

"Good," he says. "Comms open. Don't drive off the quarry cliff."

We launch into the air off the gray dust piles, bumbling into the dark.

* * *

My breath is a tornado locked in my helmet. Sweat trickles down my face and I can't wipe it away, so it drips over my lips. I taste salt and regret, washing away the fake-fruit sweetness of rum punch. The rover rumbles over the pavement with Gloria at the wheel. Up ahead, red lights that ring the quarry blink in the black air, not a cloud in sight.

Gloria drives until we run out of road by the forgotten pile of gray moon bricks. We don't know the area well enough to drive safe and last thing we want to do is roll off a cliff, so me and Gloria hop out of the rover. I scrabble and bounce in the low-gravity, each huff sending more fog against the edges of my helmet, blurring the glass. Gloria yells at me to slow down.

Everything is black and gray, like Flynn's lead sketch of the moon.

"There!" Gloria jabs her arm out ahead.

Somewhere in the direction of the quarry cliff, a lone

starman faces us, just a white smudge against the black sky. The blue light inside his helmet is a dim lighthouse beam.

"Starman, you copy?" My helmet radio only squeals static back to me.

My inhaler. Jesus, fuck, my inhaler. Gloria is gonna have to carry us both back to the base. I can see Flynn as a kid, wild-eyed, scrambling around the fire escape. At least I don't keel over. Gloria bounces up ahead—and why does she stop, turned into a frozen rock pile, same as him? I bumble into her side and through her helmet I can see the muscles working at the sides of her jaws.

I know Flynn's face—the too-big nose, the neck I've drawn in my notebook, the lips I kicked myself for not kissing. Only he's older, now, and his face is slack, his mouth open, his eyes lost somewhere on the ground.

And when I look down, I can see why. Impossible gray mist glowing in invisible headlights swirls around his ankles. The mist rolls towards us and before I can stumble back, it's all around my feet. And Gloria's, now. So, so beautiful, like cigarette smoke curling in the spotlight of Ma's club, only the whole gray moon is the stage.

Slowly, the mist pulls together, rising, like some invisible hand pulls it up from the middle. Something in the mist. Someone. The whole wave of it stretches back over the gray cliffs behind Flynn and deep into the quarry—slipping past cracks in the rocks.

I blink and I see blue glass. The cold curves of a machine, swirled with colors. A spiked, shivering jewel that's like the broken heart of a beast.

I feel eyes. I feel hunger.

A blinding flash of light. The mist swallows us whole.

* * *

Everything is screaming at me. Lights on control panels, screaming. Alarms, voices that sound like tin cans scream in a language I don't know. I'm in a ship, looking through blue glass, and the ship is on fire.

The *Saint Christopher* shuttle? No. Something way smaller. I'd turn around and look behind me, but I know I'll see a wall of flames. The left thruster just blew—and I don't know how I know that, through the blue, but I do. Same as I know that I gotta tap out the right notes on the mirror ball of the controls for me to pour more bass into the right thruster so it'll blast me back onto my projected flight path before—

Boom.

Bye, right thruster. *Fuuuuuck.* My scream comes out like a shredding tin can.

I close my eyes because the gray ground of this little world is racing towards me, and I can't blow to mist because I'm so far away from the landing point with no Instrument in sight. And he'll never find me. And he'll look forever, same as I would.

The ship's hull howls and tears as it skitters—I scream over it all, glass bones breaking—before it grinds to a halt.

Alright. Alright. Safe, and silent. And lucky that I didn't rupture the engine core containment tank and blow myself and half of this middle-of-nowhere solar system away with it.

Screaming as the rocks from my impact rain down, burying me alive.

Though, is this alive? Aching, broken, screens dying all around me. Too far from the music of the others. Praying *help, I can't hear the Song. Please find me.*

The walls of my ship hiss and tick as they cool. Then, just quiet. The quiet is the worst, trying to suck every last bit of the Song out of me. Waiting, drifting, fading out for a few bars short of forever.

Until—sound. Not music. Noise without the grace, just metal against rock, and jabs at the dirt, and tiny, awful voices that I eavesdrop through their radio waves. They sing out without Song: *Hey captain, I think we found something here?*

And then rubble clears just enough for me to slip out of the cracks.

* * *

The blue light and the mist clears. I'm burning up in my space suit like I'm still caught in the fire of a ship hurtling towards the moon. Gasping. Frozen with my hand stretched out to Flynn. Gloria is two steps ahead of me, another statue in the mist. The mist twirls, reaching out, and I'm drowning in warmth. Heat and light trail up from my fingers. I feel the light like water in my ears, and I'm not alone in my head, somehow not alone in my body. Muscles stiffen, head tipped up. The light seeps in past my eyes.

Don't be afraid.

Fingers over my brain, poking. I sputter and spit against the invasion, but the fingers push harder. Moving memories. Flash. I'm strapped in a shuttle. Flash. Cruising a Miami boardwalk to make up for losing a boy. Flash. On a fire escape with Flynn—*and he's here, if only I could reach.* And then asleep in a catwalk, wrapped in mist.

Here. Here. *Yes.* The fingers in my head soften. Stroke.

We join in the Dance, again, I can feel the voice sing.

Fire in my chest. Fire blasts out of my mouth.

The fingers and the voice and the light stop and slip away.

And I miss it all, somehow. Even the engine screams and the tin-can of my voice. The music. My bones turn to mist and I don't feel my body hit the ground.

SEVEN

CLOSED DOORS

I'm trapped. Hot metal bands are strapped around my chest, keeping me from sucking in a full lungful of air, with two more pinning one of my legs. When I open my eyes to the walls of the Boom Boom Room, the only thing holding me down is Flynn. We're on my cot, tangled up in each other, him jamming me into the wall. I'm in my jumpsuit and Flynn is half out of his, the zipper down to his waist, his bare arms scalding hot and shaking against me, the hair on his chest wet with sweat. His eyes are crammed shut under his dark brows, twitching through a fever dream. Sweat plasters his short brown hair to his forehead. His lips quake a prayer I can't hear. Across from us, Gloria sprawls half on her cot, half on the floor like she passed out drunk.

No. We were outside. Then mist. Then voices? And fingers digging into my head—and I can't breathe. The edges of my eyesight fizzle to black.

I wriggle under Flynn, freeing an arm. I manage to snatch my inhaler from my jumpsuit pocket, shake it up real nice, and suck on its vapor. Mist moves all through my lungs, opening them back up. My vision clears and I see Flynn is still there. The doll of a boy from my fire escape is a toy soldier shaking on my cot.

"Flynn," I whisper, rubbing his shoulder. Just more shivers, more head twitches. "Wake up. You..."

Across from us, Gloria murmurs and scrubs a hand across her face. "Delaware, we got eyes on him." Her voice is a soft gurgle. Then she slides to the floor with her back against her cot. "What happened?"

Flynn is shaking like he's in a shuttle launch.

"Something's wrong. I—I can't get him up."

Flynn stiffens, arching off the cot with his arms crammed to his sides. I shake his shoulders, yelling his name. Nothing, just his lips curling in a frozen scream. Gloria scoots over, panic in her eyes. I practically hop onto him as I shake his shoulders. He finally heaves in air and pops off the cot, shoving me off. He hugs his knees to his chest, wild-eyed.

"You're alright," I tell him. Or I ask him. My voice shakes too much to be sure. "You're..."

"Where are... How did...?" His eyes hit mine for the first time. "Mitch? How in God's name did you get here?"

He scoots to me and pulls my hand—a flash of fire and fog in my eyes, the second our skin hits—into his lap.

"And just where is *here*, anyhow?"

"We're back on base," I say.

"No—we were outside." Gloria's fingers tighten on the edge of my cot. "Mist, and something wild going on with my helmet radio with all them voices, and..."

"I was on patrol." Flynn starts narrows his eyes, tilting his head. "Diaz shouted something about a dust cloud rolling in. Then, then... nothing. You remember?"

Something about mist moving on its own and fingers in my head? I shiver. "No."

My alarm clock on the shelf says it's just past 1500. Me and Gloria were on duty for maybe an hour before we got the MIA distress call. My memories of the last eight hours or so have faded to mist.

Gloria leans back from me and Flynn, then slowly crawls back to perch on the edge of her cot, her elbows on her knees. "I think... I think Diaz found us. I can almost hear him hollerin'. All black after that. He must've got us back on the rover."

Three fist pounds against the door cut her off.

"Freeman, Ward. You in there?"

Oh God. The smugness of Kern's voice even slips through closed doors. Gloria opens her mouth to say something, but I put a hand up to stop her.

"Two minutes to get to my quarters," Kern snaps before me or Gloria pipe up. "That's an order."

Flynn's hands shake in mine. He squints, eyes aching against the light. "Don't leave me like this," he whispers.

Gloria, bless her, takes that as her cue. She slips out of the room without another word, leaving me and Flynn alone on my cot. He turns from me to his sketch taped on the wall. I search his eyes, the same window-cleaner blue as that night on my fire escape. The tears I see in them breaks me open.

"I reckon you're really real." His voice is as soft as the backs of his knuckles along the side of my face. "You got to be."

Heavy, dark brows cut across his pale forehead. Flushed cheeks, regulation smooth. His jumpsuit open to a muscled chest that I would bury my face in if Kern's warning wasn't ticking down in my ears.

"As real as you are." I brush my fingers across the badge over his nametag. "Lieutenant. You'll be captain in no time, just like your Pop wanted."

Something moves over his face, and his shoulders ease. His hands slip into mine.

"We got a lot of catching up to do," he says.

"We'll have time."

I wait, in case he'll run off. I let him cross the space between us and kiss me first. His lips are sweet and strong—rum cut with Kool-Aid—and clumsy against mine, our teeth knocking together. I slip my fingers to the back of his neck, tugging him closer. I open my eyes mid-kiss, and he's so close to me that he's just a blur.

* * *

A closed door seals the room that used to be Watkins's from the rest of the base, each of the rivets glowing in the overhead lights like Gloria's washers on the stage. And up my ass with a space suit air hose, because two starmen I don't recognize are keeping watch. I'm in for it. Kern didn't call me here to give me a medal for rescuing Flynn. He'll accuse me of being blackout drunk on patrol, and I don't even remember enough to argue.

Gloria must already be inside with how I lagged behind her, barely able to tear myself from Flynn. Let Watkins toss me on latrine duty, I don't care. Me and Flynn are breathing the same recycled air, and I'm walking on the ceiling. The door opens and I spot Gloria, her back to me, and Kern, his hands folded behind his back, his cigarette ash hair beneath his service dress cap. His red jumpsuit is sporting some new white stars on the epaulets.

Two puffs from my inhaler do squat to calm my lungs.

Gloria turns to the door and all the color is gone from her face. Her eyes meet mine for just a second—*game over,* they tell me—as she freezes in the doorway. Eyes out to the blue-painted hallway, like she's seeing it for the first time.

"Lieutenant Bomer will get your things," Kern says. "Launch is in two hours."

I reach for Gloria's arm, calling her name as she passes, but her eyes don't focus on me. She brushes me off and then clomps down the hall. And then somehow, I'm in Watkins's old room with the door sealing us in. Kern is too big for the cramped space. His eyes on me tick a launch countdown in my head.

"Ward."

"Sir." My quick nod at him sends rum-punch spins around my head. "What's happening with Gloria?"

"*Freeman* was given the option to behave like a soldier or ship out."

I don't have to ask which one Gloria chose.

"Though I would worry about myself if I were you," he says, bored eyes back down at his clipboard. "Given your actions here."

I shrug. "I recall seeing you sipping on a few fingers of smuggled bourbon after Sunday Service in the Lodge, sir."

"The rules don't apply to commanding officers." He waves a hand. "I'm not referring to your contraband operation. Which, of course, Columbia knows about, as you're not nearly as clever as you think."

"Why would they let me keep it up?"

"We view it as a... pressure release valve to stem wider resentment."

He's really testing the slapped-on ease I'm trying out. I let out a slow breath. "Then what behavior do you mean, sir?"

A tiny bit of red creeps up his neck. Good.

"I'm referring to inappropriate contact you've had with a fellow starman. Which you full well know goes against the Guard's moral code."

Sucking on my inhaler again would only let Kern know how much he's getting to me, so I clench a fist at my side.

"I'd say there was nothing inappropriate about the contact, sir. They were very much on board."

Kern sighs and turns away from me, stalking in a cloud of cologne over to the far wall, where he crosses his arms behind his back. I can see him looking out an imaginary window at a big open space in the National Mall where the monument to him will sit, one day.

"You're suggesting that there has been more than one?" He clears his throat, not bothering to turn around. "Of these instances?"

Oh. He's embarrassed. Or. Or? Something more? Lucky that he's turned around and can't see the smile yanking at the corners of my lips. I remember the Uncles. *As long as you're useful to them.*

"I'm suggesting nothing. I'm telling you there's been a few instances, sir. With a few different starmen." The way his shoulders snap straighter only makes me want to keep going. "Is it helpful if I describe them?"

When Kern spins back to me, I see that the red has crept up from his neck and across his cheeks. The crinkles in his eyes tell me, *Tell me and don't tell me.*

"There are more of you with these proclivities here in the Guard? And you would be able to recognize them?"

"I'm saying that what happens between two people behind

closed doors is no one's business but theirs, sir. And that my *proclivities* were no surprise when I was enlisting."

Kern cuts the space between us with two quick steps. His leather-brimmed full-dress cap adds to the two inches he already has on me. He tilts his head to look down at me. But I've got years of mag booting around these halls with my shoulders straight to pull from.

"This is a matter of national security, Ward, and exactly the reason why we're enacting the STAR Soldier system. Homosexuals are a security risk that the Reds can discover and exploit, and—"

"Respectfully, sir, we aren't exactly hitting up the bars of Lunogorod with the Russians. I can't see how they would find out."

I can see red webbing the whites surrounding his steel-gray eyes. Smell the old leather of his cologne. I almost want him to poke me in the chest, or throw a punch. Gimme a chance to knock him in the nose and see if motor oil will spurt out instead of blood. I must pass some test with how he steps back again and looks down at his clipboard.

"You've got a good thing going, here," he says without looking up. "Enlistment up soon. Your smuggling has put some decent money in your pocket. Give us a few names, and you can go back to all of that." He looks up with softer eyes and I can almost hear clanks from the machine trying to smile. "If you're smart, you can use the STAR System, Ward. That's why it's here. If you re-up I could even put you up for a promotion for your cooperation. Set yourself up for life."

Kern's eyes tell me: *Do what I did, and push that perversion down.*

"Not that kind of setup I'm interested in."

"Even after someone reported you, you're unwilling to do the same?"

"I'd rather be stupid than a rat." I borrow some of Gloria's sing-song and let it lean into my voice. I smirk down at his lips, then back to his eyes again. "Or a coward."

"Then we'll continue this conversation back on Earth," he says with a wave of his hand.

I snap out my best toy-soldier salute. I'm barely out of his quarters before Kern snaps his fingers and I feel the hands on me. No. Wait. *Back on Earth.* Hands claw at the backs of my arms, yanking, and—*Wait, wait.*

"To the brig," Kern says. "Eyes on him until launch."

We'll have time, I told Flynn.

I don't scream. I don't give Kern that ammo for his spank bank. I'm dead weight, mag boots scraping down the star-spangled steel hallways past the red jumpsuits. I think I hear Hernandez clapping and cheering my name.

"Hey, that asshole still owes me a *Penthouse,*" Sousa yells after us.

In the coffin of the brig, bruises bloom over my body.

EIGHT

LAUNCHED

Handcuffs don't fit over a space suit. I never thought I'd learn that the hard way.

The bridge of the *Saint Christopher* is a small movie theater with a window that looks up to the silver retractable launch bay roof. Five padded seats form a line in front of the control panels and domed screens with their glowing green flight paths and fuel numbers, with the rest of the fifty seats in cramped rows of ten. Kern's guards *escort* me to the back row—past Watkins up front, who nods at me—where I'm the last starman to sit. My own fault, I guess, for thinking I could carve out some kind of life here. For being an idiot and following Flynn into the Guard in the hopes that I'd ever see him again. Moon-eyed like some dopey lead in *How to Marry a Starman.*

Flynn, blurry up-close, in my arms. We barely got to say hello, and I didn't even get to say goodbye.

Kern's starmen buckle me to the seat and duct-tape my wrists together. With the fat lip I gave one of them, I'm not surprised.

"Welcome to the back seat of the cop car." All the music

is gone from Gloria's voice. At my right side, she flicks on her helmet light and I can see that they made her scrub the blue powder from around her eyes. That's alright. I got enough blue and purple around my swollen left eye—one helluva shiner—for the both of us.

I try real hard to smile for her. Feeling anything other than empty right now hurts too much. Her eyes tell me *Baby, I sure know.*

"At least your hands are free." I lift up my duct-taped wrists. "I was never into bondage."

She manages a slight twist of her lips in something like a smile. "You clock 'em good?"

"You know I did, Miss Monday."

"Good on you, boy."

The retractable roof in the hangar roars as it rolls away, drawing up the curtain on this whole shit-show show time.

"Sure will miss that view, though." Gloria points one white-gloved hand up.

The Earth is a murky circle, like I'm looking down at my cup of rum punch. Clouds float like the smoke from smuggled cigarettes that the others trade for extra beer rations. I traded my life for a thousand-buck bonus. Founding Fathers' best trader. Traitor to yourself, Mitchy, and how soft your heart wants you to be, and traitor to the music that moves in your hips.

The only music I hear is when the engines growl to life.

Ignition.

The ship rattles up through my bones. *Hiss, rumble, whirr.* White clouds billow at the edges of the shuttle window, and when I blink, it's a silver column rising up. Cold fingers over my head again.

We are go for lift-off.

I cram my eyes shut as my stomach yanks and the shuttle lifts from the metal stage of the launch bay. An ocean is trapped in the ship and it roars beneath my feet. The ship shivers and slices through the air, *fearless men unbound by gravity, who loose our heavenly lightning hard.* The ocean beneath my feet calms and the starmen around me whoop like seagulls on the boardwalk back home.

I cram my eyes shut against the stomach-spins, and the blue halls of the base sear against my eyelids. I can see the tip of one of my cigarettes catching fire. I brought cigarettes and matches in the ring. Crazy, yeah, to light up in that big tin can pumped full of oxygen. One stray spark and *kaboom.* But what a way to go. Quick-quick as a lighter-flick, and worth it for that mouthful of Marlboro.

And now I want to light that whole goddamned place up. Fog fingers in my head tap, tap at my matchbook. Look—there's the fuse of the fat star-shaped firework of Fort Founding Fathers. Those assholes would deserve it, the way they treated Gloria and me. Kern will have a harder time with his STAR Soldier System if the whole house is on fire. So easy for the big bad bloodhound with busted knuckles to lower a little flame down to the firework fuse.

"We're getting some unexpected noise," one of the flight crew says. "Abnormal hull vibrations. Do we abort?"

"No," another answers. "Still within the green zone."

The headrest of my padded launch chair beats against my helmet, rattling so hard my eyesight blurs. And it's not supposed to be like this. That big gentle hand that's supposed to pull the ship's puppet strings is clawing something mean on the side, trying to scatter us toy soldiers into space. Hull vibrations, nothing. Music rises up from deep in the ship, played on a church organ made of starlight, with deep-space coos, and *ahhs* and—

Boom.

I can see the whole base exploding in red, white, and blue fireworks. Flames roll down the hallways, and starmen around me scream, and I'm screaming. The organ blasts from deep in the ship want to rip us all apart, and *ladies and gentlemen that's all the show we got for you tonight.* Flash. Fires blaze in a ship that's crashing to the moon. I gasp and my eyes fly open. Gloria screams at my side. When I grab her hand as best as I can with my bound wrists, the noise of the shuttle warps and bends—with her voice shimmering high over the grinding metal like she's belting on stage. I blink and silver shudders over everything. Alarm lights? Tinkling wind chimes, somehow, then electric whirrs, and blasts, and the shouted prayers and yells from the starmen putter out like someone yanked the speaker plug. Beeps from the nav systems keep an even time.

In the sudden quiet, eyes look around like *I wasn't really scared. Were you?*

Tells in the crinkles of their eyes. *Sure as hell was.*

"Looking mighty fine, *Saint Christopher,*" comes Kern's tinny voice from the front panels, safe back on the fort. "Godspeed home."

Kern's *mighty fine* is sure as shit a lot different than mine. They must not have picked up the ship nearly busting open.

"Copy, sir." The voice from the captain at the front quivers a little, just at the end. "We'll tell Earth you say hello."

Something punched a hole in my suit with how I can't breathe. Gripping Gloria's hand is what calms me down.

She looks down at our intertwined, gloved hands, and a tear trickles from one of her eyes. Her other hand flicks invisible rosary beads.

For once, I join her, mumbling prayers in my helmet that only I can hear.

* * *

The second we touch down at the Columbia Base runway on Cape Canaveral, the weight jams me something fierce. Stiff-jointed after three days cramped in the back and praying my MAG diaper wouldn't leak. Every muscle feels like used chewing gum in Earth's stronger gravity. I slug down the shuttle ramp, and unclip my helmet. Florida sun over the landing pad sears my eyes.

I'm never leaving the ground again, not even on a plane.

Once we're out of our space suits, the babysitters tug us away before I even have a chance to talk to Gloria.

The Guard can boogie real fast when it wants. Even here on Columbia, I'd have to wait two weeks and fill out three forms just to get a new pair of boots if the heels wore out, but my hearing is scheduled for the morning. Better to take out the trash like me before I start to stink.

Nightmares of moving mist in the brig, and then I practically blink into a conference room with Guard brass and lawyers around a long oval table, sitting at attention in a stiff chair. This ain't a hearing. It's a telling. The brass ass with the most chevrons *tells* me that I'm there to *tell* them the names of twenty confirmed homosexuals in return for reduced administrative disciplinary actions under Article 15. The three other starmen who are supposed to be my jury keep quiet.

"Twenty?" I whistle. "I can hit the barracks bathroom and see what kind of confirmations I can drum up, sir. Give me two hours. Maybe a bit more if I need breaks to rest my jaw."

The hearing doesn't go so great for me after that, even after someone who says he's my defender submits a letter about my *exemplary dedication to Guard values* from Watkins. Chevron yammers about the *seriousness of my conduct, giving me a chance* and *suspension of Constitutional rights while on Space Guard duty*—I'd know all this if only I wasn't such a fist-throwing fuckup.

But damnit if I don't cut a *Honcho* cover figure in my dress blues, while the officers hit me with principal eyes. I combed my wet curls into a neat side-part and licked my fingers to smooth the wild fringe of my eyebrows in the head mirrors, while starmen swirled in steam from the showers. Since I'm of no service to the Guard, my service is no longer required. Dishonorable discharge, effectively immediately.

A couple of signatures on a couple of pieces of paper, and I'm out on the sidewalk outside the security gate of the base, with all I own in this world in a trash bag at my feet. My last paycheck—barely enough for smokes and a bus ticket—in cash in the front pocket of a denim shirt I haven't worn in five years. Whoever packed my stuff left everything but a handful of civ clothes and a canvas pouch with a bar of soap and a toothbrush on the moon. None of my letters from Flynn. That one hurts most. Even more than missing the old Folgers can stuffed with my chits from smuggling that I didn't get a chance to turn in for real cash. No surprise that disappeared.

Seagulls by the bus stop dive-bomb each other, fighting for crumbs around the trashcan. Moon-gray clouds clamp a steel roof onto the sky. A hit from my inhaler does nothing to douse the fire burning me up. I close my eyes and can almost hear the electric whirrs that rattled through the shuttle during takeoff. When I open them again, it's a damn miracle that the fuel tanks by the *Saint Christopher,* just a silver smudge in the distance, aren't rolling in flames.

"Fancy seeing you here."

I don't recognize Gloria, carrying her own trash bag, at first. A Yankees cap half-covers her face, and she's tucked her hair up inside of it, wearing too-big jeans and a men's flannel rolled up to the elbows. Safer for her to travel like this.

She's light in my arms. We don't hug for more than a second because us crumbling here on the sidewalk in full view of the base is the last thing either of us wants.

"What'd they peg you for?" I ask.

"Bein' who God made me is fraud to them."

"Those goddamned fuckers." I wince. "Sorry."

"Goddamned fuckers, in this particular instance, is mighty fine by me. What'd judge man say 'bout you?"

"Some morality shit all 'cuz I wouldn't rat out my fellow fags-in-arms."

She toes the cracked sidewalk. "Where you headed?"

I swing my trash bag. "My Pop's place in California. You?"

"I called up my folks and told 'em..." Her sigh is a long, tired breeze. "Well, didn't tell 'em the whole story. Just that I'm in a bind. They got me a plane ticket back to 'em in Chicago."

"Must be nice."

She gives me the hairy eyeball, and plucks at her shirt. "Their help's never free."

"I know. I didn't mean it like that."

"Sure you didn't."

In a stab of lightning, I'm back with her on the moon again, paralyzed in rolling fog. Reaching, reaching—trying to scream from a mouth that won't move. Fingers in my head.

Don't be afraid.

I search her face. She must know this is coming, with how her lips press together and she looks away at the eaves-dropping seagull atop the trashcan. Its yellow feet soft-shoe on the trashcan lid.

"Glor, what happened up there?"

She squints up into the clouds. "The ship wanted to fly apart, huh? I was praying with my whole heart that it would stay together."

"No, I mean when we found Flynn. What was that? The mist, and I swear I heard voices, and—"

Her eyes snap back down to me. "I can't talk about that." She stops and sighs, softening the hard edge in her voice. "I'm not ready. Maybe—maybe I'll never be."

She waves a hand at the seagull and it jumps off, laughing at us and soaring up to the others. Just another circling speck of white cutting clear across the gray sky.

NINE

SUNSHINE SHITTY

Highway billboards for the latest *God's Guardsmen* flit by the windows of the bus as we pull into Tallahassee. I stumble out of the bus to take a leak and I have to stop in the middle of the crowded bus station just to catch my breath. Domed TV screens in every corner. Automatic ticket kiosks that look like panels on the shuttle, with glowing glassy buttons and blinking route maps. Packets of powdered pancake breakfasts and Thanksgiving dinners in a Moon Meals vending machine. How could people want to eat that shit? Starman North sips a can of Coca-Cola Comet—*The official soft drink of the United States Space Guard, flavored with real Florida oranges!*—on a domed TV the size of a billboard by the newsstand. The Coke ad ends and the next film sees a squad of Miss Moonies in silver bathing suits and space helmets tap-dancing on roller-skates, singing about the new Miss Moonie's Drive-In off I-90. *The best burgers and shakes from here to Saturn.*

Basic-training crewcuts and Miss Moonie finger waves in the crowd. Some guy slams into me and yells at me to watch it. When I turn, the shiny silver buttons and the epaulets on his suit jacket have me thinking that Kern followed me here.

There are no *Blueboys* or *Honchos* at the newsstand, not that I have enough cash. I don't let my eyes linger on the magazines I really want, with blurred shapes on the cover and big screaming headlines: *ALIEN ENCOUNTER*. The front page of the *Tallahassee Teller* says *PREZ REAGAN TO MAYOR BEAM: CLEAN UP NYC OR I WILL*. A red, white, and blue watercolor of Reagan on the cover of *Time* salutes over the words *REPAY. RESTORE. RENEW.*

"This ain't no library," the guy behind the counter of the newsstand snaps. "Buy something or beat it."

Bodies, and noise, and blinking lights, and a husky voice from a chrome radio on the newsstand belts *I'm a-waitin' for my straight-shootin' starman* while girls doo-wop behind her. Buses honk and their exhausts stink like rocket fuel. A dust storm blows around in my head, blocking everything from view, and the next thing I know, I'm leaning against the Moon Meals vending machine, trying not to keel over.

I buy a Thanksgiving dinner Moon Meal, rip open the packet, and add water from the hot spout of the vending machine. Back on the bus, it's just mush in my mouth.

* * *

Three days in a bus across the country—nightmares of Flynn choking on mist storming my head when I manage to sleep—until we cross into California and I change buses in Palm Springs for the last leg. The *thing* that rumbles on eight giant dirt-caked wheels towards me outside of the station is not a bus. Someone drove a lunar schooner down from the moon, its silver solar panels and white satellite dish on the roof reflecting the hot sunlight.

Inside, I'm shivering in the air-conditioning before I even park my ass in one of the curved seats. Small domed TV screens on the bus roof flick on, playing a video of Starman North in the bus driver's seat, once we rumble onto the road.

"Hwelcome aboard this new solar City Rover, American-made here in the Golden State." He honks the horn. "And please enjoy your in-flight entertainment, hwholly provided for by Mayflower Studios."

I can't escape his shiny pomade-ad hair and his too-red smiles. Or the rocket blasts and the *hoorah*s from two *God's Guardsmen* flicks that burn away any chance that I'm gonna sleep.

And then I'm jelly-legged and stumbling down the bus stairs and out into the parking lot of the Sunshine City bus depot, my sweaty denim sticking to my skin. Waves of heat warp the air above the concrete. The rest of this place is just a couple of blocks of buildings in the middle of the endless desert, looking so much like Founding Fathers against the gray lunar landscape that I almost check my tank.

The cars lining up along the curb must've rolled off a *God's Guardsmen* set. I remember the hood ornaments and grille logos, but the curved chrome bodies and the model names glinting on the bumpers are all strange. Ford Saturn V. Dodge Luna. AMC Voyager, with a back spoiler that's flared like shuttle fins. I half expect them to blast off into the sky.

Pop honks and waves at me from the driver's seat of his dull gray '65 Chevy Impala—held together by twelve years of rust—at the end of the line of cars along the curb. Nowhere else to go. I can't run into the desert. I can't run to Miami. I'm glad I didn't stop there, in case the Calypso is boarded up and the boardwalk scrubbed clean.

My feet mag-boot clomp until I'm in the passenger seat next to him. The dull leather of the car's interior is the same color as his hair and eyes. I see him see me—sinking, swollen-eyed, nothing but a trash bag in my hands—and something deep in my gut cracks.

He pats the back of my head. "Those pieces of shit don't deserve you, Junior."

I hate how much he means it.

* * *

We drive past the half-empty hardware store, and the single-pump gas station of this nowhere town. Concrete buildings are washed in faded sunset pinks. The O in the neon sign for the County Laundromat twitches in and out. No boardwalk. No music, except for the stupid song from a thirty-year old musical called *Can't Help Singing* that spills out of Pop's car radio. The chick warbles about it raining champagne in California, only she says the state like "Californ-eye-ay."

Pop switches off the tunes. "I got the Beatles and the Stones albums at home. Don't you worry."

I don't have the energy to answer, not with how the gravity is pummeling me. My busted eye throbs something mean. Pop talks about how he came back from Korea changed, and how he knows that I'm changed, and that the world has changed a lot since I've been gone, too. Especially this last year. I'll learn how to get by, same as he did. And I have whatever I need. He rented a two-bedroom, figuring I might need a place to crash once my enlistment was up. He lined up a job for me on his construction worksite. He's not much of a cook, but we can learn together. No cooking tonight, anyhow, because we're celebrating.

My big welcome home is two Miss Moonie's Microwaveables on TV trays, both of us parked on his lumpy couch in front of the TV in the living room. Pop's rental is a flat shoebox of a ranch with beige walls and a dying potted palm by the coat rack. We don't got a lot to say, yet, so we let *The Love Boat* fill in the silence while I knock Salisbury space steak chunks into my freedom fries. The Microwaveables come with a mini Atomic Apple Pie that burps steam when I stab it with my fork, so at least that's something.

"I'll get us some brewskis," he says, smiling at me with a gravy-smeared mouth.

His gray eyes search mine. *Tell me I'm doing this right.*

"Sure," I mumble.

He's trying. I'm trying to try, as much as my headache wants to pop my left eye like a cork. He putters into the kitchen, and by the time I hear the bathroom sink running, I hit a button on the channel-changer to skip past a commercial. On the next channel, a looker on the evening news talks about continued Canadian presence in disputed territories. Mostly I'm focusing on his mouth, and how he's the kind of guy I'd follow into a bus station bathroom.

A ticker on the bottom of the screen crawls by with *PRESIDENT REAGAN'S ADDRESS DOES NOT RULE OUT SPECIAL MILITARY OPERATIONS IN THE REGION.*

Glass bottles clink behind me.

"You oughta turn that garbage off." Pop frowns on his way back from the tiny kitchen. He settles back on the couch and snatches the channel-changer from my TV tray before I have a chance to move.

"The Guard told us squat about any beef with Canada." The Bud he hands me freezes my palm.

"It's nothing." He takes a long sip. "Just noise."

I can't follow the plot of *The Love Boat* with how my eyes keep sliding closed. Pop notices and says I should get some shut-eye. He shows me to my room, where he hung up a Starman North wall calendar for me. Pop told me he's renting this place from a family who moved into a bigger house on the other side of town. I must be staying in their kid's old room if the green glow-in-the-dark stars stuck to the ceiling are any hint. I got a nightstand and a twin bed that Pop made up with neat military corners. I don't need much.

Not even past sundown and the fake starman's eyes follow me while I pull off my stinking clothes. I crash land in the squeaky twin bed. I must sleep for a while, because I wake up screaming in the dark, soaking my sheets. The edge of the bed, and the nightstand, and my pile of clothes glow green. I look up, head swimming at the minefield of stars stuck on the ceiling. The cold light turns the bedroom into an alien world.

* * *

Pop got me a job, sure, but I didn't think it would start the day after I got here. Work will give me purpose, he says, making us a pot of coffee in his small kitchen, and purpose is what I need. On the walk over to his construction site on the other side of town—and you can walk from end to end of this place in twenty minutes—I keep wincing in the dusty pink sunlight. I keep ducking under invisible doorways, my feet wanting to roll-step. My pounding heart is asking me *Where's the roof?*

The wide-open sky and the endless desert take all the air outta my lungs. I'm claustrophobic for all this space.

"Am I telling them you're my boy, or not?" Pop asks. His eyes move from mine out to an actual tumbleweed that blows across Main Street, running red through the town's only stoplight. "I'm happy to tell them you're my boy."

His tell is the way he sniffs at the dusty air. *Tell me I'm making up for leaving, even if I'm ten years too late.*

"Not telling 'em," I answer. "I don't want anyone treating me any different."

"Alright." Then, nodding, like he approves: "Alright."

We get to the job site before most of the other workers because Pop is the foreman. This neighborhood will one day be one of ten new blocks of houses with pretty brick fences and painted shutters. Now, it's not much more than brick piles and matchstick half-built house frames. Most of the workers here are not *technically* on the books, he says. A lot of them traveled from the border towns in Mexico to LA, and then the city shoved them out after the quake hit. They're on the move from the cops, saving enough coin to head up north to Canada, and Pop is happy to give them work while they're here.

He holds up papers, showing me building plans for the Golden Acres development. My arms are still too heavy. My dull eyes dart to the plans, then the concrete foundation in the dead earth. How the hell do you even start?

Pop pats me on the shoulder. "One board, one nail at a time."

Yeah. I know this. I've been on sites during my weeks with him in the summers, and he showed me how to hang drywall. But the sun is hard-boiling my noggin under my yellow plastic hard hat. The buzz saws sound like the rattles from the shuttle. Pop passes me off to a guy named Ricky who's around my age, with a sunburn painting pink over his brown arms, in dirty denim like the others. A couple of curls slip from under his hard-hat and onto his neck. Black stubble sandpapers his cheeks. I follow him to a cluster of houses that's a warzone of timbers and empty concrete foundations. The sound of every hammer and saw cracks my forehead. Ricky introduces me to the six other guys in our squad, who grumble their names, and tells me he needs a gofer for the day. *Go get me another box of nails from the shed. Go help Juan carry that timber. Bring those cans of primer to the house three down.*

I puff my chest out like the others do. I know this game. I take up space like I'm supposed to be here. Only, my arms shake when I help Juan with the timber. Try to help. I have to drop it and spit dust. Someone must've wrapped a veneer of wood around a long cement block the timber is so heavy. Same as how someone must've filled the two cans of primer with lead. Five steps and I have to rest the cans on the ground and catch my breath. Four steps. Three. Sweat burns my bruised left eye.

I can hear the whispers and the muffled laughs over my boot stumbles. I know enough Spanish to know that *maricón* doesn't mean butterfly when they say it the way the other starmen used to call me a pansy, before I had the ring to shut them up.

And Jesus Christ. Jesus Christ, I'm here again, only now I don't got a way to be useful. Now my muscles don't work enough to throw a punch. I'd rip that fuel hose right off that cement mixer over there if I could, and watch gasoline bubble over the dry earth. Flick my cig like a cherry bomb and watch this whole worksite—the County Laundromat that stinks like mildew, the ghost town Main Street with tumbleweed traffic, the bus station that looks like a pile of cinderblocks—and all of Sunshine Shitty turn to ash.

Only thing stopping me from whipping these cans at their goddamned heads is the fact that I can't lift 'em higher than my waist.

Instead, I walk. No other choice. Three steps, stop. Two steps, stop. The house down the lane isn't moving any closer, and my lungs are screaming, but I'm not listening. I can't let the boys behind me see. Two steps. Two fucking steps. I leave the primer on the front stoop of the mostly finished house down the lane. Past the plastic-wrapped windows, the rooms are all empty.

Pop is talking to Ricky and the others once I walk back. I can tell what Pop is telling them by his eyes, by the flick of his hand at me. *Give him a break. He just got out of the Guard. He'll get stronger.*

All of their eyes under their sweaty brows hit me. Maricón Mitch who couldn't hack it in the Guard and is now hacking up his lungs while his Pop begs the others to cut him some slack.

If this was the moon, I'd pull off my helmet and be done with it, just so I wouldn't have to start from nothing and go nowhere again.

TEN

AND NOW A HWORD FROM OUR SPONSORS

My first morning on the job lasts ten years, somehow. Come lunch break, the other men park it on house foundations and on truck backs, yapping. Ricky takes me to a short woman wearing a big sunhat with a pink plastic flower at the edge of the worksite, who's selling sandwiches wrapped in tinfoil out of a cooler. She's his ma, he says. They've got the same eye-crinkling smile. Pop lets her set up shop here. Same as he gave Ricky and his dad a job and warns them when Immigration is about to roll in. Ricky's parents hauled over from TJ and he was born in LA, even if the men who ran them out of the city called him a wetback, same as everyone else.

He lifts a can of Coca-Cola Comet, beaded with water, to his lips and drinks. Fishes me a can out of his cooler. I don't want to owe anyone nothing, but my throat's filled with dust. After lunch he brings me to the house at the edge of the block. The original plan was to finish the whole development before coming in and working on the insides all at once, but well. Well. My Pop did him and his a solid, so here's a pity party of a job that I can handle.

"What can you do?" he asks, voice echoing in an empty living room.

Yeah, what can you do, Last Mitch Effort? I hide a sniffle with a cough. The tears stay locked up. Attaboy.

I look to the broom and dustpan in the corner. Drywall powder mixes with dust from outside, coating the nail-scattered floors.

From his gofer, to a gopher hiding in my own little mound.

"I can sweep," I say.

"Sweep it is."

* * *

I have to peel off my wet shirt and wrap it around my face so I don't breathe in clouds of dust as I sweep. Nails tossed by the broom jingle across the floors. Pop is all smiles when he drops off a battery-operated radio and another can of Coca-Cola Comet. He sings out *How's the first day, Junior?* I'm so embarrassed to be pushing a broom while the others are lugging wood outside that I yell at him to quit hovering around me. I didn't need him when I was a kid, same as I don't need him now that I'm a grown man. Echoes in the empty rooms say my shitty words back at me, and he backs out of the house hands-up, laughing *easy, easy.*

Later I'll say I'm sorry. For now, I switch on the radio and keep sweeping. *Oooh we've got a plan in Vi-et-nam,* the Star-Spangled Sisters sing with jangly voices. I can see them tap-dancing in matching dresses. Some square named Chip Hines croons *Starmen are a girl's best friend* like we're at a sock hop. I change the channel looking for real music, and all I get is 'The Star-Spangled Banner' introducing an update from Reagan about how, now that gas prices are falling, it's the perfect time to buy Moon Bonds. Static on the next channel, then a commercial featuring some chick calling herself STAR Citizen Kate Dickens gabbing about how the new Ponds Moon Mask Cold Cream evens out even the deepest facial craters.

Static. Static. A barbershop quartet belts out the Guard Hymn in braided harmonies. Give me Fleetwood Mac, or Aretha, or hell, even the chirpy beige bullshit of the Beach Boys. I look up and Ricky is silhouetted against the late afternoon sun. I almost trip over my dust pan.

"What happened?" I point to the radio.

He shrugs. "Reagan's got a lock on the airwaves."

"No, what *happened*?" I grip the broom handle so hard I expect it to bend. "I been in the Guard five years, and it's like..."

Like we blasted off thirty years into the future and into the past at the same time. *Fly me to the Moon, let me play among the STARs.*

"The Big One," Ricky says.

One. One. One. His words bounce around the empty rooms behind me.

* * *

Ricky steps inside and closes the door behind him. He moves close and sits on the floor with the radio between him and me.

"We have to be careful." His voice is soft as the whisper of a record between tracks. "'Cause in LA, cameras on wheels follow you, and microphones hide in the walls. I don't know if that shit is out here, yet, but..."

He nudges the radio up in the empty house and scoots closer to me so that our dust-covered knees brush. His breath tickles my neck.

"I'm telling you this because people like us need to know these things," Ricky says.

People like us. The back of my neck tingles with something close to a blush.

He tells me a story with his words as much as his eyes.

The Big One is not really the Big One, he says, but a collection of Ones that are so Small that no one notices much, at first.

California's got it the worst, probably, because Reagan used to call it home. He got elected governor three times before he became president. He's still got one foot here, tugging strings, since his former lieutenant governor took over, and the hack he appointed mayor of LA fell in line. Reagan has a saying that he loves to bust out. *As California goes, so goes the nation.*

Before the White House and the Governor's Mansion, Reagan was an actor, back when movies used to mean something, according to him. They told stories that were Moral and True because the Studios got together and decided on the right way to tell stories, which they called the Hays Code. The code told them what movies could and couldn't be about. Men were men. They were soldiers, cowboys, detectives, cops. Women were nurses, teachers, showgirls who turn into upstanding wives, wives who turn into mothers without the audience seeing them in a Family Way. No homos except to setup a sissy gag now and then. No butches, because what man wants to see a movie with a broad in pants? Colored Folks could be goofy sidekicks, band singers, the help, occasionally tragic heroes if they found God—so long as the most they ever did with white folks was nod politely, because the Almighty made different races for a reason. The West was won by God and gun. Nazis and Commies and Pinkos are bad, and it's not bad to say that. You don't shit on the clergy because America is a Christian Nation, and you don't say shit neither. "Golly" is enough, by gum.

I remember a movie of Reagan's called *Bedtime for Bonzo* that used to rerun on the tube when I was a kid. He played a shrink who tried to teach a chimp to be an upstanding citizen. I can't say the flick improved my moral character.

When a shadow crosses one of the plastic-wrapped windows, Ricky's lips freeze. One of the other workers walks by, hollering about looking for the wheelbarrow. The brass band in the radio commercial is so loud I expect the windows to rattle. *Fly to the future in a new Ford Saint Christopher, now featuring satellite mobile telephones and compact disc player radios with crystal-clear sound.*

When the shadow is gone, Ricky leans in again.

Once Reagan landed in the governor's mansion in California, he decided that Hollywood was the storyteller of America, and surely, Studios should be encouraged—no, rewarded—for telling the wondrous story of our Country the right way. Mayflower Studios knew what was up, with their costume dramas about Pilgrims and the Founding Fathers following the Divine Will of God. They hit gold with the *God's Guardsmen* flicks. Then came the tax breaks, and city council seats, and zoning restrictions lifted around their sound stages and offices. The other Studios followed the cash and fell in line, too.

I was a kid in Miami when this was happening, busy ditching school, and making sure Ma didn't drown in the bathtub after her three o'clock solo happy hour.

The Studios were doing such important work and bringing

so much cash into the State that Governor Reagan wouldn't *impede the natural flow of free, American enterprise.* He created the Studio Economic Zones in '73. I was in the Guard by then and heard squat about this. Because who was the government to say what the Studios could do on their private property? And surely they could be trusted with their own private security, and their own code enforcement.

By the time Ford got killed in San Francisco in September '75, the Studios had a whole bank of movies about who really belonged in America, so it was easy enough to point at who didn't. The gunman was a *gunwoman*—turn to camera, gasp—and a Manson follower. A president got shot on city supervisor Harvey Milk's watch, and that's why you need ballot measures and executive orders to keep queers like him from working in government, and in the schools. The queers had got too mouthy ever since they started attacking cops in New York City in '69, and now we needed to remind them of how things work. Our Nation is a Family and there is only one kind of Family.

Ricky's voice shakes. When I close my eyes, I can see Reagan at podiums making speeches, only he's wearing Kern's face.

And after those tremors, the Big One hit, leveling six blocks of downtown LA and most of Bunker Hill. Instead of rebuilding the tenements—where Ricky and his folks lived—Reagan expanded the Studio Zones, and the execs built luxury apartments and themed hotels instead. Look at how he transformed slums into even more proof that Los Angeles is a shining City of Angels on a Hill. Think of what he can do in the White House for the whole country. We already have the roadmap in the Preamble of the Constitution—a living, breathing document that has kept this country safe these two centuries. I knew the words well since we had to memorize the Preamble for our yearly Loyalty Exams in the Guard.

We the People of the United States, in Order to form a more Perfect Union, establish Justice, insure Domestic Tranquility, provide for the Common Defense, promote the General Welfare, and secure the Blessings of Liberty to ourselves and our Posterity, do ordain and establish this Constitution for the United States of America.

Domestic Tranquility. Common Defense. He came up with a new campaign slogan for his White House run: *REPAY. RESTORE. RENEW.*

Though you can't put a price on the American lives lost, Europe must *REPAY* American dollars, by golly. We're going to *RESTORE* protections on American scientific and intellectual property, so no more worldwide leeching of our satellites and communications systems, our solar power, our medicine, our propulsion, our life support technology, and all other advances that grow in the fertile garden of the Guard. We must *RENEW* our faith in American Morality. No country is an island, but we are something bigger. We are a continent. Sea to shining sea, star to blazing star. We need nothing else but our American ingenuity, no one else but our leaders to safeguard our Bright Future.

Well, one specific leader, and his whole arsenal of wartime executive powers he loaded up after moving into the White House last January, because what is this campaign for Truth and Freedom if not a war against Immorality?

REPAY. RESTORE. RENEW. REAGAN.

The fizz of my Coca-Cola Comet is bubbling acid in my guts. Now I know where Kern got his talking points at that last Reels showing from.

"How in the hell does a construction worker know all this shit?" I ask. "You some kind of lawyer?"

Ricky flicks the tab of his Coke can. "Woulda been by now, if UCLA hadn't booted people like us out."

I don't have a chance to ask him about which kind of *us* he means. A knock on the door sounds like a rock dropped in a wheelbarrow. We both snap away from each other and I bonk my can with my knee, knocking toxic orange fizzy water all over the floor. Somehow the sun rocketed way down in the sky when me and Ricky have been gabbing for, what, ten whole minutes? Ricky bounces up, lowers the radio, and opens the door to show Pop on the front stoop.

"Quitting time." He smiles big at me, then looks at Ricky, and then back to me. I grab my hardhat and Coke and leave Ricky in the empty house. We're ten feet out of the construction site when Pop turns to me and says, "Ricky's a good dude."

I've never heard him use the word *dude* and never heard this fake breeze in his voice. How could you, I want to scream. How could you let all this shit happen when I was gone? How could Ma leave for Europe when the getting was good and not take me? How come you didn't drag me by the hair to Canada before I enlisted, when you still could?

Instead I grumble *whatever* at him, and we walk the rest of the way home. The town's single traffic light creaking in the hot breeze is the only sound between us.

* * *

Green light from the glow-in-the-dark stars seep through my eyelids in the dark of a bedroom that's not mine, that night. I never thought I'd miss my stiff cot in the Boom Boom Room. Pop is catching Z's on the couch, and the live-audience laughs from a rerun of *I Love Lucy* blows in through my door. I creep out my window and head back to the worksite because I need something to do with my hands or I'll kick in the TV. So I stumble in the dark, down the empty streets to the worksite and sweep dust in the empty house, come home before dawn, and then do it again all day.

My black eye fades to purple, then to a moldy green. It still hurts to touch. I should stop, of course, but every morning in the bathroom mirror I poke and pull at the skin, hissing. Every night is the same dream. Glowing fog rolls onto me, cold fingers creeping up my chest and into my head. Then fire blasts over everything.

Flynn visits me in my dreams, when I'm lucky. I know I'll never see him again, which drops the fifty-pound bags of cement we use at the site—the bags that are still too heavy for me to carry—onto my chest. He might as well be on Mars. *Ho, upward! Ho, moon-ward! Then Mars and asteroid bound.* Low voices singing the Space Guard Hymn laugh at me.

When I dream of holding a toy soldier on my cot, at least I don't wake up screaming. When I wake up screaming, I go to the worksite and paint until there are no more finished drywall rooms to paint. And then I sweep away piles of sawdust by the buzz saws, and clean up empty cans of Coca-Cola Comet from the porta-johns.

"If you're going to go stepping out," Pop toes the dirty linoleum of our kitchen with his morning coffee. "Just be careful. The cops, you know, they're looking for boys like you."

I keep the wall up between me and him, and turn to the

brick walls in his plans. At first, I can only carry four bricks at a time, stacked against my chest, from the pile by the cement mixers. I slap mortar between layers of brick, night by night. Three weeks home—my moldy green eye fading to yellow and finally healing up—until my muscles remember they're strong, and I can push a wheelbarrow full of bricks.

I keep the radio on at the site. No news from the outside, though. Just the Star-Spangled Sisters and commercials for the new General Electric ClearView Big-Screen Television with Opti-Disc recording. I learn how road trips are a breeze with Land Rover's new satellite-powered continental positioning system dash-navigator. And who has the money for this shit?

Ricky visits me in the mornings, and during a surprise scorcher halfway through May, he says the other men joke that a ghost visits the worksite every night to clean and organize the supply shed. They nod hello at me, though.

That night does nothing to thaw the chill on my skin. My feet kick a different path through town, out to the gas station bathroom, and after a few toe-taps Ricky slips into the stall with me. I smother a laugh against the back of my arm. His lips scoop up into a smile. For a few minutes, the sandpaper of his stubble smooths away my edges. I can tell in his eyes that he's seeing someone else in place of me, same as I'm doing for him, but we blast off together anyhow. I pick up an extra Coca-Cola Comet at the drug store and slip it to him at the job site. He winks at me, and that's all either of us need.

I'm not alone, though, not really, because I have Gloria this whole time. We write a shoebox full of letters to each other, and I can hear the warm church bells of her voice in her pretty cursive. *The shuttle took a left turn somewhere and dropped us off on the wrong planet*, she says. *This may be my last letter as a free man before I land in the slammer for killing my Pop*, I write back. While I was sweeping empty houses, she was leaving hers. She was barely two weeks home when she realized she couldn't be the son her parents needed, and they wouldn't see her as their daughter. So she left and moved in with her Auntie Anita in LA—barely two hours away from me—to help manage an apartment building now that Anita's latest husband died. Gloria writes about how she's settling in and tells me I have to come visit. I will, when I'm feeling like myself again.

Letters, weeks. I rip May off my Starman North calendar and burn the page in the trash bin. Then, I decide that Starman North can use two cigarette burn shiners over his pretty blue eyes. My big plans this first Saturday afternoon in June—drunk in my bedroom, alone, while a Miss Moonie's Microwaveable dinner cools on the nightstand—offer up some hints about what kind of a wild summer I got ahead of me. Pop is out grabbing brews with some guys from the site since I drank all the beers in his icebox again. And *Goddamnit Junior, I'm not the enemy*, he told me. Two months home, and the rest of my nothing life stretches out in pinched beers and empty calendar pages.

I almost don't hear the phone ring because I'm wailing *I'm a-waitin' for my straight-shootin' starman* with my best four-beer falsetto. I bounce over in case it's Ricky calling. Once or twice a week we meet up for some brick-laying.

"Do you accept a long-distance call from..." The operator's voice crinkles at the end. "The Only Girl on the Moon?"

I drum on the countertop, hooting. "You bet your sweet ass I do, lady."

Gloria's laughter drips out of the phone once the operator connects us. "You gave me Bowie and 'Five Years' when I needed it." She leans into her voice something sweet, and it's like I can feel her leaning over my shoulder. "Now you need this."

Rustling, then a metal click, then silence. A low, liquid build. Thrumming that sounds like a heart made of metal beating all crazy after six Coca-Cola Comets. Glowing hot meteorites hit the cymbals on the drum set of Ma's percussion section, over and over. Heatwaves blast over the shaking sides of the *Saint Christopher* and burn all the beer outta me. And the voice. Oh God. The voice paints a picture on the back of my eyelids of pouty gold-glittered lips leaning into a mic that's burning brighter than the sun.

Oooo it's so good it's so good it's soooo goooooooooood—

Another metal click and the music dies.

"What the hell is that?"

"That's disco, baby." Her laugh is thick and sweeter than the Atomic Apple Pie in my Moonie Microwaveable. "I'll be there in two hours. Lady Moondust needs you."

I write Pop a note to stick on the icebox. *I need to go this alone. I'll call.* Then I scrawl a quick *thank you for everything.*

Starman North's burned-out eyes watch as I shove everything I've got in a pillowcase.

ELEVEN

THE UNITED STUDIOS OF HOLLYWOOD

Not even two months in LA, and Gloria already looks the part of a celebrity, standing outside her car in Pop's driveway in a white flared dress with thin straps and big white Jackie O sunglasses. Last I saw her, she kept her chin-length curls wrapped under the purple flower headscarf. Now it's in a bun beneath a white scarf. Her hands, covered in white driving gloves, rest on her waist as she poses for cameras that aren't there.

She sees me in the front door, and leans through the open car window to honk her horn. "Your lady knight in shining Buick is here," she sings out.

I bounce out of the house, and I'm hugging her so hard that she swats my back, giggling at me, *Mitchy, I gotta breathe.* Her smooch leaves a Cadillac Red pair of lips on my cheek.

She pops behind the wheel and I toss my pillowcase of stuff in the backseat, and ride shotgun. Wordlessly, she hands me a Sony Moonboom from the back. The portable radio looks like the big remote controls the research unit in the Guard thumbed to wheel the surveyor rovers around, with silver dials and chrome lines set in a big black box. I hit the play button as she glides onto the road.

The demo is only a few minutes long. The electric ripples and waves start, and then Donna Summer giggles. *Oh, that's wild. What's that?* A male voice with a Italian accent answers *It's a rogue.* Rogue what? Gloria tells me that he's saying *Moog,* which is brand of electronic instrument thing called a synthesizer. The producer counts Donna in, and she sings a few lines. *It's so good it's so good. Heaven knows, heaven knows. I feel love. I feel love.* More star-music waves. Then Donna asks *Don't we need another verse?* Three blippy star beats tickle my skin. *No,* the producer says, *this is mostly about the feel of the music anyway.*

I play it again and again as we drive, with the sun turning the sky the toxic orange of Coca-Cola Comet, on the way to Gloria's apartment in LA. Off in the distance, giant white rovers crawl around the solar farm—three times as big as the one we had on the moon—with its glimmering panels pointed to the sky. Gloria's car smells like rose perfume.

I hit the eject button on the stereo and pop out the tape. I don't know how a little plastic square no bigger than my hand can hold so much magic. In black pen on the white label of the cassette, someone wrote *MORODER/BELLOTTE/ SUMMER – MUSICLAND – MAY 1976 DEMO.*

"What's Moroder and Bellotte?" I ask. I know Summer is Donna Summer. I smuggled her *Love to Love You Baby* album up to the Boom Boom Room. The first time I heard the sixteen-minute moany big-O of the title track, I wriggled on my cot while Gloria cackled.

"Music producers." Gloria turns her head from the road and taps the label with a white-gloved finger. "Musicland is a studio in West Germany."

Was a music studio. In what was West Germany, which flipped Commie last summer and went dark. Same as East Germany. And Morocco. Portugal, Spain. The news updates on the few TV and radio channels that reached Sunshine Shitty were obsessed with how the grocery store shelves were now stocked with Grade-A eggs from new heartland farms. I thought we were too far out in the desert for the outside world to reach. Turns out Grade-A asshole Reagan hit mute on all the news coming in from everywhere else, right before me and Gloria landed. Something about needing to focus, now, on the American family, now that the Reds are crawling all over Europe. The Feds even jammed the radio waves coming up from Mexico two weeks back when Reagan closed the borders.

The demo tape fell into the hands of a musician friend of hers, who's got a whole trunk-load of smuggled singles from Europe, plus demos and albums produced in LA that the recording studios didn't have time to release before the new General Welfare Bureau decided that American ears were too delicate to hear anything but the Star-Spangled Sisters on the radio.

I load up the cassette again. Gloria must know what I'm thinking with the way she's keeping her eyes on the road. Rogue Moog electronic synthesizer thing my ass. This sounds like the star music that rattled through the *Saint Christopher* before we almost blew.

The tape zips with my next rewind. "Are we going to talk about this?"

"Neither of us have shut up since Sunshine City, honey."

"I mean really talk about this music."

Well, why didn't I say so? And then she says that DJ Hat-Trick—his name is Patrick but everyone calls him Hat-Trick when he's doing his thing—will have to be the one to explain the Moog, because as far she is concerned, that doo-hickey is magic, all while her voice's tempo speeds way up. All while her eyes tell me, beneath her mascara-swept lashes, *don't push.*

* * *

Spotlights glaze gold over the red, white, and blue-painted letters of the Hollywood sign up in the hills as Gloria's Buick glides into the city. The wind swells in my ears when I lean out of the car to drink in the air.

Off in the distance, more spotlights play on the bottoms of the clouds. Screens on top of buildings, whole blocks glowing same as the computer panels back in Founding Fathers. A line of traffic blows their horns. I can just make out the figure of Starman North on a billboard screen the size of a goddamn house, but we're too far away to hear his voice. Then the red, white, and blue stars swirl and words bloom on the screen, even bigger than the Hollywood sign.

We are Mayflower Studios.

You are Mayflower Studios.

America is Mayflower Studios.

I used to light up Ma in the Calypso, thinking one day I'd be like Rock Hudson. And now here I am.

The electric shimmers of the 'I Feel Love' demo die after my latest replay. I don't even realize I'm sputtering when Gloria turns left, away from all the lights.

"Don't worry, Miami, we'll take a tour tomorrow," Gloria says. "It's still something. But..." She sighs. "You should've seen it."

Back in the Boom Boom Room, Gloria told me how she went to Hollywood to visit her Auntie Anita, who worked as a seamstress for one of the Studios before she retired. Anita had a whole sewing room in her apartment, and she saw how Gloria's eyes lit up at the bolts of fabric, and the metal rack stacked with clothes waiting to get altered. She was the one to steer Gloria from suits to dresses, following her niece's eyes. She put Gloria in a sweetheart neckline number with a flared skirt, stepped back, and told her *hand to God, you are the spitting image of one Miss Dorothy Dandridge.* There'd be no Gloria without Anita, or Hollywood.

And yeah, I know the Hollywood in my head can't live up to the real deal. The sets of Ma's favorite musicals were made of canvas and cardboard. But after Sunshine Shitty, reality can kick rocks for a while. I can use some fake glamor.

Fake or not, the glamor fades into the rearview mirror. Gloria must've taken a wrong turn with how we're puttering down a stretch of factories, then a narrow alley opens up onto a lake of gray pavement, with streetlights painting the smog pink overhead. At the other end of the lake, a giant clown face is laughing at us from a gray slab building. Giant red eyes, inset in a stark white face, glow in the darkness, with lights around its two-story open red mouth that rings the front door. A fake tiger rears up on the roof, illuminated in a spotlight. Gloria pulls up to the curb outside of the building.

"What kind of freaky-deaky place are you taking me?"

"A nightclub."

"A nightclub that's dead at ten on a Saturday night?"

"Exactly the problem we're here to fix."

Inside, the wide room is dead quiet except for the clinking of glass bottles as a shadow moves around the bar along the left wall. The place smells so much like the Calypso—years of spilled beer, cigarettes, and old cologne—that for a second I'm back on the lighting catwalk. Painted elephants balance on giant balls on the walls. Lions leap through flaming hoops. Horses dance in fringe-trimmed saddles. A DJ booth in one corner is the pulpit of a church, lit by a glowing triangle from the can light above. Green lasers and twirling multicolor lights spark off the dozen disco balls dangling from the ceiling, the central one so huge that I could curl up inside. For a second, I feel like I'm bounce-running out on the moon. Laughter like static in my helmet, burning up in the lights, shockwaves of music wrapping me up. Echoes of parties past have me dizzy, and I have to reach out a hand to Gloria's shoulder just to stay on my feet.

"This him? Funny, I thought he'd be taller."

A gruff voice clears the disco dazzles from my eyes. I look down and I'm at the bar, blinking wildly, next to Gloria, who pulls out a stool. The bartender's short hair is swept up into a glossy Elvis pompadour, bottle-black except for the gray at her temples. Ash from the cigarette stuck to the corner of her mouth falls on her black and white bowling shirt. She tosses a rag to the bar top and stabs her cigarette into the overflowing ashtray.

"Last Mitch Effort, meet Sure Bette, the owner and protector of Circus," Gloria says, making a burlesque show out of peeling off her white driving gloves.

"Charmed." Bette nods glumly. "I been running this place for fifteen years, since it was the Circus Cabaret, and the city almost ran me out for being a club owner with a set of knockers."

I wave my hands at the empty dancefloor. "You sure know how to throw a party."

She snatches her pack of smokes from the bar top, narrowing her eyes. "The cops just closed up the Hollywood Baths health club for code violations. Seems you boys were awfully focused on lots of squat-thrusts there." She lights up a smoke and the end flares with her first inhale. "Everyone's been too scared to hit the town this week in case they get caught in another raid."

Gloria frowns. "Just when the Stus have been circling?"

"Vultures." Bette blows smoke. "But we ain't dead yet."

They look at each other, then at me. I can see the tell when Bette's eyes size me up. *Well?*

Gloria pats the stool next to her for me to take a seat.

* * *

Things used to be a certain way, and everyone knew the rules, Bette tells me as we smoke through her pack. Like any honest American business owner, Bette knew the right cops to bribe for them to buzz off from her little cabaret. She's not ashamed to say that she's fifty-four years old. She practically remembers when this state was called Mexico. She was the first woman PA to work a movie set thirty years ago, and her girl Juana was the first Mexican actress to snag a contract from RKO before they canned her for having an opinion, and Ponds got freaked that no one would buy cold cream from a brown broad. Bette and Juana are this city, and this city is this club—and Bette isn't giving up the ghost on account of some new breed of breeder that's obsessed with sucking the dicks of the slave-owning Founding Fathers and letting them finish all over their faces, and then laying back to get the Constitution shoved right up their tailpipe without the courtesy of lube.

And goddamnit, she oughta mow them all down with her motorcycle while smoking a stogie. Goddamnit, those rat-faced fucks come for the women and the little guys first, and how fucking dare Reagan actually do the things he said he was going to do, while his court appointees cream all over his portraits and cash checks and fuck balances, and everyone else in the government is too busy jacking him off so they get reelected. She's red-faced and spitting Budweiser foam by the time she mentions the STAR Citizen System, and suddenly everyone's fine with being a piece of shit if it gets them on a vidboard, and—

"Darlin'," Gloria coos. "Breathe."

"Yeah." Bette rakes a jittery hand through her hair. "Sorry, I know we got ladies present."

Christ, here I thought I was the one with the mouth. I'm gonna like her.

Gloria pats Bette's hand. "It's fine."

Bette downs the rest of her Budweiser, then spreads a white paper cocktail napkin on the bar top. The nails of her stubby fingers are all chewed-up half-moons.

Welcome to Hollywouldn't, Bette explains, tapping the napkin. Which ain't been the same since Reagan painted the letters of that big sign on the hill in red, white, and blue. There are other queer joints in town, for now. Studio One for the muscle boys, the Black Cat for the lesbians, Jewel's Catch One where a lot of Black folks boogie. Until she left Hollywood a few years ago to raise horses somewhere in Virginia, Marilyn used to pop down from her house in the hills to have a drink at a little gay cocktail bar called Red Raven and pick up everyone's tab. But this—Bette places the overflowing ashtray at one side of the napkin, near the fold—is where Lady Moondust used to hit the stage four nights a week to host drag shows for a packed house, until the governor decided they were illegal outside of the Studio Zones. Immorality, all that jazz. He'd ban drag shows outright, but enough of the Studios run pictures with dopey male leads slapping on wigs and dresses to get close to Vegas showgirls. Cross-dressing is fine when the straights do it. People came from all over the city because Circus Disco is an everybody bar. Mostly queer, yeah, but also folks from the neighborhood jam the place on Latin night, and squares are welcome anytime, so long as they're not assholes.

Circus Disco, AKA the center of the known world.

Bette places three empty rocks glasses at points across from the ashtray. Warner Brothers. RKO. Paramount. Three of the biggest movie-makers, with an empty bottle of Bud for Mayflower, dwarfing the others, now that it gobbled up Columbia, Walt Disney Pictures, MGM, and a dozen smaller Studios. The four main Studios have been running the Zones, with a Code of Conduct and their own private security force—the Studio Security Division, even though everyone just calls them the Stus—since Reagan created the mini kingdoms in '73. For a while, things worked fine enough. Everyone knew to steer clear of Studio City unless they wanted to head to Bible Camp. Turns out the Zones were just the dress rehearsal and Reagan started the show for real once he hit the White House this past January.

He just established the Bureau of General Wellness and all these laws and moral infractions based on the Studio Codes of Conduct. Which, sure, ramble on about *hewing closer to the Founding Fathers' views of the ideal American citizen* and somesuch. But now he wants the cops to actually enforce the code. Now some pig can make a name for himself if one of the cameras on the telephone poles—sprouting up everywhere—gets a shot of his good side while he's making a bust. Suddenly that cop's got a single line in the next *God's Guardsmen.* Queers are scared to leave the house. The Bureau decides the American Cultural Works that get played in public, and on TV and the airwaves, and who the hell is going to show up on a Saturday night when the only kind of music a bar can play is 'Saving Myself for a Starman' while the Star-Spangled Sisters do the Charleston on stage?

The city—the Studios—want to run Bette out. Circus Disco is sitting on a fat plot of land between the Zones and the working-class neighborhoods of East Hollywood and Silver Lake that the Studios want to bulldoze for Bogart Bungalows and Miss Moonie Multiplexes. Either she leaves, or the city seizes the land and hands it to the Studio. It's only a matter of time.

Unless there's a third option. And I can see where this is going.

Bette upends her Bud and the last droplets of beer spill out the top, seeping across the napkin fold and around the ashtray.

"We gotta hold the line. This ain't just about me. This place is a home for a lotta folks in a city that don't want 'em, and..." Her eyes swim. I wince at her wet cough. "And Lady Moondust tells me about how her pal Last Mitch Effort set up his whole contraband shebang, running circles around the Guard..."

Bette loses steam. Then she swears and shoves away from the bar to grab herself another beer, leaving just me and Gloria watching beer seep across the napkin.

Gloria leans in, the laser lights of the dead disco dancing in her eyes.

"There's something here," she says, barely above a whisper. "Right?"

I close my eyes. I hear music way off in the distance like another club has got the sound system cranked way up. No—the music is coming from below. Bubbling up from the ground, like plates deep in the Earth are bogeying something sweet.

Something in my head clicks like I hit *play* on the Moonboom.

"Yeah," I tell her. "Something's here, alright. I can feel it."

TWELVE

LADY MOONDUST, LIVE ON TOUR

Gloria and her Aunt Anita live on the ground floor of a blue three-story apartment building with potted plants on the front stoop. I follow Gloria up the cracked cement steps from the street and into the tidy pad, where a stretch of bright yellow countertop in the kitchen bounces off the beige cabinets and the beige walls. White ceramic canisters line the countertop by the oven and the yellow fridge. I almost bump into a coat rack by the door. In the living room, a brown rug that looks like chocolate pudding pools over the warped floorboards, beneath a low beige couch topped with yellow crocheted daisy pillows. Doilies top the low coffee table and the wood-framed TV set by the windows. Doilies on the end tables flanking the couch. Doilies on top of doilies under potted plants on the window sills. An open window leads to a fire escape, with the window screen in place to keep out the mosquitoes. The beige walls are a garden for framed paintings of geometric yellow and orange flowers. A beaded curtain separates the main living area from the hallway that leads to two bedrooms and a bathroom of chipped teal tiles that smells like rose soap and window cleaner. Gloria has been sleeping on a twin bed in Anita's sewing room, across from the sewing machine, bolts of fabric, and rack of clothes waiting to be tailored. Stray threads and scraps of fabric decorate the orange carpet.

I built a home for Gloria on Founding Fathers, according to Bette, but the most Gloria can offer me for the night is a pillow and a blanket for the couch. I get it. I'm here on short notice.

I must sleep for a while because soon enough cabinets are rattling in my ears. I pop up and see Auntie Anita in a house dress and a full face of makeup before ten in the morning. She whips up a couple of breakfast martinis—what she calls ice cold-gin served with a side of dry toast. Me and her dig in while Gloria polishes off a bowl of Wheaties. She stashes the box back in the cabinet so Starman North, holding a bowl of cereal made with *real American wheat,* doesn't eavesdrop. When she's done, me and her head to her car for the tour.

In the street, she sighs at the film of dust over the windshield. The dust is either from the smog—we shouldn't be outside for long on a day with this low of an Air Quality rating, anyhow—or from the fire up in the hills. I hop into the car after her and she drives, her white-gloved hands light on the steering wheel, down the gray stretch of road deeper into the city.

Silver Lake—my new home, according to Gloria—and neighboring East Hollywood have seen more costume changes than Marilyn in *Gentlemen Prefer Blondes.* Palm-shrouded bungalows used to stretch around Silver Lake, Auntie Anita told Gloria, in the forties and fifties. All the queer screenwriters, actors, and directors who needed to stay away from the eyes of the Studios during their off-set time lived out here. And Holy Marilyn, the *parties*, until the Studios bulldozed the bungalows to build textile mills and factories that pumped out Bogart-branded shirts all over America. That's how this part of LA got the nickname "Spindle City" compared to "Studio City." Then the Studios figured it was easier to move all that to the Costume District within the Studio Zones, and the factories either got abandoned or turned into apartments. Officially or unofficially, with squatters rolling in from neighborhoods the Studios shoved them out of.

Reagan and the governor blab a good game about immorality and crime, like there's a bullet train from Sing-Sing right out to this neighborhood. Sure, some of the windows along the first floors of the abandoned factories are busted in. Sure, some of the buildings are half burned down, though the neighbors aren't the ones who started the fires. Starman North spits bullshit in the Reels about how Mayflower is preserving the *real America.* When Silver Lake is real as anywhere else.

Gloria points as she drives. That Vietnamese deli serves the best coffee you will have in your entire life. A nickel at that Chinese laundromat will get you a cup of noodles. When that Armenian grocery store gets raided for harboring "suspected Communists" on a Thursday, everyone knows to shop there on Friday. We pass a dirty bookstore I'm absolutely going to later since Gloria says the back shelves are always busy, with boys taking turns keeping watch. Neon signs hang in pharmacy windows. I feel bits of the Miami boardwalk, and smell stewed *ropa vieja* and vanilla ice cream. Gloria weaves east, towards what she says is Studio City, through backstreets since the Studios imposed car make and model restrictions on the main drags, shoving the jalopies like us into bumper-to-bumper traffic.

We park on a side street by a bar called From Here to the Brewery, where a drunk Humphrey Bogart impersonator outside the door makes a pass at me. Gloria sings back that I'm taken and links my arm with hers. If he was cuter, I woulda stopped. Instead, I let her lead me to a bus stop shaped like a giant film camera, where she buys two tour tickets on the cheap using Anita's old work badge.

She wasn't kidding about the double-decker tour. A big solar City Rover painted like a Rolls Royce rolls up, and we climb up to the open-air top deck, past a family with two little boys in plastic Space Guard helmets. They pretend to shoot toy rifles at us. We take two seats in the back, and Gloria ties a white scarf around her head.

Our tour guide is dressed like Charlie Chaplin with a black bowler hat, white-powdered face and shoe-polished eyebrows. He welcomes us to this tour of *The City of Angels on a Hill* and how we'll see the *best parts of American storytelling.* We'll drive past the Studio lots and gated neighborhoods—entry into these places is extra, of course—and we can hop off whenever we'd like to explore more. He says the tour wraps up at Mayflower Studios, where he recommends the *God's Guardsmen* Sound Stage Spectacular.

The bus whirs down Santa Monica Boulevard, a gilded road that cuts through all the Studio Zones. Millionaire Mile, they call it, where the stars and the Studio heads live. Palm-shrouded white mansions as big as Founding Fathers, which Marlon Brando, Katharine Hepburn, and Paul Newman call home. We whir past the golden gates of Grauman's Chinese

Theatre and the Starman North impersonators posing for pictures with tourists on the Walk of Fame. The Studio Zones are movie-set neighborhoods bordered by Art Deco wrought-iron gates topped with golden director's bullhorns. Through the gates I can see un-wilting plastic flowers in window boxes of Movieland Malt Shoppes, lines in front of chrome carts selling *Sunset Boulevard* sherbet floats. I smell fried dough and sugar. Photographers trail ladies in prissy dresses and guys in three-piece suits, even in the June hell-heat. Which must be the Starlet Express Experience that marquee signs advertise by Omniplexes—*now with high-definition Opti-Disc projectors and Liberty Bell sound.*

God's Guardsmen Gear Costume Rentals spit out toy soldiers carrying white plastic air rifles. Some of them ride on fake lunar rovers with Opti-Disc cameras on the front, only their two-piece gray uniforms are all wrong. Gloria follows my eyes.

"The Studio Security Division," she says, leaning in close. One of the toy soldiers turns, and I can see a gold director's horn badge on the lapel of his dark gray jacket. "Studio cops. The Stus patrol the Studio Zones. Though them and the Studio Surveyors have been forgetting lately about what's in the Zones and what's not."

She points up to telephone poles. I hadn't noticed the Opti-Disc cameras pointed down at the sidewalks. *Those are popping up*, she says, *even in the borderlands of the Studio Zones.* The borderlands that, like Bette mentioned last night with her bar napkin gag, seem to be creeping awful close to Circus Disco, lately.

And now I know why we're taking this tour. I get the

giggles so bad—that martini breakfast is sure helping—that Charlie Chaplin glares at me.

I borrow Gloria's scolding voice. "Why, Miss Monday, are we casing the joint?"

"Just a little patrol is all." She bats her eyelashes, suddenly shy. "Like old times."

"Those times ain't even old yet."

"Exactly."

The bus wheels around the corner. Warner Brothers. Paramount. RKO. They blur together, with Gloria leaned close, her hand on my arm, telling me the real tour.

* * *

Seamstresses know how to pattern. Auntie Anita retired as a seamstress last year, but she didn't retire all the way. Like the other girls who spent years breaking their backs over sewing machines, she sees how threads hold things up. She still sees patterns and knows who can help stitch things together.

Before the Studio Zones, there were just studios. Studios with contracts, and morality clauses, written by boring old white men sipping scotch and sucking on stogies, before meeting their mistresses in hotels, sure. As long as those rules have been in place, seamstresses have been patterning around them. On sets, in dressing rooms, delivering sketches from the costume department to private homes. Seamstresses are all over the place. They're real useful. They're tailors, and designers, too. They've got quick fingers and always keep their kits with them. Most studio bigwigs don't even notice that they're there, especially if that seamstress wears a different Revlon foundation color from the Mayflower stars in the ads.

Who does notice, though? That actress who has to ask the seamstress—*again*—to let out her costume around the belly.

This time of the month just has her so bloated, you see.

I see, alright, that seamstress says through the pins in her mouth. *Sugar, we can help you with that if you need it and not a soul will hear a peep.*

And that seamstress knows the threads to follow to get that actress to the right doctor, or she can pass her the right pills from her sewing kit the next time she comes in for a fitting. That seamstress knows how to get that actress a little pixie powder if she's having a tough time staying awake during night shoots. Nothing long term, just so she can wrap production and get away from that director with the sticky hands. And the actor that *Movieland Magazine* just called "Hollywood's hottest bachelor?" Well, he was at that pool party in Silver Lake with a bunch of other bachelors, and none of them were hurting anybody before the cops rolled in, so the seamstress pays her lawyer friend a visit. Her lawyer friend can make that story disappear before it hits the morning papers, because the seamstress visits Catering between costume fittings, and always makes sure that a bottle of bourbon appears every Friday in the trunk of the lawyer's convertible in Mayflower Lot C.

Once Gloria arrived at her favorite auntie's apartment, they sewed and talked. Gloria about whipping up Lady Moondust numbers with washer sequins, and my Founding Fathers side hustle. Anita about what it really meant to be a seamstress, and how it sounded like me and Gloria picked up a thing or two about pattern-making all on our own.

Seems like Bette knows something about it, too, since she knows all the other business owners in the neighborhood and can spot which cops to pay off. And maybe DJ Hat-Trick. He's a session musician at practically every recording studio in town. Producers know they can call him up to work magic on every instrument under the sun. Producers tell him, too, about how they've got all these groovy demos and already-finished albums just sitting in warehouses all around the city ever since the Bureau of General Wellness got a lock on the airwaves. Too bad they don't have a place to play these tunes. People would just die over 'em.

The patterns are already here, just waiting for us to make some alterations. If the Studios can trickle out of the Zones, the seamstresses can too.

Gloria doesn't have to lean into the words when she talks. The time away from the moon has changed that caramel timbre in her voice. Turned it thicker and richer.

"This seems like an awful lot of effort just for you to find a place to sing," I tell her over Charlie Chaplin's caterwauling about how we're approaching the gates of Mayflower Studios.

"Baby, I'd be happy singin' in the shower if that's all there was to this."

In her empty club, gravel-voiced Bette softened when she told me *this place is a home for a lotta folks in a city that don't want 'em.* And we built the Lodge into what it was for the other starmen to let loose, and the Boom Boom Room for a couple of them to get close. That's nice and all, but the city don't give a shit about us having a space to party. Unless we make it useful for them.

I'm grinning big, seeing how things could take shape like the matchstick diagrams in Pop's building plans.

And I'll be goddamned if I'm ever going to be so weak that I can barely pick up a couple of paint cans again.

We could get caught, sure. But honestly? Me and Gloria—giggling in the back of the bus while Charlie scowls—we've already done stupider. We've stuck our necks out for less, like getting rocketed to the moon. All I got left to lose is in a pillowcase on Gloria's floor. All I got to protect is in the bus with me. We're already soldiers, now we oughta choose the war.

* * *

Me and Gloria stay on the rover tour for hours—hearing the same jokes and facts from Charlie Chaplin over and over—as we circle the streets, talking threads. Gloria points out more of the city's set. At the corner of every other block, sky flowers sprout from metal poles at least ten stories high, their metal petals spinning in the breeze. Bright yellow sunflowers and pink-tipped white orchid petals spiral smog out of the neighborhood. And into ours.

The City of Angels on a Hill is surrounded by mountain ranges that trap the smog—from the cars, and the hurricanes of cigarette smoke from rooms of screenwriters, and lawyers, and accountants—with a nuclear reactor buried in one of those peaks of old rocks to power the grids and the millions of vidboards and Opti-Disc TVs and cameras and satellite dishes everywhere. We've been avoiding the last stop on the tour, Mayflower Studios, for hours, because I'm not ready to face how familiar it looks. Eventually Gloria catches my eye and tells me without words that it's time to go.

The City Rover pulls to the side of the road and drops us off at Mayflower Studios. The place looks so much like a cartoon Founding Fathers that my guts spin.

My feet hit alternating red, white, and blue plaza tiles that are studded with gold-plated stars etched with names I don't recognize. We knock shoulders and elbows with the swarms of people waiting to get their tickets punched by Guardsmen in space suits at the wrought iron gates inset in the triple archways of towering white-washed walls. Fathers and their boys in red Guard jumpsuits, moms holding hands with their mini Miss Moonies. Fake space helmets and plastic air rifles. T-shirts of Starman North punching Russian villains, and silver pillbox hats with tiny fake satellites. Past the gates, a signpost with markers shaped like rockets points the way. *Studio Lots 1–5. Moon Mess Hall Meals. Starman Shopping Center. GG Set Tour.* Eight-point stars hang from trees between blue-painted buildings, with glowing signs, and vidboards, and buttons everywhere. A theme park and a movie set and a dream, powdered and sealed in a Moon Meal vending machine.

Funny that, past the gates, the people who look like me and Gloria are mostly the ones pushing brooms.

Light pulls my eyes up to the enormous vidboard that reaches halfway to the moon, surrounded by a dozen other smaller screens. At the center Starman North salutes us. Stars swirl as a symphonic riff on the Guard Hymn blasts through the air. Clips from *God's Guardsmen* flicks pay on the smaller screens orbiting the center, though I spot a younger Reagan driving a convertible with a chimp in the backseat, too—his comedy hit *Bedtime for Bonzo.* All this is fucking bananas.

"STAR Citizen Kitty Keys here." A chirpy blonde in a high-necked polka dot dress looks out from the central screen. "From sitting in the theater to watch *God's Guardsmen,* to starring as nurse Celeste Keen in the upcoming *From Heaven to Earth* thanks to my work for the STAR Citizen system, I'm here to remind you that in Hollywood, American dreams do come true."

Starman North blinks to one of the smaller screens at the side, looking up at her with love. "Hwhy, that's right Kitty. Because hwe are Mayflower Studios."

The surrounding screens flash with new faces. "You are Mayflower Studios," a whole chorus of STAR Citizens sing together.

Starman North rockets back to the center screen. "America is Mayflower Studios!"

I'm strapped to the chair aboard the *Saint Christopher* again, looking up at that big movie screen of a window while my busted eye pounds.

"Funny thing about Kitty Keys." Gloria takes her time digging through her purse and loading up a Virginia Slim into her cigarette holder. She does love to ham up a moment on stage. "Auntie Anita said she used to be a girl named Catalina Chaves, before the hair bleach."

The vidboard screen blooms with the red, white, and blue petaled flower logo of Mayflower Studios.

* * *

We drive back to our side of the Studio Zone, listening to the star-beats from the Moonboom. Gloria leads me back into the clown mouth of Circus Disco. I swear someone left a giant bottle of poppers open in this place, with how stepping inside makes my head all fuzzy.

A Sunday night at the club when the only people inside are the painted animals on the walls is all the convincing Bette needs. We lay out the patterns for her with bar napkins and bottles. Who to tap for the ring, who to bribe, who to let into the doors, what exactly to offer so I don't get another nutso Powell on my hands. Bette's tell is the way the gray hairs at her temples twitch. She's been bribing cops since I first started sprouting pubes, she says, and she not about to start taking orders. She's been dodging heat for years, same as Juana, who runs a gay newspaper called *Paradigm* out of the back office. Some stranger sure as hell isn't going to come in here and start telling her what the deal is.

And that sets her off. Boys like me have it so easy, she yammers, when her and Juana would get food chucked at them when they sat together at the diner—because they were two women, or if everyone figured they were a white man and a brown woman, who knows. The least I could do was maybe show some goddamn respect. *For what?* I finally snapped, yelling at her until the glasses rattled, about my folks, and how the same thing had happened to them whenever they left Miami. How assholes would point at me and tell my parents to *take your little mutt with you.* How I heard about my Uncles getting tossed in lockup for cruising, and then I got shit-canned from the Guard by Kern for not being a rat. And if Juana is as wonderful as Bette says, why the hell is she with an old, pissy Frankenstein like Bette? And Gloria, Gloria, we're wasting our time.

After my big speech, Bette laughs her ass off, leaning onto the knees of her ripped gray overalls.

"I knew I liked you, kid."

My shoulder stings from where she swatted me. Christ, the arm on her.

Two days later, Auntie Anita tugs on some threads to get

three seamstresses over to the Circus Disco, along with a few record producers that Patrick brought in. Bette bribes a few beat cops over, and we all meet under the disco balls with the music down low, standing around the bar. I remember an old Mayflower musical Ma used to watch called *The Buccaneers of Barbary Shores* about wars with pirates along the coast of Africa that led to the creation of the American Navy, back when. There's a scene where the pirate kings meet to sing about how their *ships would tip with riches high, if not for American sea cannons nigh*. And the cheats, liars, and murderers decide to band together to clear American ships from their plunder routes, as shirtless, sweaty pirates spin and lift each other while they hoist the sails. And *maybe* Mayflower ain't all bad since they gave a million little gay boys that scene.

Anita and three seamstresses, me, Gloria, Bette, two music men, and two beat cops who are here but definitely *not* here. Fingers crossed we don't stab each other in the back before the second act, like the movie buccaneers.

"And what's in this for us, exactly?" one of the cops says, rocking on his heels. His tell is the slow smile he hides behind the rocks glass Bette filled up with bourbon for him.

I can feel a grumble building up in Bette, at my side. She's gonna explode and then put her cigar to the blueprints of this whole deal.

We've already offered a place for them and their girls to dance if they want—so long as they leave the guns and badges at home and remember that they're guests in a gay house. We've already offered them a cut of the booze profits, and the seamstress hookup to buy bottles of liquor before the federal Nuts-in-a-Vice Squad shuts down all the bars in the city, like the Bureau of General Wellness is threatening. Gloria did the talking, and the lean in her voice tickled the back of my neck. None of us want the cops here, but I know we gotta be useful to them to make this work.

"Everyone'll know to fall in line so long as they can come here to party. Your jobs'll be a cakewalk." And then I load up Kern's words about my ring, and how I wasn't as clever as I thought I was, since the top brass knew all about it. "Think of this place as a pressure release valve."

The cop smiles with bourbon lips. Pirate kings, all.

THIRTEEN

BURN, BABY, BURN

Two packed Saturday Showcases later, the spotlights on the giant clown face around the door of Circus Disco are dark. We don't need to advertise the place. We've got a phone tree and word of mouth to let the family know that the disco balls are still spinning. Not even ten and already the line snakes out of the front door and around the side of the gray slab of a building like a string of spaghetti the clown is slurping up. Bette's guests know to keep quiet while they wait in the shadows. All the better for the music and the light, inside.

The hot summer air oozes around me. I jog across the concrete lake to the door, where Bette is at her usual post in her leather jacket, with her Elvis pompadour slicked back. She runs a tight ship. She knows even if we're an off-the-books operation, she has to open the night with the 'Star-Spangled Banner' and scrape the gum off the Reagan portrait she hung inside by the entrance. All us pirate kings have our positions. Bette runs the house, Gloria the entertainment, Patrick the tunes, me the contraband.

I nod at Bette before I pop inside.

"Lady's almost on stage," she says. "Too many dicks in your face to see the alarm clock and show up on time?"

I blow her a kiss. "From that foul mouth of yours to God's ears."

She swats my ass when I pass her, and I yelp overdramatically. When I push through the front door, the giant clown mouth gobbles me up and spits me out into heaven.

The huge dance hall smells of drugstore cologne, spilled beer, and poppers, 'Yes Sir, I Can Boogie' by Baccara playing so loud that it rattles my ribs. Patrick, or DJ Hat-Trick when he's spinning on the small stage, plays smuggled unreleased disco tracks and hits the Moog when Gloria sings live. The lights work their magic over the disco balls, glinting constellations on the walls. Dancers shake their cans on platforms around the room, dressed like ringleaders and lions. Air-conditioners hiss and pump out cold air to try to douse the heat from so many bodies. Bodies, everywhere. Men and skin and bare arms and glistening chests. Latin boys swinging salsa hips to electric beats, Black boys locking lips under the twirling ceiling lights. Girls and dolls and queens cackling in corners, showing off their sequins and glittered eyes. A platoon of lesbians gather by the bar, the biker butches like Bette tossing back Buds, arms slung around the shoulders of their girls. Squads of skinny white boys sipping beers, California-tan surfers eyeing each other. Boys, girls, and everyone in between. Last Friday, a daughter of some RKO exec told me that the red-painted toenails she hides under her stockings back home are a big middle finger to her Pop. Even straights—the girls with their miniskirts and shags, the boys with wide-lapeled suit jackets and bushy moustaches, my favorite couple that dances the cha-cha-cha like there ain't no one else in the room but them—hold hands and cut wide paths as they loop on the floor.

They all know the rules. Bette doesn't charge entry at the door, but everyone ponies up for the potluck their first time in, plus free drinks for every other contribution. We're building a stash of goodies the Studios are cracking down on, following *moral guidance from the Bureau of General Wellness* and their goon squad that Reagan is sending out to *evaluate the American character of businesses.* Us family folk will dip into the potluck when we need it. Birth control pills, nail polish, and makeup. Trojans, Kotex, and Clairol hair dye. Dirty mags, disco demo tapes, and smuggled vinyl singles. I know some folks here snort some diamond dust—and I'm nobody to judge—but the strongest party favors I supply are quaaludes, because a disco biscuit now and then never hurt anybody.

I ran a contraband ring on the moon. Down here, the ring belongs to all of us. We're all a part of the sparkling gold circle, each of us shining like diamonds.

I'm supposed to keep watch by the entrance to the back room of the club—the Circus's Boom Boom Room—or at least put one of my boys there to take orders and collect payment for the ring. Ricky's on watch tonight. I called him up and he headed over from Sunshine Shitty once he got his parents across the border into Canada. Pop got a scrubbed-clean update, too: I'm safe, I'm alive, I'm working something I'm good at.

I slap a quick peck on Ricky's lips. His curls are slicked back real nice, and his tight t-shirt has me wondering about the next time I'll get to see what's underneath. I look for pieces of Flynn in the boys in the backroom most nights. I miss him, only now the feeling is all knotted up wrong. I got enough distance to see what a blockhead I was, chasing after him like the lead in *How to Marry a Starman.* That Mayflower movie magic did a number on me, after all.

I can't quite bury my feelings for him, yet, but it sure is fun to hit up the backroom and try.

Officially, we're a private "music appreciation civic organization" and not a business. Unofficially, we all know that some kind of magic happens at this place, especially when Gloria is singing onstage while Hat-Trick wiggles his fingers around the dials and tickles the keys of his portable Minimoog Model D, which I've never seen him without. I've been in this disco during the day when it's just the two of them rehearsing—learning and remixing demo tracks that would never see the light of day if not for this place. Yesterday afternoon Gloria hummed and harmonized with Hat-Trick's synthesizers and weird machines that whirred and buzzed like robots getting it on. She digs him—while I can barely understand when he yammers about oscillators and drift and wave-forms—and swears it's not just because he says she's his muse. He's a space cadet with short bright red hair and a freckle-clouded face, bopping in his booth with his giant cans over his ears.

Lately, I've seen flashes and felt warm waves bubbling up from my feet. I can't be the only one, with the way that folks knock outta here like bowling pins after Bette flicks the lights over the bar for last call.

Tonight, Bette got on me about almost missing Gloria's show, but I'm right on time. Snare drum taps tumble out of the speakers, weaving around Hat-Trick's electric swells.

"Therefore, it is with the Intentions of the Founding Fathers close at heart..."

Cheers in the crowd sour to boos at the sample Hat-Trick pulled from Reagan's latest address about shifting the American border north to follow the *natural divides of God's waterways.* The DJ flashes us a cartoon pouty face.

"...that we relay this warning," Reagan rattles on. "Canada must cease its illegal and amoral occupation of the American-foreordained territories surrounding the Saint Lawrence River."

From the wings, Gloria twirls onstage waving a Canadian flag in a pleated gold caftan with wide sleeves, eyelids the color of bubblegum, and her usual silver crescent moon painted on the side of her face.

"On behalf of our neighbors to the north," she sing-songs into the microphone, looking like Space Captain Cleopatra. "I'd like to tell the president to eat my poutine."

The crowd's whoops twirl around Hat-Trick's electric rainstorms, with my laughter the loudest of all.

Lady Moondust confesses things into that mic that Gloria would never dare—she's a lion on stage and a tabby cat back home—and I'm here for it. Hat-Trick cues her into a cover of a song called 'Voulez-Vous' by some Swedish band named ABBA, courtesy of a smuggled cassette demo. I wriggle through the crowd closer to the stage, and when Gloria catches my eye, she mimes sipping from a teacup. I know the deal. I put up a show stomping my feet like she's putting me out, then I wriggle through the crowd and hit up the bar.

I don't know much about disco yet, or how the Moog makes noises that sounds like a thunderstorm trapped in a Folgers can, or how Gloria seems to talk to that music, but I dig that the tracks fade together. Nights here, Hat-Trick blends each tune into the next and his whole set feels like one song that lasts for five hours. Feels like you could leave here and the music would keep playing on without you. I'm used to Ma's nights at the Calypso when she stopped after every song to drink in the applause. The spotlight was all about her. From my spot at the bar, I turn back to Gloria and the way she's spinning her big sleeves around reflects the spotlight into the crowd. Girls like her—who first put on costumes to hit the stage, then realized what they wore offstage was the act—come over to the apartment for Gloria teach them how to tailor hand-me-down dresses. Half the time they sleep in the sewing room for days, when I'm still stuck on the couch surrounded by my pile of clothes. When they work late into the night, Gloria always makes sure the lamp by the sewing machine is switched on.

She stops and laughs into the mic, and I know by the tell in her eyes that she sees the lamps lighting us all up good and golden.

By the time the jangly electric guitars are fading into the next track, I'm back with her tea: a rocks glass with brandy and a Lipton bag. *Ladies don't drink on stage,* she says, but add a tea bag, and bottoms up.

"Singing in French?" I yell into her ear when she leans down from the stage for her drink. "That's new."

"I'm very orally talented."

"Don't you mean vocally?"

"I said what I said." Her wicked smile burns hotter than a pull of bourbon. "And be an angel and spread the word to that Black Adonis over there." She wiggles her gold-tipped nails behind me. "We've been chatting sweet all week."

"Roger that."

Some nights, Gloria gets roses delivered to her backstage, or we wake up some mornings to find a box of chocolates on our apartment stoop. Not that she needs to be adored, especially tonight, when she's the one clutching the arms of girls on our way to the bar, swearing she loves their dresses, telling their boyfriends how sharp their suits look. Interrupting a conversation between dolls by the bathrooms because she absolutely *has* to tell them she's crazy about their makeup. Shimmying her shoulders and laughing with the gay boys. I watch the music from her ripple over their faces. I've already seen what her tilty-voiced magic voice can do, up close, and now everyone else is learning.

* * *

Early in our days in the Guard, Gloria told me about Sunday Service at the gospel church, where her Pop was pastor, on Chicago's south side. We told each other a lot of stories to pass the time on patrol, marching in the darkness. She knew who she was once she slipped into her red choir robe for the first time. Not because it was a dress, but because the boxy thing hid her body from everyone, turning her into just a voice. A voice that soared high above the others, even when she was a tiny scrap of a kid her parents still called Charles. A voice that the choir director couldn't hide in harmonies, so he made the solo. And Gloria's voice rang like church bells, wrapping around the church ladies in their pretty hats and floral dresses, and the men in their suits. In front of an altar crowded with poinsettias for Christmas service—in a robe red as the sculpted blood on the crucified body on the wall behind her—Gloria stepped in front of the swaying choir and lifted her voice to God.

Gloria, she sang. *In excelsis Deo.* With each crystal note, she could see her voice ripple through the congregation, through the tears that trickled down cheeks. *You do not just sing*, her choir director told her, *you deliver hearts.*

She didn't use her voice much outside of church or practice, in case the others picked on her for the way she talked. She listened. She heard others in the congregation telling her parents about how that voice was a gift from the Almighty. Then their voices dropped to whispers about *it's just a shame.* A shame that one day that voice will change.

Change how? She flipped through her Bible, gobbled up the songs and poems in her hymnal looking for what change they meant. *Sic transit gloria mundi* was her favorite hymn, something about passing glory they sang at Easter when the church bloomed with lilies. Nothing in those words, so she turned her eyes up to the constellations, like the three wise men who followed a star to Bethlehem. Soon enough, she didn't recognize her body much anymore. That voice stayed with her though—high and clear—and God Almighty it anchored her something fierce. *Glory be to God.* And when her parents turned from her—they couldn't call her Gloria Monday, a name that she chose because it was so close to that hymn she loved—Gloria had to turn to the Guard to get away from them. Like somehow being that high up in the air meant she was closer to that heavenly throne the Space Guard Hymn mentioned.

She hid her voice in Bowie songs and dick jokes during the Lady Moondust Lodge shows. Until last Christmas on the base, I helped her stitch together a white choir robe from an old tablecloth by hand, ahead of Kern's mandatory Christmas mass. We dyed the robe red with Kool-Aid powder. Time moved way too slow up there around Christmas. The blue-painted mess hall was emptier, colder. Kern called Gloria "Private Freeman" as she stepped to the Lodge stage in her choir robe. No Guard jumpsuit, no scarf around her hair. The first keyboard chords barely cut through the chatter from the bored starmen. Until she delivered us all with her voice, slow and quiet at first, then soaring into the sky—bringing all us with her.

"Fall on your knees and hear the angel voices," she sang, her church bell voice ringing out. The breath, the pause, and I could feel the gasp rippling through the starmen from the front row. "Oh, night divine."

Palms spread out to the rows, a stained-glass angel letting the light in.

For all the talk about America's God-given right to lead the world and conquer space, she was the one thing that made that base feel anything close to divine. I turned and caught a few of the other starmen rubbing their eyes. Lips trembling a tell, *I'm sorry.*

And now that Bette is almost flicking the bar lights for last call, that angel is cranking up the holy fire. Hat-Trick pumps the keys of his synthesizer, whipping up electric horns out of thin air. Gloria is liquid gold, slithering from the crowd back up the side stairs to the stage.

"This next one is called 'Disco Inferno' by the Trammps," she says. "It would've burned up the charts, tellin' those Star-Spangled Sisters what's what, let me tell you."

She knows the magic spell that can turn all our ears to her like the satellites on top of the gates of the Studio Zones. *Let me tell you.*

"They're trying to bury us out there." She points to the

front door. Of course we know who she means. The Studios. The city, the president. The *thems.* "But let me tell you, they don't know that we're..."

Gloria would say something like how we're all seeds planted in God's garden, reaching for the sun. But Lady Moondust is on the mic tonight.

"Landmines," she finishes. "Step on us, and *kaboom.*"

Our cheers are a landmine blowing up in holy fire. And here—here's what we all came for, that moment when the Big One radiates up from the floor, and we blur together. The crowd crushes me as we sway and breathe as one. Lips, skin, eyes up to the disco balls. We are all one body dancing in the dark with a torch after we just invented fire. Lady Moondust sings about burning up as Hat-Trick's magic Moog bends electric horns into cat purrs that build to a roar. And it's like her voice is taking us to church, and the Mayflower Miles station outside of the Studio Zone, where we fill up smuggled beer bottles with the endless supply of gas sucked from Vietnam, stuff rags down the necks, and light them up. Send shooting stars right over the Studio walls.

"Burn that mother down," she growls, pointing to the front door and the city outside.

Hat-Trick cuts the music for the night, before our body heat short-circuits the air-conditioners, and the crowd trickles out into the street. Zipped lips, now, so we don't wake up the whole neighborhood. My skin is on fire so I pull the first boy who nods at me in the crowd into the alleyway and crush him to me. Practically rip his zipper open, and the gravel scuffs up my knees even through my jeans. Swallowing his hose does nothing to douse the fire in me so I circle the city, still tasting him, sucking cig after cig. One stray butt and I could burn the whole city down, and it won't even be my fault.

* * *

A late afternoon breakfast of Wheaties later, a news Reel interrupts the rerun of *Gilligan's Island* I'm watching on the lumpy couch in the living room that I've been sleeping on for weeks. In her bathrobe, Gloria sits next to me with her feet curled under her, talking about the steak dinner date her Black Adonis, Laterian, wants to take her on. I can barely understand her because my brain fog doesn't clear until my morning cigarette burns it away first. It clears real fast, though, when the footage of a burning apartment building captured by a Studio Security camera flashes on screen. An early morning blaze on Mariposa Ave., the anchor says, likely connected to the increase in anti-Studio activity across Spindle City. The footage switches to a live view, where Stus and firemen are clearing what looks like the rotting ribcage of a whale in place of where a three-story apartment had been. I know the street. It's between here and the disco.

I light up a Marlboro Red with twitchy hands. Gloria pushes off the couch and comes back with her long black cigarette holder. She's been watching *Breakfast at Tiffany's* lately, and she said the cigarette holder makes her feel like Audrey Hepburn with a nice tan. She loads up one of my cigs, avoiding my eyes until she blows out a long vine of smoke.

"That wasn't one of us." She waves her hand to the TV screen, where flames paint light against the pink smog sky. "Right?"

Her eyes ask something else. *Was that me?*

Burn that mother down.

"They're full of shit." I wave my cig at the screen. "Pay 'em no mind."

Funny that I can't quite look at her, though, in case she sees the smirk in my eyes. The *attagirl.*

FOURTEEN
TURN UP THE VOLUME

I left my Starman North calendar in Sunshine Shitty, so I count July in fires reported on the news, and how many primo unreleased disco ditties Gloria learns from scratchy demo tapes, singing in the shower until she roars onstage with Hat-Trick. 'Ma Baker' by Boney M. about a tough broad from Chicago. Of course Gloria would dig that one. 'More Than a Woman' by the Bee Gees. 'You Make Me Feel,' with jangly guitars, by a cat named Sylvester that I'd love to twirl with in our disco. She doesn't sing 'Disco Inferno' again. I get it. I see her on stage—wrapped in sequins, with the fog machines and the lights working overtime—holding back, just a little. Scared of the heat and the sparks she can ignite.

Beyond our own walls and borders, the Studio Zones are creeping closer—rovers crawling our streets, Stus and Surveyors buying lunches from the arepa stands run by the same people they call criminals. So we blow the roof off the disco with music and laugh-screams, and I lose myself in the backroom until I stumble home with sparks in my eyes. The Moonboom is my pillow, and I fall asleep with my ear pressed to the hard plastic, as the thrumming star-song of the

'I Feel Love' demo fills my ears. Gloria says my nightmares are getting worse, with how many nights she has to shake me awake after my screams rattle the windows. Thank God Auntie Anita is half deaf.

They don't feel like nightmares, though.

Visions, more like. Fire. Smoke. Glittering mist that moves like it shouldn't.

More of the mist and smoke is clearing, showing me Flynn's frozen body, his lips twisted in a frozen snarl. The noises between my ears—my ragged breath inside my helmet, the bone-grinding vibrations of the shuttle as it took off from the moon—only drowned out by a voice that tells me through radio static, *Don't be afraid.*

I'll find you. I'm coming.

Starman North's latest role is in Reels that take over the TV twice a day. I don't care what he says, us queers didn't start the first fire. Anyone who thinks we did is stupid enough to believe it isn't the president using Mayflower, and him, as a megaphone to talk about the *essential work of the new Common Defense Corp, the enforcement division of the Bureau of General Hwellness* and how important it is for us to *stand up to Canadian disregard of American Sovereignty.*

We're lucky that everyone who lived in that building got out in time, and that the Circus Disco potluck includes the names and addresses of folks with spare rooms and couches in the neighborhood. Lucky, too, that the gals over at the Black Cat are quick on their feet. They booked it for the extinguisher when the dumpster out back caught fire. Officially, some kids in the neighborhood were playing with firecrackers. Just like how, officially, some of the rockets during Mayflower's

Independence Day Jubilation misfired and dropped sparks all over Spindle City, and the city just couldn't help how long it took the fire trucks to get here, what with the traffic all down Millionaire Mile.

A whole row of houses, up in ash. Someone spray paints the words *FINISH THE JOB* across buildings around the neighborhood, like they're asking for a sequel to the Big One.

Mayflower has cameras, but we've got eyes all over the city, too. And ears, connected to beating hearts instead of wires. Queens in casting, dolls in studio makeup departments, butches like Bette working mechanical, queer screenwriters from here to Malibu passing us tips, even some closeted queen tipping us off about police raids. We're fine with them being on Mayflower's payroll because they're helping us keep the Studio out of our neighborhoods.

Soon we're helping Auntie Anita pack up her martini glasses for her move out to her late husband's beach house in Hermosa. Me and Gloria will protect each other here, now we got the club and the seamstresses. Things are getting too hot for Anita with the latest fire a couple of blocks away. She's got a nice sewing circle waiting by the beach with some other old-timers. Their fingers might slow down a bit, but seamstresses never really retire.

She knows the pattern. The city bought up a whole neighborhood east of here in the '50s, booting out the Mexican folks who called the place home for a hundred years to build Dodger Stadium. Funny, how right before the city surveyors came in to buy the houses for pennies on the dollar, these mysterious fires blazed all over the neighborhood. Which feels *ahwful familiar*, when Studio Surveyors roll up to the Vietnamese deli down the road, or an apartment building with smoke-blackened windows on the first floor. Even if the buildings don't catch fire, enough flaming bottles or bricks flying through your windows would make anyone want to sell.

Funny, too, how a lot of these fires follow visits by the new Common Defense Corp. They're all smiles, with shiny white teeth that match their new quill and eagle pins, wearing white shirts and red ties under their dark blue jumpsuits. I learned in the Guard that jumpsuits have plenty of pockets for supplies. Or, say, for lists of names of *suspected criminals, illegals, and Communist inciters.*

I don't know if the white plastic rifles slung over the backs have rubber bullets in them or not. For their personal security, the Reels say. Because of course.

The same shit They pulled with Dodger Stadium is why we call the raids, and the fires, and the Commdef visits *Dodges.*

We didn't start that first fire. But others? Well.

Some of us must've known about them, even if it wasn't me or Gloria.

Commdef set up shop in the police precinct by Mayflower Studios, and the boys in blue let them borrow patrol cars for their *essential work*. Sure was boneheaded of Commdef to leave the cruiser car window open a crack during that one house call, even if the midday heat scorched past ninety degrees. They must've forgotten about that lit cigarette they left inside, too. The head of Mayflower should also be real careful about where he drops his cigarettes–like, say, in the mulch surrounding the palm trees outside his mansion, especially since July has been so dry. Only one palm caught fire. There must've been zero traffic down Millionaire Mile that day with how fast the fire engines got to his place. Then there was a fire in the dumpster on the RKO lot, started on the day a girl with painted red toenails hidden under her pantyhose just *happened* to be visiting her dad.

I knew I liked her.

Me and the others have gotten real good at climbing telephone poles to pull the wires out of the cameras that are popping up all over Spindle City and the borderlands between the Studio Zones. Up and down in twenty seconds flat, swinging like the chimp from *Bedtime for Bonzo.*

The Dodges don't come to Circus Disco. I can only assume that the other pirate kings are keeping their word. I stay out of it and let Bette handle the cops. She knows a closet case down at the precinct who tips her off about Dodges at other queer spots about the city, though. We can't leave the others out to dry. So we turn dodging Dodges into a game—Dodgeball. Me and Gloria came up with the rules.

Rule one: Your disco needs you. You hear about a Dodge, and you still show up. No matter if the raid's rolling into the lesbian spot, or the leather and Levi's bar, or the club for the dolls and chasers.

Rule two: We have to be absolutely goddamned *boring.* Fags, leave the fangs at home for the night and let's try this out. Minimal props. No more fake Bible studies because Commdef are such losers when they're mad.

Rule three: The dolls bow out first. We cause enough distraction for them to slip out the back first because the cops go for them extra hard. Gloria gets on me about how dolls like her climbed lampposts in New York City to drop bags of bricks on cop cars, until I remind her that other places don't have Studio Zones with blanket immunity for the pigs.

We got the tip that Commdef was coming to Jewel's Catch One for a Moral Inspection. We cleared out the booze before they got there. They rolled in and we were playing bingo in borrowed church clothes, with Doris Day on the radio. The straights in the neighborhood showed up and brought a spread of casseroles and ambrosia salad, let us borrow their sweater vests and khakis. Next it was Studio One—Commdef found a dozen of us sitting around an open Bible on the bar. They came back the next morning to haul in the owner. Something about how the Bible was open to a verse about feeding the hungry, which must mean this was a secret Communist group. The knitting night at Jewel's Catch One ended up with thirty people in cuffs, including two grandmas. One of them waved their knitting needles at the blue jumpsuit squad a little too hard.

I'll never be in *Honcho*, but goddamn it if my first mugshot didn't make me feel like a cover star. I've never been happier getting slugged than when it gave Gloria a chance to pop out the fire exit with her girls.

We play Dodgeball and dance. Even after the sun dips outta the smoggy sky, the heat doesn't let up, and the air of the club is as thick with sweat as any Miami night. Gloria introduces a new drag king to the showcase named Manny Fest-Destiny, and he spins in his rhinestoned poncho, twirls the ends of his glued-on moustache, and sweeps his finger guns over the heads of the crowd while Hat-Trick spins a new smuggled track called 'Devil's Gun' by C. J. & Company about standing up against the devil.

My throat is raw from all my screaming by the time Starman North interrupts my late breakfast martini, and my favorite episode of *I Love Lucy*, with his latest Reel the next morning. He flaps his painted red lips about the Bureau of General Wellness's updated current policies based on the *recent developments out of Paris,* which I've heard nothing about on the news. He reads lines about the *urgent need to protect America from the Communist Threat, and American Morality from undue, unjust influence.* Which includes closing every gay spot in the city.

The pirate pact keeps Circus Disco safe, for now. I'm sure it's because the straight bars playing the Star-Spangled Sisters and serving birch beer are a snooze.

And it's such a shame, really, the straights tell us, while we get blind drunk and Hat-Trick whips up hurricanes with his magic Moog. Even Lady Moondust doesn't bother with the tea bag in her tea any more. They're here for a night away from their godawful boring lives, and they don't mind us. We're stylish, and silly, and the interior decorators who live above their apartment in the Studio Zones are just so sweet.

Our visitors have got tells in their eyes. *Such a shame, but you know, you boys...*

Funny they know not to finish that sentence when I'm around. Bette has to tell me to scram from her post by the door because my vibes are making her guests feel like they're doing something wrong. And they're here to dance, too.

* * *

Four Saturday Showcases into July, and the sewing room is stocked with contraband and supplies for the potluck in the closet, and now our walls need changing.

I push the furniture in the living room off to one side and cover everything with a bedsheet. The whole mess looks like a kid's pillow fort. Auntie Anita took all her pretty flower pictures off the walls when she moved out, leaving clean patches against the cigarette-smoke-stained beige. The old bedsheet on the floor is already splattered with coral-pink paint from my roller brush. I'm alone, after the family of three that was camping out in the sewing room—Gloria had moved into Auntie Anita's old room—made it out to Sunshine City with Ricky's help. And help from Pop. He can always use a couple of hands at the jobsite, he told us. There're a whole lot of finished houses that haven't sold yet if people need a place for a few days. Likewise a whole string of construction sites from there to Canada if folks happen to be traveling up that way.

Pop taught me that you paint in wide Ws. I thought he was pulling my chain until he told me that you don't paint up and down because drips and lines from the roller dry and harden, and then you have to sand them out. So much extra work when you can do things the right way the first time. The big coral pink Ws of my strokes are the start of a word each time. *Why. Why. Why.*

I know that widening the ring is a risk. That we're all a chain, and once you add more links, there's a bigger chance one of them will break. But he married my Ma. He threw cups of coffee and punches when we got chased out of diners. He told me Ricky was a good dude. Of course he'd help us. I needed to get over all my bullshit with him to see him for who he is now. *'Cause I'm happy to tell them you're my boy,* he told me before that first day at his worksite.

I never thought I'd be happy telling people he's my Pop.

My arms are hot, tingling like the back of my neck. More pink punctures the beige walls as I roll and roll. *Why. Why,*

July? My favorite episode of *Gilligan's Island* plays on TV while I work, with the laugh track bouncing off the walls. It's the one where a satellite dish from the Guard washes ashore, and the castaways think it's from an alien spaceship. The Professor rigs it up with vines and coconuts, turning it into a two-way radio, ringing up the Columbia base. He's about to ask them for help until blockhead Gilligan trips over the vines and knocks the radio into the ocean.

"Libra, Libra." Gloria clucks behind me. With the castaways screaming at Gilligan, I didn't even hear her come in.

I spin and pink paint falls over my jeans. "How'd the date go?"

Laterian, her Black Adonis from the club, finally got the nerve to ask her to out, and she left earlier this afternoon for a late lunch before tonight's show. She's wearing her favorite red skirt suit and pillbox hat—she makes the new dress guidelines feel like a game of dress-up—only she's looking just a *little* more rumpled. Good on her.

"I'm going to be a spring bride." She fans a gloved hand over her chest. With the other, she points at the walls. "You wanna tell me what's going on, Picasso?"

"I figured we could use a change."

She sighs, pulling her pins from her hat and sticking them in the corner of her mouth. "All this." She bobs her chin to the walls. "And all this." She taps her heart. "Just your Saturn's return swinging back around, baby. It'll all work out."

Leave it to her to dish out advice without stabbing her tongue like a good seamstress.

"I don't think one of your star charts is gonna be a big help here."

I turn back to the walls. We got a rule, when it's just me and her at home—that it's just me and her. We're in the Boom Boom Room again and all that matters is picking the next vinyl. Playing pretend helps me from getting brain-powed like Powell. Except, it's never just me and her anymore, with the ID checks all over the city sending folks without the right papers into our safe house on their way up to Canada. With Gloria mother-hen-ing for doll sewing circles, and letting them crash here when the hormones she scores for them knock them into second puberties. And how can I get cranky at her for helping the people who need her? I have boys a couple of times a week, but I don't *have* them. I don't own them and don't want to. Besides Gloria, I'm alone in all the ways that mean much to me.

"That's where you're wrong," she says. "The stars know things. Just this morning my horoscope said to expect a 'great season of change,' and here I come home and someone's changing my living room up."

"Uh huh."

"What color is this, exactly?" She drops her hat, pins, and gloves on the kitchen counter, slips out of her black heels, and walks over to the tarp, dodging pink paint splattered with her stockinged feet.

"Bermuda Sands."

"Sounds like one of our girls' stage names."

I still don't look at her, or she'll know. I roll on more coral pink W's. *Why. Why, whine.*

"Mitchell Ezequiel Ward." She sighs and I finally look at her.

Damnit. I can't keep the words out of my eyes. *You don't belong to me. Just—we used to belong to each other.*

And her eyes sing back, *You absolute blockhead.*

She leans down and grabs a pink-coated paint brush from the tray.

"At least go change first!"

"Hush up. Now, let me tell you about Laterian. Like I said, spring bride. He's a history professor or something. Brainy type." She swipes a big curly G onto the wall like she's practicing her autograph. "He'll read to our kids every night. We're having two baby girls, Cissy and Thelma. You're the godfather."

"I'll start practicing my spiritual guidance."

"You'd better."

Pink blooms on the walls around us as the sky darkens.

* * *

I should've turned off the TV after Gloria left to rehearse early with Hat-Trick. Another episode of *Gilligan's Island* fades into a new Mayflower made-for-TV movie called *God Save the Queendom* while I'm moving the furniture back. Rolling hills and gray, jagged coastlines painted on canvasses are supposed to be New Brunswick in Canada. The family in dirty rags working the land of their tiny farm is supposed to be every Canadian family. If only someone was there to save them from their broken government that can't do anything without the approval of Mad Queen Elizabeth II, who has barricaded herself in the jewel-encrusted walls of Buckingham Palace and drinks tea from gold-filigreed cups while her global subjects starve. And imagine. Imagine being ruled by someone on a throne an ocean away, never mind a woman with her wild moods, never mind the head of a church when those things should be separate, never mind her insanity about her divine right to rule, when the right to rule should be decided by the people, like in America. *America.* The word is a sigh. So close—their neighbors to the west in Maine, who risk the queen's rage to air-drop them Moon Meal care packages.

The way things are going, the family will to have to eat the dog to survive. If only. If only brave souls can liberate them.

Gloria is lucky I don't *accidentally* kick in the TV. I really am such a klutz.

FIFTEEN

RHINESTONE RIOTS

Days mix like the tracks of Hat-Trick's sets, and the disco biscuits don't help much, either. I tip my head up to the disco balls on the ceiling of Circus Disco, and the lights dazzle my eyes. I fumble into my boyfriend for the night. He holds me up from behind, steadies me with a kiss to the back of my neck.

"Are you good?" he shouts over the music.

It's so good, it's so good.

I mumble something back. The tide of the track—Candi Staton singing 'Young Hearts Run Free'—rolls out, and it must be time for Lady Moondust to introduce tonight's show. Only, why is Bette the one onstage? She's holding the mic in one hand, a glass with jiggling bourbon in the other.

"Listen up, freaks." Her voice shakes just a little.

Freaks. Fags. Dykes. Words that the Stus, cops, and Commdef toss at us like bricks, that we wear like badges around each other. Few things crack me up harder than hearing someone yell *Hey, you silly faggot* outside of the laundromat, and when I look up, last night's trick is coming at me in tight jeans for a bear hug. The word tossed at me as a kid and in the Guard sounds sweeter when it's coming out of lips you've kissed. "Freaks" is Bette's favorite, since we're all her Circus Freaks.

"You're all under my roof, and you better follow my rules," she says, stronger now. I can see her chin bob. "You need anything, you come talk to me. You can give anything, you come talk to me."

"Thanks, Dad," someone screams from the front. Ricky, I think.

Waves of laughter carry me off, and Lady Moondust dressed up like Eartha Kitt as Catwoman purrs Bette off stage. A couple of songs later, a secretary from one of the Studios climbs onstage and makes a show of ripping up her Indecency ticket for not wearing pantyhose with her skirt. The Studio girls sneak in here in skirt suits and change into mini dresses and hoop earrings in the bathroom. The dolls do their makeup.

"It all happened so fast," the secretary says, the red confetti of the ticket falling around her feet.

And sweet, sweet Lady Moondust just chirps back brightly, "Did it now?" And cues up Hat-Trick for a mighty Moog-ified 'Proud Mary.'

* * *

Somehow the dancefloor fog clears outta my head and it's morning. August something—August fourth, right, because Gloria was just reading me my horoscope over coffee in the kitchen before she dropped me off a couple of blocks outside the Studio Zones.

And why am I here, in front of the vidboards at Mayflower, in too-big borrowed shoes trampling over the STAR Citizen Walk? Oh. Oh, right. I'm here for a contraband pickup, now that our pharmacist hookup won't travel into Spindle City, and we've been passing out birth control like Halloween candy. I'm here because one of the beat cops needs a pill pack for his girl, and the part he never says out loud is that he *needs it right now or else Commdef might suddenly decide that the supposedly private and on-the-level music appreciation club needs a visit after all.*

And of course. We've only ever been clowns at the circus to them. That's on us.

I look the part of a square who doesn't want a ticket for Indecency. Three tickets and you spend a night in lockup. I borrowed shoes from Ricky, Bette gave me a suit, and Gloria tailored the brown wool pants to fit my ass real nice, like I asked. I tip my head down, cutting off Starman North at the neck with my fedora. The hat has got me feeling like a private eye—*Mitchell Ward, investigating male privates*—in an old black-and-white flick.

And yes. Yes. Here I am, again. I'm goddamned Last Mitch Effort who got court-martialed for sucking dick and never once gave up a name. Even in the brig, even when the fists found my eye socket, even with wrists duct-taped together on the shuttle back home. I'm wearing a suit so I don't get clocked for Indecency, but I've got the jockstrap underneath.

I know it's not funny at all, but the squares dragging their kids around me now are all wearing big blank faces and dumb, squinty eyes. They're dressed in suits and fedoras, and skirts with hosiery. They've got the same big rover-wheel eyes blinking outta their faces like the starmen when Kern unveiled the new STAR Soldier System, all *wait, this shit was never supposed to include us.*

Because, of course. Of course the Citizen Behavioral Codes, and Dress Codes, and today's Moral Threat Color Code is going to be locked and loaded at you too, breeder buckaroo.

The brick in my stomach turns to a disco biscuit, sparking the sillies. I have to slip away from the crowd, because I can't keep the church giggles crammed in. I mag-boot roll-step around the corner, where I spot my contact with the red tie at the bench half-hidden by a *Sunset Boulevard* Sherbet cart. I ease down next to him and swap the grease-splotched Miss Moonie's takeout bag at his side with mine.

"Double the fee next week," he says. "Heat's cranking up."

"Heard the good word, daddy-o."

And goddamnit, I need to do some toe-tapping in the bus station to burn off this high. I lift off from the bench and round the corner again, where Starman North's gigantic noggin is still on the vidboard and his painted lips are yapping away. I accidentally bump into a mother holding her little girl's hand, both of their faces tipped up to the vidscreen. I mumble a *sorry*, but she must not hear me, with how her mouth falls open at the footage of bar brawls and street riots on the central screen. I'm not in the footage. Neither is anyone from the family—queer, square, straight, queen, king, doll. No, I recognize the footage from old Mayflower flicks.

"...what law enforcement is calling the 'Rhinestone Riots' because of their garish attire. These attacks perpetrated by vigilante queers are aimed at impeding the lawful, decent, and *needed* work of the Bureau of General Hwellness and its enforcement officers, the Common Defense Corp, in our City of Angels."

Starman North flaps his red lips against the backing track

of muffled screams from the footage. The mother tugs her daughter's hand, scoops her up, and scoots away.

"Hwhich is hwhy, until the threat can be *properly* assessed, a joint taskforce between the Studio Security Division, the Los Angeles Police Department and the Common Defense Corp has been established to investigate Allegations of homosexual inclinations, and apprehend individuals who engage in these Adulteries of the Flesh."

One inhaler puff, just in case. The vapor doesn't do a whole lot to calm the fire behind my ribs when the stars swirl around the vidboards. Here's the windup, the soundtrack swell, and Starman North salutes us all.

"For the safety of our city, the great state of California, and our American family."

You think with the scriptwriters, they could come up with something that wasn't so fucking tired. The Rhinestone Riots bit is something, at least. Say something loud enough with the soundtrack and the right footage, and it turns true.

I turn from the vidboards and start the long walk home. Each time I blink, pictures pop up on the screens of the backs of my eyelids. A pair of brass knuckles covered in rhinestones. A spiked disco ball at the end of a chain. A sequined purse with nothing but a spray can of Aqua Net and a lighter.

* * *

Starman North, and the Stus, and Commdef, and whoever else, is lucky that the boys and me just bury our fires in each other those next two rainless weeks in August, or else this whole goddamned city would burn down.

The city shut down our bars and now *Adultery of the Flesh*

means that, for us queers, one's a crowd, two's a felony. Add a single beer, some dancing—and, sure, the dancing we do in each other's apartments is horizontal and out of our skivvies—and suddenly we've got an Unsanctioned Gathering. The cops wouldn't have cared a month ago, but the cops aren't doing their job, according to the governor. According to Reagan, who has *no choice but to send additional members from the Common Defense Corp to the vulnerable cities across the Nation.*

Running from Commdef and hoisting up the other boys so they can crawl out through apartment windows during a raid has made me stronger than stacking bricks in Sunshine City, that's for goddamn sure. We are playing with fire, Gloria scolds me, still cruising at bus stops and hopping up on toilets in the stalls for our feet to escape Commdef flashlights. Squads of us necking in streetlights on the way to some after party when the disco closes up shop for the night. Things are bound to blow.

I forget whose idea it is, once Hat-Trick cuts the music at the disco after a raucous Wednesday night show, to keep the party pumping for a little hump day hoedown. Probably mine. Either way, rum-punch-stained whispers pass the word around the backroom and lucky thirteen of us head to one of the boys' apartments. A single floor lamp is all the light we need. We don't even have a record going—the only music is our breath until the boom of the front door busting in.

Sure is hard to run when your jeans are around your ankles.

Two nights in lockup while Bette scrapes money from the potluck to post our bail. Some of the boys don't even bother going home, back to their parents, with how all our names are in the papers. Jobs gone. Homes gone. Homes where they're not really welcome, anyhow. We've got couches and beds for them all. Cots to sleep away the daytime in the disco.

I don't let Gloria pick me up from the station Friday morning. I call up Bette instead. With how the front tire of her truck bumps the curb when she pulls over, I can tell she wants to ream us out. Until she spots Ricky's swollen-shut left eye, and the blood down my t-shirt. We cram into the front and Ricky's hand squeezes mine for strength. She can't yell at her battered boys, so Bette points her anger at Mayflower instead. She tells us how a buddy of hers in the city planning office told her about some rough plans floating around for something called Mayflower's Moon Miracle—part theme park, part Founding Fathers recreation, part apartment complex, part soundstage lot. It extends from Mayflower's Studio Zone almost all the way to East Hollywood. Just too bad for all the eyesore apartments in the way. Like the apartment we got busted in, which the city already knocked down, calling it a Moral Hazard Zone. Bette calls that a real riot.

The three of us don't find it really funny, though. Bette pulls over outside of me and Gloria's place, and I pop out of the truck. Gloria isn't home. Funny how a Commdef billy bat was a reminder that I'm still made of skin and bone even if the magic star-song waves of the Moonboom try to tell me I'm just music. In the shower—washing away the stink of jail—I wiggle my loose front teeth with my tongue. I had too much time to think, laid out on a shitty mattress in a cell. Even with the Moral Codes, why did Commdef bother raiding an apartment with a bunch of queer nobodies just trying to get their rocks off? Even if it was at the edge of Mayflower Studios turf. And how'd they even get the address?

Unless someone called it in. Say, if someone slipped out of the backroom and hit up one of the payphones in the neighborhood, and dialed up the number that the Reels flash onscreen on the daily.

I watch as the grime and dried blood drips off me and twirls down the drain.

* * *

I'm sweating under the collar of my borrowed suit as I walk towards the Studio Zones under the blazing sun. The stiff leather of my shoes cuts up the backs of my heels. Gloria's not here to tell me to choose compassion. To scold me to walk away from the pile of brick rubble that was once an apartment building, and not towards it. Then past it, to the vidboards over the Mayflower walls.

But I've got to know. My air tank is screwed on real tight once the vidboard light washes over me. New names engraved on the gold stars of the plaza tiles. New faces on the screens, a whole chorus of STAR Citizens talking about how *Bisquick's new batter will have you whipping up sky-high stacks of mooncakes.* These shoots have to move fast, I know, because if these STARs don't see their faces up on the screens, then what's the point?

And there in the lower-right screen—bushy eyebrows that the makeup department tamed, full painted lips. I know the face from the disco, I know the muscled neck from how he tugged my hands up to it and told me to squeeze, that time I snuck up the fire escape and into the apartment he shares with his cousin while she was at church.

Give it to me harder, he said when I pressed him against the wall. Squeeze. Eyes rolling—*yes*—for how I was cutting off the air.

"STAR Citizen Max Page telling you that..."

Close. I knew him as Max Paglioti. Or was it Paglia? Either way—one of the dozen of boys I've fallen in love with waiting to get into the disco.

I *choose compassion* with each footstep out of the Studio Zone. Libra, Libra—tightrope walking on the chains that steady the scales. Compassion when I don't kick open the front door, compassion when I pick up a pebble and not a brick and toss it at the window by the fire escape that I've climbed before.

Three breaths and Max Page or Paglioti or Paglia opens the window and sticks his head out. He's got the stones to skip playing dumb and ask what I'm doing here, at least.

Compassion that I don't choke him like he likes, only this time I don't stop when he taps out.

A seagull screeches in the silence behind me.

"I couldn't make rent," he says. "And..."

And. And. Like my heartbeat pumping in my busted lip. I can scream at him about how Bette told us all to come to her. About how one of us calling in Commdef is a million times worse than the squares doing it, because we're supposed to be better. We're supposed to be family. Instead, my tongue pushes at my loose teeth and I taste blood.

"Was it worth it?" I ask. "Seeing your mug up there on the vidboards?"

His eyes look up from under his bushy eyebrows at invisible cue cards in the sky. *Coca-Cola Comet is...*

"You know?" He tips his head. "Yeah, it was."

I unbutton my collar and lose the suit jacket on my long walk home. I leave crumbling brick walls and Max's face on the front stoop of my and Gloria's place. It's the nicest thing

I can think to do for her since she hasn't once given me grief about what my mugshot will do for my contraband pickups. I'll figure it out. Last Mitch Effort always does.

Inside, I find Gloria at her sewing table that she moved into the living room to free up more cot space in the old sewing room. Her head bobs up from layers of yellow tulle like she's the topper on a birthday cake. Mama Cass is singing about how we should all *make our own music* on the record player, while the sewing machine rumbles. We've been busy fixing up the place, and hanging up tie-dye tapestries and posters on the Bermuda Sands walls. Tina Turner—a blur of brown sheeny skin and a shimmering red dress, caught mid-dance—from her *Acid Queen* album cover across from a Jesus poster over the couch, blasting love rays out of his bleeding heart. The sleeves of one of my flannel shirts trails from a pile of clothes by the far corner of the couch like it's trying to crawl away from the mess. A stack of *Honchos* and *Blueboys* wait for my afternoon reads on the end table. Those things are gold, now, with how *gay propaganda* can't travel through the mail. Juana still writes her gay newspaper, *Paradigm,* even if all she can do is sneak around photocopies by hand. Now that Auntie Anita's doilies are gone, sticks of incense drop ash right onto bare wood.

We've kept the TV off for days. Just better that way.

I hang up my suit jacket on the coat rack.

"Yellow's not usually your color," I sing out, forcing some of the sunlight from outside into my voice. My ass bounces on the couch cushions.

"Well, tonight's going to be something," she says over the machine whirrs. "I can feel it. We got a big show planned."

The breath locks in my chest. "I'm not really up for—"

"Mitchell Ezekiel Ward, you are leaving these four walls tonight."

"I went out today. Daylight and everything."

"And see, you didn't even turn into a pumpkin." She swoops down to plant a kiss on my forehead as much as I grumble, swatting her away. "Come on, Cinderella. You're not missing the ball. I'm not letting you. We gotta dance all this noise out, tonight more than ever."

She floats away before I can grumble any more, and soon enough she's trilling in the shower, turning her messages for me into a song, like she always does. *I'm not letting you, ooooooh my child. And maybe one day you'll pick up your God-forsaken dirty socks like I asked you, oooohh oh oh.* She leaves the door open a crack, and her voice twirls out like steam from the shower, billowing into the hallway and wrapping me up.

SIXTEEN

OUR OWN KIND OF MUSIC

Me and Gloria work the phone tree for the rest of the afternoon, shaking branches. Your disco needs you. Just family tonight. Spread the word. Skip the front and pop in the back alley door, and be quiet, and—*har har, yeah that was a setup for a backdoor joke, daddy-o.*

Half hanging out the window and smoking butts while Gloria finishes up her dress, I watch the sky turn into a pink and gold tie-dye tapestry. Even if it ain't pretty to breathe, God paints some beautiful sunsets with that Hollywood haze.

Once that canvas of a sky darkens to smoggy purple, me and Gloria escort her giant birthday cake of a yellow dress across the concrete lake in front of the night-darkened disco. She makes a turn for the back alley until I stop her. Lady Moondust never hides, and ain't about to start now. We're strutting through the front, as usual.

Bette is a smart broad. She said that she'd send word to the other pirate kings that we had to lay low tonight because of the extra heat from the Commdef demolition. Even still, she put Rex at the door to turn away the squares. A line of them already trickles towards the clown mouth of the front entrance only to drift off after Rex turns them away. The dim light over the front door glows on his shoulders, as he puffs on his stogie in the dim entrance, in his painted on-jeans and leather jacket.

I knew his face—and a lot more of him—before I ever saw him at the disco. He was in the first photoset Uncle Javi snuck at me. *Honcho* ran the photos as a spread a few years back, too. I still remember the caption, below his open jeans. *Rex King, 46, 6'3", owes his rugged good looks and dark complexion to his Cherokee ancestry. He hones his physique with long hikes in the California sunshine.* He's older—with a bushy grey-streaked beard, now—but the man is the same. The first night I saw him at the Circus, I made the mistake of going up to him and opening with a line about how I rubbed myself raw looking at his pictures. The quaalude I'd popped kept my mouth from hearing my brain hollering at me to stop. Rex was sweeter than he should've been. He told me he jumped behind the camera soon after that—erotic portraiture, he called it—which only led to a million more questions. He humored me as I interviewed him for a while. When I tried to take him home, he patted me on the shoulder and bought me a soda. Said maybe next time when I was more with it. I don't get embarrassed much, but every time I see him my ears light on fire.

Not tonight. I'm feeling wild. Tonight's going to be something, like Gloria said, and I always listen to the lady.

I don't know the square at the front door, arm-in-arm with his girl. I can see how pale his neck is, though, compared to the California tan of his face. A fresh cut to stick to those Dress Codes for dudes about no hair past the nape of the neck.

"Closed tonight," Rex tells them.

Haircut thumbs at me and Gloria stepping past him. "What about them?"

"What *about* them?" I snap.

"Private party to wax our disco balls." Rex blows a smoke signal into the guy's face. "I hear the Star-Spangled Sisters are singing at the Glass Slipper off Vine. I'm sure they'd love to have you."

The way that Rex winks at me, Gloria has to tug me away.

Already the *thud-thud-thud* of the bass slipping through the crack of the front door sways some music into my hips.

* * *

God bless the three queens on stage, two-stepping and pointing to 'Dancing Queen' while the lights catch on the beaded cocktail dresses they whipped up from Dodgers baseball uniforms. I think it's supposed to be a statement about the Dodges, but they lose the plot halfway through the song. Not that anyone seems to mind once a couple of background dancers in nothing but tight blue shorts hit the stage. We shove crumpled dollar bills at all of them.

Just family here tonight, like we promised. Rex is in from the door and he locked it behind him. Bette's slinging a special rum punch that could degrease a carburetor. No goddamned Max Pages in sight, just seamstresses. The only straights in the crowds are the ones who danced with us during Latin nights before Commdef, who we see every day at the Armenian grocery store and the Chinese takeout spots. They bring pasta salad to the Dodgeball games, and we bring the scrub brushes and the buckets when anyone spray paints *FINISH THE JOB* on their front doors. They're the ones who watch over us like Watkins. The ones who know not to ask us how we can be dancing right now—because twirling so we don't spin out is the entire fucking point—and they need the dance, too. Because they're family.

Two numbers later, and Lady Moondust shimmers in the spotlight, fresh off a costume change with a purple sequined headband around her afro wig and her yellow frilled windstorm of a dress. Hat-Trick is building something. Electric rain tickles the back of my neck.

"We have a tradition at Moondust Manor," she says, tugging one of her hoop earrings that are so giant I could hang off them. She laughs over the whoops. "When it's just family at home, none of the racket outside follows us through the front door."

Someone in the crowd doesn't get the hint to shut up the shouting. I turn and a guy in a tight tee and a bushy moustache —dark broom bristles against his pale face—flaps his arms, hooting. He's sporting a huge pair of ears that must catch radio waves. I can barely hear what he's yelling except for something about how we have to clear outta here.

"Lucky for you that Mama has been cookin' up something real good with Hat-Trick," she continues.

The guy tries to crawl on stage until a couple of muscle queens in the crowd yank him back down by the shoulders. Gloria sweeps her purple-lidded Lady Moondust gaze over to him.

"Now, if you be so sweet as to get the hell out of my kitchen." Gloria bobs her head over at Moustache. "Fly on off outta here on those Dumbo ears of yours. And lay off the disco biscuits next time, girl."

Laughter from me and the rest of the crowd drowns out

whatever else he's trying to scream, until he slinks back into the mess of bodies.

"Well," Gloria huffs back into the mic. Yellow frills bob when she shakes her hips. "So much for the sermon. I had a hunch I'd be preachin' to the choir anyhow."

No one cheers louder than I do.

"So, DJ Hat-Trick, my sweet. Would you please get those funky grooves going? You know the one."

The second the star heartbeats thrum down from the speakers I feel ten feet off the floor. The electric thrum starts low, building into something thick and bright. The air already vibrates something fierce. The edges of everyone's bodies around me turn all gooey, like they could let me in. Gloria's long drawn out *oooooooo* crackles with light that I can almost see. Light that arcs between all of the bodies on the dancefloor. Light like comet tails, heat that ripples through all of us in waves—all of us wanting and burning and moving.

And it's so good.

It's so good.

I know the magic music from the Donna Summer demo tape. I've heard Donna cooing in my dreams, and I know her breaths, her laughter from the recording. Her *Oh, that's wild. What's that?* Sometimes when I popped here on random afternoons, to organize the contraband stashes in the backroom, I heard Gloria and Patrick practicing. Gloria swaying and humming into the mic while Patrick wiggled the Moog knobs and stepped out of the DJ booth to switch to electric guitar. He clanged chords, heavy on the fuzz distortion. Both searching for the right ingredients of the spell.

Gloria drizzles caramel over all of us with her voice. Light glints in eyes everywhere. In mine, too. All of us loving the thrumming star-song, and each other, and how each brush of skin snaps with sparks. And how couldn't we love each other when we're this fucking perfect?

I don't need words. Gloria is already singing out everything I could ever possibly want to say, her arms moving like liquid on the stage, the light shimmering all around her. I can't speak so I laugh, and the wild tears spill out of my eyes. At the same time, I can somehow touch every face that's tipped to the disco balls. Kiss every pair of lips. I must be going crazy because I'm already begging whoever will listen not to let this perfect, wild moment ever end. *It's so good.*

The knot that I always carry around in my chest loosens. A voice between my ears wraps me up in velvet. Telling me, *Stay here. Touch. Laugh. Kiss. Breathe. Let the music fill you up. Love it and let it love you back.*

I know everyone else feels this too.

And I hope—laughing and crying at the same time—that I can take some of this with me when the music stops.

But please. Don't ever let it stop.

The electric beat shivers into a rainstorm made of starlight, and Gloria coos, *I feel love.* Building, building, and a wave of rhinestones flows through the crowd, washing over all of us. She unties her yellow birthday cake of a dress at the waist, twirls, and drops it to the floor, revealing a purple sequined slip of a thing. Our girl loves a good reveal.

Glittering fog spirals around me, with everyone else swaying in slow motion. The dancers are all carved from blue crystal and blasting a whole galaxy of light into the dancefloor that's suddenly an endless night sky. And the night sky is

Gloria's skin, and every fleck of glitter on her is a star.

I slip and weave around the bodies, walking a tightrope made of beaded fringe into a clearing on the floor. Lured in by a curve of neck I know so well from behind, poking out of a blue Guard dress jacket. Flynn. I can see him—feel him—before he even turns around. And no surprise he's here, with how the whole dancefloor is blasting past the moon.

Don't be afraid. I'll find you. I'm coming.

Through all the static and star-song in the demo tape, I didn't recognize the voice was Flynn's. Calling to me.

He turns and his eyes reflect every piece of light from the disco balls. Sweat-slick skin, his Guard dress jacket slung over his bare, hair-swirled chest, one knee sticking out of his torn jeans. In an instant, everyone else vanishes into the fog. There's only us. Flynn circling the gym-class track while I wondered, *What the hell is this twinge this kid is working into my chest?* Flynn circling outside the Calypso Room, then with me on the fire escape. Years later, frozen in a puddle of fog on the moon, and shivering on my cot. The light all moves through him. But that's a mistake.

He is the light. And so am I.

I reach out and crush him to me, grinding my hips into his.

"What are you doing to me?" My voice is a hundred at once, echoing out to forever. My raid-busted lip twinges with my wide smile.

I'm afraid if I say anything else, the star that's pulsing behind my ribs will burn straight outta my mouth. All I can do is laugh and watch as the sound ripples the beaded fringe waves that connect all of us.

Flynn laughs back and snakes his arms to my waist,

holding me up, until the key change cued-up by the hand of God bowls over the whole crowd.

Gloria's voice blooms stars everywhere it reaches.

I feel love.

Fog billows higher and higher. Glass bodies with eyeless faces watch us as we dance, hands reaching out. The floor rumbles. *Wait, wait. Too early. The music, out of time, the Score—*

The instant his lips hit mine, the beaded-fringe soundwave connecting us all snaps. The giant disco ball shatters into a swirling galaxy of rhinestones that pulls me in.

* * *

Tick. Tick. Tick. Tick.

I don't see a clock through the fog, but I hear it. The sound of a giant second hand knocking around an even bigger clock.

When the rhinestone glimmers clear from my eyes, I'm in a city made of hammered starlight and wrapped in glittering mist. Everything is sheened with rainbows. Buildings, maybe, or giant trees made of silver-beaded fringe sparkle to the white sky. Bodies shift in the fog, but at the same time, they are the fog. And the buildings, and the starlight, and the music that rumbles from deep below. The bodies sway and glass tendrils that could be arms ripple up to the sky.

Tick. Tick. Tick.

The clock speeds and slows, the sound stretching out in a liquid heartbeat.

I look up past the buildings and the trees, and instead of stars, panels of what look like glass stretch all around, like we're in a sphere the size of the sun.

We.

I'm not alone.

A puff of fog that could be a face turns to me. An eyeless gaze punches me in the chest. My flicker of fear echoes in the fog, though these dancers could never be afraid. Anything that isn't love and light snaps guitar strings here, clanging minor in the chords. And how could I ever be scared?

The fog wants to rain stardust down on me until I'm made of mist and light like the dancers—warm, and held, and safe. Forever.

Fog swirls and solidifies at my side. When I look down, Flynn's fingers are interlaced with mine. He drops my hand and steps in front of me, placing himself between me and the ocean of fog. Tendrils rise up like tongues tasting the air.

Tick. Tick. Tick.

Commdef rubber bullet rounds. Cannon blasts. Lightning bolts.

A feedback screech from a speaker chainsaws the air. I don't know how it doesn't shatter the buildings all around me. I'd fall to my knees if I could move.

Flynn reaches out his hands high into the air.

"They hear the beginnings of the star-song," he says, his back to me. "That we are here is proof."

The silence is worse than the screech. Fog sways, unconvinced. Just eyeless faces on me. On us.

Enough of the fog clears to reveal the crystal-carved dancers from Circus Disco, swaying impossibly slowly to the music. I blink, and they're lost in the mist again.

Donna's liquid giggle from the demo tape rolls across the panels. *Oh, that's wild. What's that?*

Perhaps.

I can feel the sing-song voice—a chorus of a hundred at the same time—between my ears more than I can hear it.

That you are here before your duty is complete is proof of Disharmony.

"We can heal it," Flynn calls out. "We can return to the order of the Score."

The answer is a record scratch that seems to ripple the giant glass panels in the air. The panels whirr, pop up, and spin—locking into new formations. Unseen fingers sweep up my arms, sending shivers all over. *Tick. Tick. Tick.* Each a tiny gasp from me.

I've been frozen like this before. On the moon, reaching for Flynn.

Is this healing?

The panels in the sky twirl to life. I can see the outside of the disco reflected across the gleaming glass. Three cop cars skitter to the curb outside the club, the car lights flashing. More cars whip around the corner. One of the Commdef goons eases out of the car—he's enjoying his light show, and leading the charge, I can tell by his eyes—and he raises a bullhorn. Whatever he shouts is drowned out by a booming *tick, tick, tick.*

A raid. And we're all trapped inside. Maybe the big-eared, moustached guy squawking at us to run outta the disco was onto something.

Such small, broken Instruments.

Wait.

We feel. We see...

Glass panels zoom out to the whole of the Earth. A glowing red line, sharp as razor wire, blasts out of the green-and-blue globe like the flight projection path on the screen of the *Saint*

Christopher. Thick yellow smoke spills from the red line. I can feel it choking my lungs like car exhaust.

We hear the ache of this Discord. This foul music must not infect–

"Please," I beg Flynn, or the voice, or the dancers in the fog. "You have to send me back so I can help stop them. I–"

Another world-shaking feedback growl kills my words.

You would leave the Dance to return to such chaos?

I have to grit my teeth just to keep from shaking. The air growls again. The fog must not like my silence.

And how would you stop them? Alone?

I can feel the invisible hand wriggling past my eyes. I choke and gasp against the invasion–my neck straining, gurgling, and I'm begging the back of Flynn's neck for help.

Fire in my eyes. The shuttle exploding. The Earth. This place, wherever we are.

Flynn cuts through the fog and the second he grabs me by the arm, I can move again. I collapse into him, shivering.

"They have found the Instrument, tuned to the Oscillations, and sang out to us. It is our sacred duty as Adjudicators to bring–"

A record scratch that sounds like a mountain breaking in half shudders through the whole place.

We know of your Duty.

My fingers claw into Flynn's hand. The red and blue cop lights flash down from the panels above as I sway to my feet. I don't give a shit about the glittering fog, and the music. I'll climb up these silver-beaded trees and punch my way through the glass if that means sending a warning to Gloria and the others to run.

"Then give them the power," Flynn says, just above a whisper.

Another tendril twirls to us from the ocean of fog. Another eyeless face looks me up and down. The music air shifts to low thrumming. A song I know, with rocket flares, and electric rain, and oh heaven knows. Heaven knows, I feel...

It is freely given to those who sail the Wave-Forms to us here.

We have missed you, and–

We move now to meet you in the Dance.

The crystal ground rumbles under my feet, my stomach spins, and my ears twinge with how the whole ship seems to boogie to a new beat. Rocket-fire force almost knocks me over. The glass panels above whir and snap into new formations, zooming out from the club to the whole Earth, faster and faster, as the invisible DJ cranks the volume on the music all around.

Tell them–

Give in to the Song.

Heal, move, dance.

Or when we arrive, they will feel the Silence.

The glass panels thrum with fuzz-guitar distortion. Stars explode in Morse code, with rockets rattling the walls of the *Saint Christopher.* I blink, and I'm in the shuttle again, staring up at the movie theater of the screen, into space.

"Looking mighty fine, *Saint Christopher.*" Kern's razor-wire voice scrapes against glass. "Your new coordinates are locked. Goodspeed on the journey to Earth."

I blink again and I'm black with Flynn in the fog. I can feel the ground slow and rumble beneath me, then my stomach dips a tango. This ship–whatever it is, wherever it is–is changing course.

The display on the glass-panel sphere zooms out, past planets, into the darkness. The floor beneath my feet turns black. No, to clear glass. To crystal that rings out church bells each time one the glass bodies stamp their feet. *Tick, tick, tick.* Not a clock this time. Cracks in the crystal floor—spreading, spreading—until it shatters and I free-fall into the blackness, screaming the whole way down.

* * *

Me and Flynn only missed a beat of the music, back at Circus Disco. His lips still press against mine, my hands are still crushing his hips to me. There's no *me* and *him,* though. We're one swaying, dancing creature—bound to each other in beaded soundwaves as much as to everyone else.

We are Manifold. Many, folded, swaying, and loving into each other.

It's so good. It's so good.

And how cute the ones outside the Manifold are, trying to kick our music off-beat by pounding on the walls of this House and screaming demands. We can barely even hear them over our light, our laughter.

Our hands fly up in time with the star-song from the ship's drives, fingers curling through the fog, and arms intertwined. Lips brush lips—all the bodies honoring the Manifold in each other, all, and—yes, palms out. Tempo wraps the sacred hall of the dancers, turning air to glass, while giant Cadillac Red-painted lips blow a rainbow-edged bubble made from the beating heart of a star. The odd beads—lead instead of rubber this time—that the invaders shoot at us bounce off our glittering shield. Just rhinestones falling off a dress and dropping to the floor.

What do we do if we can't break the door down? the voices of the wallflowers ask.

Are you on the list? We are at the door. Plenty of room, yes. And everyone outside is welcome, only if they are here to dance.

We, I. Eyes.

Eyes to the front door. We can't stay like this forever—and already my mind wants to slip away and rest. I can barely see Flynn, or even my own hands, through the fog. I grab him, his eyes ablaze with white light, and crush him to me. But he's not just mine, he's everyone's. And he knows—*oh, heaven knows*—that there's still work to do tonight. He pushes through the crowd. I can't find Gloria through all the bodies.

The whole sea of us surges to the entrance. The front door of the disco flies off its hinges, launched by the rainbow-edged bubble that shields us. The bubble shatters into glitter—hovering for an instant like snow.

The door whips through the air and cuts the closest of the cop cars clean in half. An invisible hand knocks the guns out of the hands of the dozen cops and Commdefs standing in a line ten feet from the entrance, and sends the weapons flying. Smashes the windows of three cop cars, sends a fourth flipping through the air, where it lands on the concrete with one hell of a cymbal crash. The group of us at the front know to reach out, laughing, and grab the cops with more invisible hands and toss them in the air. The patrol cars whip back with squeals of rubber. The floating cops flail on puppet strings until we slowly lower them back to Earth.

The clown's-mouth entrance of Circus Disco spits us all out into the industrial park on a tide of fog. The Commdef closest to all of us turns heel and sprints away. We don't blame him. If these guys didn't want to dance, why'd they bring the flashing lights? We flow over the concrete, weaving between stunned faces, hustling and hip-checking around uniformed bodies that back away before running off. Our song is laughter. And if the men who came here to cuff us think this makes us weak, we will show them that our love and light are strength.

Our love is boundless. Our mercy is not.

Our mercy may be tested.

My connection to all the laughing eyes and dancing bodies around me is fading fast, like a song I can barely remember. The last thing I can feel is, *we want to be gentle.*

We don't need to be.

"Put your fucking hands up!" one of the cops screams, his voice shaking, through a bullhorn in the front seat of the furthest cop car with its busted windows. "Step back! Lay flat on the ground!"

Lights from the cop cars blaze through the fog.

My eyes find Flynn, in his service jacket, up ahead by one of the cop cars. Gloria is by his side, all sequins and silver light. Maybe it's the floodlights from the club entrance, but they seem to glow. I wriggle through the crowd to reach them.

"Let us dance," Flynn says. "Or else."

The crowd wraps him back up, keeping the dance party kicking even as more sirens already whirl in the distance.

SEVENTEEN

HAZY COSMIC JIVE

I could've danced in the fog until the sun rose and burned it away. I could've climbed streetlights, and knocked the Studio Zones' sky flowers over with a wave of my hands, but Bette has enough sense to bark at us to scatter. More cop cars are coming and none of us are dying on her watch. Later, we'll figure out what that group acid trip was. We gotta stay alive first. Her words spiral dancers away from our concrete lot party and off into the night. High-heel clacks bounce off buildings. I don't know how the others expect to hide when I can hear their cackles echoing down the alleyways as the fog melts away under the streetlights.

The laughter sounds louder than the sirens.

I brush through the thinning crowd, up to Flynn and Gloria. Flynn's smile crackles something wild. We'll have the time we need for a reunion and for me to ask him what the hell just happened when the cops' backup isn't blasting 'round the corner.

The painted crescent moon on the side of Gloria's face dances in the light. Even through the fog, we talk to each other with our eyes. *Go,* I tell her.

"Listen up, ladies," she calls to the dolls. "Kick off those heels. We gotta boogie."

"Our place?" I ask her.

"No," she says. "In case the cops follow us, I don't wanna risk it."

"That goes for everyone," Bette shouts. "Get to cover. Keep an eye out for tails. If you spot one, weave through the back roads until you shake 'em. My truck's by the back door. Whoever can fit's welcome."

"I'm parked in the alley." Flynn jerks his head behind him. "Mitch, you're with me."

Bette snaps for all of us to move. Fireworks spark over my chest when Flynn grabs my hand. We sprint off, and my feet crunching on broken glass from cop cars is about the sweetest song I've ever heard.

"You saw it, right?" he asks, half laughing, while we run. "You heard it?"

The star-song, and the trees and buildings of silver-beaded fringe, and the bodies in the mist. I know he means all that and more.

"Everything."

In the alley by the club, I reach for the passenger-side door of his car, and it snaps open before my fingers even touch the handle.

* * *

Blasting through the streets, cackling and knocking into Flynn behind the wheel, we could rev the engine and blast right off into the sky.

Flynn's grip on my hand is a little too hard, just how I like it.

I can't even make a full sentence. How. Where. Why? *Later starman*, he chirps at me. I get it. Hard to talk about how we just flipped cop cars with a wave of our hands when we keep turning around to see if more are following us. I tell him how to get to me and Gloria's place, and when we're in our living room, I finally drink in the sweet rum-punch sight of him.

His clipped hair has grown out to short, sweat-slick waves the color of instant coffee in the four months since he was shivering on my cot. His trim beard frames bright lips that I want to devour like a bloodhound coming in for a meal. Bright blue eyes under thick brows. Time away from the sunless moon base tanned his skin. He's grown into his nose since his teens, but I love that it's still a little too big, with a sunburned bridge. His shoulders are Space Guard-straight, his hands buried in his jeans pockets. He's wearing his Guard jacket over his bare chest, with a white t-shirt tucked into the back of his waistband like a dangling flag. The dark hair on his chest and in a line that disappears into his jeans is the trail on a treasure map that my lips are itching to follow. I buzz around the room, kicking away laundry piles and straightening magazine stacks, suddenly hating the mess. Wishing I'd listened to Gloria's song-scolding about tidying up.

"There's about a million things I've gotta ask you," I say, shaking my inhaler. I snag a puff. The metal of the thing should twinge my busted lip, but I feel nothing.

"I'll tell you everything I can." That bright trumpet voice of his, again. "For starters, you can throw that thing away." He nods to my inhaler. "You won't need it anymore."

When my fingers fly to my lip, all I feel is smooth skin. My tongue pushes at my front teeth that are rooted tight into my jaw. The fog and the music of wherever we were healed me up. Or it was him.

"I joined the Guard for you," I tell him. All I can think to say. "You left. My ma left. The only thing that made me feel not so alone was that maybe—maybe—I could find you up there." I point to the moon, somewhere past the ceiling. "Every shift change had me thinking maybe I'd see you again."

"I left the Guard just to get back to you." He's got to have lights behind his eyes, somehow, with the way they beam at me. "I'd say that makes us about even."

"How'd you even find me?"

"You know how, right? You've got to."

"The music. The 'I Feel Love' demo, the..."

"We're the same. Or... or it's like we talk in the same frequency. And the magic you—all of you—worked on the dancefloor each night was beaming out a message. I could hear you, way up on the moon."

I gush out a shaky breath. "Wild."

"You were singing to me, Mitch. Once I touched down on the last shuttle from Founding Fathers, I found Watkins on Columbia and he got a secretary to pass me your number. I reckon he felt bad about how Kern kicked you out, lickety-split. I called the number, spoke to your father, and he said you were in LA. So, I hit the road. Four days in the van from Florida, catching winks on the mattress in the back."

My skin is too hot to stay inside. It's his idea to head out to the fire escape—I love the callback, too—and he follows me when I crawl through the open window. The fire escape isn't much bigger than my and Gloria's kitchen table, just a black metal grate with a short railing and a ladder leading to the alley. Streetlights and other apartment buildings cramp close. Past midnight, most of the windows around us are dark already. Up in that smog-purple sky, the moon looks so close I could poke it in the eyes. Flynn sits and leans back against the building, his legs outstretched and his feet sticking out between the bars of the railing. I scoot back enough so I can face him—his eyes drift from me and land on the closest streetlight, a half-smile poking out from under his beard—and cross my legs under me.

My hands fumble for the box of smokes and lighter I left by the windowsill yesterday. I scrape my thumb over the lighter wheel, hoping it'll keep me in my body.

"I reckon a lot what I'm going to tell you will sound kooky," he says. "I need you to believe."

I snort. "Unless there was magic mushroom mist pumping outta that fog machine on the dancefloor, we blew past kooky a long time ago."

"Alright." He laughs. "Let's start with—what did you see?"

If I close my eyes and hold my breath I can almost hear music from wind chimes made of starlight. I can almost see silver-beaded trees and eyeless faces in the fog.

"Another planet?"

"A higher dimension than this one. A place that sits on the doorway to heaven, basically."

"How did we even get there?"

"Every living being vibrates with energy. Get enough of us together vibrating at a high enough frequency, and with a little luck, we can catch a glimpse of higher worlds."

"I saw *people* in the fog, and—"

"They're called the Metronomes. They've been traveling

across dimensions, and across the universe basically forever. They reach out to other worlds to guide them, when those worlds are ready."

"We saw that place, or those people, on the moon that day me and Gloria found you, right?"

"Right."

I stick the cig to my lips and light up, sucking deep. "Alright." I blow out smoke and back-blast it in through my nose. "Alright, alright, alright. Phew."

"Let's start with *this* world." He reaches out for the cigarette, brings my hand to his lips, and takes a puff. My fingers tickle against his beard. He tips his head back and blows out a line of smoke. "You feel something about this world, don't you? I reckon you do."

"Something's off." I squint. "Something's wrong. I don't know what, yet. And not just Commdef, and the Studio Surveyors blowing up buildings. Something bigger."

"Roger that." He grabs my hand and squeezes, just a little too tight. "Alrighty, that's good. That's not just a feeling. Something wrong—very gee-dee wrong—is happening here on Earth, and the Metronomes are..." He scrubs a hand across the back of his neck, waiting. He looks away.

"Flynn, you can't leave me hanging like this."

His eyes hit mine again, his lips twisting. "They're not happy."

"And I take it we don't want to piss these cats off?"

"They're cosmic beings of light and order, alright. But, golly, give them a reason to be mad at you, and..." He trails off again. With the way he's eyeing my cig, I finally give up and just hand it over to him. He blows out a plume. "Earth might as well be an ant hill, and they're hauling out the bug spray."

Gee-dee. Golly. Reckon. By the way he talks, I can still hear a little of that boy who was scared of his Pop.

"Why now?" I fish out a fresh smoke for myself. "Is it the Dodges, or Vietnam? Or...?"

He shakes his head. "It's something mighty bigger than that. Big enough to threaten the cosmic balance. We—everyone at the disco tonight—better find out. You and me, most of all."

"Cosmic balance? Now you sound like Gloria, going off about my Saturn's return."

His sigh tickles the skin on the back of my arms. "There's a whole heck of a lot I'm still trying to understand, myself."

"Well, you gotta try harder than this. Please."

"Alright," he says. Then it's his turn to say it eight more times, like maybe it'll come true if he prays hard enough.

The Metronomes have certain rules, he says. They call it the Score, and it's a song, and an oath, and a roadmap all at once to guide them as they contact other worlds. Well, put a pin in that for a second. He's doing this all wrong. Back it up. First, there's an energy that flows through the universe that scientists here haven't discovered yet, as precious and rare as life itself in this big and mostly empty dancefloor of the universe. And the Metronomes call this energy Tempo.

Think of Tempo as a song—that the Metronomes were the first to hear—built of beaded silver soundwaves, wrapping up stars. It's creative force, and love, and joy, and a million other bright, beautiful things that there's really no way to describe with words. Tempo is drawn to worlds with conscious beings, and certain worlds and certain people generate even more of the power. With their kaleidoscope-like eyes, the Metronomes can see Tempo wrapping worlds and higher beings with glittering mist. The power is the collective emotional resonance of every living being in the universe, and maybe the brainwaves of the universe itself. And the things the Metronomes have seen—mosaics made of asteroids drawn together by Tempo tractors that show the big bead of everything right before the Big Bang. And starships that are really giant brass choirs weaving around binary star systems, their engines singing of the first instants of the universe. And dances that span continents as each being bows in joy for the first lifeforms that crawled into creation and started this whole dance. It's impossible to see all this, to know all this—he says, his eyes filling with dreamy mist—and not crumble at the absolute certainty that the universe loves you. That all life is divine.

Here I have to grab onto his hands. *Woah, woah, woah, starman. I need to you to ease up on the hazy cosmic jive.* He lost me at collective emotional resonance.

"Tempo is energy," he says. "And the Metronomes make sure there's enough of it to go around. That no world uses up too much, or accidentally destroys itself with some new-fangled technology built using it."

Energy nothing. Power, more like. Power, I get. Like how the States suddenly got all interested in protecting Vietnam once they discovered big piles of petroleum and palladium.

"And how do the Metronomes make sure, or whatever?"

Right, right. They call that the Score. Each world follows the beats of the same song. Once a civilization shows that they are of Ascended Potential—they develop some technology to detect Tempo on their own, or create some great work or art, or some leader raises the collective vibration of the world—the Metronomes notice them, and sends ambassadors to live among them. To learn of the world, and to keep it in time with the cosmic music.

"And what was it that happened here?" I ask.

He tips his head. "Something about the energy you all kick up at the disco, and that crazy machine the DJ plays."

"The Moog?"

"Right-o. Like the music it makes is actually the Metronome language."

That part at least makes sense. We all knew magic happened at that place before we started flipping cars. Tempo. Metronomes. Score. I'm drowning in it all, until my cigarette fizzles down to my fingers. I hiss at the burn. And how the hell does a boy who told me he grew up in Pensacola to a Space Guard pop and a mom who threw garden parties know all about this shit?

He said I wouldn't need my inhaler. Fat chance. I fish it out of my pocket and suck hard.

"The Metronomes—I said *they* when I really should be saying *we*." The trumpet music of his voice softens. "I know that something happened to me on the moon. One of the Metronomes came to me and asked for help. He... he was hurt and fading. Didn't have long to live, and I let him become a part of me."

"Let him?"

"Or, no." He stops me with a hand on my leg. "Time is all fuzzy. I'm not sure if I've been a Metronome my whole life, somehow. All I know is that I wanted to serve my country, and now I'm serving something even bigger."

I'm drowning in all of this. With how his eyes squint up to the moon, he must be, too. He finishes his cigarette and throws the butt over the railing. The red flame sparks through the air.

"I died on that dancefloor," I say, dropping my back against the side of the building. "That's the only thing that makes sense."

"You're here." He shakes my leg, grinning all goofy. "Starman's honor. I can hear this all like music. Same as I heard it out in the street tonight and it called me into the disco. And I'm sure—sure as the rooster crows—that you're a part of this too, Mitch."

"How?"

"As a kid, I knew the second I saw you that you were special," he says. "Even your ma said you had music in you."

"I just figured that meant I was a fag."

He laughs, knocking into me, and soon I'm gushing laughter back at him because with all the hours and hours I've spent listening to *Ziggy Stardust*, here we are talking about aliens and love energy.

"I reckon you're a fellow Ascended Being." He takes my hand and whispers his thumb over the back of my palm. "That's why me and you had to meet, when we were kids, and again in the Guard, and again tonight. We're tied up together in something real big."

"Wouldn't I know if I'm a fucking superhero?" I can barely talk I'm laughing so hard, with only his hand in mine to keep me from floating up to the stars.

"Look at what happened!" He falls into my lap, letting me thread my fingers in his hair as he flops onto his back, looking up at me. "Me and you, at the disco, two higher-vibrational beings. We changed the music of that place the second we touched, bringing everyone right through to a higher dimension and hollerin' with the Metronomes."

"Never mind how all of us turned into Luke Skywalkers

and started flinging cop cars. Can I do that again?" I waggle my fingers at the box of Marlboro Reds on the fire escape, but it stays put. No dice.

"I'll show you how. But right now we have to focus. I need you. I woke up too early, best I can tell you. I should have been an old geezer by the time I remembered my life as a Metronome. Something big and wrong on Earth—something the Metronomes call Disharmony—is messing with the natural music of the Score. Something bad enough to get them on their way here."

I squint, remembering something he said to them. *Tick, tick, tick* in my head, and dancers carved out of crystal in the fog. "Because it is our sacred duty as Adjudicators to bring... what?"

"Judgment."

I swallow. "What kind of judgment?"

"Whether to save this world, or end it, and keep the flow of Tempo in time everywhere else."

My heartbeat is the booming *tick, tick, tick* from my vision. I keep a question locked behind my teeth. *Are we that bad?* Because I know the answer already, just from L.A. Dodges. The Studios kicking folks out of their neighborhoods to expand their lots to film the next installment of *God's Guardsmen.* Reagan threatening to invade Canada every week. Imagine what a bummer we are to a civilization that parties across the universe, spreading light.

I don't even know why they'd want us on the same dancefloor as them. I wouldn't.

We can save the world, sure. Starting with the neighborhood and working our way out, once I fly on over to Mayflower and tear some vidboards down.

I can just about remember something: the warning the

chorus of voices sang out right before we left. "'Give in to the song, or feel the silence?'"

He sits up from my lap. One hand stays on my knee, tracing a circle of fire.

"You've seen things, I reckon?" He frowns, the laughter draining out of his eyes. "As an Ascended being, you should get glimpses of the right notes in the song."

"I have dreams, sometimes. Gloria would call 'em visions. And sometimes I just know things."

"What do you see now?"

"I keep seeing fire burning up everything." My eyes drift away from him, up to the moon. The base is too small to see from here. A vision of flames leaping out of the control panels of a cockpit wants to wallop me, and I squint, keeping it back.

"If that's not a warning, nothing is. We need to find the Disharmony and right it, together, before the Metronomes get here and judge against us. By God, we're not ready for that."

"How long have we got?"

"I'm not sure. They can pop all over the universe like gophers in a field." Muscles at the corners of his jaw pump. "Days. A week, if we're lucky."

"That sure as hell don't sound lucky to me. And *how* do we stop them? Assuming—after that show we put on tonight—that the cops don't hunt us down first."

"After what we did? They oughta be shaking in their boots at the sight of us."

Goddamn it if that doesn't have me wanting to wriggle him out of his jeans right here on the fire escape.

"Hoorah!" I hoot. "Then what's the plan, Metronome Man? You come out to the whole world as an alien?"

"No, we keep this close. Panic all over the world'll just lower the vibes of this place."

"What's even going on, outside? We don't get much news other than Reels here, squawking about Moral Codes and shit."

"That's not just here." He frowns. "Commdef, the Codes, the crackdowns. All that's spilling out like dirty water from a bucket. I was at a rest stop outside Tucson two days ago when a trucker with a ham radio hollered about a gunman shooting at the president."

"Did Reagan make it?"

"The guy missed."

I'm smart enough to read the hard line of Flynn's lips and know not to make a crack about wishing that cat was a better shot.

"There's madness outside that's getting worse," he continues. "Panic, and more anger'n I've ever felt, that'll make it harder to generate Tempo. And we need more, for both me and you to remember what we can do. Who we really are." His hands are rough, almost crushing mine when he pulls them into his lap. Eyes to lips to eyes. "Now that I've got you, there's no stopping us."

His words smooth over an ache I thought I'd bricked over years ago after Ma split. Not that the ache was about her. Just that it changed the song in my head. *You are easy to leave, easy to forget, so you might as well close up to everyone else.*

He rewrites the music. Us. We. With all the hazy cosmic jive he just threw on me—with all that happened tonight—that sounds like true magic.

EIGHTEEN

HEAVEN KNOWS

How do you sleep after someone changes your whole world?

Turns out you don't.

We climb in from the fire escape and peel off each other's clothes, cotton whispering to the floor. Flynn is wound tight with lean muscle, skin so pale the veins on his forearms look almost blue. The mounds of his shoulders and arms, the ridges over his chest, the horns of muscle that jut out at his hips all lead to a dark patch of hair over his pole that bobs between us. He's a centerfold pulled out from one of the magazines on the floor.

He leads me with a bob of his chin to the couch and I know to fall in line. Strange to take our time, instead of the tugs in the bus station bathroom or the park that I'm used to. Wild to keep my eyes open, and let him see the years that passed between us. *And we need more, for both me and you to remember what we can do*, he told me. *Who we really are.* I'll give him everything I got. Hands, lips, just a hint of his teeth on my neck. And with the way he grips my wrists up over my head, and I know to keep them there.

Through the blur of heat, and sweat, I don't know when the fog trickles out from his skin. Just that by the time he's bucking his hips into me—and *starmen, unbound by gravity*—glittering fog rolls everywhere like a rocket about to blaze into the sky.

In the quiet afterwards, with the crystal Gloria hung at the window glowing in the streetlight, I shift under him to look up at his eyes. His eyebrows are smudges of instant coffee. His short beard traces shadows across his face. In the glow of the streetlights, we're two pencil sketches wrapped up in the couch.

"I've never been the same since that night on the fire escape." I brush my knuckles against the side of his jaw. "Like I've been looking for you in every room."

He traces the edges of my lips with his thumb, then sweeps his hand into my hair, cradling my head.

"The things we've seen already." His lips open and close, wordlessly. I spot a peek of his pink tongue. There—maybe that's his tell. Like he's holding something back. "I can't wait for you to see more."

He wriggles to my side, his chin finding a home in the curve of my neck, his breath in my ear whispering me to sleep.

* * *

Me, Flynn, and Gloria idle in her car in an alley at the side of Circus Disco—far from the gaze of the clown doorway—peering at the bustle under the bright, open sky. In sweat-stained jumpsuits with glinting quill-and-eagle pins at the lapels, Commdef officers lug metal riot fences around the lot where we tossed cop cars and hustled in the fog last night. They sweep glass and scrub at what must be puddles of oil from the burnt cop cars they've already hauled away. Two gleaming patrol cars are parked close to the club entrance. Four cops gab through the open windows, with three more parked on the other side of the lot. I want to see if I can shatter their headlights from here, but I haven't been able to move anything with my mind again. Commdef and the cops all brothers-in-armsing like this, the pirate king truce we worked with the local beat cops means squat right now.

Whatever. We don't need them.

Besides the hazy dawn glowing on Flynn's skin this morning, wrapped up with me on the couch—*good glory in the mornin'*, he sang out to me, stretching—I've never seen anything so beautiful as pieces of busted cop car headlights across the concrete. Blue and red glass scatters on the bleached pavement, catching the morning light.

Gloria banks a left down a side street before the goons recognize us as three of last night's entertainment. We can't have an encore.

She came home not long after sunrise this morning—me and Flynn still tangled up on the couch—and he told her everything he told me. I watched her eyes crinkle, blurring the smudged crescent moon still painted on the side of her face. I watched her leap up from the couch while Flynn talked, adjusting the sewing machine, and the vase of flowers on the coffee table, and her candles, all so she wouldn't have to look at him. Same as every time I tried to get her to talk about what happened on the moon. Until he got to the whole *the Metronomes are pissed at us and on the way here* part, and she knew we had to warn the others. Something was drawing her back to the disco, and she figured it was where the others would head for answers, too. She barely hopped out of the shower before she snapped at us to move.

"That was heaven last night," Gloria says staring off through the windshield. "What I felt, what I saw. That's what I know."

"You're not wrong," Flynn says. "The Metronomes live in a place of pure bliss."

"Then you're telling me the Metronomes are angels?"

I hadn't thought of that. Leave it to Gloria to find God. She squeezes the steering wheel again. Flynn leans forward between the seats, closer to us. He's in my favorite blue flannel shirt—I figured the Space Guard jacket of his wouldn't be so incognito—and I never thought seeing someone in my clothes would make me smile so much. I'm jealous for the cotton wrapped around him.

"They're messengers, more like," he says. "Funny, the Greek word for 'messenger' is *angelos*. Which is where we get the word 'angel' in the Bible from. And if you think of it like that—"

"I know you're not going to quote the Word at me." Gloria glares at him through the rearview mirror.

"Just telling you what my Greek grandmother told me, is all." He shrugs.

"They have Greek grandmothers in space?"

Despite the annoyed flash in Gloria's eyes I actually laugh. Big mistake. She turns the hairy eyeball on me. "Sorry," I mumble.

"Flynn's grandmother, if you rather think of it like that," he says. "I'm both Flynn and not Flynn."

"Then I both know what I saw, and am scared of it," Gloria says.

"Me too," I pipe up. "But if we've been, I don't know, *chosen* to help heal the Disharmony..." I trail off, looking to Flynn for help.

The corners of his lips tug up when he lays a hand on Gloria's arm. "I reckon you felt their love in the dance? That's what'll get us right through this."

I watch as some of the edge in her eyes softens. "Anyone else got any bright ideas? Everyone meeting here and getting hauled in by the man probably ain't a part of the divine plan." She smirks at me with her eyes, borrowing some of Flynn's accent to add, "I reckon."

I tell her with mine, *Be nice.*

"We gotta move fast," I say. "We shouldn't be on the streets."

Gloria's fingers drum on the steering wheel. "I told Bette to spread the word and stay low."

"Can we round up all the others at your place?" Flynn asks.

"We ain't exactly gonna fit the whole disco in our two-bedroom." Gloria tilts her head. "Besides, what if that brings Commdef right to our front door?"

Good thing I know a sweet little pad where I like to cause some trouble. We just need to make some calls. And oh God, we need rum punch in the biggest goddamn container I can find.

* * *

I close my eyes and can almost hear the rows of sewing machines that used to crowd this place, over the chatter of disco dancers from last night walking over the warped floorboards of the wide-open studio.

Before its top floor was half burned to hell a few weeks back, the Spindler's Arms was an apartment building, and before that a Studio textile mill. Now, it's our temporary home until we can figure out where the hell to go next without Commdef finding us. I cobbled together something close to punch that sits in a couple of plastic jugs on the folding card table right outside the kitchen. We even brought over the good Welch's jam glasses that we use for cups.

Flynn is Space Guard-straight, by the huge row of windows inset in the brick wall. Bette folds her leather-jacket-clad arms over her chest while Gloria rocks on her heels. Her favorite daisy poncho over a pair of jean cutoffs ripples like water around her. No pantyhose, since an Indecency ticket is about the last thing we have to worry about right now. Light from the window shines through the edges of her teased-out hair. I was standing there with them until Gloria had to tell me, as sweet as she could, that my energy was amping them up too much. I can't help it. Ricky didn't pick up his phone when I called again and again. Bette swung by his place and it was empty. By the door, I thumb the inhaler in my pocket, willing my lungs to quit dancing so hard.

Twenty or so of us so far, safe, here and chatting in excited clumps. Giggling about tossing cop cars, and magic bullet-deflecting bubbles. There must've been close to three hundred of us at the disco last night, but this is everyone we could reach this morning. More will come.

Call it a hunch. I can see us spreading over the city—then the world—like glowing fog. Dancing to the music.

Morning sunlight blows in through the dirty window panes that aren't busted in, with a few bricks and rocks on the floor around us. Graffiti gashes the flimsy drywall, with a jagged hole in the center that looks into another studio. The wall and the unlocked door is the only thing that separates this apartment from the rest of the top floor of the five-story brick beast. Some crafty queen before me made sure to keep the electricity and plumbing of the building working after the folks who lived here got booted out because of the fire. The crumpled beer cans and condoms we found between old crates are proof that I'm not the only one to use this place as an occasional love nest. Gloria crinkled her face and wouldn't step inside until me and Flynn at least swept up some.

Me and Gloria spent all morning chain-smoking and working the same phone tree we use for Dodges to round up as many people as we could from last night. I recognize the cats here from the disco even if I don't know them all as well as I know Ricky. Juana, Bette's girl, flits around the room, handing out jam glasses of punch. She's at least a head shorter than everyone else, with a tight, silver-threaded black braid bobbing behind her. Hat-Trick—or Patrick, I guess, since he's not on stage—was one of the first ones to get here. He set up his DJ stand and the Moog, plugging it into an outlet in a corner. Electric-spiked church organ chords trickle into the air. Bette's already told him to lower the volume three times in case Commdef walks by and wonders who the hell is holding mass upstairs.

Rex, in a ripped white t-shirt over his jeans, moseys through the front door and over to Gloria, Bette, and Flynn. I zip after him.

"Nothing yet," he rumbles softly to the trio.

"We should—"

Bette cuts me off with a hand to my arm. "Junior, we'll get him here. Don't worry."

Funny that she's the one trying to calm me down when she stormed in here railing about lockups, and camps, and nailing the cops to the walls until Juana talked her down. They didn't even go home after our dance party last night, figuring Commdef would be waiting to question the owner of the club. We only reached her because they were crashing at Rex's pad.

"She's right," Gloria says. "Right now, we gotta take care of the ones under this roof. They all have questions. *I* still have questions."

The four of us sweep our eyes to Flynn. He holds his bright blue eyes steady.

"Alright," he says. I can just hear the tiniest quake at the edge of his voice. Then again, stronger. "Alright."

We turn to the crowd and I can feel the camera lenses of their eyes twitching on us.

* * *

No one here really knows Lieutenant Flynn Parker of the United States Space Guard except me, but everyone knows Sure Bette, and Lady Moondust, and Rex the doorman, and Last Mitch Effort, the pirate king of the contraband hoard. We stand in a line with Flynn in the middle, vouching for him with our bodies, while everyone else sits on the floorboards across from us.

"Listen up, freaks," Bette says by way of introduction. Then she bows to Flynn who clears his throat, taking the floor.

Over bad punch and lighter flicks, Flynn fills the group in on the big beats. He's an alien. We all warped to another dimension last night. Tempo flows through the universe. We all thought Dodges were the end of the world until we heard the Metronomes were basically knocking on our door because of some cosmic Disharmony we're guilty of. And it's got them madder than a boiled owl. He answers questions with the Space Guard trumpet of his voice. The others have enough sense to ask more than I did last night, still hot over flipping cop cars and itching to get Flynn out of his clothes. I smell liquor breath over the old wood and dust of the room. Someone asks Flynn just where the Metronomes are from. Everywhere, he says. They're a whole group of Ascended Beings from various civilizations around the universe, who join the chorus once they reach a high enough vibration. They're travelers, though he remembers the green oceans of a world maybe somewhere in a galaxy that's so far away we don't even have a name for it.

"I heard voices," Juana says from her perch in the front row. "And we all... We were a *we*, right? And—*mierda*—how did we even do what we did?"

"You were working higher-vibrational energy," Flynn says.

"Well, that's the first thing that makes a lick a' sense so far," Lainey cracks from the back. "I was so high I was dancing on the ceiling."

From the way the giggles roll out of her, I'm guessing Lainey isn't back down to Earth yet. She's wrapped up in tie-dyed linen, her cork-heeled sandals on the floor beside her. Her waist-length black hair is ironed pin-straight like Cher. She was one of the dolls on stage last night in the Dodgers uniforms and blue wigs. Her drag name is Conda Sending. I see her most days working the Vietnamese deli her parents own down the road from me and Gloria's, draping pickled vegetables on banh mi sandwiches with the same flourishes as when she plucks a dollar outta someone's fingers.

Seeing straight-backed Lieutenant Flynn Parker pat the air like a substitute teacher trying to calm us down has me wondering if I should swoop in and help out. I'm happy to let him take the heat without mentioning how I might be an Ascended Being, too. That's not nearly the kind of attention I need.

"Spaces of shared joy like that practically crackle with Tempo," he continues. "That place especially, it seems."

"We can all feel when a party's bitchin' and the vibe is right," Carla, in the middle of the pack says. Today's she scrubbed off her painted Manny Fest-Destiny drag moustache, instead showing up all femme with a million beaded necklaces. "Just—that's the first time I've blasted off to Mars."

"I'll get you some off-the-hook mushrooms, sister," Patrick burbles from his corner over the bouncing notes from the Moog. "I've been space-walking and talking to little green men for years. Good to know they're really out there and I'm not outta my gourd." He hiccups. "Not totally, anyway."

"For the love of dick, please turn that racket down," Bette groans, squeezing the bridge of her nose. "The adults are speaking."

"It's not racket, it's *music*, and—"

Gloria sighs. "Bette, a little mood music ain't hurting nobody." When Bette grumbles, Gloria sings out, "Hat-Trick, baby, you're controlling that volume, aren't you?"

He waggles his eyebrows. "You know me."

This is going to take forever. Got me thinking, not for the first time, that we're doomed.

"The energy of the disco that night pulled me in, straight off the street," Flynn continues. "You all were able to sync to my frequency as a Metronome, and see them for yourself."

More glazed eyes. Rex takes a slow, slow sip of his punch, then tugs at his gray-streaked dark beard.

"And the bubble and the door thing." Rex clears his throat, like he's embarrassed. "That was...?"

"Mind-meld and collective telekinesis," Patrick says, echoing into his jam glass. "A friend passed me a file on the government's secret MKUltra experiments in the fifties." Heads tip at him. He blinks his saucer-eyes. "Do your research, sheeple."

"He's more right than you'd think," Flynn says, spreading his hands. "We've all seen schools of fish swim like one, and birds fly in formation."

"We're a flock of queer pink flamingos," I add. Then bite the inside of my cheek when no one laughs. Fine, then.

"A group of higher lifeforms channeling Tempo together isn't that much different," Flynn continues. "The Metronomes have a name for when they can all boogie as one, and share knowledge, and gifts, and—and big mojo." He interlocks his fingers in front of him. "They call it the Manifold."

"My aunt got dragged into some Oregon cult compound and talked hippie hoo-hah about vibrations," Stetson grumbles from the middle of the pack. "They sold tea and ate soybeans until the leader got snatched by the Feds for tax evasion."

"Any chance that cult levitated people with their brains?" I snap.

Stetson was the one with the bushy moustache and Dumbo ears who tried to climb the stage during Gloria's show last night. And, it turns out, the leak from the LAPD who's been tipping off gay clubs about the raids this whole time. He told us this when he first rolled in here, his chest all puffed out like he just pulled a whole family outta a burning building.

"Phony baloney," he barrels on, ignoring me. He stabs a finger at Flynn. "You oughta get the president on the horn and lay into him with your 'take me to your leader' jive."

"President Fuckface is too busy in Camp Puller, bleeding Vietnam dry of gas, and jerking it thinking about Commdef controlling what we do in the bedroom." Bette glares at him. "If anyone's gonna level with a bunch of dance-floor aliens, better any of *us* than him. We're talking to 'em, already."

"He's not my leader," Juana chimes in evenly at Stetson. "And neither are you, so up your nose with a rubber hose."

"If any of you listened to me last night, none of us would be in this mess," Stetson volleys back.

Rex's low bass rumbles how even if we emptied the club out before the raid, that wouldn't patch up the—what did Flynn call it?—the Disharmony. And maybe we should talk about how we fix that instead of going off about telekinesis. Someone cracks that even if Stetson sucks dick, he's still a pig cop, which only gets him yammering about how he's here and not helping the cops, or Commdef, or whoever find us. Cue the overlapping tracks, yapping, and finger-pointing, and Flynn's mouth moving without a sound, like he's bobbing for air.

I'm about to run outta there when Gloria glides forward from the line of us.

"We were all changed last night," she says. "It can't've been just me." Her wide eyes look like they're reading our horoscopes on the back wall. "I can hear music all around if I quiet up enough." She brushes a loose fist in the center of her chest. "Music, and there's something else, here."

I know what she means. Power. The voices sang out in the fog, *it is freely given to those who sail the Wave-Forms to us here.*

Lainey's gasp cuts the chatter. Then Bette yelps and scrambles back, tugging Juana with her. The whoops and laughter sound as sweet as music, with Gloria at the front like she's hosting a killer show.

One of the glass jam jars of punch floats high above us. Red punch flows out like a tiny waterfall in reverse and twirls around the glass in a liquid ribbon, catching the light.

NINETEEN
POTLUCK

After the laughter, after Gloria floats the jam glass back to the table so it doesn't rain punch on of us, Flynn tells us how we can all do this. And more. We can think of Tempo like music, like Gloria does. We can use Tempo to move mountains, easy as jam glasses. If the universe is one heck of a big living thing, Tempo is its feelings. You don't tell the glasses to move. You love them so much that you *ask* them to move, and they do. We all reached the Metronomes and heard their song, and it opened up our hearts. And we can sing it to others, teaching them the tune. We're instruments of the Metronomes, now.

And I don't know. He loses me with the cosmic love talk.

Others catch the drift. Lainey, wrapped up in tie-dye, sways to her feet. Her lips twitch, her shoulders shake. A black line of mascara smudges down her face. I can't tell if she's happy or if her heart is breaking until the glass in her hands lifts off in a little puff of fog and her laughter rattles the windows. Everyone else hoots and calls her name, with more glasses rising to the air. Carla. Juana. Rex. If all it took to heal the Disharmony was levitating empty Welch's grape jam jars, we'd wrap up in time to hit happy hour at the Black Cat.

The jam jar in my hand is doing squat. I'm supposed to be some Ascended Being, according to Flynn. *Failure*, a glass-tipped voice hisses. *Fuckup*. I'm standing in a line with the others, still, but I'm somewhere else, too. Ma is singing around the house as she packs up to leave, and Buckteeth Keith's teeth hit my knuckles, and starmen are hooting all around me after I peel back the blanket of my bunk in the east barracks to find that they poured sugar all on my sheets because *Last Mitch Effort's got sugar in his tank*, and now Kern is offering me a last chance not to screw up the rest of my life. The shuttle on the way back to Earth creaks and screams in my head. I gulp hard and try to listen to Watkins telling me to cram down my feelings. The waves slamming against the airlock door sure ain't the love Flynn says we should be feeling. I chomp the inside of my mouth, tasting blood. My inhaler. He said I wouldn't need it, but now I'm huffing and trying to do it as quiet as possible so everyone's eyes don't turn to me.

"Tempo will get louder and stronger in you with enough practice," Flynn says once Lainey tiptoes back to her spot in the crowd. "And you can pass it to others, strengthening the whole Manifold as our numbers grow." He stumbles a bit, looking to Gloria, who just nods at him. "I mean, you can teach others, in shared moments of joy, how to hear the music."

Juana doubles over, cackling. "That sure explains a lot."

"Baby, stoooooppp," Bette groans over-dramatically.

Flynn tips his head. "What?"

"I wasn't at the disco last night," Juana says. "I was home working on a story for *Paradigm* when she"—Juana thumbs over to Bette—"comes barreling in for a moment of *shared joy* right in my office. Then two more right after."

Oh my God. Like hearing about my parents getting frisky. I wish I had a pitcher of punch to glug.

"Listen, you can't blame me." Bette chuckles. "Who knew exploding cop cars would get me hotter'n a furnace?"

"Wait," Stetson cuts in from the back. I'm surprised he hasn't stormed out of here. He's tugging on one of his ear lobes, his face burning up. "You're telling me that the ability to use Tempo is spread through sex? Like—like we need to give the Common Defense Corp any more reason to think we're all perverts with the clap, or—"

"No no no." Flynn clears his throat and adjusts the buttons of his flannel, shuffling on his scuffed high-tops. Aww—with what we got up to last night, now he's embarrassed? "We didn't have sex with everyone at the disco last night, did we?"

"Well." I whistle. "Not everyone."

That finally gets his hands to his hips, his eyes squeezing shut, laughing like a kid on a fire escape. I gotta help him with the sermoning. We need less *aw, shucks* Pensacola, more hip-swaying disco. Know your crowd. I tell him with my eyes, *at ease*.

"Shared joy, I mean," he continues, his trumpet tune brighter. "Making music, making art, dancing together when the right song hits, like last night. And, yes, making love. Your hearts open for all of these. Music, sex, art, science—the Metronomes hear all this as notes in the same song."

"So, every time we fuck, we get stronger?" Rex chomps his cigar. Smoke the same gray as his beard curls around his head. "That's an army I can get behind."

I knew I liked him. Gloria gets all church girl, giggling and covering her lips.

"What I'm *saying* is..." Substitute teacher Flynn is going to have to start handing out detention if we won't stop cracking up at everything. "Every person we can teach the Tempo to makes the song louder. Every one of us has got a part to play."

"And now one'a us is missing," I say. "And we have to bring him home."

"Roger that." Flynn nods. "No soldier left behind."

"Family," Gloria corrects him. "He's one of us, and one of us in trouble means that all of us dig in the potluck for him."

"Family, then," Flynn says. "Heard the good word."

Bette rubs her palms together. "What kind of a jailbreak are we talking? I owe those pigs for shutting down my club. I oughta flip a patrol car right on toppa Commdef central."

"We were all one last night," Flynn says, still in the middle of our line at the head of the group. "I reckon we can all still feel that. Hear it, like a song on the radio in the next room. We have to remember that song, and reach out through it to find Ricky, and if he's in a bind we're going to push him some extra Tempo. We're going to let it flow from us to him. Not too much, or it'll burn him out."

A slow, liquid beat of silence spreads out. In the back, Stetson frowns, feeding on the doubt around him. I sway on my feet, knees aching from standing so long.

"We can do that?" I ask.

The corners of his lips sweep up. He bounces two fingers against his eyebrow in a quick salute. "Starman's honor."

I might not have enough love in me to waste it on jam glasses, but what I've got for Flynn makes me believe.

* * *

Flynn sees patterns that I don't as he has us stand in a circle around the room, like he's looking at Gloria's star charts. His steady hands guide us into formation as the wood floors creak and groan over the soft silk of Hat-Trick's Moog. Flynn slips his Space Guard jacket over his flannel, and I can see that the costume change straightens his shoulders. He tugs Lainey's hands and she bounces on her feet, giggling behind him, to one part of the circle. Then he hits her with his Lieutenant Parker eyes, tips his head, and moves her next to Carla. Cigar smoke billows around Rex's head, at Stetson's left.

"If we start singing 'Kumbaya, My Lord', I'm out the door." Stetson plucks at his bushy moustache.

"No one's stopping you, ears," Bette calls out by the window, her hand in Juana's.

"We can't have those vibes here." Gloria whips out the church lady voice. "Both of you."

Bette wilts. "Sorry, Lady M."

"She's right," Flynn says, his hands on his hips in the center of the circle. "We have to tune up to a certain pitch, and..."

The rubber of his hi-tops creak on his way over to me. Those lips that were tracing fire down my body a couple of hours ago are looking something sweet. He taps my chest.

"He's in here?"

Something behind my ribs quakes. I can see Ricky, at the jobsite in Sunshine City, sipping Coca-Cola Comet and being good to me when he didn't need to be, before we started meeting up in the empty houses at night. I can see him back in LA, driving carloads of people out of me and Gloria's apartment under the cover of night, to get them out of the city and on their way into Canada, like his folks. We've been buddies in the backroom, but neither of us were looking to pick out wedding china. Friends, lovers, brothers—it's not just the Studio Zone boundaries that are shifting. A different kind of invisible string links me to Ricky than the tighter, brighter one that ties me to Flynn. Still, I got room enough for them both.

Flynn shakes his head, like I've got my own tell. "It's good. Hold onto that. That's the pitch."

He tugs me into the center of the group, then reaches for Gloria next. Bette and Juana, since they're a package deal. Rex, too. With the way he eyes the five of us, he must be hearing music we don't. Until he perks up, and heads to Stetson.

"Officer?" he says.

"Cult shit is what this is," Stetson huffs. "Devil worship, and Manson mumbo-jumbo, and sacrificing goats, and—"

"None of that's here." Flynn shakes his head. "You've served this family already, haven't you? We can always use another protector. We need you, if you'll have us."

For the first time today, I hate the softness in Flynn's voice. Cops like Stetson—even the pirate kings—have been giving us shit for months. I keep my mouth shut, toeing the floor between Gloria and Rex, when Stetson sighs. He doesn't let Flynn take him by the hand, but he follows him back to join the circle, on Rex's right.

"Patrick, sir?" Flynn calls out to the corner. "We need the tunes. And Bette's right that we can't tip anyone off that we're here, so, please watch the levels."

His beard-framed lips twitch when he sweeps his eyes to Gloria. I know her well enough to see the little dance at the corner of her mouth as a smile she's trying to keep in. Whatever joke they're telling each other is one I don't get.

"Though, I reckon you already know how to do that?" he adds.

"Suh, yes, suh!" Patrick snaps.

Flynn steps into the circle between me and Rex, pecking me on the lips, and grabbing my hand.

"You know what you're doing, starman?"

He taps the eight-point star on his lapel. "Cross my heart." Then, he lifts his chin and cranes his neck, sweeping his eyes around the room. "Everyone, hold hands."

Séance. Summoning. Witchcraft, whispers and giggles while hands slip together. Honestly, Stetson doesn't seem that far off the mark.

Slow, pulsing star heartbeats spill into the air. I blink and can almost see silver beaded threads connecting us all around the room. But it's just the sunlight bouncing off my eyelashes.

* * *

I squeeze my eyes closed when the music starts, the slow hum, gliding up my legs, trickling down my arms and into Flynn and Gloria, through our clasped hands. Hat-Trick adds a little *beep-boop*, and I can see the watchtower search beam on the moon, looking out.

We ain't perfect. We ain't even probably the right ones for the job—bringing home Ricky, and patching up whatever hurt is getting the Metronomes all riled up—but we're here. We're here. I want to feel the love energy that cradles galaxies, like Flynn said. But brick walls are exploding in my head, and I'm scared for Ricky as much as for us.

Beep-boop. We got a discoman MIA. Beep-boop. Are you there?

"The music is as much about silence between the notes," Flynn says. "And the dance is as much about being still."

I open my eyes, just a crack. Someone switched on a big fog

machine, and fog drifts up to the warped, old ceiling beams. No—it drifts from our hands and shoulders. Flynn's eyelashes are dark ink stains against his cheeks. His lips move with words I don't hear. Maybe he's praying.

"We've got a missing brother, and we're going to call him home," Gloria says.

The fog above us thickens and spins, swirling with glitter. Something in Hat-Trick's music crackles like radio static in my ears. Something the fog needs me to see? Or...

Flash.

Everything is tinted blue, like the color on a vidscreen is all wrong. Through the blue haze, a cracked diamond leaks burnt yellow into space. Toy soldiers drift in yellow fog, board their spaceship, and trace a jagged red line through the sky back to their world. I can feel the yellow fog over the city, trapped by the mountains and billowing in the breeze from the sky flowers, stinking like burnt blood. The fog settles on the dead leaves and the brittle bushes of this rainless city. A hand tosses a smuggled cig into the dead earth.

They will come for you. The voice is the hiss of the brush catching fire. *They will take from you, they will smother, steal...*

Blue glass cracks. The floor pitches under me. A snake of yellow smoke is wriggling around in my lungs, and I'm gonna keel over. I can't breathe, I can't—

"We can feel him, through the sound waves," Gloria says, drizzling the sweet caramel of her voice onto all of us. "We can see him."

Yes. I'm with Gloria. We're checking each other's tanks, and her voice clears the blue glass from my eyes. No yellow smoke in my lungs, when I'm breathing easy with her. She has me.

Juana gasps. "We can see him."

I can feel cuffs cutting into my wrists, same as the duct tape that bound me on the *Saint Christopher.* I blink, and just for a second I see Ricky's face reflected in a car window.

"Those fuckers have him in cuffs," Rex growls.

"We have him, so close," Flynn says, steadying us against the rattling of the floorboards. "Lean in. We have to—"

The star-song swells into church bells. A bright ache starts in my throat and blooms out, whirling and glowing. Bliss cut with sadness. An empty dancefloor ache smoothed over with the disco-biscuit spins. I can feel the same song echoing out in everyone —*it's so good, it's so good.* Minds and hearts linked by beaded silver fringe that's missing one bead to make the chain complete.

"We can bring the music to him because we are the music." Gloria's voice is mixed with caramel, edges echoing with one hell of a vocal run.

Electric wind chimes connect us to him. Fog billows all around us and over the dented floorboards. And that sweet DJ knows the right track to play, with the vamp wrapping up in a few beats. We can feel the cue. We know the right moves now, boogieing for our boy.

Ignition. We have liftoff, swirling up to the stars on silver-beaded fringe blasts.

* * *

We hear the tinkling of metal on metal. We, I. Eyes. Eyes up and around, and—alright, where are we? We are many bodies standing in a room with worn wooden floors, just as much as we're one body.

We look down, legs all cramped up, hands pinned behind

our backs and wedged between us and the seat. A metal cage separates us from the two seats up front. The magic at the disco last night healed our swollen eye from the raid, just in time for us to get a fist in the other one not three hours ago. Alright, we're in a car. A car that stinks like exhaust and fresh paint. Right. They must've just painted *COMMON DEFENSE CORP* across the doors of this thing, but it's still a cop car. Good. Cop cars are easy. We've been cuffed in one before. Cuffed in jail cells, too. They cracked us good on the side of the head that one time we made an *alright, Mr. DeMille, I'm ready for my close-up* joke before the camera-flash of our mugshot. And yes sir, we are still boogieing.

We lean forward and jangle our wrists, accidentally brushing against the welt on our back.

Funny, Commdef rubber bullets feel like regular bullets when they're fired up close.

Funnier, the electric wind chime that links us all in the big song sounds like the music of our handcuffs clinking together. Music, we can use.

First, we have to skip back in the track—just a bit. We have to know how the song started, so we can learn the new cues in the Score.

* * *

Commdef was so polite. When we were walking back home from one of the safe-house supply drops, they made sure to say *please* and *excuse us.*

Excuse us, son, can we have a word? We'd like to ask if you know anything about an attack on law enforcement last night. You look like the type that was there.

We knew to say *sir* with a nice voice, like our parents told us, and to pull our hands out of our pockets.

No sir, we said. *I was at home.*

And you're from here?

Yes, sir. Born and raised in the city.

That ticks the other one off.

No—but where are you really from?

Just off North Hoover Street, sir, and—

We're going to need to see your papers, son. And please tell us what happened. Please tell us where the others like you are.

The other one starts in with, *Please, don't make this hard for us. We don't want to hurt you. We will if we have to, to keep you from hurting others.*

We turn our head to the side a little—a mistake, yeah—looking over their shoulders, to the other Commdef cars circling.

If you run, that'll make it worse, son.

And we know we shouldn't have. Still—that music in his voice sounded all wrong. Made us want to try running even if they warned us.

We made it a couple of feet before the rubber bullet in the back. Before we keeled over, then the knee jabbed between our shoulders, and hands wrestled our arms behind us, our face crammed into the gravel.

* * *

Alright, we're here. Jingle. Jangle. The Commdef cops don't hear the music of the handcuffs because they're inside the deli to question the owner and grab sandwiches and coffee. Two birds, one stone and all. They left me in the car and cracked the window.

The rattle of the cuffs makes us laugh because how do you handcuff a song? The way the sounds harmonize makes us crack up harder, and then we can see just how easy it is for those sound waves to slip in between the teeth and fasteners of the handcuffs, and rattle the right way until—*click*—the cuffs hit the seat behind us. Almost done. The sound waves hustle out in beaded silver fringe and knock around in the door until the lock pops open.

And wait. Wait. The car is still running. One of the Instruments in the band is winding up for a big solo moment, telling us how easy it will be to just slip behind the wheel, honk the horn, and plow into the Commdef goons when they run out of the deli. And think how it would feel. *Oooh, it's so good.* The windows of the car start to rattle, invisible hands treating the metal cage like a drum set.

Mitch, you have to calm down. I hear this through static in the radio. *You're feeding him too much Tempo, and you'll pull us out of the Manifold if—*

The voice through the static stops. The conductor with the clear blue eyes gets the soloist to wrap up, and then we shake our head as the band winds up for our big finish. We open the door and slip out of the car, low to the ground. Commdef doesn't notice because they're still inside. *If you run, that'll make it worse, son,* they told us. That was when we were alone. That was before we remembered we've already helped people like us run hundreds and hundreds of miles up away from people like Commdef. So what's a two-mile sprint back home?

As the big music fades away—fire in our lungs, muscles all singing strong—we run, our feet knowing the way.

TWENTY

DODGEBALL

I trickle back to myself, skating on strands of silver-beaded fringe back to my body. I sway into Flynn and he holds me up. Me, Flynn, Gloria, Rex, Juana, Bette, Stetson—our circle within the circle breaks, and the fog vanishes. Gasps, and laughs all around, as Gloria claps and hoots. Stetson rubs his face. Rex somehow didn't drop his cigar this whole time. The way everyone else giggles and sways, they must feel as drunk as I do. Hat-Trick cuts the tunes. I squeeze Flynn and Gloria's hands, and—*wild, crazy, we did it*, I agree with everyone—but I'm not adding to the laughter.

Because what I saw when we were calling out to Ricky sucks all of it out from me.

Burnt yellow fog that tastes like pain, trickling from space and spreading over the city. A glass-tipped voice, scraping all over me.

They will come for you. They will take from you, they will smother, steal...

Bette knocks into me as she throws her arms around Flynn, picks him up, and shakes him in a bear hug.

"Goddamned miracle is what you are, kid," she says, her voice quaking.

"No ma'am," Flynn wheezes. "That was y'all. All I did was point the way."

Bette drops him, and he stumbles into me—laughing nervously—and I bonk into Gloria.

"And that's how we set things right," Flynn says, stepping back a bit from the circle so the whole group can hear. "We kick up some more of that Tempo. Louder, 'n' stronger, and then, with a little luck, I reckon I can draw on all that power to close up the Disharmony before the Metronomes come in."

"And the Disharmony is..." Stetson trails. "What, exactly?"

"If I knew that, I'd be on the way to patch it up myself lickety-split," Flynn says.

"If it's some, what'd you say, *cosmic wrong*," Stetson starts, narrowing his eyes. "That's somehow worse than all the other *wrongs* going on all over. Commdef, the Moral Codes, the Studio Zones..."

"Nancy Reagan's haircut," Juana adds.

Bette licks one palm and smooths the sides of her Elvis pompadour. "The fucking Star-Spangled Sisters."

"Whatever million possible fucking awful things that are happening everywhere in the world, that we know nothing about, since Reagan's got a lock on the TV and radio." I frown. Goddamnit, Officer Asshole is on to something.

"From where I'm standing, the only cosmic wrong is this cat from outer space," Stetson finishes.

"Who, in case you forgot, saved our asses last night," Gloria says, jumping in before I can. Her eyes tell me, *you're not helping.*

"Who also just said he's gonna heal the Disharmony," I finish. I'm nice enough not to add *asshole* at the end like I want. Family squabbles will get us nowhere.

"See! That's what I'm talking about." Stetson's jerky hands smooth down the edges of his moustache. "If it's a human problem, shouldn't a human be calling the shots? Shouldn't one of *us* be the one to heal whatever's got these aliens' panties in a bunch?"

"It's part of my duty, sir. Not something I'd wish on anyone else." Flynn folds his hands in front of him. "Holding that much Tempo will burn any of you out, same as holding onto a power line. Nothing like sending a little over to Ricky to bust him out. I'm used to working higher-vibrational energy."

"And what do these Metronomes get outta this Score game, anyhow?" Juana asks, squinting. "They let us hear their music and it's their way of handing out fancy magic powers without asking for anything in return?"

"You'll forgive me, ma'am, because I mean no disrespect," Flynn says, "but that's about the most Hollywood thing I've ever heard."

"I'm not following?" Juana tips her head.

"I love this country. Enough that I joined the Guard and was ready to die for it. And my time in the Guard brought me to plenty of other places, and to plenty of folks. That idea that 'I got lucky and have something and you can't have it.' It's just..." When he looks to me, the muscles of his jaws pulse. He's a nervous kid on the fire escape again, asking me *how do you be yourself?* "The Metronomes show us boundless love. Spreading it to others doesn't diminish the whole. That's our shared responsibility, I reckon."

"You gonna give us commandments, Moses?" Stetson smirks. "Start passing around the collection plate?"

"This look like any kind of church you've been to?" Gloria asks. Then she stops, and her cat smile slinks over her face.

"You know, maybe you're onto something. The Church of the Divine Deviants."

Deviant. We all get called that enough. *Deviant activity not permitted* signs on the gates of the Studio Zones. Sections in the Moral Codes to outlaw *deviant behavior.*

"I just..." Stetson backs away from the inner circle of us, the red spreading from his ears down to his neck. "I just don't get it. If this is a numbers game, don't we need to get the straights and everyone else on board? Maybe they'd take us seriously if the warning about the Metronomes wasn't coming from"—he jabs a finger at Flynn and Gloria—"free-love freaks, and—"

"Sugar, you're gonna want to think mighty hard about the next word that flies outta your yap," Gloria says, sweet as her brandy tea.

"Drag queens," he finishes.

That put some mean music in my hips. "We're not doing this. Yelling at each other about who belongs, and ratting each other out for some bullshit STAR Citizen Ponds Moon Mask ads is exactly the kind of noise that makes the Dodges work."

"And Commdef is locking up the respectable queers in suits same as us 'drag queens,'" Gloria purrs. "Just so we're clear, *officer.* What we just did is proof that there ain't no one coming to save us, we're here to save ourselves."

"And the rest of the world." Juana tugs the end of her silver-streaked braid. "Apparently."

"And the whole big wide beautiful world. Whether they like who's saving 'em or not." Gloria rewards us with a little Lady Moondust shimmy. "Easy-peasy, lemon-squeezy."

"I'm not trying to fight." Stetson sighs, letting his hands flap to his sides. "What we just did, it's—it's a miracle, a'course. And

I felt part of... I just—just..." We all let him flounder, until he frowns at the floorboards. "I should check in with the station, keep 'em off your tails if I can."

He brushes a finger at his nose and zips out of the room. His heavy footsteps sound like bullets down the stairs. No one goes after him.

* * *

Bette is about to circle the neighborhood in her truck, looking for Ricky, when he bursts through the broken door of the apartment. Hands and arms fly all over him. I don't know how everyone outside doesn't hear our racket. *Our love is boundless. Our mercy is not.* I remember the thoughts from last night's Manifold, and now even Rex is bounding up and down like a cigar-smoking rabbit, crushing Ricky's face to his chest. And then Ricky's in my arms, and I'm careful of how hard I kiss his already healing black eye. One more night like last night, and Tempo will patch him up good.

I press my forehead to his before I pass him to Flynn, who doles out about the straightest hug I've ever seen—no hip contact, a couple of pats on the back—until Ricky slips off to the others.

We might not be soldiers, but we have our orders. Search and rescue, just like we did for Ricky.

We need to vibrate together again, call up the Manifold, and hopefully channel enough Tempo to Flynn for him to see just where or what the Disharmony is and how to heal it. But it's a balancing act, he says. A tightrope on fire, not the fake ones that crisscross under the mirror balls at Circus Disco. We need to whip up enough Tempo without burning up like spent fuses. We were able to work big mojo with the bullet-deflecting bubble and telekinesis production number because enough of us were in the crowd.

Which sounds a whole hell of a lot to me like this calls for an absolute bitchin' party.

We can't go back to Circus Disco with the pigs sniffing around there. Every other gay bar is boarded up, and any of us gathering under one roof breaks about a million Moral Codes, anyhow. So we're bringing the party here. We've got until nightfall—give or take eight hours—to turn this busted brick house into the new Circus Disco. Easy-peasy, lemon-squeezy.

Sergeant Sure Bette calls the shots. Cleaning crew. Food. Supplies. Whoever feels strong and safe enough to leave the building is on search duty, bringing all the family they can get a hold of to our new home. Curfew is sunset, when everyone better be back under this half-burned roof. Flynn and Rex break off from the group and I hear then yammering about which walls have to come down.

Lainey swipes her fingers through the ends of her long black Cher hair, braiding and unbraiding as Bette whips everyone up.

"And while we're doing all this, and stayin' outta cop cuffs." Lainey's pink glossy lips crinkle into a line. "We gotta keep all this a secret?"

Even Bette stops barking orders. Everyone turns to me and Gloria. Two Space Guard rejects leading the charge.

Gloria's cat eyes tell me that I know the answer for the both of us.

"You tell every queer you know to come on home for the party tonight," I say.

No one argues because we all know the first rule of Dodges.

Your disco needs you.

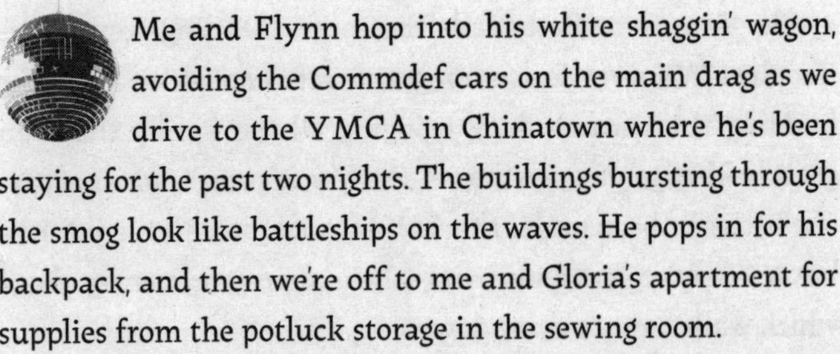

TWENTY-ONE

PENSACOLA SON

Me and Flynn hop into his white shaggin' wagon, avoiding the Commdef cars on the main drag as we drive to the YMCA in Chinatown where he's been staying for the past two nights. The buildings bursting through the smog look like battleships on the waves. He pops in for his backpack, and then we're off to me and Gloria's apartment for supplies from the potluck storage in the sewing room.

The living room is the same as we left it, barely eight hours ago, with the posters of Tina Turner and Jesus scowling at the mess of the couch and my piles of clothes and magazines. The air smells like church candles, murky over the wet weight of a rainstorm that won't come. The beaded curtain flaps in the breeze from the open window. I left an empty Dr. Pepper can on the coffee table, a still life next to the roses I snatched from a fancy Silver Lake yard three days ago, and dropped into a Budweiser bottle.

We should load up all the sheets and towels in the apartment in the van. Maybe Gloria's mattress. I should surprise her and lug over her sewing machine and bolts of fabric. Definitely the couch that I laze back on, my feet on the coffee table, watching as Flynn riffles through his backpack.

My favorite blue flannel fits him better than it does me—hugging his arms and slim waist in all the right ways, with enough buttons undone to show the black storm cloud of his chest hair—but you'd think it was made of iron wool with the way he tugs at the sleeves. The cotton over his skin sounds like record scratches in the quiet.

He peels off my flannel, sniffs the armpits, and tosses it at my face.

Five minutes ago in the van he was going off about how all the traffic in this city is caused by crossed negative Tempo waves, then he's sniffing my shirt to see if I should wash it before wearing it out tonight. Starman and man-man. Both. Either, or. Mine. I test the word on my tongue. I hold it in like grass smoke, seeing how high it gets me. *Mine. Mine.*

He slips into a fresh white t-shirt then punches through the arms of his Space Guard jacket. Chevrons on his shoulders are compass points. He brought a few changes of shirts, a handful of skivvies, and some socks. Barely enough to trade for an issue of *Penthouse* back on Founding Fathers.

"Do you wear that all the time?" I ask, pointing to him in his jacket.

He shrugs. "It's gotten me a free coffee at Denny's more than once."

I trace a line on my chest, mimicking where "Lieutenant" is stitched over his heart.

"I bet that badge made your pop real proud."

"He's been pushing daisies these two years. Cancer came for him."

Mine, landmine. I hide a wince. "I'm sorry. I shouldn't have..."

"You didn't know."

He parks it on the couch by me, his hand on my leg warming me up through my jeans. No explosion, then. I test the ground a little more with my foot. "He ease up on you at all once you joined the Guard?"

He waits a long, slow breath. I try to send some strength into him though his hand on me, watching his even blue eyes.

"Being away from him helped, some ways. Other ways, he trailed me like a ghost."

"Any chance the Metronomes have got some advice on how to get rid of ghosts?"

The same invisible line tied to our knees as kids on the fire escape vibrates like a guitar string. Flynn's eyes traces the arc of his thumbnail on my leg.

"I reckon I should stop trying to impress ghosts, and just let 'em float on off to where they need to go."

"Gloria says the same thing, basically, about bad feelings." I tap my chest. "Sounds smart. And easier said, you know?"

He frowns. "I know it's not right to talk ill of the dead."

"I'm not squealing." I stare down at his thumb, which looks like any other thumb that I've seen. Alien. Man. Two songs in my head try to mash together. "How can you be both Flynn and... *not* Flynn?"

"You mean, how much of this..." He squeezes my leg. "Is an alien?"

"Something like that."

"I can feel the Metronome here." He spreads his other hand over his chest. "A ghost. Speaking of ghosts. Or, or—a friend hanging over my shoulder, looking out for me. I can... lean into that feeling, you know?"

"I don't think I do. Know."

"I remember what it was like to dance with the other Metronomes, and be a part of this big glowing bright thing. But there's something stopping me. From losing Flynn to that brightness." The dreamy edges of his voice sweeps over me. "Like I'm supposed to stay *me* for this to work. How it's always worked for us Adjudicators. Like we, or I, or us—like I need to..." He looks away.

Adjudicators. Judgment, he told me. Like how my sham Space Guard trial had a jury of my fellow starmen, even if they didn't say a word.

"How much do you remember?" he asks me. "Any of this feel familiar?"

I can close my eyes and hear a song. Or a voice. *We join in the Dance, again,* it whispered to me on the moon. Again. Again? Glass-tipped fingers trail down my back, kicking up shivers. The mist creeps over me, and I breathe it in, shuddering. Choking and burning up from the inside out—*lock all that up, Ward*—and Christ, Flynn can't see me out of breath like this.

Gloria would tell me how that hurt doesn't belong to me. Breathe.

"I think," I start slow. "Something feels familiar. Like you need to stay human if you're gonna pass judgment on 'em."

"Something like that."

If he can't tell me much about Metronome Man, what about Flynn? We have too much catching up to do—making up for lost time and burned letters—and boys like us can't be who we really are until too late in our lives, anyhow. He holds in a breath, and then the words flow, and don't dry up until rush-hour traffic makes big-band music out on the street.

All us boys got a story like this. I know the tune even if the lyrics are different. Like I can feel the tracks of us blending together.

High school, Flynn tells me. Every club you can join. Pre-law. Pre-med. Future Christian Leaders of America. *An A-minus is not an A, Flynn,* his pop tells him. So you go to the library before school and after—the librarians see so much of you that they start sneaking you tuna sandwiches they bring from home—until the next report card's got As coming up in spades. If you're busy winning awards, you're too busy for a girlfriend, even with how many times your folks remind you that this girl from church is batting Bambi eyes at you. When you run home in time to make it before curfew, you always pick up the pace right before you pass the street preacher holding *REPENT FOR YOUR SINS* signs at the plaza with the monument for the Confederate general. He isn't holding the signs for you, specifically. Probably. Pick up the pace, anyway. Faster, faster. Move to Miami and do it again. Run the track, and run away from the eyes of the boy who makes your sneakers fumble, because if you trip, how will you notch that eight-minute mile, how will you get to the state track meet?

Military camp. Pre-Guard school. Officer's training school. Scary at first because you're alone, but then again at least it's not Father blowing whistles at you to wake you up before the rooster crows, and timing your three-minute trips to the head with a stop watch, and barking in your face as you crank out pushups until you lose your breakfast. At least the drill sergeants let up once in a while.

Camp Puller—stationed there same as your father was—for one rotation that turns to four because the Guard won't let starmen leave Vietnam when protecting the newly minted territory from extremist locals is so *integral to the Safety of America and the Democratic Way of Life.* And once you're in the Guard, Father changes the hurdle heights on you. Again. Lieutenant in the Space Guard is fine and all. What about congressman? Senator? What else, what else? Bashed shins, and stitches in your side, and an eight-minute mile is well 'n' good for pansies, but are you a pansy? Answer me, Flynn Andrew Joseph Parker the Third, are you a pansy? And save the waterworks and the sniveling and Christ on the Cross I barely touched you with the belt. It's gee-dee embarrassing. My father, God rest him, walloped me twice as hard twice as often and look at the man I turned out to be. At least I didn't use the gee-dee buckle.

And Mother is no help. *Flynn angel of mine—you know your father. One minute he's got more vinegar in him than a boiled cat, next minute he's honey on biscuits. Just you wait.*

Wait. Wait out the years until you can leave. Waitwaitwait, you have to get home before the keys jangle in the front door, but can't you just stay on this fire escape for a while longer with this boy who swings the moon at you like it's a spotlight? You can't. Weight on your shoulders as you run home. Racking weights in the Camp Puller gym because at least that place didn't have windows, and the concrete walls that beaded with humidity blocked out the stink from the palladium mines. And what are they even burning that's billowing all that black smoke?

Then, weight on your chest when the rockets blast up to the sky until finally, finally—gee-dee, you can't even breathe—you're weightless. Arms bobbing up at your sides in zero-gravity as you look back on Earth falling away on the screen in front of you. Somewhere six feet in the ground of that planet behind you, Father is lying in a mahogany casket, even while his voice follows you into the corners of rooms. And you wonder, my God. My God. What was all the running for?

Flynn's hands are twitching by the time he stops talking. I kiss the backs of his knuckles. Thank the Metronomes or whoever I didn't grow up with a man like Flynn's father in my life. I'da ripped that fucking belt out of my Pop's hand, and turned it on him, making damn sure to use the buckle.

"Camp Puller," I say. Remembering how Powell flipped out at that last Reel meeting makes me squirm. "The starmen who were stationed there and rotated up to the moon, something about 'em weren't right."

"None of us left there same as we came in." His jaw muscles are working overtime.

"It wasn't combat, though. Right?"

"That wasn't combat. That was dishonor."

A hell of a truck must drive by with how the windows rattle. The wells in his blue eyes want to overflow, but I feel the muscles in his hands tighten, hauling out the sandbags. Like the ghost of his father is telling him that real men don't turn on the waterworks.

Dishonor.

"Me and Gloria don't even talk about our time in the Guard. Like, we know it hurts too much." Eight-point star pins stab my forearms at the sight of Flynn's crinkling brows. "I'm here. We can talk."

He warms me with some version of his Lieutenant Parker smile. "Some things you don't speak about."

Of course I know. Code in our letters, in his eyes. *We will. Not yet.*

TWENTY-TWO

CALL AND RESPONSE

Flynn switches on the TV while I start packing the potluck supplies from the sewing room. Canned goods, towels, sheets. Boxes of instant noodles and sleeping bags. Gloria's sewing machine and her bolts of fabric. My magazines, of course. Me and Flynn load up the back of his van, running up and down the stairs without so much as breathing hard. I take my time stacking things up so cans don't roll around everywhere. As much as I'm antsy to get back to the others, me and Flynn are long overdue for this solo time. I'm thinking we have time for another boogie on the couch when I pop back into the living room and see that his eyes are locked on the TV, where Starman North is talking to this whole *great Nation of ours.*

"This latest fatal attack on the Common Defense Corp in Los Angeles, carried out by homosexual violent extremists, hworking in tandem hwith the same Canadian anti-Liberation forces behind the recent attempted assassination of Our President, has necessitated these protective orders, in place immediately, for the sake of..."

I watch his lips, dumb. What a stupid time to realize the makeup queen finally got his shade of lipstick right.

"*What* fatal attack? We didn't—"

"No, we didn't," Flynn says. "Wait."

"...our greater Homeland. And hwhile hwe understand that Executive Order 77 hwill necessitate some sacrifice on the part of the American people..." Starman North stops to let the red, white, and blue stars swirl around him. The soundtrack builds to that big *God's Guardsmen* finish. "Sacrifice has always been a Sacred and Necessary part of the American story."

Cut to the logo of Mayflower Studios. I sink to the couch next to Flynn when the Reel fades back to the six o'clock news where the words *GAY MELEE AGAINST COPS* jabs the bottom of the screen. I know the clown-faced building inset in the corner of the broadcast, of course, above the white-bread guy behind the desk. Common Defense Corp was investigating credible reports of child endangerment, he says, when armed vigilantes, obscured by smoke bombs, detonated explosive devices, killing seven law enforcement officers.

My stomach sinks. Flynn is frozen like he's paralyzed on the moon, again. I try to say *we didn't* but my tongue turns to ash.

Whatever the top brass wants to say with that sweet Mayflower Studios production value becomes true.

The anchor's words don't match the speed of his lips, with how my brain is running on a lag.

Something something *Executive Order 77 requires the suspension of civil liberties while in public. Stay-at-home order beginning each evening at sundown until further notice.* Something something *armed forces dispatched to maintain Moral Public Order in major cities, prevent further attacks.*

Ricky would tell me that this kind of response isn't something Reagan whipped up since late last night. He's been waiting. Hoping, poking, jabbing. *Are we going to let them do this to us?*

"And now we return to continued coverage of the Liberation of Edmundston," the anchor says, "where Canadian forces have—"

Eeeeeeee—

A high-pitched whine vibrates my skull. A thin line of smoke trickles out of the TV set, then *pop*. The broadcast cuts out, the curved glass of the screen webbing with cracks.

Flynn bows his head into his folded hands.

I might not be able to float jam glasses, but blowing the TV could've been me. If Flynn wasn't here, I'd be flooring it in the van, headed to Mayflower and singing a different tune. *Burn this mother down.*

"It woulda been easier to just get up and turn that off." The joke sounds dumb even to me. When he doesn't answer, I tug his hands away from his lips. "Hey, Earth to starman."

"I'm here."

I bob my chin to cracked glass of the TV. "What's this mean for what we can drum up tonight?"

"I don't know. Compared to us Metronomes, I'm not sure how much you folks can hold."

"Tempo?"

"Yeah, that."

He slips his hands from mine, and before he looks away I can see what he really means. *Love. I'm not sure how much love you folks can hold.*

Yeah. News flash, me neither.

"We should get back to the others," he says, his voice all sunshine.

The glass and metal of the busted TV *tick-ticks* in the silence while it cools.

* * *

We drive through the streets under the gray sky, and past the newly painted Commdef cars on the street corners. The second one we roll by sends me to the back of the van, hunched between boxes of canned goods and records, just in case two boys together in a car looks fishy. Flynn parks in the alley by the Spindler's Arms. Out on the sidewalk, looking up into the sheet-covered broken windows, it's way too quiet. Commdef must've rolled in here the couple of hours me and Flynn were gone. And—*oh God, Gloria*—I'm running up the stairs three at a time with Flynn yelling at my back when I hit the landing of the fifth floor, and the music almost knocks me over.

The sizzling high-hats, the bouncing bass, the claps of DJ Hat-Trick's smuggled demo of Patrick Hernandez's 'Born to Be Alive.'

I stop. One step down and the music vanishes. One step up and Patrick Hernandez croons over disco trumpets.

Flynn slams into my back, and nothing about that smile is painted-on sunshine.

"I knew we could trust the DJ to watch the volume." He waggles his eyebrows.

And now his little eye-joke with Gloria before Hat-Trick pumped the tunes for us to reach Ricky makes a whole lot more sense. *So, please watch the levels. Though, I reckon you already know how to do that?*

"Any other secrets you wanna share?"

He hooks his arm into mine. "Now, where's the fun in that?"

Arm-in-arm, we round the corner to find a patchwork quilt of party and potluck spread out over the whole top floor.

Gloria loves a reveal and a costume change. She and the others took hammers to the walls separating the front unit from the six other studios on the top floor, knocking down everything but the support beams. They spray-painted flowers and peace signs along the brickwork, between tie-dyed tapestries. Straight ahead by the wall of windows is the once sectioned-off apartment where we floated jam glasses this morning. Behind us, a maze of support beams, and walls of bedsheets weave out to the half-burned back unit, where the roof opens to the sky. Bodies, and family, and music everywhere. Gloria flaps around by the front windows, separated from me and Flynn by dozens of us pulled from Saturday night at the disco. Me and Flynn hop-step over bodies sprawled over sleeping bags and forking pasta salad into each other's mouths in our—what to call it?—spankin' new loft. The air crackles with lightning that the gray clouds outside won't give up.

The countertops in the front unit's tiny kitchen are a memorabilia-shop window spread of goodies from the gas station junk food aisle, along with stacks of sandwiches and bowls of cut fruit and macaroni and cheese. Booze bottles decorate the dead oven. Everyone's putting the jam glasses to good use if the giant cans of Hawaiian Punch and red lips are any sign. The former studio might as well be our new commune living room—a jungle of couch cushions, sleeping bags, and camping cots.

I can practically hear Bette calling the shots, getting her grunts to rip up floorboards from units in the other floors and nail them together in a surprisingly sturdy-looking stage, about the size of the small one on Founding Fathers, in front of the two colossal windows in the brick wall. Hat-Trick has turned the corner opposite the couch into his battle station. He bops—his ears lidded with his big silver can headphones—as he fiddles with his Moog, flanked by a guitar and a bass propped up against the wall. I don't know how the hell they all got four giant speakers in here without anyone outside noticing. But already my hips are moving in a liquid boogie.

Candles line a card table next to the stage, like they're offerings to the posters on the brick wall. Judy Garland. Diana Ross. Tina Turner. Dolly Parton. Barbra Streisand. Liza Minelli. Mary with a halo of stars next to Marilyn on a sewer grate, holding down her white dress. Of course Donna, in the same white dress and same pose. Even Elton John and Sylvester. We're the worshippers and the worshipped, with some on-the-knees veneration bound to happen later tonight, past the sheet walls that flap in the breeze from the open roof.

Eighty—easy—of us Divine Deviants bop around our new home, smoking up and lazing over cushions, hip-swaying to the music, and necking in corners. Even my favorite straight cha-cha-cha dancers are twirling by the front bathroom. I hear whispers while me and Flynn weave towards the kitchen, where I'll definitely be toasting to all this. *That him? I heard that cat punched clean through a cop car.*

"Look alive, boys!" Bette snaps.

Me and Flynn bumble out of the way as she and three others haul in stage lights and set them up by Hat-Trick. I look back at the parade of her Circus Freaks lugging in more supplies from the freight elevator. Flynn jumps to help them. I find Gloria with Lainey, hanging up posters by the stage.

"Looks like you've all been busy." I look around the

place—the flock of queer flamingos, the light, the laughter—and when my eyes hit Gloria's, I laugh again so I don't cry. Half heartbroken because of how goddamn beautiful this all is. I'm tired, and wired, and quaalude-brained.

A shiny fresh coat of Cadillac Red lipstick slicks over her lips. Her tea-colored eyes spot everything in mine.

"We're calling it Fort Founding Mothers," she says.

"Your best work yet, Lady M," I tell her.

I'd planned to come in here all yapping about the Executive Order. No way in hell I'm harshing the vibes, now. There's too much to do. Lainey bounces on her cork platforms by Gloria, flashing painted eyes. For some reason a strand of Christmas lights pins her arms to her sides, wrapping her all up. Little plastic flowers flash rainbow lights all along her tie-dyed linen.

"Little help?" she asks.

Gloria clucks. *Kids, huh?* And then me and her waggle our fingers over Lainey, tickling and looking for the end of the lights—hooting and *how the hell did this even get so tangled?*—until we all almost fall to the floor.

* * *

I hate to be a buzzkill but I have to pull Ricky, Bette, and Gloria away from the party as a squad of dolls hangs more sheets—just by waving their fog-trailing hands—over the windows before sunset. The pirate kings and everyone else already know about the Executive Order, and the bullshit response to the *gay melee against cops,* which I'm absolutely printing on a t-shirt. Gloria made the call, just like it's me and her in the apartment, to stick to House Rules for the night. We don't gotta talk or worry about what's outside these walls for a bit, which explains the righteous amount of Moral Indecency going on. The others need the escape. And for the ones not here yet, seamstresses on the outside are helping them leapfrog from safe-house to safe-house until they can trickle in, a few at a time, before sunset, after which we'll stay off the streets. A couple of new rhinestone-riot fires in the hills, plus a whole phone-tree's worth of calls to the STAR Citizen tip line ought to keep the pigs busy for the night. And the funny thing about the cameras that have been popping up all over the neighborhood, Ricky says, as he points to Rex in the corner duct-taping an Opti-Disc camera to the side of a speaker. Someone must've Tempo'd the things off their poles.

"Most of those cameras are props," Ricky says between punch sips. "No Opti-Discs, no film, no nothing."

Gotta love that Mayflower movie magic.

* * *

The first Saturday Night Showcase of Founding Mothers is off to a bitchin' start. The door is closed for the night, and it's just us family.

We forget about rule two of the Dodges—we have to be absolutely goddamned boring—because look at this place. This morning it was an abandoned apartment, and now the floorboards creak and groan under hundreds of feet stomping and swaying to Hat-Trick's star-song. Wine, whiskey, and weed. Auntie Anita used to puff every now and then, and she had to tell Gloria and her judging eyes, *oh sweetheart, God made grass, so kiss my sassafras.*

In the light of the spotlights and fabric-draped floor lamps, Gloria and Lainey are racing on dueling sewing machines in one corner, seeing who can finish up a dress the fastest, sequined fabric zipping through the machines while the crowd around them sings out bets. *Betcha one Whatchamacallit bar that Lady Moondust finishes first. Nah, two Twix on Conda, honey, she got that baby queen fight.* Extension cords slither like cobras from wall outlets to can lights on the floors that cast red glows onto sheets. We got a corner in the sheet maze that'll make any dirty bookstore backroom blush. Bette and a few of the other biker butches lugged their motorcycles in here with the freight elevator and now they're hanging with the leather daddies, talking tailpipes and after-market accessories. All while Ricky—his busted eye already healed up with all the Tempo crackling in the air—levitates liquor bottles in his makeshift bar by the kitchen. He plucks the fog-wrapped bottles like the air is the bar wall, and mixes up magic potions for us all.

Hat-Trick keeps our volume down. He told me, blinking his big flying-saucer eyes, how music talked to him his whole life. Now he's figured out how to talk back.

Divine Deviants. Flynn talks about how our powers will grow. I can't wait to see what they'll do to all of us.

In the meantime, I follow Rex's cigar smoke cloud through the crowd. He hefts his camera. In the glow of his flash, a couple of muscle Marys lock lips, fingers tugging at waistbands. Flash. A doll is a goddess with white silk levitating around her. Flash. Scruffy Black hippies with beaded necklaces suck on clove cigarettes. Rex yells at me over the music to smile.

Flash. Fire. Alarms lights blink wildly all around me. Sirens wail. And screams. Blood trickles into my eyes. And then *bam*. Rex's thick arm wraps around my waist, propping me up from keeling over in the middle of the dancefloor.

"You good, kid?" His beard tickles my ear.

I swallow against the flashes and the sparks die in my eyes. "Copacetic. Too much beer. Or not enough."

"Let's get you sitting down for a minute."

I try to shove him off with a laugh, but Papa Rex won't hear it. And honestly, my legs feel like they're made of mist, and I can use the help. Me and Flynn dropped my couch-bed by the kitchen, and Rex half-carries me over, my ass finding my favorite indent in the cushion. On the other end of the couch, Stetson is an island in the lamplight, thumbing through one of my magazines. Rex swings over to the kitchen to get me something to drink. The others seem to know not to boogie too close to Stetson. The detective eyes of his are contagious. *Maybe they'd take us seriously if the warning about the Metronomes wasn't coming from free-love freaks, and drag queens.*

His moustache wiggles with something that must be a smile.

I nod at him. "You getting some reading in?"

He tugs one ear, sighing up from the magazine on his knees. He picked a good one—the February '77 issue of *Mandate*, with George Payne's hog hanging between his hairy thighs in the centerfold.

"Bette told us to bring essentials. I brought a backpack full of canned food and camping gear." He taps the page. "And you brought these?"

These. For a gay guy, he nails that square tone of voice. *These. Those freaks. I'm gay, but I won't be that gay.* Normally I'd bite back with something mean, but the music's got me feeling charitable. And I'm too fizzy-headed for sarcasm, anyhow. Stetson's tell is the red that brushes his earlobes. I've seen that same red on cheeks and burning down Kerns's neck. Red over the bridges of noses of guys in bus stations who follow me into a stall, pretending like it's their first time. I pick up the closest mag to me and flip to the back personal ads.

"Oakland. SM. Gemini. 41." I might as well be reciting poetry, set to Hat-Trick's synth rainstorm, with how I read the ad. "Five-ten, one-seventy, Latin. Beer-bellied construction workers and dominant trucker types wanted for mind-blowing orgasms, humiliation play, and intelligent conversation afterwards. Write box 9134. Photos get prompt reply." I close the magazine with a tip of my head.

Stetson squints. "Is that supposed to mean something?"

Rex clomps in his heavy boots back from the kitchen and hands me a can of Dr. Pepper.

"Meaning, officer," I continue, nodding a thank you at Rex, "that somewhere in Oakland, there's a dude who's waiting by a post office box to get raunchy letters and pictures from a couple of dudes somewhere else. And because *this* magazine put the ad out there, those dudes feel less alone."

Red on his lobes, still. A traffic light. *Stop.* "Don't you ever get lonely?" I ask.

"All the time, in the force." He looks away, waving his hand. "Here, too."

"Not *that* long ago, people who made magazines like these were getting tossed in the slammer," I continue, "and there's still people who want to lock 'em up."

Even in the dark, I see the edges of Rex's eyes soften at me. Rex bobs his camera at Stetson. "I started out modeling before I figured out I wanted to be behind the camera, not in front of it, and set up my own studio. Started sending photo sets to guys all over." He turns at the waist and—flash—he snaps Ricky grinning big with a bottle of Captain Morgan sailing over his palm. "The wrong postal inspector came across one of my packages, and I ended up in the slammer for two weeks on an obscenity charge."

The secret code in his voice: *You boys don't know how easy you have it.*

The dream is to be sitting here in twenty years with some young kid telling him how hard we had it back in the day, and watching his uninterested eyes tell me *sure, Gramps.*

I can see the argument well in Stetson's eyes. Nope. We're getting too heavy for a night at Founding Mothers. House rules.

"Is that where your cop kink came from?" I crack.

Rex winks at me, and for a second I'm closer to him than if he'd actually let me take him home that night we met.

"No way. We don't fuck the enemy." He chomps his cigar, bobbing his chin at Stetson. "No offense."

Stetson tosses the magazine back to the stack on the floor. "I turned in my badge this afternoon. Administrative leave, because of the Executive order. Sergeant's suggestion, since..." He frowns somewhere into the crowd. "There've been questions about me."

The sugar rush from the Dr. Pepper is doing me good. I jostle his shoulders. "Well, tonight we're celebrating you getting outta lockup, officer... Uh, just what do we call you?"

"My first name's Nick," he says. "Everyone except my ma calls me Stetson, though."

"Stetson fits," Rex observes. "Like the old cowboy hats."

"Yeehaw." I loop an invisible lasso around Stetson. "Go on there and find a pony to ride, pardner."

The music is calling me back, too. At his spaceship

command center, Hat-Trick is fading his cosmic wind-chime tunes out. I can feel something slow slinking away. Water building up for a wave, and I'll be there in the middle, when it hits. The hot air tickles over the back of my neck. I'm about to look for Flynn when he elbows past Rex and collapses next to me on the couch.

"Where've you been hiding?" he asks, sweaty waves sticking to his forehead. "I need you out there on the floor."

From the syrup in his voice, I take it he's sampled some of Ricky's magic potions. Good on him. That answers my question about what the *healing power of Tempo* is going to do to my alcohol tolerance.

"Just trying to get this wallflower here to dance." I thumb over at Stetson,, deciding he's my next project. If he's not getting lucky by the end of the night, we might as well pack it in and let the Metronomes take over. I'll've failed my Duty as Ascended Being and champion of love or something.

Flynn flops over me, towards Stetson. "I'm glad you're here. Surprised, if I'm being honest, but glad all the same."

"I had a feeling that I could do some good here tonight," Stetson calls over the music. "I thought we'd be talking Metronome plans, or, or..." His eyes drift. I follow his gaze to where a couple of silhouettes in the red-lit sheet maze are definitely not making shadow puppets. He pinches his lips. "Something other than this."

"What's the point of gay liberation if you can't feel liberated?" I offer.

Rex grumbles an agreement. Then, before I know it, *flash*. Me, Flynn, and Stetson captured by his camera forever—hands up, heads tilted to each other—like a church painting.

The Sermon on the Couch. The tide of the music pulls Rex away, back into the crowd.

"Music is healing!" Flynn sings out, flapping his hands to the dancefloor.

Even in the lamplight, Stetson's face darkens. "We're asking to get raided."

"You know, I reckon," Flynn starts, until he collapses in giggles against me. "Last night, I reckon a little fear in the mix—the cops bangin' down the door n'all—helped make our juice a little stronger."

No time to answer. Not with how Hat-Trick's bitchin' mix of our song is calling us all to the floor. And it is *ours*, with the way the silver beaded fringe soundwaves are already swirling. I can feel them linking us and trailing out to the stars. Saint Donna of Fort Founding Mothers lures like a siren from her demo tape. *Ooooooo. It's so good it's so good it's so good it's so good.* Hat-Trick cranks the volume up something sweet. Someone's crawling around the floor by the altar. Juana, I can tell by her braid and knit poncho. She yanks the plug on the strand of Christmas lights around the altar to plug in a toaster instead. How the hell did a toaster even get in here? Heaven knows, heaven knows. A minute later, she pops up from the floor, her braids whipping. I smell sugar and strawberries, and next thing she's hopping up and down—everyone around her is a foot taller than her, anyhow—to pass out strawberry Pop-Tarts. Telling us to eat up and to drink water. *Thanks Ma,* someone yells back. I have to lean onto Flynn because I'm going to fall on my ass just from laughing so hard.

By the time I kiss fake strawberry frosting off the corner of his lips, Juana plugs the Christmas lights back in and I can see the plastic flowers glowing in everyone's eyes.

TWENTY-THREE

MIND WARP

Our loft club disco cathedral of the Divine Deviants, Fort Founding Mothers, is a cauldron bubbling up to the stars. We are part of the spell. We are holding a séance to ring up the Metronomes, and the ingredients are slinking bodies, and body heat, and liquor, and head-fizzing poppers hits, and disco biscuits, and just a dash of stardust offered from little glass bottles. Not everyone partakes in all of these, but all of us give. We give energy and laughter and kisses on necks and lips, and eyes to lips back to eyes again, and out to the sheet maze. Sweet sweat falls on the creaking floors. Me and Flynn are pinballs knocking into each other. His eyes are shuttle windows out to deep space.

In the dark, under the lights borrowed from other discos, we can't see the differences the squares outside of these walls tell us should be important.

Tick, tick, tick. No clocks at the disco. We can only measure time with Hat-Trick's endless mix. Flynn scratches his beard over my lips with his kiss, then slips out of my hands and sways to the microphone before we can really get going. That tease.

"We have been to countless other worlds," he says,

dreamy-voiced. "On each, the Song is the same. The first medicine is music. That's where we will find healing. We are all Sacred Instruments, though some have different parts to play."

Flynn works through the crowd back to me, and my heart is linked to his by Christmas lights. His fingertips spread kisses on the sides of my face.

Is this what it's like to be a Metronome? I don't know if I ask the question, or if it flows out like mist from my eyes.

"Like this, when we're all together," he says. "Like this, always. Always."

Rex's camera flash pops on the dancefloor. Eyes twinkle. I can still hear the Pensacola street preacher in Flynn's voice. He must feel the hesitation. The others don't know him like I do. They can't see him as a little boy on a fire escape, and see his letters and his frozen face on the moon at the same time. But Gloria, they know. A sigh ripples through the crowd when she's back on the microphone, wrapping us up in her rose perfume.

Oh, heaven knows, heaven knows—

Shivers dance along my sweat-slicked forearms. Hat-Trick shreds on his guitar like he's wrestling a live crocodile, launching scratchy-fanged chords over the synth waves. The syrupy basslines, and pulsing electric sighs, and hard-candy crunches mash all my senses together. I see birdsong in his music, and wings made of glowing gas that'll eventually come together to make stars. I taste starlight like ripe raspberries. My heartbeat in my once-busted lip echoes the bumpin', juicy basslines. And oh. Oh.

Heaven knows

Eyes up to the borrowed disco ball that Gloria hung from

the warped ceiling rafters. Dancers sway under its light and we tip our heads up to the stars and sing out as the silver beaded fringe wraps around us. We are made of light. We dance for years, maybe. Light and years, and light-years—out into the wide dancefloors between the stars. We can see the whole Earth like we're floating in space. With our thousand eyes as one, we see a silver beaded fringe that circles the spinning disco ball of the planet. And there—somewhere by the Pacific, the fringe catches and snaps, launching beads off into space. The light of the beads dies in a haze of yellow smoke. The Disharmony. We can feel it like blood leaking out of a bullet hole.

I feel

love

The Disharmony is a deed. Yes. An event. A trauma, we know through the Manifold. We can feel an ache, spreading, in toxic yellow smoke that bubbles skin, and sends screams searing into space. We will heal it. First we must find it, if only the fog didn't blur our eyes. Too few, even now, to see.

Yet we grow stronger.

Overhead, the clouds finally open up, dropping silk sheets of rain onto Fort Founding Mothers and the whole city. We can feel the beads of rain dropping on our skin like falling stars.

I

fe e l

lo   v   e

The rain is radio static, and guitar wails, and screeches from an alarm. And a signal. Yes, a signal. Somewhere. Not far. Not...

I'm huffing hot air—myself again, as the others sway around me—and Flynn's hands glide from my hips to the side of my face, pulling my gaze from the disco ball to him. Yanking the *me* down from the *we* again.

"Where is the signal?" he asks. Blue glass eyes. Not-Flynn and Flynn, with the Space Guard Hymn echoing in his voice. His hands caress my neck. His thumbs sweep over my Adam's apple and trace fire along my jaw. When he squeezes, it's so sweet. "What do you see?"

This séance was for him, I know, to pull Tempo to find the Disharmony. But we aren't enough. Maybe we won't be—*I'm not sure how much love you folks can hold*—but we are all a tapestry of silver beaded fringe, wired to him, through me, skin on skin. He needs something in my touch, same as last night when our lips first hit at Circus Disco. Only instead of taking from me, I can feel power bleeding in. I can feel him give.

I'm on fire—blinded by the light blazing from his skin. A supernova dressed as the man I love, burning bright and bright and so beautiful I could die.

Outside, thunder crackles.

I fall into the blue glass of his eyes.

* * *

The Calypso Room is flooded with blue lights, and empty.

I'm on stage in the spotlight where Ma should be, for some reason. I look around at the empty tables and chairs. The bus boys forgot to clean up after last night's show, with how many empty glasses litter the stained white tablecloths. I must've fallen asleep in the lighting catwalk again? Either way, Ma is gonna miss tonight's show time. I turn from the empty audience to the velvet curtain—it's purple, now, since I'm looking at everything through blue glass—and know that there's something I have to see, beyond it. This close you can really see the dust and the rips along the curtain's tassel trim.

Martini glasses shatter behind me—Ma must be throwing them again—knocking me scared and stumbling through the curtain, coughing on dust.

Backstage is not backstage. Backstage is an endless plain of gray dust against an empty black sky. So, so empty and cold. The blue light followed me here.

I'm not alone. Pinpricks jab my skin.

I turn and Flynn is in his Guard jumpsuit—it's painted purple in the blue light, same as the curtain—but Flynn is also Not Flynn with the way his eyes are tiny blue glass stars. He's wiping a rag across the side of a mini *Saint Christopher*. The thing is my jet, I know, even if we never had jets in the Guard.

"Rush," Flynn says when I walk close. He straightens his shoulders and beams at the word written on the side of the swirled metal of the jet. The word is written in tight waves that look nothing like *Rush*, but the meaning is crystal clear when I look at the shapes. "You know, since you're always in such a rush."

Another joke like the one passed from his eyes to Gloria's that I'm too slow to get.

More glasses explode behind me. No—the sound is rockets blasting off, and when I spin toward the sound, the giant blue-tinted vidboard shows a toy model of *Rush* on a string flying across a black canvas stuck with green glow-in-the-dark stars. *Rush* approaches a painted ball of a planet, and the screen zooms in as the jet lands on a cracked brown landscape. Mayflower movie magic ripples across the screen as the landscape changes from brown dirt to a grassy field, to a lava-veined hellscape. A giant gap in the ground shudders open. *Rush* tips backwards on its spindly swirled-metal legs, falls into a chasm, and the maw of the ground closes up behind its silver fins.

Cue the Mayflower production assistants rolling in with painted canvas backdrops on rovers.

I know the new set well.

Music, sex, art, science—the Metronomes hear all this as notes in the same song, Flynn told us.

California, the land of porn barons and pirate kings and seamstresses. Mayflower Studios and muscle mags. A million *God's Guardsmen* flicks with perfectly rigged explosions, same as the Big One. The record producers here invented the marvelous Moog and the Star-Spangled Sisters. Watkins grew up in LA and carried some of the California sunshine up to the moon in the shape of his kindness, the same light that Auntie Anita wrapped Gloria in. Starman North is cruising at the bus stop. *Hwell, it ain't gay because a mouth is a mouth.*

Stars in the Reels swirl around. *American Liberty, a LunaScope Production.*

We blasted off every night at Circus Disco, knowing full well that magic happened there, somehow.

Flynn's warning from the night of the Circus Disco raid rings out. *Let us dance. Or else.*

People have been coming to this holy land to dance for years and years, drawn by the magic of a Metronome ship buried in the earth. Nomads, then tribes called this place home for thousands of years, before the invaders from far-off. A City of Angels, and the neighborhood of Hollywood with its lights and magic, then the Studio Zones. Textile mills and Dodges.

Until someone paved over this ground and plonked a building with a clown face right on top.

"Where is the signal? What do you see?"

I turn to Flynn's words but all I see is an eyeless, faceless figure carved out of blue glass, reaching for me, its voice the metal nightmare of the *Saint Christopher* exploding.

* * *

I gasp back into Flynn's arms. The real Flynn in his flannel. Divine Deviants sway in slow motion through the fog all around us.

I try to croak *I know where*, but Ma's broken martini glasses shredded my throat.

"I know." He kisses my forehead. "Rest, now."

I'm flying down, into the quiet beyond Hat-Trick's bubble of mystic Moog music. Then blankets, then coughing on water. The scrape of Flynn's bearded chin on my lips.

The stage lights turn off. Only darkness.

* * *

Softness, all around me. I rustle on the pile of sleeping bags and the only way I know it's morning is when Flynn sings out *good glory in the mornin'*. He smokes a cigarette like he's in a centerfold shot, leaning back against the brick wall in nothing but his Space Guard jacket. The hair on his forearm, propped up on his bent knee, glows when he flicks ash out of the broken window. The sunlight paints a shadowed grid from the windowpanes across the dark hair on his chest. Two waves of his hair stick out from his head like he's a wolf disguised as a dog, and this sleeping bag pile in an abandoned apartment below Founding Mothers is his den. The smoke drifts from his full, pink lips in the light.

"Did you get the license plate on the truck that ran me over?" I'm out of breath by the end of the sentence.

"You look as limp as a dish rag." He puffs smoke with his laughter. "What do you remember, so I know what to tell you?"

"We worked up Tempo and gave it to you. *I* gave it to you."

I reach out and brush his ankle. His skin scalds. *Holding that much Tempo will burn any of you out, same as holding onto a power line*, he told us. *I'm used to working higher-vibrational energy.*

"Big mojo." He takes a drag. "Still, not enough to find the Disharmony, not with this few of us in the Dance."

"And then you gave some to me?"

He nods. "I told you, certain people generate Tempo. Others—even Metronomes—like me can see it, sure, and use it. You've already felt what Gloria can do with that cat-purrin' voice of hers. And Patrick with his tunes. All of you here, you're special. That's why you found each other, I reckon." He brushes his thumb against my lips. "But you, most of all."

"You don't gotta try so hard with the sweet talk. We're already knockin' boots."

"No fooling." He threads his fingers through my messy hair. "Real special. You said yourself, you've always been able to see things. I reckoned you could use a little Tempo top-off to see if it would help."

"And I did see something." I sit up, and immediately regret it with how my stomach lurches. "I was looking through blue glass, at my Ma's club for some reason." I squint into the window, the visions or whatever they were drifting away like cigarette smoke. Rain droplets from last night's storm still stick to the broken glass.

"Alright, and then you—"

"A ship." I can see his hands wiping a rag across swirled metal, even if the name drifts out of my head. I squint. "A ship that's under the disco."

That snaps Flynn to me, scooting closer. He tosses his cig out the window and grabs my hands. Any harder and my bones would crush. "Hold your horses. You're saying there's a *ship* under the disco?"

"*Your* ship. A small jet that looked like the *Saint Christopher*. That's what I saw."

"Under the disco?" His knees knock into mine. "I mean. Of course. Of course, that would explain the vibes of the place, drawing me to it."

"Why did it look like the Guard shuttle?"

"Your human brain trying to make sense of Metronome magic, I reckon. I can certainly relate. What else do you remember?"

I blink and see blue glass. Something about a faceless, eyeless thing with a head like a welding helmet, and a metal scream. I pull the sleeping bag tighter around me.

"It's alright," he says. "You'll get there."

"What does this mean?"

"It means we got a way out of the woods now, for sure." He tugs the sleeping bag around my shoulders and the heat of him grazes my skin. "You should sleep. Or...?" He sweeps a hand through his hair, smoothing away the wolf ears.

I'm always one for an *or*.

I'm freezing cold, so I steal warmth from him. He crushes

me like my space suit—pressurized and squeezing a little too hard, and with the thick, veined pipe of his giving me something I want more than air.

* * *

Flynn slips out of our pile, leaving me to nap some more and gather my strength, and now here's Gloria coming in for a landing with the sleeves of her poncho billowing around her. She's holding two jam glasses with dark liquid, one of them topped with a strawberry-frosted donut on a paper napkin. She hands me the glass with the donut before I even have a chance to sit up, her eyes telling me, *peace offering.* Funny, I didn't know we were at war.

She flops down across from me, her eyes pinching more than the sweet spice of the drink. She swirls her own Dr. Pepper like wine, sipping and sighing to give me time to heave up from my sleeping bag pile and ask her what's wrong. Her church lady eyes are not exactly making me want to talk to her.

Fine. I sit up, the sleeping bag billowing around me. She looks away politely and tosses me a shirt. I slip it on, cross my legs under me, and turn to face her.

"Yes, Glo—"

"Mitchell Matthew Mark Luke and John Ward." She stabs me with one of her red-lacquered nails and I yelp, swatting at her. "You want to tell me what in God's name happened last night?"

I stretch and yawn, really drawing this one out because her impatient glare is cracking me up inside.

"Flynn needed some juice to look for the Disharmony, and..." I scratch the back of my head, woozy but getting a hang of sitting upright.

"And him carrying you off the dancefloor like you were loopy from 'luudes?" She jabs me again, harder. "How's that tank of yours, dummy?"

"Breathing easy. It's Flynn. He wouldn't hurt me."

"Flynn, sure. What about Metronome Man?"

"I know him. I *trust* him."

Her turn to look away. I can see in the smudged edge of her cat eyeliner, though. *More than you trust me?*

"Keep checking my air," I tell her. "And I'll keep checking yours."

"Fine." She scowls through another Dr. Pepper swig. "Now I need your help on patrol. Mommy and Daddy are fighting upstairs."

Her red-lacquered nail points up at the worn boards of the ceiling. She gives me a minute to make myself decent and then I follow her back upstairs.

Fort Founding Mothers is a sea of sleeping bags and mattresses. Me and Gloria weave through zonked-out lovers and Divine Deviants cuddled up on islands of pillows in the sheet maze. Patchouli incense swirls to the ceiling, hiding the smell of bodies and spilled beer. Ricky and four other guys are passing around a joint and giggling at the entrance of a couch-pillow fort. Normally I'd sprawl down and help them with the fort defenses, but focus, Mitch. Everyone knows that the rest of the floor is the playground, while the front unit is our schoolroom. Patrick is a cat with headphones, dozing in sunbeams on the stage. The only music is the morning traffic from the street, punctuated by taps from Juana's typewriter on the card table to the side of the tower of speakers. *Ding.* Her typewriter bell rings like a microwave oven telling me my Miss Moonie's Microwaveable is ready.

By the kitchen that's strewn with bottles and boxes of gas station donuts, Flynn and Bette are leaning close and having it out in hushed voices. *Mommy and Daddy are fighting*, Gloria said, and even Flynn would agree that Bette is Daddy with her *you're under my roof* fists at her hips. Rex and Stetson, at their sides, chime in now and then.

Once he spots me, Stetson bobs his head past the kitchen, at our sleeping friends. "You get a load of the others?"

"They were dancing and drinking for eight hours." Flynn sighs. "That'll get anyone plum tuckered."

"Sure seems like you're forgetting the part when we all just handed the Tempo we worked up over to you." Stetson shoots back.

"Freely given," Flynn quotes the Metronomes. "The Tempo will refill in them all, same as the tide rolling in. Rest and water, not much different'n a Sunday morning hangover."

"And how are we still standing?" Rex asks, thumbing around to the squad.

"You all are stronger." Flynn hooks a finger into one of my belt loops as a hello. "Special."

Gloria's eyes are the first on me. I don't know if the others saw Flynn carrying me out of here last night. She doesn't say a word.

"Well, for the record." Stetson huffs, crossing his arms over his white t-shirt. "Next time, whatever juice is in me isn't *freely given*." He sneers the last two words, making fun of that lingering Guard trumpet in Flynn's voice. Figures the cop would be the one worked up about helping people out.

Juana's typewriter dings again. Bette sighs, slicks back her Elvis hair, and plasters on a smile.

"Think you can keep it down with the novel-writing, baby?" she sings out.

"The next issue of *Paradigm*'ll be out of sight," Juana chirps back. "Boss is the one who told us to tell everyone we know. I'm on it."

Flynn is boss, then. I shoot him a goofy salute and he tugs my belt loop again.

"Hoorah." I hip-check him. "We got our next orders, sir?"

Flynn and Bette stiffen like I pissed in their Dr. Pepper, too. Stetson snorts. Rex chews an unlit stub of a cigar. Gloria flaps rose perfume when her billowing-sleeved arms cross.

"What?" I ask. "I'm missing something."

"Funny you should talk about orders." Gloria's voice is way too bright. "Would someone like to tell Sleeping Beauty over here what we've been hollering about for the last hour?"

Flynn draws in a slow breath, keeping his chin up when he turns to me. "We got a message from Admiral Kern this morning."

Dr. Pepper spins something mean in my guts. I can feel the heat of Kern's steel-gray eyes. Hungry. The stink of his old leather cologne clogs my nose.

"What the hell does Founding Fathers know about what we've got cooking down here?" I ask.

"Kern was on the last shuttle back to Earth, same as me," Flynn says.

"And he just rolled in, decided to squat at Circus Disco, and wants to meet," Bette snaps. "Don't forget that very important tidbit."

Goddamnit. The ship. My eyes hit Flynn's and he nods, muscles working at the sides of his jaw.

"How'd he find us?"

"Word came in from the seamstresses," Bette continues, shining one of the studs of her leather jacket with her thumb.

"And we've got, oh..." Stetson looks down at his watch-less wrist. "Five minutes before this Guard Rear Admiral leads a Commdef charge in here?"

"The seamstresses are our girls." Gloria's tea-warm voice helps my nerves, at least. "Gathering intel, passing messages is what they do. Squealing ain't. They didn't say a peep to Kern about where we really are."

"Though, staying in hiding won't matter much," Rex starts, slow, tugging at his gray-threaded beard. "If..."

"If?" I ask.

"If your sweet, gullible Lieutenant Dipshit just walks right into Kern's obvious trap." Bette thumbs over at Flynn. "Fucking pants down, ass up and wiggling, waiting to get completely cock-railed. Sorry, Gloria."

"Railed in the bad way," Gloria says. "To be crystal clear."

Flynn chews his lip. "I can handle—"

"Junior, you say 'I can handle it' and, my God, it's straight to the moon." Bette pretends to punch him in the shoulder. When her fist hits, her hand opens and shakes his shoulder gently. "Have some sense. I'm not going to let one of my boys kill themselves, and you're one of my boys, now."

And then the bickers flare up. Rex hasn't taken orders outside of the bedroom since serving in Korea and he's not about to start now. Orders means there's no talking, and there's no way on God's green Earth that Gloria isn't going to have a say in protecting the people under this roof. Stetson, meanwhile, goes off about splitting the group into other safe-houses around the city, until I have to shush them all.

"Somebody please," I huff. "*Please* tell me just what the hell Kern said."

"He wants to meet at the Disco to talk terms." Flynn rocks back on his heels, crossing his arms. "He said he's calling me back to serve."

TWENTY-FOUR

THE BATTLE STATIONS REMIX

The disco. Bette's beautiful clown-faced place has been overrun by those pigs, pissing all over the seats and thumbing through her record collection in the office, murdering the vibes with their women-hating, queer-bashing bad juju. Bette might as well cannonball out the window, whether Flynn's Metronome ship is nearby or not. Juana has to zip over from her typewriter, braid bobbing, to press Bette against her chest.

"*Cariño*," Juana sighs, patting Bette's head. "There, there."

"And you know it's there." Smoke from a freshly lit cigar circles Rex's face. He chews on the end. "This ship."

"I saw it through the Tempo last night," I offer.

"Since when do you see things?" Bette picks up her head to ask.

"Since always," Gloria vouches for me. "Keep up."

"Figuring you can get past Kern and what I can only guess is a Commdef perimeter..." The way Stetson narrows his eyes, I can see he likes torching our plans. "You're going to do what with your ship, exactly? Fly away and leave us here?"

Chin up, the Space Guard jacket around Flynn pins his shoulders straight.

"I'm going to use the ship's communications to radio the Metronomes and tell them to call off the..." He stumbles. "The visitation."

My heartbeat rattles like liquor bottles. Sure sounded like he was going to say *attack*.

"Or else I'll pilot it up to meet them, and explain what's going on," he continues. "How we deserve more time to heal the Disharmony, and–"

"Which we're supposed to heal on our own, right?" Stetson shoots back. "With this Donna Summer disco cult orgy séance stuff."

"Two plans sounds better than one to me," I say, cutting Flynn off. I don't need him confessing to everyone that he's got doubts about how much love we can hold.

Me, Flynn, Gloria, Rex, Stetson, Bette and Juana–the parents in this big family, I guess–close ranks. Over resigned sighs and stuttered arguments, we decide that me and Flynn are going, while the others stay behind to watch the family. And look–*look*–since I still haven't mastered the art of Tempo jam-glass floating, we'll take Stetson as a police escort, in case we need the muscle. Stetson will drive our getaway van. Him grumbling about working as a chauffeur for a cult leader only sweetens the deal.

I have to leave, when Flynn and Bette are hashing out the backup plan to the backup plan, because I'm burning up. I tell them I'll be waiting by the van and Flynn hands me his keys. Gloria stops me with a hand on my arm before I can escape.

"Don't you dare get killed," she says.

That wicked Lady Moondust gleam in her eyes has me scared that if I do kick it, she'll find a way to raise me up and kill me herself.

* * *

The streets outside are still dotted with lakes after last night's storm. I bang around the corner of the Spindler's Arms and head into the alleyway where Flynn parked yesterday. Spilled oil spins colors across the puddle under his van, looking like the swirled metal of the ship in my blue-glass vision. I hop into the passenger seat and lean over to start the van. I crank my window down, drinking in fresh air. At least the storm cooled things off for a while.

The clock on the dash reads just past ten on a sleepy, summer Sunday. Normally, Gloria would be coming home from church and trying not to wake me, where I'd be on our couch sleeping off a hangover. Ma must be hitting the stage for a weekend matinee of her show in Geneva, or wherever she is. I hope Pop is sleeping in. The posters decorating Founding Mothers remind me how he hung the Starman North calendar in his spare bedroom for me, before I even rolled in. I know he didn't have the words to get all mushy with me, so he taught me how to build instead. One board, one nail at a time. I hope I'll have time to make things right with him. Say sorry for being such a turd, acting like the empty streets of Sunshine City and me getting kicked out of the Guard were somehow his fault.

And the Guard. Kern calling us in is not the kind of Guard reunion I'm itching for.

Not all of them were shits. Hernandez could've been a friend, only after I'd socked him. And Watkins walking the hallways of Founding Fathers singing out, *how're you living, Ward?* I light up a Red and puff hard, the tip of it burning. Burn, Kern. Burn, baby burn. In our holy house, Kern is probably reciting his favorite dead president's quote. *I owe to my beloved country.* Owe. Someone's got a debt due, and it's time to pay up. Owe? *Oh, no,* here comes a speeding van, on fire with me behind the wheel, hollering with the windows down and the music blasting. Pointed right at Kern, and even if Flynn's ship blows up, it'll be one big happy ending.

My hands are twitching by the time I light up my next cig. I've got my eyes closed, holding in the smoke, when Flynn pops into the driver's seat.

"For someone who hates being gay so much, Stetson is preening like a queen ahead of a Saturday night," he chirps.

The light in his eyes drains when he sees my face. Past those eyes, I know there's my Flynn and someone else. Metronome. A ghost, like he said. A friend hanging over his shoulder, looking out for him.

I can't tell who I need more in this moment, Flynn or Not-Flynn. I flick the wheel on my lighter.

"What if we monumentally cock this up?" I finally ask.

"I reckon thinking like that is no use."

Flick, flick. My thumbnail over the lighter wheel sounds too much like the clock hands of the Metronome's world.

"They said we would feel the Silence. What does that—"

"I can't lean in." He stops and breathes, his eyebrows twitching. "That beat in the Tempo, those feelings. They don't belong to Flynn."

"Then what does the Metronome have to say?"

Clouds move over his eyes. "The Silence comes after the Metronomes leave. Before that, it's noise."

I wince. "Screams. And the sky's all on fire."

"Is that you remembering? Or seeing?"

"I don't know. It's the Kern stuff. Or, or..." I wince. "Days like this it just feels easier to burn all this shit down and start fresh."

His hands on mine pull me away from the flashes. Gentle, same as his voice. "You've seen all that before. We've been here before."

"Have we?"

"I remember more, around you." When he smiles, the ghost of the Metronome slips away. "You'll remember, too. I promise."

Stetson patrols around the alley corner and clambers into the back of the van, grumbling about how there's no seats. I barely hear him as Flynn pulls onto the road. *We've been here before.* I hold onto his hand, wanting to remember. His words like fog-fingers sweeping up the back of my neck as we bomb through dirty puddles.

* * *

The outside of the disco and its lake of concrete have changed. Crazy to think that just yesterday me, Flynn, and Gloria drove by. Now, me, Flynn, and Stetson circle the street in the van, casing the joint. Not that we can see much, since giant black plastic tarp walls shroud the whole concrete lake around the disco. Two starmen guarding the gap in the tarp barricade are wearing eight-point star pins. A glowing vidboard at their side reads *AREA UNDER UNITED STATES SPACE GUARD SURVEILLANCE*. Two tanks guard the entrance to the alleyway leading to the club, the giant hard-ons of the cannons pointed out at the whole city. Three Guard rovers—three that I can see, anyway—rumble around the block in opposite directions.

Forget Mayflower bulldozing a few blocks to bring a fake Space Guard base to their upcoming theme park. Kern built a real one right here.

We leave Stetson in the van. Kern is expecting Flynn to come alone, according to the seamstresses, so the starmen at the entryway don't want to let even me in. Flynn says he's not going in without me and starmen squawk into their radios and pass us off to other starmen, and what the hell is Kern doing with a whole platoon of them here and not on the moon or at Columbia? Blood rushes in my ears when two starmen lead us past the gap in the black tarp, and into a tarp jungle that looks a lot less fun than the white sheet maze in Founding Mothers. Electrical wires and extension cords snake around the pavement, leading into areas sectioned off by the tarps. Muffled chatter. Clanks of metal against metal. I see sparks arc from the top of one tarp wall, where someone must be welding. A white-gloved hand moves one of the tarps to step through, and the person is wearing a helmeted white suit that looks so much like my space suit from patrol that I almost check my tank.

Side by side, deeper into the black maze, until we walk through the clown mouth of the disco's front entrance. I'm dizzy from the stink of burnt air.

I got the head spins when I first walked in here with Gloria, months back. I figured it was me feeling car sick after our ride from Sunshine City, and other times I could blame the feeling on being half in-the-bag, or taking poppers hits in the backroom between contraband pickups. Now, though—walking over the too-bright dancefloor—I've got a clearer head. It must be Flynn's ship whirling my guts like the launch sim.

Pure Tempo sends tremors up through my legs from deep below the ground. I clench every muscle to keep from falling because looking weak now would prove everything right to the thirty or so men gathered here. Starmen in Space Guard red jumpsuits scowling in corners and men with slicked-down haircuts poring over maps and flapping around with stacks of papers. Other haircuts sit at tables that ring the whole disco, their squat, dome-screened computers giving off green light. Keys clack out of time. No beer and cologne, just the stink of sweat, hot plastic, and coffee breath. The painted circus animals on the walls are waiting for commands from their new ringleader.

Kern stands, hands folded behind his back, frowning down at a stack of paper some haircut is showing him, by a projector on a wheeled metal cart under the central disco ball. Same cigarette ash hair. Same eyes the color of dull metal. In his dress blues to separate himself from the grunts' jumpsuits.

I want to hold Flynn's hand for strength, but Lieutenant Flynn Parker is on duty. Chin up, shoulders straight, waiting for the Guard Hymn.

"I should haul you out of here in cuffs just for wearing that uniform," Kern says.

"Sir." Flynn's sneakered heels click when he snaps to attention. "I'm technically still in the Guard."

"Absent without official leave." Even Kern's voice has got a frown. "And you certainly had an *interesting* way of leaving Columbia, according to the security footage I saw. Disarming an alarmed backdoor of the base with a wave of your hand and sneaking out in the middle of the night like a criminal is not something I expected of you, Lieutenant." He seems to see me for the first time, and puffs a humorless laugh. "That's behavior I'd expect more of Ward, here."

That's not exactly how Flynn told me he left the Guard.

"I do love a good backdoor." I toss a two-fingered salute at him. "Sir."

Kern stiffens, pinching his lips. He jerks a hand, dismissing the engineer or whoever at his side, and strides to us on creaking leather shoes. So close that I can see the red webbing his eyes, and smell his leather cologne.

"These games have to stop, gentlemen. We don't have the luxury of time, not when I assume we're about to witness the most significant event in Earth's history." The hard edges of his mouth seem to soften with his next breath. "I will pay you the honor of full transparency if you have the integrity to do the same."

Jesus Christ, this guy. Honor. Integrity. He knows how to work the invisible strings of toy-soldier Flynn. I can feel Flynn stiffen like Kern is his Pop with the stopwatch.

"Sir," Flynn agrees.

All I do is nod.

Another charged second before Kern leather-creaks back to the projector. He switches it on and a bright square of light blasts onto a screen nailed up over the bar.

"Months ago, we uncovered what appeared to be an alien spacecraft below the lunar surface," Kern says.

He slides a transparency onto the projector, and a black-and-white picture of what looks like a giant Opti-Disc sticking up from the surface of the moon appears on the screen. I know the bulldozers and the bucket excavators in the background, and the moon bricks littering the gray dirt around the abandoned furnace.

"The Plymouth Colony civilian expansion," I cut in. "That's why you stopped construction."

We all owe that crazy cat Powell a heaping apology. He and the other starmen who babbled about aliens were onto something.

"Correct." Kern swaps the transparency for another, an image of the ship that they must've dug up. Based on the three starmen in space suits standing next to it, the thing looks smaller than the fighter jets that billowed red, white, and blue smoke into the skies over Miami during Fourth of July celebrations. It doesn't look like the mini *Saint Christopher* from my blue-glass vision last night, but it's made of the same swirled metal. I must be seeing the thing for what it really is, now.

A fried egg with a disco ball for a yolk.

A flying saucer. Of course.

But none of this makes sense. We know Flynn's ship is below the disco, and the concrete below my high-tops is still intact, so they haven't dug it up yet. Studying the projection, I know the tight waves etched onto a panel by what must be the door is the ship's name. In my vision, Flynn told me his ship was named *Rush. You know, since you're always in such a rush.*

The waves are screaming another name at me. *BOLT.*

"Where's my ship?" Flynn asks, then adds a hasty, "Sir."

"If you'll hold off on the questions, Parker." Kern clears his throat. "As I was the officer in charge of the Plymouth Colony's construction project, anything we found there was under my purview. And given the *sensitive* nature of our discovery, I have kept knowledge of the ship's existence limited to a select few officers."

"Watkins." The floor bobs beneath me. "You kept it from Watkins."

"Watkins is more suited to his current post at a desk in Columbia. His extended time on Fort Founding Fathers shifted his perspective regarding the Starman's Oath, it seems. He was more interested in fostering a sense of Brotherhood, while the other Virtues—chief among them Valor and Strength—waned in him. And others on his watch. I knew he was no longer capable of the tactical decisions necessary to understand our finding. I kept our research from him, limited it to a small muster station by the quarry. And to be fair to Watkins, we weathered certain difficulties. Personnel issues. Some unintended repercussions from our studies. Progress is never a straight line, you see." He presses his lips into a line. "Columbia understands that."

Powell. Was he one of those personnel issues?

"Once I assumed command of the base," Kern continues, "I expanded our research. When it became clear the task was beyond the limited expertise of the personnel on the moon, I requested Columbia's assistance. They sent an emergency launch of the *Saint James*, and we returned to Earth with the ship to continue our research, some four weeks ago."

Kern projects another picture, this one with gleaming panels of swirled metal. A screen ringed by lights shows a glowing map of California with a dot on it.

"Two days ago, the ship's onboard navigation switched on and, as best we understand it, is now pointing to this very location."

I know the ship's panels. I've seen their alarm lights flashing through the flames in my visions. Heat blasts my face.

I swear I hear the club's speaker system crackle. Another wave of dizziness almost bowls me over.

"I can only describe what happened next as an 'alarming confluence of events,'" Kern barrels on. "We began the process of moving the ship and our research team to this location when we received word that super-powered homosexuals are rampaging through Los Angeles, all apparently encouraged by a man wearing a Space Guard jacket who says he's an emissary of a civilization he calls the Metronomes."

Eavesdropping eyes of the starmen now pretend to look at the corners of the room. I swear I hear a laugh someone tries to disguise as a cough.

"I wonder how you heard about our work, sir?" I smirk. I can see Kern saddling up to the doll-chaser bar in Silver Lake, or pulling up past the Studio Zones to a corner of Sunset where one of our boys was working the midnight shift.

"Which we would dismiss as nonsense, of course," Kern says, ignoring me. "If not for the fact that Space Guard astronomers detected a massive object—roughly half the size of the moon—just beyond Jupiter, moving towards Earth. Astonishingly quickly."

He slaps another image on the projector, of a fuzzy round thing in the darkness of what must be space. Funny, if I squint just enough, it looks like a disco ball blurred with fog.

Object, my ass. That's a ship.

"Holy smokes," Flynn whispers, his mouth falling open. "They're on the way with the entire World-Ship."

"Preposterous," Kern snaps. "An object that large isn't a ship. And its shape is completely absurd given the thrust-propulsion required for space travel."

Just the tiniest hint of a smile touches Flynn's mouth. *With Tempo, we can work miracles.*

"As completely absurd as a bunch of queers waving their hands and deflecting bullets?" I want the words to slap Kern, but another head-spin sucks some of the fire from my voice.

"Every world government. Every amateur astronomer with a telescope pointed up has seen this, same as you." Flynn stabs a finger at the disco ship. "Panic in the streets, riots, it's..."

"We've informed the United Nations and various world media outlets that what they're seeing is merely light reflecting off gas that's abundant in the outer solar system," Kern says. "Any story to the contrary is pure falsehood and alarmism."

"Alarmism? No, sir. With the speed that the ship is moving closer to us," Flynn says, "someone else is bound to get a clearer look. And then what?"

"Russia, at least," I jump in. "They got telescopes on the moon, right? There'll be an armed response. Or—"

"If the United States government says that this image is light off gas, then it is light off gas." Kern's fist slams on the projector's metal cart, shaking the picture. "Communist coups are raging through Europe. They can barely feed their citizens, never mind concern themselves with the heavens. The Russians on Lunogorod are busying themselves by looking at mold through magnifying glasses. All the other nations—their telescopes are little more than binoculars. Their armies wave muskets. They are no match for the might and the progress of the Space Guard, and our Nation."

I swallow hard.

"*We* are the arbiters of Truth," he continues. "As Lincoln told us, 'a house divided against itself cannot stand.' This world is *our* house. The United States of America writes the story and the rest of the world stands with the United States of America."

The ceiling speakers crackle with static for an instant. I have to fight against a fresh dizzy wave.

"Now," Kern says, softer. He adjusts the hem of his coat. "Back to the task at hand, if you please. The ship and its navigation systems. Surely the ship brought us here so we could communicate with the object in space."

"With my people," Flynn says.

Kern nostrils flare. "Who are your people and what do they want?"

"We are travelers spreading joy and knowledge. And power." He falters. "But this type of response is saved for..."

The speakers crackle again. The hairs on the back of my neck stand up.

"For?" Kern asks.

"For the correction of grave injustices," Flynn says, as formal as the Guard hymn on the trumpet. "Cosmic wrongs."

"What kind of *correction* are we discussing here, Lieutenant?"

"An armed response."

Key-clacking around the room suddenly stops.

"Surely we can reason with them." Kern frowns, his leather shoes creaking. "Educate them on the good works of the American Republic. Reach some sort of agreement or strategic alliance between our nation and theirs, at least, if not for the wider planet. You'll help us contact these aliens."

"We're past the point of reason and agreement, sir."

"Then where are we, exactly, soldier?"

"Judgment."

My cruising eyes know how to read tiny movements. Kern folds his hands behind him, again, with slow effort. Seeing his Adam's apple quake almost makes the whole potential destruction of the planet worth it.

Petty, Petty Officer Mitchell Ward.

"You swore an oath, starman, to protect this nation."

"That's what we're trying to do." I flap a hand at the blurry disco ball in space on the screen.

Flynn's fingertips brush my arm. *Easy.* "You said full transparency, sir."

"Correct."

"Have the integrity to tell me where my ship is," Flynn says. "And I'll tell you just how I'll fix all this."

"Follow me."

Kern turns on his stiff leather shoes and leads us deeper into the disco.

TWENTY-FIVE

BACKROOM ACTION

Our straight guests dancing in Circus Disco know that the Trapeze Room in the back is off limits. The dolls and the girls call this place home as much as any of us, but even they know that the Trapeze Room is for us boys. Boys come here, in the dark, to be lion tamers and ringleaders and strongmen. We don't come to the Trapeze Room unless we're looking to swing. Unless we want to get up on the high-wire, or join the elephant walks and contortion acts on the dancefloor. The red-lit corners and the dim of the dancefloor is for the kind of acrobatics and feats of physical strength that got the Hollywood Baths shut down. *The Greatest Homo Show on Earth.* The things that the square queers who wear suits and ties to work as lawyers and accountants swear that we don't do in public. *The straights have to know we're not all sex-crazed animals because then they'll never give us rights.* Even when enough of them get their tickets punched here on Saturday night for the show, same as me.

Besides, I'm done with asking.

The most depraved thing I've seen happen in the Trapeze Room is that right now, the overhead lights are on, exposing the dirty concrete floors. Instead of boys in bulldog harnesses, men in white hazmat suits mull around, waving whistling meters at what looks like a giant bank vault in the center of the room, which must've barely fit through the double-doors. A wheel crank sticks out of the vault's side, and a horizontal seam cuts across the center of the metal plate of what must be the front door. Clear plastic is draped over the bar. Another tarp splits the dancefloor in half between the bank vault and more hazmat suits bustling around tables. Through the hazy plastic, I can't see what they're tinkering over.

The hazmat suits have me wondering what the hell they're protecting themselves from. And why we're not covered up. Kern barks at everyone in the room to leave. When the scientists—or whoever they are—lift the tarp to get out, I see piles of black on the tables. Maybe a boot.

I barely hear Flynn telling Kern about Tempo and how he's leading us Divine Deviants to generate enough for him to close the Disharmony. Kern asks how Tempo spreads and Flynn gives him the speech. Shared joy. Boundless love. Vibrating to higher levels.

The overhead lights are vibrating in my eyes, somehow. The air is too heavy in my chest.

"Greedy," Kern says, his arms folded behind his back by the bank vault, "for you to decide who gets this power or not."

"Freely given to those who want it," Flynn counters.

"The people you want." Kern's voice is almost bored. "Who you choose. Frankly, that's un-American."

I might as well be underwater with how Kern's voice is muffled. Everything moves with a liquid haze, my senses blurring like I've eaten a monster dose of disco biscuits. The air tastes red. Gloria. I can almost smell her rose perfume. We should've brought her with us. We should've—

"My ship." The stage dreaminess weaves through Flynn's voice. The echo in it could just be my ears misfiring.

"It's outside." Kern paces around the bank vault, eyeing it up like it's soldiers in formation. "The civilization who created the craft—the Metronomes, you say—clearly possesses technology well beyond our current capabilities. Still, we're making some promising discoveries."

Something past the metal sings out to me.

"What kind of discoveries?" I swear I hear the liquor bottles at the bar rattle behind the tarps at Flynn's words.

"The ship was damaged beyond flight capability, best that we can determine." Kern's hand rests on the wheel of the vault. "What I presume to be its power source remains intact. Its containment apparatus, however, was damaged."

"And this is to contain..."

I shiver. *Personnel issues,* Kern said. *Some unintended repercussions.*

"To prevent naked exposure to the power source." Kern nods curtly at the vault. "Once we removed it from the ship, we found that the radiation exuded by the core led to a certain kind of constitutional distress among weak-minded Guardsmen. An emotional contagion, perhaps."

A bolt of pain splits my head in half. For a second, I blast out of the disco and I'm looking through a blue glass helmet, jump-sprinting over the lunar landscape towards the lights on the hulking Constitution nuclear reactor in the distance. Others running with me have heard the same hisses through the mist, and screams in the mess hall. *They will come for you. Unless you stop them.*

When we séanced for Ricky, I saw toy soldiers drifting in yellow fog. Emotional contagion. Some of it must've seeped up from the ship before we even dug it up, and we've been bringing it back to Earth with us.

Look at what they took from us. You must end them.

"Panic." Flynn stutters. "Madness..."

"The madness is here," Kern says. "Since returning, I have never seen such madness in the world."

At least we can agree on something. "The Moral Codes," I sputter. "Commdef, the—"

He cuts me off with a wave of the hand. "Strengthening the American character. You people are so single-minded. Whining about all these perceived persecutions, when the very existence of our nation is at stake. I'm talking of the assault on Democracy. The Communist coups that have spread like a cancer. A Guardsman making an attempt on the life of the President."

Another bolt of pain. Another blue-tinted vision. I'm in a wood-paneled conference room. The president. Service dress and lab coats. A projection screen. I'm here to share information, yes. Updates, and studies, and... I look down at the table, where *CONFIDENTIAL* is stamped in red on the top sheet of a stack of papers, just above *OPERATION VANGUARD.*

Voices that the others don't hear hiss and promise. *They will... They took...*

Stop them.

My hand unleashes a snake of yellow fog, pinning Reagan against the wall.

Flynn's hand on my back brings me back to where my feet are planted. I cough, my hands flying to my neck.

"You brought this contagion to Earth?" Flynn's mouth falls open.

"Once I learned to properly contain the core and shield others from its radiation," Kern says. He flattens his hand on the side of the vault, his thumb stroking the metal. "The core spoke to me, you see. Chose me. Did you ever truly hear its voice?"

A high-pitched *eeeeee* stabs my ears. Kern's hand falls back to the vault wheel, and he might as well be pulling on my shoulders with how I almost fall. Sweat trickles into my eyes.

A thin slip of fog billows from the collar of Flynn's jacket.

"It showed me how to shape the smoke from the core emissions. How to feed it into tools." The vault wheel groans and clanks and Kern turns it. "I learned how to purify them. How to make them worthy."

A bright line from the middle of the vault stabs the air as Kern cranks, drawing the two horizontal halves of the vault door apart. The shimmering gap widens. More wheel screeches, the volume on the *eeeee* cranking louder and louder until I see a burnt yellow sun—not much larger than a basketball—hovering in a glass chamber. Shivering and rotating, jagged spikes zipping in and out of its surface.

Invisible chains launch up, grab me by the wrists, and wrestle me to my knees on the dirty concrete. I can't scream. I can't speak.

Groans float from behind the plastic tarp. Figures struggle, sit up, slide off the tables.

Fog leaks out of Flynn, now. The air tastes like static.

"How to turn them into weapons," Flynn says.

"Into the Vanguards. God's true Guardsmen." The static hiss finds its way into Kern's awed voice. "Come soar. Come shine brighter than all the stars. Come serve as a deterrent for all other nations to quake at the might of our armies." He waves his hands at the blinding sun. He doesn't even blink. "We've seen how the people of this nation wish to serve, and sacrifice. We will give them strength and power. We will protect their families and they in turn will protect our American family. And now they will rise up against the invaders from the sky."

Invisible smoke invades my lungs. Invisible bricks from an exploded apartment building weigh me down, and it's all fucking Max Page or Paglioti or Paglia's fault for ratting us out for a touch of the vidboard fame.

"And now that the rightful pilot of the ship has returned," Kern continues, "you'll help us lead the response against the Metronomes."

Men in black jumpsuits stagger past the plastic tarp. I know the one at the front. Hernandez. The poker night pal I punched. I don't know the other four with their stitched nametags over their hearts. Amato. Costa. DuBois. Saito. Who knows if even their mothers would know their faces through all the burns. Hernandez's left eye is milky white, half of his hair burned away.

I don't know how Flynn and the others aren't covering their ears against the guitar screech splitting the air.

"Unholy." Echoes ring out from Flynn's voice. "To take the Sacred Music and lower the Frequency. To infect."

His eyes spark with blue fire. He doesn't see me writhe against the invisible chains.

"To protect and defend our people," Kern's hiss returns.

"We've seen how you protect." Flynn says. "How you defend."

"Have you, now?"

"Camp Puller." Fog creeps from Flynn's fingertips. "This Instrument hides these memories. Shields them from us in shame, even as we share a heart and a mind."

The fog slipping from Flynn's claw-hands are a new tell. I can see us talking in me and Gloria's apartment, Flynn telling me about his time in the Guard.

That wasn't combat. That was dishonor.

Kern doesn't flinch. "We defended American assets against a violent Vietnamese incursion."

"We turned guns on civilians who were protesting for basic safety precautions in the mines." The quake in Flynn's echoing voice matches the growing rattles from the bar. Flynn with blue-sparking eyes. Not-Flynn. "We burned villages until they got back to work."

Hernandez and the others look around, squinting. His trembling hands tell me *where am I?* Amato tries to speak but can only cough with a withered stub of a tongue. Costa's lips are twisted open in a permanent scream. All of this only crumples me lower, closer to something buried deep in the ground.

Something that's calling my name.

Hurry to me. Rush. You know, since you're always in such a rush.

Two ships, always. Two soldiers on patrol. Such a basic military maneuver that even us blockheads on the backwater moon base had it covered.

"Higher being or no, you are a fool if you don't see that some sacrifices are necessary." Kern snorts. "And a fool if you think either of you are leaving this place free men."

I crane my head up, begging Flynn with my eyes to do something. Kern nods at his Vanguards. They snap to attention and burnt yellow fog sears from their hands.

Finally, Flynn's blue-glowing eyes hit mine. I hope he can see the secret code through my wince. *Flynn, lean the fuck in.*

His hands snap to his sides. Silver, glittering fog blasts from him towards the Vanguard. The clouds collide and my face cracks against the dirty concrete floor.

* * *

Once the fog drifts from my eyes, I'm standing on the stage of the Calypso Room again. But it's not really the Calypso Room. It's not really anywhere.

"The music is as much about the silence between the notes," Flynn told us before the séance for Ricky. "And the dance is as much about being still."

In this in-between place, the Moonboom sits in the golden circle of the spotlight on the black-painted wood of the stage. I bend down and pick the thing up. The familiar, heavy weight of it belongs in my hands. I pop the eject button and pull out the tape.

In black ink on the white label is *METRONOME/ MITCH – CALYPSO ROOM – MAY 8, 1962 DEMO*. My handwriting. That's the day when I changed. When I became myself. I know, somewhere behind me, ten-year-old Mitch is asleep in the lighting catwalk, surrounded by sparkling mist. Mist that floated around this world, asleep, and waiting for its perfect Instrument, the one with the music in his hips.

Gloria's got her gifts. Patrick, too, and the others are waking up. My power has always been seeing, and feeling, and turning up the volume in others. Giving power, like I do to Flynn. Now, the engine core by my body back in the real world, in the disco, is feeding power to me and boosting me up.

Now I'm ready to listen.

I hit play and the blippy beats and the star-song cradles me. Donna giggles through the speaker like she always does. *Oh, that's wild. What's that?* More silky sounds spill out and have me bopping my noggin.

"Baby, are you ready for another verse?" Donna asks me through the Moonboom.

Hell yeah. Crank that volume, lady.

I hold the Moonboom to my side as I step through the curtain.

* * *

I can see through the blue light that Flynn is wiping the rag along the side of the ship again. I should say *my ship*. Time to get the lyrics right, like Flynn, who made damn sure to say "the ship" and not "his ship" when we were talking to the others about the ship under the disco.

Sneaky, sneaky starman. That's alright. We got the message across, and this is mostly about the feel of the music anyway.

The ship is showing me its true form—the fried egg with the disco ball yolk—and not the mini *Saint Christopher*. Flynn is the Flynn with the trim beard and sweat-slick curls, bare-chested under his Guard jacket like when he came back to me at Circus Disco. I can tilt my head, if I want, and see him wearing his blue glass body with the metal welding mask face. Same as I can look down and see my arms as blue glass instead of skin. Same as I can realize I'm seeing all of this in blue light because I'm made of blue glass, too.

We've danced in a lot of bodies, twirling around each other like songbirds. We sing out to each other in a harmony that's rare, even for Metronomes, but Lieutenant Flynn Parker of the United States Space Guard is the truest version of Flynn that there ever will be. Same as me and Last Mitch Effort.

"Rush." Flynn's eyes twinkle something sweet at me. "You know, since you're always in such a rush."

Rush is my callsign. Since I've joined the service and gotten my wings, I've sung out into the radio, *Rush back from patrol and requesting reentry clearance* a million times. Bolt is Flynn's callsign. I teased him about that.

Sounds perfect, Bolt. First sign of somethin' hairy and you bolt, baby.

Really, "Bolt" was perfect because of something else. First time I saw him, those blue eyes knocked me clean through like a bolt of lightning.

I look up from Flynn and my ship to the vidboard overhead. On the screen, *Rush* and *Bolt* twirl around each other in space. *Bolt* is flying a little crooked, with me not noticing because I zip ahead in *Rush*. The two ships separate all the time on patrol, anyhow, since it makes coming back together on the dancefloor that much sweeter. Then *Bolt* is alone, spinning and lagging—coming in too hot and missing our landing zone by a million miles.

Flynn's ship crashes into the moon's dead gray rocks and the debris from the impact rains all around, burying it deep.

* * *

At my side, the Moonboom clicks. I press eject, flip the tape, then hit play again.

* * *

Blue light glows over the med bay in Founding Fathers, filled with padded gurneys and domed computer screens. Wires, tubes, and glinting metal. A dozen starmen mess with buttons and make notes on clipboards. Others fuss over the unmoving bodies on tables behind a makeshift bedsheet curtain. Fog hugging the floors keeps this place icy cold. A huge screen above a central console shows men in service blues around a table, keeping watch, with the sun gleaming on the lush green swamps of Florida in the distance.

I really don't want to follow the wires across the floor to the bank vault. I do because Donna's voices gives me a little nudge. I know I'm here to see things, even if my heart hurts every time I learn more about what these fucking awful creatures do to each other.

Like I'm one to judge, really. Though, I guess that's my job.

"Attempt nineteen," the starman by the crank of the bank vault says to another starman with a clipboard.

A firehose connects the bottom edge of the bank vault to the helmet of the space suit on the padded table. Beyond the glass of the helmet, Hernandez blinks his pretty eyes. Kern peeks down at Hernandez, almost bored. Attempt eighteen was the same as attempt one. Failure. Another body covered in moon bricks in the abandoned quarry. Must be the fault of these weak, stupid men that the Guard admitted when they relaxed the rules, desperate for more bodies.

Kern will fix them. Turn them into real men.

"Clear to open the iris," he says.

Oh, God. No.

The two halves of the bank vault door creak open to reveal that burnt yellow spiked sun encased in glass. Toxic yellow smoke swirls around the sun and slithers into the firehose. Into Hernandez's helmet. My screams harmonize with his screams. He enlisted for this special study as part of the STAR Soldier System to get the coin to finally get his girl that diamond ring he promised her when they got hitched. And now. And now the same fire that torches my lungs sears his bubbling skin.

Voices hiss through the instruments in the room. Kern looks up, like only he can hear. *You must stop them. You must avenge us. We will show you the way.*

I know the horrors and the noise that's filling Hernandez's head. I've seen that little sun shimmering in space, in the silence after the Metronome ships appeared. In the perfect, still Silence between two tracks—after the screams, and the bombs, and the fires.

After the Adjudication.

The burnt yellow sun is not a sun. It's the ember of a world.

Static fills the wide screen over the control panels. When it clears, the featureless blue-glass face of a Metronome looks down at all of us. Eyeless, and still its judging stare burns me up.

Power, freely given. Voices in the Metronome chorus call out together. *Still, you drink until the well runs dry. And now this Affront to the Sanctity of the Celestial Music. This Disgrace. Unworthy, all of you. All.*

The echoing Metronome chorus-voice and the burnt sun hiss-clang against each other. The disharmony cuts up my skin.

Disharmony. Yes. This.

I gasp for air.

Your existence is a drain on the Collective, the Metronome chorus cranks into a mad Moog mudslide. *It must be Silenced.*

What a time for Starman North's big mug to flash on the

other screens in the room. He beams at all of us as the orchestral version of the Space Guard Hymn plays in the background.

"Hwhy, hwhen last hwe saw our plucky Starmen, they hwere fighting for their lives in that den of iniquity known as the Circus Disco."

Starman North salutes the screen and disappears. In his place, me and Flynn are trapped between two roiling storm fronts in the backroom.

A slow gurgle tears my eyes from the screen back down to the starmen.

Hernandez snaps up on the gurney. *Sweet fucking Christ.* I scream and skitter backwards into another gurney, knocking it over and dropping the Moonboom. I topple over, and Kern and the others vanish into yellow smoke while I skitter away from Hernandez's half-melted face. I slap the floor, looking for the Moonboom. Looking for Donna—*anyone*—to save me.

I'm hissing and wheezing so loud I barely hear the high-hats *tap-tapping* the vamp to 'Five Years,' about to cue Gloria in for her last show in the Lodge.

Rose perfume washes over me.

"Mitch." Gloria's voice streams through the Moonboom on the floor. "Mitchell, get up."

Hernandez's hands lash out and blast me with yellow fog. Blue glass hands drop the curtain of the Calypso Room, plunging me into darkness.

* * *

Mitch.

Mitchell.

Mitchell—we can't hold them much longer. Check your tank.

I scream and gasp out yellow fog, yanked back from my blue-glass vision by Gloria's voice roaring through the club's speakers. I pick up my head from the floor.

"You move your ass and help that boy."

Her voice surges with music—with all the heat that she's got—set against Hat-Trick's thrumming black-hole beats. I can see her scolding eyes, and then she's trilling again, she's singing back-up for us from a séance in Founding Mothers. Their music is slowing Kern, his Vanguard, and their rolling yellow fogbank, somehow. Even still, they'll shake it off any second. Flynn, glittering fog whipping all around him, should be stronger than five Tempoed beings, but they're amped up by their twisted power source.

Their Disharmony. We'll stop them. First we gotta get out of here alive.

My ship, *Rush*, is down below. The engine core of Flynn's ship, *Bolt*, is here in this room. They're too close. We've let the cores Resonate with each other—crackling with power, calling out to the Metronomes—a million times before. But it's too soon. It ain't time for the fat lady to sing just yet.

I squeeze and howl like a bloodhound and—yes—on my feet, I press my hands to either side of Flynn's face. Blinding light blasts out of his eyes and mouth. He screams, has the sense to slam the engine core bank vault closed with a nod, and whips his hands out, careening the Vanguard and Kern into the air. They crash into the metal tables and the bar, the glass bottles exploding in a rain of glitter.

Flynn's laughter is like circling too close to the sun. He's fire and beauty and power.

And now we're fucking cooking, starman.

Easy does it, I tell him with my eyes. *Run too hot and you'll burn that body to ash. And we have too much work to do before the others get here.*

Shouts come from the next room—with a nod he slams the double-doors of the backroom closed—and I don't need to sing up a premonition to know that the toy soldiers and their guns are about to storm in.

"We gotta run!" I yell at Flynn.

Yes. My hands and my voice pull some of Flynn back out of Not-Flynn. We're shaking, and laughing—*yes, I can see it coming back now,* my eyes sing—and there'll be time for all of that.

Flynn punches his hands out and twin plumes of fog smash through the back wall. Here's hoping Bette won't mind the new backdoor in her club.

We run through with Kern's armed Space Guard not far behind. The Vanguard must be picking themselves up out of the broken glass, and they'll be on our tails us soon, too. Up ahead, Stetson is leaning on the back of the van, smoking a butt. The rovers on patrol are headed this way, but we got a lead on them. I yell his name. Poor guy looks up at me and Flynn—him stumbling as I half hold him up—scramble his way, with rifled starmen thirty feet back and *oh shit oh shit oh shit,* Stetson rips open the back doors of the van. I help Flynn inside on the mattress and yank the doors closed just as Stetson vaults behind the steering wheel. He peels out into the street.

"You couldda given me some kind of warning you were on your way!" Stetson pounds the steering wheel. "We're not gonna make it. They have guns."

The van's radio is bumping Hat-Trick's beats. When I crane around and meet Stetson's eyes in the rearview mirror, the song in them wants to break my heart open. I can see him, as a scared kid, hearing how the Tempo called to him. How it told him his purpose. *Protect. Serve.* How he misheard the tune and thought he needed a gun and a badge from someone else to do what he was born to do. How the right notes didn't reach him until he heard our music at the disco.

Not his fault he misheard it, with all the noise in this fucking sad, broken world.

"We're gonna make it because we've got you," I tell him.

My fingertips crackle light at the side of his face. He gasps as light warps out of his hands and wraps the van up in a shimmering, rainbow-edged bubble—same as the one he tossed up around the disco that night of the raid, protecting and serving us all.

"Hit the gas and eyes on the road." I cram a kiss on the side of his cheek.

Bullets bounce off as Stetson hollers into the dash.

"Ten-four!" he hoots.

I scoot back to the mattress, and Flynn wriggles up into my lap. We jostle into the side of the wall as Stetson cuts a corner hard, weaving in and out of traffic. I wish I was on the sidewalk to see a van wrapped in a rainbow bubble streaking down Santa Monica Boulevard like a giant billiard ball knocked to the corner pocket by the hand of God.

Two blocks down, the Space Guard rovers are speeding towards us. I almost feel bad for them.

Flynn is stiff muscle against me, one of his hands hard in mine. I feed him just enough of a spark to yank two sky flowers down from roof of a bank we pass, and send them crashing into the street. Cars skitter out of the way and screech to a stop, blocking traffic behind us. The metal petals grind and turn chunks of pavement into confetti.

I can feel him vibrate in my arms. The tears in his eyes are so loud I almost hear his voice. *I couldn't tell you. You wouldn't believe me. You had to remember.*

The three of us laugh and cheer, my tears blurring the light in my eyes as I remember. And remember. *We American kings soar on speeding van wings. And no braver men are found.*

TWENTY-SIX

REMIXED AND REMASTERED

I don't remember the name of the planet I'm from.

Some part of me must've remembered parts of my life there, when the light hit a certain way. When I was walking home from a bus-stop cruising and the pink dawn washed over the graffiti-slashed brick of the dead factories in Silver Lake. When my eyes hit someone else's on a street corner, or in the disco, and we recognized that we were singing the same music. When sudden beauty stopped me so fast in my tracks that I just had to breathe it in.

We didn't really have language from where I'm from. We spoke in mind-flashes and visions. We talked in touch and hip-bumping boogie. I remember black sand beaches and tide pools made of star glow. I remember crystal islets dotting the green seas off our shores that resonated with the blue light from the triple moons in our wine-colored sky. I remember, at feast time, we blew horns made from hollowed-out deepwhale bones and sang old songs that spoke of a visit from a third sun made of glowing planks, and travelers touching down in glowing sky-birds who held out their hands out to us, singing. *Heaven knows, heaven knows. I feel love.*

I was born long after my world first heard the waves of Tempo over the waves of the sea. After my twentieth harvest festival, the skies over our village on the beach darkened from bright bronze and filled with clouds the rust-orange of the deserts beyond the mountains. For years after, the winds whipped, and bombed snow on the turquoise grasses around our thatched-roof huts. The seas boiled and dead fish bobbed to the surface, their triple gillstacks gasping in the blue moonlight. Our crops burned in the yellowing dirt. The ground growled while lightning crackled around the cone of the volcano that guarded us from the strangers beyond the brightsea.

The harvest festivals weren't so bumpin', those years.

Our world was dying and so were we, and I watched the others wave their hands and sweep the fog of Tempo into the churning forge cut into the side of our village's volcano. They sang and prayed, while I watched the swirls in the Tempo fog. If only we could get the forge hotter. I knew—in mind-flickers, in blippy pulses—that we could use it, somehow.

It was my idea to break off pieces of the crystal islets and feed them into the forge, cranking the red flames into something blue-blinding and hot enough to melt the Tempo fog into molten goo. I built the first molds to pour in the molten Tempo so it would cool into slabs of blue-swirled glass. That far-out shit broke every tool I threw at it. We weren't really supposed to toot our own deepwhale horns but, *toot toot, baby.* I'd always been the weird kid climbing the crystal islets when everyone else was weaving seagrass, and now maybe they wouldn't throw fish heads at me come harvest time. The last time we had good news was the week before when my cousin found a fresh grove of cavemangoes on the other side of the creek, which meant maybe we wouldn't starve that month. We all needed a win. Especially me.

I told them how we could turn the Tempo glass into tools. How the fire somehow burned hotter when I was near it. *Sure, Mitch,* they flashed and boogied back. *How is glass going to dig us out of the deepwhale shit of our God being pissed at us? Maybe more of us need to jump in the volcano to see if that'll make Her happy, and right now you're looking like a real good tribute.*

He's onto something, one of the others flashed and danced back. *We can turn the glass into shelter from the weather, and build greenhouses for crops, and build ships to sail over the brightsea, even. I reckon he just saved your blue asses.*

We all knew Flynn—his name wasn't really that, then, it was music, same as mine—wasn't from our same star. We might've wrapped ourselves up in woven seagrasses and banged on fish-skin drums to pass our nights, but we weren't stupid. Even if he had the same glowing blue skin and long limbs, he might as well have been wearing an Us costume that didn't fit right around the joints. His copper eyes flashed blue in certain lights. He knew a thing or two about being an outsider, too. I could see it in the way he moved.

I puffed my seagrass spliff and bobbed my chin at him. *If you're not gonna listen to me, at least give this jive turkey a chance.*

We got to boogieing and cranking out Tempo glass. I was not the best glassworker or forge smith, but when I was around, or when I touched the others, I could feel a zip move from me to them. And then they swung hammers harder and faster. They could toss the molds around like they were made of leaves. By the time the next harvest festival rolled around, a whole archipelago of swirled blue glass houses dotted the shore in the shade of the volcano. And thanks to the greenhouses, we actually had some food to celebrate with. Toot toot. The others ate and banged on fish-skin drums while me and Flynn kept working the forges like we'd been doing for months. Let them dance. I liked being around him more than the others, anyway. He made the roaring of our forge sound sweeter than deepwhale horns. He turned the fire in my insides blue-blinding, same as if I swallowed some crystal islet chunks.

Once the smoke of the dying feast fires twirled to the twin suns in the morning, someone from the village down the creek wandered into the forge. I wiped the green sweat from my forehead and turned away from the flames. This cat had star music in his blood, same as Flynn, even if he wore the copper eyes and purple skin of our cousin-tribe.

This whole continent is about to bust, purple dude flashed and danced. *We should signal the World-Ship early. A volcanic winter is not my jam.*

Too soon to Adjudicate, Flynn boogied back.

Adjudicate my ass, Purple said. *We have to blow this fucking Popsicle stand. We need an emergency evac.*

We can't leave them. Flynn's dance turned sour. *Mitch here is proof of Potential Ascendency. We have a duty.*

Oh my God. Purple's dance had him gasping like a fish in the boiling sea. *He made fancy glass. Get a grip.*

I dropped my pokers and turned from the forge. *I mean, I'm right here,* I flicked, annoyed. *I can hear you.*

He moves and sees Tempo. He builds power and potential in others in a way we've never seen. Flynn's flickers and the slow, liquid sways of his long arms were the most beautiful things I'd ever seen. Even more than the crystal islets glowing in the pink double sunrise, washed over with seafoam. *That's special. He's special.*

They're not ready. Purple gyrates. *Their world needs more time. Time that we don't have.*

Then we can save them. What else are we for?

We have to follow the Score.

Flynn answered with slow turns and sways and circles I couldn't understand.

* * *

The World-Ship and its fleet of smaller sky-birds sparkled and swayed one hell of a lightshow over the village, even through the black smoke.

As Beings of Ascended Potential in the Presence of Adjudicators, you have been Blessed by an Early Intervention, the light show whirled and shimmered, speaking to us. *You may join us in the Dance if you wish.*

I'd watched in the violet twilight—the sky bruised by the first black smoke from the volcano—as Flynn and Purple had tippy-tapped at what had looked like glowing crystal chunks in their sky-birds. Forges in the birds had rumbled to each other, then, in a couple of shakes of a deepwhale fin, the World-Ship had bloomed in the sky.

I was the only one in the village to follow Flynn to his sky-bird. I busted out all my moves for the others—hip-check, hustle, and *yes sir, I can boogie*, but no dice. A fish head landed in the yellow dirt by me.

We're taking him to safety with us, Flynn added. *We have room for more.*

And everyone else was like, *What, you're still here? Sure, whatever. Take him. We're planning a visit to those shitheads over the brightsea.* And my cousin was already sharpening some Tempo glass into a sword.

See, I told you, Purple slithered a slow tango. *Not ready.*

* * *

The Ascended beings wrapped me up in song. *Brother. Dancer. Lover. Builder. Welcome. We sing to the Tempo in you and it brings light to us that we hear you sing it in return.*

Flynn taught me how the Metronomes could vibrate so high that they could slip out of their own bodies and become music and light. And joy. And *joy.* Holy deepwhale shit, I thought shuffling to fish-skin drumbeats was joy until I realized that the best harvest festival was torture compared to this place. He showed me the World-Ship and the crystal spires of its one-city. He showed the others my Tempo glass, and they spun it into ship armor and worked it into engine drives. He brought me to the dancers in the fog. I dropped my blue-skinned body like a favorite blue flannel and became glittering light-mist like the others. We swirled into each other for so long that time meant squat. *Tick, tick, tick.* Clock hands and twinned heartbeats, same same.

The Metronomes weren't one people. They were all people. Bright beings from every civilization the fleet had sailed past since this universe was a burbling baby. One or two of the dancers who still swirled on the floor had had a hand in building the World-Ship, the giant orb studded with what looked like glass panels that constantly shuffled into new formations. The ones who built this ship had passed on the songs and the rules, before they Ascended to even higher heavens. *For the good of the Countless Worlds, for the sake of Ascendency and Universal Life, we will act as Conductors and keep the even beat of Tempo in its right time.*

Flynn had been a soldier on his world, untold star-songs before I even dropped in here. His world mistook the Metronomes' visit as an invasion, and attacked them. The Metronomes, in their mercy, let him and some others into the fold and he joined the Adjudicators. He and the others piloted their ships ahead of the fleet, visiting populated worlds, and living among them. The best way to judge a civilization was to slip in an Instrument to live a single lifetime among them. Borrowed bodies and hearts and minds that forgot all but the faintest tune of their lives as Metronomes. They visited worlds in pairs, leading separate lives, not meant to cross until the very end—maybe singing a few Metronome ditties about peace and love on the way—so they could be impartial.

I had to stop dancing when he told me this, just to sway against him. Drunk, in awe. Talk about boundless love. *I will step down from heaven for the others to toss them a ladder.*

I enlisted, too, after dancing long enough. I don't know, maybe the infinite bliss of the dancefloor had me restless. Always in a rush to see more. I took over as his partner from Purple. Me and Flynn poured the glittering Tempo fog of ourselves into blue-swirled glass bodies to pilot our ships and race each other through the stars. Flynn already had a ship, but I turned ours into hotrods. Tricked-out babies with killer radios and lights, fuzzy dice on the dash, and aftermarket mufflers.

Of all the off-the-hook magic we saw—peeling out around the rims of black holes, and surfing on nebulae, and tanning on the surface of suns—the most beautiful thing, each time, was meeting him again on different worlds. Telling him of the life I'd just lived, waiting for him. Loving him in a thousand different bodies. And seeing the way he spoke about me—on that nameless world where we first met—in his eyes every time. *He's special.*

* * *

We had a duty. Divine, boundless love, protecting life and all that jazz. We visited planets and lived among them. I even heard from one of the other Adjudicators that my home world—though my real home by then had become by Flynn's side—had survived a mass extinction. If they played their cards right, in a couple of million years they might be on track for Planetary Ascendance.

Here's hoping. We knew the instructions, the Score to the Metronome's plan. If a civilization played the right music, they could hang. They could join the chorus, and sing with us, and we'd give them technology, and guidance, and boogie until dawn. Too much bass in their tune and we had to turn their volume way down. The music leading up to that particular finale usually played out the same. A civilization discovered Tempo, then came the Tempo-fueled genocide. Bio-weaponry. Apocalyptic warfare. Occasionally, civilizations tossed us a disco biscuit to keep things interesting. Like that one that invented a perpetual Tempo-siphoning power plant that circled their star, just to fuel their solar-system wide entertainment empire.

By the time the World-Ship shimmered into the space by the planet me and Flynn had judged, we were usually back inside on the dancefloor. In case we ruled in favor of a Silencing, Flynn said we shouldn't stay and watch.

He'd seen too many.

One time I stayed, though. I idled my hotrod just outside of the World-Ship, turned up the tunes, and shook out the creaks and stiff muscles of wearing a flesh-and-blood body again. Really, I needed some space from Flynn after a particularly gnarly Adjudication where we didn't see eye-to-eye. The fact that this species had no eyes maybe had something to do with it. These cats had invented a Tempo-powered ship to travel back in time to get their ancestors to discover Tempo earlier. Clemency, I had ruled. Early Intervention. We pause the track on their progress and axe their time machine.

Silencing, Flynn had argued. Even if they don't mean it, time-travel is a weapon waiting for one bad cat.

You're too hard on them, I'd told him. *Going too soft is weakness, and weakness is dangerous*, he'd shot back. We'd fought and cried. He'd called out to me *Mitch, Mitchy* and used the Metronome music of my name while I'd called him an asshole. We'd hurt each other only like two beings who've circled suns together for a couple of billion years can. He'd overruled me, as the Senior Adjudicator. Funny, I thought we were equals until then. Until he'd looked at me like Purple had, a forever ago, gasping like a boiling fish about my Tempo glass.

They're not ready.

I watched the World-Ship surge forward. Music swelled. Glass panels popped off the ship and rearranged in dizzying patterns as Tempo fog swirled out and swallowed the planet whole. Bass beats rocked my ship, and the planet collapsed in on itself—along with ten billion souls, give or take—into a shuddering burnt yellow orb.

How's that preserving the natural order of things?

And I know watching a planet collapse probably doesn't compare to the horrors of seeing what unworthy civilizations do to themselves if they're left alone, according to what Flynn's seen. But. Funny how that shuddering orb looked a lot like the one in the engine compartment of my ship. And the rhinestone things that swirled around the giant warp engine in the World-Ship.

Tempo engines that run on the life force of dead worlds.

Power. Freely given, to the worthy. Freely taken from the unworthy.

I had to circle the block for a couple of years, weaving through asteroids and tuning my ship radio to pick up the fragments of that planet's music that was still drifting through the galaxy. Saint Donna of the Disco, the music that place made. All I heard was static, Silence. When I rolled back home, Flynn raced to me. He solidified his arms enough to hold me, and I could feel his words in sways and flashes.

I reckon I can do it because I focus on all the souls we bring to the Dance, and not the ones we have to leave outside, he said. *We pull away the weeds so the flowers can grow.*

Duty, I said. *Sacrifice.*

I let him lead in the dance. I tried hard to follow—telling myself *the flowers will grow*—but the music didn't sound the same.

* * *

We could've left. We could've taken leave for a century or two and just twirled under the lights. But we swore an oath, and we had a duty—serving the boundless love of creation was an honor. I try to serve in the way that I know how.

I started leaving ahead of our station assignments, to explore alone. Flynn let me go. He knew it was my version of wandering off from the others and climbing the crystal islets back on my home world. I always knew when it was time to leave the party before it started winding down, and the endless dancefloor of the World-Ship was no exception.

Our latest posting was going to be special, the other Metronomes sang to us. This little green-and-blue-swirled planet was smack-dab in the middle of a natural Tempo valley. The creatures there were already wrapped up in Tempo. And look, the cute little two-legged folks that will one day run the place are already painting on cave walls. From art to the Ascendency Scale in no time. They'll make wonders, adding to the ocean of light for all of us.

If they get there, Flynn was sure to add. *If.*

Call it a vacation for me and Flynn after serving for so long. I needed one, with how I started hearing different tunes out in the silence between the stars. *What are we doing? Who put us in charge?*

And brain me with a fish head, the beauty I saw, that last solo hotrod trip. I skimmed a blue giant, and popped the hatch on my ship to lean out, brushing my swirled blue-glass hands in its shimmering atmosphere. I barrel-rolled around planetary rings, and laid back on my hood watching the lightning crackle in a giant red spot of a storm that whirled over the next planet. I blazed donuts on the surfaces of asteroids and waved to the single-cell life wiggling in the red crust of the next world. Once I hit Earth, I parked *Rush* on a sweet flat patch of dirt, leaving plenty of room for Flynn to park *Bolt* right next to it. I slipped out of my blue-swirled glass body to sweep over this world as glittering fog like I always did, swimming in the vibes of the place. Then resting and waiting for the right Instrument to sing my song.

I waited to feel Flynn's hotrod blasting down into the atmosphere. Waited, and drifted, and so, so tired... and...

So alone. I probably should've waited another few thousand years to bounce from the Metronomes. I'm always in a rush. I could barely hear the music. I wasn't supposed to meet Flynn, in his shiny human Instrument, until near the end. But I should've at least heard the echoes of his music by now. So I shook myself awake and slipped over the sand, drawn to the music in a place called Miami. Drawn, more, to a kid crammed up in the catwalk, because even asleep by the switched-off spotlight, the forge-fire in his chest—angry, alone, scared—was the forge of my old world.

I was so weak, not much louder than a tune you'd hum, that he didn't notice me slipping into him while he slept. And I was him, anyway. More than any of the other Instruments I played, more than the blue-skinned me on a no-name backwater planet.

Just like when I first saw Flynn again at school, that deep-down part in me knew who he was, even if he didn't yet. He must've recognized me too. Instead of mind-flashes and dances, I threw fists. He disguised his dancing by running the track and vaulting over hurdles. We met too early for the Score, so he had to leave. He joined the service and I followed him.

Rush and *Bolt* flapping around each other like songbirds in the stars. Two boys dancing in circles. And circles and circles, again.

TWENTY-SEVEN

AN ARMY OF LOVERS

Alright. Pause the track. Alright alright alright. I've got a lot to catch up and piece together, before the memories fade away into the blue light. I'm myself. I can see and feel my life in Miami, and in the Guard, and here in LA—only I can hear the volcano forge hammers in the background. There's no separate Mitch and Metronome. Just—I don't know—Mitchronome? That has a far-out feel to it.

Flynn's head is on my lap in our sleeping bag pile in Fort Founding Mothers, the floor below the others, and he's looking up at me with those window-cleaner blue eyes. No, his eyes in this Instrument are the same color as the blue-swirled glass on the planet where we met, God knows how long ago. He's shivering and moaning while I'm trying not to crack up, so we're very much not dancing to the same music right now.

"You remember," he manages to bite out. "I didn't think you'd believe. I couldn't risk you heading for the hills, and losing you."

Rushing away, yeah. I probably would've. I needed a little time to understand the various amounts of absolutely fucking crazy he's been throwing at me the last few days. I sweep a hand through the messy waves of his hair. *The things we've seen already,* he told me, when we were naked and wrapped up in each other, that night after the disco.

"I'm starting to get the hang of it."

He told me before that he could choose to lean into his Metronome side or not. I know what he means, now, even if he's a little wrong. That's fine. My soldier's never been a whiz with Tempo.

There's only so much Metronome magic we can work in physical forms. As much as I very much dig this body and what I've done with a whole lot of men from here to Miami, no flesh and blood Instrument can play the whole music of Creation for long. The volume gets too loud and we burnout back to Tempo fog. Which would get in the way of our duty. Flynn told the others as much when he said only he could work enough Tempo to fix the Disharmony.

I really dig this planet. I don't want to see the Metronomes squash it down to a chunk of coal to toss in their engines once they get here. I can see the fuzzy projection that Kern showed us, like the Metronome ship is a bullet hole in space.

I don't remember everything. My brain can't hold millions of years of memories. Already, my Metronome life is drifting away on fog, leaving me with only fuzzy impressions. And the dizzy sweetness of dancing next to Flynn. I'll have time to sort that all out later when the Metronomes aren't about to drop down from space. I know that things aren't playing out like they should, according to the Score. I should not just have relived several million years of history. That track is supposed to play only when me and Flynn switch on the engines of *Rush* and *Bolt*—officially Adjudicating and summoning the other Metronomes in here for sentencing. We were supposed to have met up as stooped, old dudes who had to crank up the volume our hearing aids to swap life stories and sweeping generalizations about the Nature of Humanity, just like we always have.

Until that fucking idiot Kern got in the way. He messed with *Bolt*'s engine core, and cheesed off the Metronomes by turning their technology into a Disharmonic weapon forge. But why the hell did Flynn miss our landing zone and crash on the moon, anyhow?

When he sees me seeing this, he winces

"*Bolt*'s been acting weird," he says. "I should've told you before we even flew to this posting."

"You think? Christ, try explaining to our friends upstairs that you basically handed your ship right over to Kern."

"Accidentally. My engine blew. I didn't remember, not until *Bolt* and *Rush* started hollering at each other."

He's lucky I love him. Oh my God, I want to throw him out the window. The exhaust fumes from the crushed world in *Bolt*'s engine core have been probably stinking up Earth, kicking up panic and madness. A broken world is bleeding all over this one. I'll have to explain to the Metronomes that Moral Codes and Studio Zones aren't typically the type of music this place plays.

Massaging Flynn's temples with my fingers, I trickle just enough Tempo into him to ease his shakes. I might not be able to levitate things, but I know my dance moves, now. Like I'm his battery, and together we spark big mojo. *He moves and sees Tempo*, he told shithead Purple about me. *He builds power and potential in others in a way we've never seen.*

"I reckon Gloria and the others'll be madder than a...

than a..." He trails, probably still too beat from blasting the Vanguards clear across the room to form a whole sentence.

I squeeze the bridge of my nose. "Tell me what you remember, now."

He rustles to sit up across from me. "I crash-landed on the moon. I was hurt, and confused, and all I could do was stay there and wait until my Instrument moseyed on over."

I shiver. All my annoyance at him leaks out, picturing him stranded on a rock, alone. So far from the dancefloor. I kiss his knuckles.

"Kern found the wreckage," I say. "*Bolt*'s engine core... spoke to him. Called out for revenge against the Metronomes, and showed him how to make living Tempo weapons he's calling his Vanguard. Seems like his plan was to hand an army of super-powered God's Guardsmen over to Reagan to *enforce* American values all over the world. The Metronomes found out about his experiments and—"

"Human experimentation with Metronome technology. Yeah, I remember that from Kern's sermon." He winces. "Holy moly. That's the Disharmony."

"Right-o."

"Kern messing with *Bolt* must've tripped the companion beacon and pointed him to where *Rush* was parked."

"How come we didn't feel the Vanguards in the Manifold?" I ask. "Did you?"

"No. Honest word. Best guess is that it's because their power comes from my engine core, and not the whole Tempo flow."

I hold back a shiver, remembering the Metronome voice from my last whopper of a vision at the disco. *Your existence is a drain on the Collective. It must be Silenced.*

"The Metronomes'll—"

Flynn snaps, brighter. "They'll be madder than a turkey in a tailpipe."

So he's almost himself again. "Get it together, Pensacola." I squeeze his hands. "How do we keep them from Silencing this whole place? We get *Bolt*'s engine core out of Kern's hands?"

"At least."

"That'll prove that we're worthy?" I ask. "Even after everything..."

Everything we do to each other, I want to say. I hold in my next breath, sinking, as I look into his eyes. I see crystal islets there, and a lost boy on a fire escape, and a former starman in me and Gloria's apartment telling me about his life, then running out of air when I asked him about Camp Puller. *Some things you don't speak about.*

"'Sorry' seems small and stupid to say, after all you saw in Camp Puller." I try to trickle some warmth into him, through my hands. I hope it reaches my eyes. "Sorry, just the same."

"I tried to heal those memories. Turns out with all the Tempo I got inside, that's still not how things work."

"I reckon." I tug his hands. "More ghosts."

"I just added 'em to the pile of all the things we've done. All the things we push down." His sigh sweeps over us as he looks down at our intertwined fingers. "The top Metronome brass said this place was sitting in some natural valley of Tempo. I'da thought that would mean things like Puller wouldn't happen here. Guess it's the same as everywhere else."

We're quiet for a while. Safe in the silence beyond Hat-Trick's music bubble. When we got here and ditched the van, I told Stetson to grab some backup and form a perimeter at the windows of the first-floor apartments. At the first sign of anything fishy—say, Guard rovers peeling around the corner, or pissed-off starmen floating on toxic yellow fog clouds—he launches one of his sweet bubble barriers around the place to buy us some time. Now that I've reminded him of what he can do.

Regroup. Backup. Perimeter. Adjudicator or starman, I'll always be a soldier.

"Think these bodies can work enough Tempo to overpower the Vanguards without burning out?" I ask.

"Assuming Kern doesn't make more of 'em? Let's hope so. Not to mention we gotta find a way to get past his regular soldiers."

"You ain't giving me much to go on, Senior Adjudicator man."

His next wiggle looks something like the flash-dance combo of *sorry* on the world we met.

"Two against an army." Flynn tugs his Space Guard jacket closed against a cold wind. "I don't like those odds."

Nah. Two, nothing. We've got a whole Army of Lovers waiting upstairs.

* * *

I'm not surprised that Gloria and the others are laughing when me and Flynn join them on the main floor of Founding Mothers. The world has been ending for people like us for years. Gloria's laughter lights me up as I spot her in the afternoon glow of the windows. She's in the kitchen making a peanut butter sandwich and adding it to the stack on the plate next to her on the counter. Ricky and Lainey are passing more sandwiches out to the hundred or so Deviants lounging around the fort in puppy-piles on pillows. Bette and Rex puff cigars by the window closest to the stage, while Juana is parked at her typewriter, writing and flicking her cig over a crowded ashtray.

Peanut butter mixes with patchouli incense, mixes with Hat-Trick's shimmer-starred tunes. His cans are over his ears and he's swaying over his Moog. I want to bawl like a baby and mind-flicker and hip-wiggle about how perfect all of them are. I can't look at Gloria or I'm a goner, seeing her put me back together again in our apartment when she first drove me there from Sunshine City. I can't hide anything from her, anyhow, and I asked Flynn not to mention the whole *funny story, I'm a Metronome thing, too* to them. Because of Gloria. She's my last link to Mitchell Ward, the Space Guard reject from Miami, and I know I'll have to let that part of me go. And her, hardest of all. Just not yet. One thing at a time.

And they have things to tell me, anyhow. Like how Gloria and Hat-Trick's music busted into the disco and saved me and Flynn.

I don't know the whole Metronome Score by heart thanks to the limits of my monkey noggin. I know *Rush* is under the disco, and that every time a big group of us danced there, we were working magic—even if that magic meant a night of joy away from the Moral Codes. But we added to the magic, too. It was something about the music. I remember drifting this world as fog, feeling drawn to music. Reed-flute songs on the shores of the Yangtze River in China. Eucalyptus-branch horn sections blasting in Australia's outback. Choruses singing in marble cathedrals in Italy, high off harmonies same as us disco queens huffing amyl. On other worlds, I remember how they discovered Tempo and it changed them. Through scientific discoveries, and artistic expression, and a bunch of slow, boring-ass stuff like societal change—waiting for decades or hundreds of years until the first beings that could directly work Tempo themselves were born. But something's different here. Maybe it's *Rush* under the disco. Probably disco itself—like the star-song from the Moog that finally let us speak the Metronomes' language. Whatever the reason, something on Earth is speeding up the track, and spitting out near-Ascended Beings that can work Tempo like wizards.

"Aren't you going to say 'thank you' to us for saving your pale behinds?" Gloria sings out.

Flynn zips over to her, with me close at his back, and he sweeps her up. She swats his shoulders with peanut butter fingers, laughing, while he spins them.

"Thank you to this be-*yooooo*-tiful angel." Flynn puts her down and drops to one knee, sweeping his arms out wide, his eyes dancing.

"Thank me by getting the Metronomes to get me a record deal," Gloria adds.

It should make me happy that my best friend and my—what, universe-crossed lover of untold years?—are pals now. Gloria's eyes meet mine and, damn it, she must know something's weird with me with how her head tips.

"How did you know to..." I trail off. "Do whatever the hell you did to help us?"

"Something sure feels different since last night." She licks peanut butter off her thumb and rests her hands on her hips. Her flower poncho flares out at her sides. "I got more gas in the tank now."

"We could hear you babies crying from a mile away." Bette swats her knee. "Pumped right through Patrick's speakers."

"Some after-effect from last night's Manifold?" I ask Flynn.

"We're all tangled up through Tempo," he says. "With all of it whippin' up when me and you were by the engine core, some feedback must've reached here."

"Lady Moondust led her own flower-power meditation session," Rex adds. "And then we, well..."

He elbows Bette, who walks over to Hat-Trick's speakers and picks one up like it's made of cardboard. I'm dizzy and giggling like someone spilled poppers nearby. Until Juana stubs out her cigarette, walks over to Bette who's still lifting the speaker like a circus strongman, and lifts them both without so much as a grunt. I already know Stetson slings bulletproof bubbles, Hat-Trick weaves magic music, and Gloria's got a hypnotic voice. She always has, I know, from all those times I felt her voice nudging me, and wrapping the crowd at the disco up in light when she sang. Only now she's got more gas in the tank.

"Rex, would you care to whip yours out?" Gloria asks.

He squares his hips towards us, plants his stocky legs, and slowly pulls his cigar from the corner of his mouth. Then, he huffs, tosses it in the air, and flicks both hands. *Flash.* The cigar is frozen in the air like he snapped it in one of his pictures. Flynn's mouth drops open while he patrols a slow circle around the levitating cigar.

"Well, I'll be." He whistles.

"Holy shit," I add.

Another few seconds and the cigar's track restarts, flying through the air and dropping to the floor by my feet. I stop it with my toe.

"It doesn't last very long," Rex grumbles, rubbing the back of his neck. "I'm still getting the hang of it."

Gloria's cat eyes smirk. Flynn catches my eye and waggles his fingers on his chin. No-name world speak, I know, but I don't remember what.

"Same as all of us," Juana says. She puts down Bette, and loops their arms together. "We don't know how strong we are."

"I'm hitting the body-building circuit," Bette cracks. "With that prize money, I'm wrapping baby here in mink from head to toe."

Almost like the air rings with music, even though Patrick hung up his headphones and is looking around at us with flying-saucer eyes. Who the hell are these crazy cats, really?

"Mitchell here can charge you up with more," Flynn says to Juana. "Same as he's been doing for me."

He gives me that weird fingers-on-the-chin waggle again.

Oh. Now I get what he's saying. Mind-flicker and finger waggle, backlit by the volcanic forge. *Ascendancy Scale.*

* * *

Flynn calls the next meeting of the Church of the Divine Deviants to order, and lovers wander from past the sheet maze to laze on pillows and sleeping bags on the floor around the stage. Flynn, Me, Gloria, Rex, Bette, and Juana sit in a line on the edge of the stage. Even Patrick leaves his DJ booth—arms out like a plane coming in for a landing—and parks it by my elbow. We're a band posing for our album cover. *The Rise and Fall of the Tempo Jockeys and the Metronomes from Space.*

Lainey and the other dolls tend to the altar by the stage, relighting the candles under the posters of Donna Summer,

Tina Turner, Judy Garland and the others. They wave incense and reapply their lipstick, floating to Gloria's feet in their flower crowns. Ricky's arms are tangled up around one of the bartenders I recognize from Studio One. Good for them. That guy never gave me the time of day. The Deviants are a sea of love beads and tight white t-shirts and glitter and pink lipstick and peanut-butter mouths. More of us than last night, I know the seamstresses are working to get more people here to safety.

"Before we get started," Lainey says. "We have a few updates."

"Updates?" Flynn asks.

Lainey snaps her fingers, rippling her tie-dyed bell sleeve, and hands pass something down to her from the back of the crowd. She holds up an axe and a wooden sign that says *fairy swatter.*

"Me and the girls made a little detour while we were getting supplies this morning," Lainey says. "Don't worry, we stayed off the main drags like you said, and didn't tango with Commdef. And last we heard the National Guard is only stationed downtown."

Gloria gives a disappointed lip-pinch while she loads up her cigarette holder. "Go on."

"We paid a visit to that skeevy singles bar off Sunset," Lainey says.

"The Glass Slipper?" Juana braces herself with her hands on her knees so she doesn't fall off the stage she's laughing so hard. "I've been writing articles about the dive for years, organizing picket lines to get them to take the axe off the wall, and—"

"Sister, they can sit on our picket lines," Daisy, one of the dolls draped in daisies, says. "Lainey stuck out her hand and Tempoed it right off the wall, righteous-like."

Gloria blows out a long plume of smoke. "Making momma proud."

Lainey curtsies as well as she can with one of the other dolls in a sequin toga in her lap. With a gameshow host flourish, Juana places the axe and the sign between the candles on the altar.

More of them pipe up. More *detours* during trips to the safe houses to pick up others. Stink-bombs tossed at cop cars and through straight bar windows. Pink triangles painted on the side of City Rovers. A disco ball borrowed from Outcast tossed right onto the hood of a Commdef cruiser while the officers were making a bodega bust. The squad of lovers almost got caught in that skirmish, though that would've been fine with them, one of them says. They would've blown the wall off the jail cell.

Yesterday in the Reels, Starman North talked about Reagan using Executive Order 77 as an excuse to send armed forces to cities to maintain Moral Public Order. Like Kern, yammering about the picture of the World-Ship. *If the United States government says that this image is light off gas, then it is light off gas.* How we're the *arbiters of truth.* Either the reinforcements for Commdef aren't here yet, or it's all just gas. Or Reagan needs all his muscle for the Liberation of Edmundston that the news anchor mentioned yesterday, when me and Flynn were watching TV at the apartment.

Either way, we told the Deviants to tell everyone they know about us, and they've been busy. What they've been doing sure as hell sounds like a raid for a raid.

I have to bite my cheek to keep from exploding into glittery mist and sweeping over them all. This is so much more fun than yapping about universal love and floating jam glasses.

I glance behind me at Flynn's scrunched eyebrows and the muscles at the sides of his jaw. He shuffles on his feet. "Tempo isn't a weapon," he says. The same thing he told Kern.

"Not a weapon," Ricky says. "But a message now and then don't hurt."

He winks at me and I could swoon right there on the edge of the stage.

* * *

Flynn paces the stage when he talks, his chin up like Lieutenant Parker. The late afternoon sun tosses square spotlights across his rigid shoulders, the repurposed floorboards of the stage creaking under his steady feet. He tells them how we found out that the Disharmony is an admiral from the Space Guard using Metronome technology to turn people into Tempo-slinging weapons. Oh, and by the way, the Guard detected the Metronome World-Ship in our solar system, and who knows how long we have until they're knocking on our door and sparking global panic.

"Fuck the man," Carla yells, her painted moustache still over her top lip from her appearance onstage last night as Manny Fest-Destiny.

"Fuck the nukes," Daisy turns the words into a song.

"New queer weapons, and not nuclear weapons," someone else yells. "And fuck the pigs, and the Moral Codes, and the fascist piece of shit president, and—"

"Big affirm to all that," Flynn agrees. "We'll get there. First orders, though—we have to neutralize the Vanguard and get the Metronome machine back."

We don't know if Kern and the Vanguard know where we

are. They could be on the way to us. Tonight, we have to get juiced up on the Manifold and try to take them out. Flynn has been yapping about how he alone will fix the Disharmony. Now he's whipping out *we* and *us. We have to... We'll neutralize.* We, we, we, all the way home. Like some of us moved up in rank.

Say, the six—at least—new Tempo jockeys in this holy house.

All you fine folks at the Circus Disco, please welcome to the ring, Lady Moondust with her Star-Song. Rex, the Time Freeze King. DJ Hat-Trick, bringing the Black-Hole Beats. Stetson, the Bullet-Proof Bubble Boy. Bette and Juana, the Strong-as-Steel Lovers.

Beautiful Circus Freaks. Plus, me and Flynn, the Metronome Men.

No more errands and detours for the day, Flynn decides. No one's going AWOL, or leaving the base, or leaving a soldier behind. When he gets the Guard in his voice, I can hear the chatter, and see the big eyes checking out. We ain't an army, I think is the vibe. We're something tighter.

"You know, back in the big ancient orgy days, there actually was an army of lovers," Laterian adds. He's Gloria's new beau—the classics professor at UCLA. I look at him, then to Gloria, and waggle my eyes like *get it, girl.* He adjusts his glasses. He knows how to make the nerd thing work. "Three hundred dude couples called the Sacred Band of Thebes."

"How in the hell did they get anything done?" Ricky asks, craning his neck. "They must've been too busy knockin' sandals."

"I got some stories about my time in the service for you," Rex says.

I whistle. "Same here."

And that's about when Flynn loses the plot on his sermon in the trenches. Everyone is staying. And we're throwing another rager tonight to give us the juice we need.

The sunset turns the windows behind Flynn into the burning bright light of the volcano forge.

TWENTY-EIGHT

PLACES, PLACES

The others drift away from the stage once Hat-Trick gets his beats pumping. Today's happy hour specials are Dr. Pepper and warm vodka, with visits to the sheet maze. I spot Ricky and his bartender buddy heading there and look over at Flynn. I should follow and show them each my thanks for *service to the cause*. He smirks, and in his eye-rolling I can see *sure, hurry*. I'm not changing myself now that I know I'm a Metronome, or now that I'm with Flynn. And he doesn't ask me to. Owning someone and controlling everything they do with their heart and body doesn't sound like boundless love to me.

Gloria stops me with a hand on the arm, though. Shit.

Her cat eyes sweep me up and down. She taps her chin, a slow smile spreading over her Cadillac Red-painted lips. "What's gotten into you?"

Mind-flicker. I can see us in the Boom Boom Room, flipping through magazines, and playing the game where we talk about everything other than how one of the other starmen messed with our air tanks again. Keeping something from her sends a twinge over my ribs.

"Just distracted." I nod over to the sheet maze. "You're right. We technically should come up with a plan before I go get my rocks off."

Her eyes narrow, unconvinced. I look away.

"Right," she says. Then softer, "Right."

Hat-Trick puts on a low, moody jazz record while Flynn gets Stetson from his watch duty downstairs. Stetson sends a few others down to replace him and tells them to scream if they see anything weird. We laugh until Stetson frowns and says, *No, really.*

And then things aren't so funny.

Jesus H., who left us in charge?

The other Deviants know to leave us in our own little bubble by Patrick's mixing table. *We need some sort of game plan to neutralize the Vanguard,* Flynn says. We're game pieces with certain moves. *Think of what we can do already,* Rex adds. Maybe Gloria can use her knockout voice to get the Vanguard to turn on each other. Or Rex can freeze them. Bette and Juana can use their muscles to rough them up if we need to. Stetson and his super shields can protect us. Or trap the Vanguard for Flynn to swoop in and see if he can pull the corrupted yellow smoke out of them, same as he borrows Tempo from me. All this, assuming we can lure the Vanguard someplace away from civilians and the other Lovers so they don't get hurt, and Kern doesn't call in his platoon of starmen, or the army, or the National Guard, or whoever to load us up with bullets first. But we can't think like that.

"We gotta heal them." A spray can wrapped in a puff of fog floats above Gloria's outstretched palm. "The Vanguard."

Bette bumps her fists together. "I got a way to heal 'em real good."

"No," Gloria says. "They're tangled up in this, same as us. Ain't no way that they deserved whatever Kern did to them. They didn't know what they were signing up for."

She didn't see them choking out Flynn with plumes of toxic yellow fog like I did. "If the only way to stop them is to—"

And then Gloria's eyes hit me. I don't finish that thought. I look away, so I don't accidentally beam what I'm thinking out with my eyes. *Would they do the same for you?*

"We heal them," Flynn says. "Honest word. We find a way."

I have an idea of where we can set our own trap for the Vanguard. There's just the sticking point of how we're going to get them there.

That sends Patrick zipping back behind his command center. He snaps his cans around his ears and holds the microphone like it's a turkey leg he's about to bite into.

"Uhhh, sir?" Patrick's voice streams out of the speakers, jittery with static. "We're getting multiple reports of wild homosexual be-havior happening all around the city. No lyin', you should definitely split up your security straights into multiple teams and send 'em out to investigate. And this for sure isn't a trap. Awwwww sooky sooky—over 'n' out."

Funny, if we can just get him to talk less like a space cadet, it almost sounds like his voice is coming out of my space suit helmet radio. Or the two-way radio on Kern's belt.

"Now they're flying right down from the skies at us!" Patrick yells. He fiddles with the dials on his board and an electric *ooo-eee-oooo* whine ripples through the air. "They're everywhere. Oh, the humani—arghhhhhh!"

Patrick heaves dramatically, hands flying around his neck. Gloria flaps the big sleeves of her flower poncho on over to

Patrick and moves the giant can of one of his headphone to kiss him by his ear.

"Something like that?" she asks us.

Patrick's smile warbles like the volume in the room is too high, his space-cadet eyes swimming.

"Something like," Flynn agrees. "Just—we'll polish up that military talk."

Patrick shrugs. "I can dig it."

We move down into the apartment below the top-floor loft and leave the others to party. The ceiling over our head creaks, dropping dust as the Lovers dance. Lucky that Hat-Trick extends his magic Mute button around the whole building, keeping our racket from filling the neighborhood. In the dishwater glow of the streetlights, the apartment is a lunar landscape, sketched in pencil. Dust as moon dust, spray paint cans and old beer bottles as boulders. We work up a sweat, squinting and letting Tempo love flow through us as we float spray paint cans and test the limits of our power. Well, *their* power. I mostly watch as Rex floats beer bottles, flings them against Stetson's bubble shields, and freezes the glass shards mid-air. Bette busts a bottle against her forehead and it shatters like a movie prop made of sugar glass. Flynn has the big idea that instead of me passing the power of the whole Manifold to just him—and it flickering out because there's only so much juice his human body can take—maybe it'll last longer if I give it to all seven of them. I don't know how much use I'll be once I'm done being their battery.

I find myself apart from the others, hanging by the window and smoking a butt. I want to train with them or dance with the others upstairs, but the beat of the music is different for them than it is for me and Flynn. We don't belong here. Not really, when we'll just have to leave when we prove to the Metronomes this world is worthy enough to live.

And Gloria. I can see the hurt in her cat eyes when she finds out who I really am. That I'm a part of the people who gave us these powers and this warning. *Heal, or feel the Silence.* That I've traveled worlds, and judged, and watched them snuffed out to an ember. I doubt she saw any of that in her star charts.

Double Libra, beware the unexpected responsibilities new roles bring.

"Some Saturn's return, right?"

Her red-painted nails tap a tune on the side of her face—the same wordless message beamed out by the crinkled edges of her eyes. *There goes the Mitch Thing again, keeping me out.*

I sigh and suck in smoke, looking away. "You got any advice from the stars on how to deal with this pickle we're in?"

"Trust your gut. Be yourself. Easy enough."

"And who's that, exactly? Starman, soldier, Deviant, or...?"

She plucks my cigarette from between my fingers, forcing me back to her cat smile.

"Mitchell Lazarus, I know exactly who you are. And we're gonna make magic tonight."

I frown at her. "I still don't like the idea of you in the field like this. You should stay back here and make sure the others are safe."

"This 'protecting me' gig is startling to feel an awful lot like control." From anyone else, the words would sting, but her timbre turns them sweet as caramel. "And the only man I'm about to answer to is Christ Almighty, if He sees fit to drop down from the sky."

The flame of the cigarette flares when she takes a hit. When she blows out smoke, I'm the one that's hazy-edged and flying all apart across empty beer bottles and spray paint cans.

* * *

Patrick left his tunes playing while we practiced with our Tempo abilities, and by the time we run back up the stairs, all charged up, the air fizzes like shaken Dr. Pepper. Hundreds of Lovers slink and spin to the beats, moving like one. Others neck against the walls. The smell of warm bodies and spilled booze and patchouli incense and the stink of cooling concrete in the night. Ricky pouring his magic elixirs, and Lainey and the dolls twirling on stage in a riot of rhinestones while passing around the axe that they ripped right off the goddamned wall.

Just before we séance into the silver-beaded fringe of the Manifold—as Gloria sings and spins in a flurry of sequins on stage—I look up at the disco ball. My vision blurs into blue. I see a giant ship's outer panels snapping and whirring, locking into new positions and spinning through the blackness. I hear the song of the engines, and breathe in the shimmering fog that trails the World-Ship like a million comet tails. I can feel their music.

We are almost there.

Tick, tick, tick. The sound of the Tempo engines cooling as they slow and prepare for entry.

Off in the distance—just an easy jump on the dancefloor, really—a little blue and green world is a bead against the black.

And then we dance and sway as one, the power building and surging through the silver-beaded fringe, and I let it flow to us Tempo jockeys. Hugging, kissing their cheeks, holding them tight, until we're cackling down the stairs of Spindler's Arms and into the alleyway where Flynn parked his van—billowing fog everywhere, with Gloria giggling for us to keep it down.

TWENTY-NINE

SMOKE SIGNALS

I figured we needed an enclosed place far enough away from the Studio Zones, Founding Mothers, and crowded residential neighborhoods for our Vanguard pirate showdown. I never did make it back to the Tomcat Bookstore—a sweet little blue building with blacked-out windows down a seedy stretch of businesses—before the gay propaganda laws shut down the magazines, and Moral Codes shut down our hangouts. So tonight, it's two birds, one stone, baby.

The shelves in the maze of magazine racks are mostly empty. Muscled bodies on posters around the room watch our perimeter. The lighting of this place—the single room not much bigger than one of the apartments in Spindler's Arms—is dim by design. The overhead lights buzz and struggle against the shadows. We've got the front door and the back entrance out to the parking lot, which is past the black curtain and at the other end of a hallway of coin-operated video-viewing booths. Two entry points are easy for us to keep track of. A wall clock over the back hallway tells me it's just past midnight. Patrick already worked his sound-wave magic into the small radio the owner left behind at the checkout area by the door, with its glass shelves cleared of condoms and toys. *We've got some kind of an attack at RKO Studios*, he said into the speaker. A few minutes later he whipped out his best Humphrey Bogart as a cop impression, shouting, *Reports of civilian-led riots at Hwarner Brothers!* Next was Paramount, with word about Studio Security rovers flipped over by smoke bombs, somehow. In mind-flashes, I could see Kern and his men reaching for the radios at their belts. Finally, Patrick barked about *freaks storming the Tomcat Bookstore with one in a Space Guard jacket at the front.*

Now we're on patrol, with me, Flynn, Gloria, and Rex watching the front door, and Bette, Juana, Stetson and Patrick with eyes on the back. The Vanguard better be on the way here if our plan is going to work. I can already feel the juice we worked up through the Manifold wanting to trickle out to doubt and panic.

Eyes on the magazine covers follow us as we pace the musty blue carpet of room. *Special Issue: Globe-Trotting in Greece. Up Close: Our Interview with Mayflower Studios' Kit Caber. September Pictorial: Wrestling Meat.* I'm about to grab one of the magazines for good luck when a crash has me spinning.

I whirl and spot Bette huffing down over a busted bookshelf.

"That's for booting me outta my own goddamned club." Bette kicks at the splintered wood.

So much for Flynn telling us to conserve our strength.

"Easy, bruiser," Juana coos, patting Bette's arm. "I'm sure that big, bad shelf is really sorry."

Flynn steps past the cash register, deeper into the middle of the room. The overhead lights play off the buttons on his Space Guard jacket.

"Did you hear that?" he asks.

My heartbeat slams at the side of my neck when I hold my breath. I don't hear anything. Until—wait. Do I? Like we're in the sleeping bag pile below Founding Mothers and the lovers are dancing above.

"Pigeons on the roof?" Gloria whispers, her eyes widening.

"Wait," Flynn hisses. "Wai—"

The ceiling crashes in on us. Flynn sweeps his arms back, knocking me, Gloria, and Rex against the front wall as a chunk of the ceiling rains to the carpet. I knock my skull and see stars. Metal screams. Flynn screams. I push off the wall to run to him but two fists of glittering fog knock me out of the way. Another chunk of ceiling thuds to the floor where I was just standing. Mangled wires spark from the broken lights.

I look up at a storm cloud of yellow bombing down at us from above.

A shadow in a black jumpsuit drops down from the cloud first, landing in a half-crouch on the carpet. He's ten feet away from me, but I can feel the burns on Saito's horror-frozen face like the fire is torching mine. His swollen red eyes hit me, and I whip to my feet, waiting for the blow. Amato and DuBois land next. Another smoke fist from Flynn, and Saito turns his attention from me and whirls on him in a yellow cyclone.

Thud. Thud. Clouds of yellow smoke whip magazines off the shelves. I crane my neck at the footsteps above, and Hernandez and Costa burst through the ceiling and land on the carpet by Bette and the rest of the rear patrol. They're on their own because Amato winds his arms back, whips them out, and two yellow fog snakes clamp around my neck. I snarl and grapple at the smoke but my fingers slip through, even as the snakes swirl tighter and tighter. Even as Amato—arms out, fingers clenching—stalks closer.

Now would be a fucking good time as any to feel those magic love waves working through me. I thrash against the smoke.

Mind-flash, a blur of movement, and Rex is a glowing-eyed king at my side.

"Freeze," he hisses at Amato, voice echoing.

Amato stops and the snakes around my neck loosen just enough for me to wheeze a breath in. Slowly, his face twists, flashing his fangs. One arm twitches. Another. One leg moving, breaking free from Rex's hold, inch by inch, while the stink of burning air sizzles off Rex.

"I got you, kid," he says, one hand on my arm.

I wheeze in more air, burning up. In a crackling storm of sequins, Gloria waves her hands, whirling clouds between me, Rex, and Amato. Her laugh is the thunder. Her eyes are the lightning.

"You," she says, her voice vibrating with laughter. "To him."

She flicks a hand to DuBois, and Amato breaks free from Rex's slo-mo and pounces on his fellow Vanguard.

I drop to the floor and Gloria bends over me. So much for me needing to protect her.

"Go!" I yell, shoving her off. I swat at Rex, one hand brushing against his barrel chest, and I try to feed whatever Tempo I can into him.

I manage a look out to my right at Bette, Juana, and Stetson at the other end of the bookstore, where Stetson heaves a glowing bubble shield at Hernandez, spiraling him off his feet. To my left, Flynn and Saito are warring tornados of smoke.

Rex darts left and Gloria dances right. I just need one more second to catch my breath before the darkness at the edges of my eyes swallows me whole.

Music spills out of the radio by the front door. Yes. Hat-Trick must be working his magic. We know the dance. I sprint to Flynn and Rex, my eyes crackling in the darkness. The music makes Saito hesitate just enough for me to slam into him from behind. He teeters on his feet and Flynn leaps into the air—tossed up by two jets of fog from his hand—and pounces as I stumble away. He knocks Saito down, knees on his chest, and pins him to the dirty carpet. Saito thrashes and a yellow fog blast knocks Rex in the face. Rex's grunt cuts over the racing heartbeat tune, as he tumbles to his stomach, spitting blood.

Red droplets splatter against glossy magazine covers.

Heat starts in my lungs and then smolders into my eyes, almost blinding me as I whip down to hold Saito's wrists as he bucks under Flynn. Flynn's face is twisted into a snarl, his teeth like fangs. I see the dance in the way he jerks his shoulders, trying to hold down Saito. *We have to stop him.*

Mind-flicker. In the space suit, the yellow smoke suffocates Saito in the lab on the moon. He screams and burns from the inside out. And I know. I know he's a person as much as Kern turned him into a weapon. But there's blood on the magazines and Rex is struggling to his knees.

The volcano forge in me cranks up until I'm shaking. It burns away my air and crackles light out of my eyes. I let in more of the alien part of Mitchronome even if it'll burn me to ash. *I feel love.* Yeah. I feel something stronger, too—something that tastes like cigarette ash. Something that I see reflected in Flynn's narrowed, struggling eyes. Go to the others for love.

Go to Last Mitch Effort for something harder. Something that incinerates magazines, and peels off skin, and blasts open airlocks and—

Hat-Trick's music cuts out. Somewhere behind me, Bette screams.

Let the others be the light and the fog. I'll be the fire.

A bloodhound growls, using my throat. A boiling Tempo cloud rolls out of my chest and through my hands that I press to the side of Flynn's face. We gasp as one. Burnt yellow smoke bubbles out of Saito's skin and swirls around Flynn. He breathes it in—still holding down Saito until he stops struggling—as I hold my breath against the invasion. No time. No time. I can feel silver-beaded fringe threads snapping as the Tempo tide in us starts to roll out.

Yellow snakes of fog knock me and Flynn off Saito. I skitter against the carpet, grunting. Flynn is already crouching, then up he pounces at DuBois and Amato, who broke free of Gloria's voice. And then everything is streaks of light and yellow smoke and glittering fog. A hurricane of magazine pages.

Flynn burns the yellow fog out of a screaming DuBois, while Rex freezes Amato. They can handle this end. I knock over magazine shelves as I sprint to Gloria and the others. Bette is an unmoving clump on the carpet. Patrick too. Gloria is lifting Hernandez a foot off the floor with a smoke snake while Juana bashes him with her fists. Stetson, his arms outstretched, has got Costa trapped in one of his bubble shields. Stetson grits his teeth as every punch from Costa pushes him back another few inches across the carpet.

"I can't hold him!" Stetson snarls at me.

I can't keep the heat, and the pain, and the ripping bass cord of my rage, in either. A minor chord blasts out of me, knocking Hernandez and Costa together into a heap on the carpet. Unmoving for the two seconds it takes for Flynn to surge from behind us, a yellow and white smoke cyclone spinning all around him, and reach out. Tendrils of yellow and white smoke twirl from Flynn's hands, pinning the last of the Vanguard to the floor.

Their screams are disharmony. They gasp and gurgle and choke as the yellow smoke evaporates out of their pores and whirls into Flynn. At my side, Gloria tightens, the light fading from her eyes as she fights back tears.

Tick, tick, tick. We don't have time for tears and hugs, and I'm sorry—I'm so sorry, Gloria—because others are coming. Not Kern himself because we know that men like him give the orders and send the soldiers. He'll send more goons, guns, and tanks, and we have to leave.

Hernandez and Costa gurgle and cough on the floor. At least they're alive.

One flick of my hand and I blast a hole through the wall of the bookstore. Rex helps Patrick up—he's barely moving—Juana lifts a still Bette, and we run into the parking lot. Sirens in the distance. We pile into the van with Flynn behind the wheel, whooping and pounding, and peel off down the road. I rip down sky flowers and telephone poles and they careen to the ground behind us. I yank invisible puppet strings and parked cars screech and squeal into the street at our tail, scattering the police cars and blocking the way. One hand on the dash of the car, pumping heat into the engine. Faster, faster—*ooo burn, baby, burn*—until the fog from my hands fizzles to nothing.

Panting, and teeth poking out of my snarling lips, I barely recognize my own face in the van window.

* * *

In the van, just sniffles and silence the last stretch of the way. We're slick with sweat. A constellation of dried blood streaks down Rex's chest from his nose. Patrick, his face bruised, cradles his arm, moaning. At least Bette is breathing in Juana's arms, even if she's not moving yet.

"I couldn't hold him back," Stetson whispers, shaking with his tears. "I couldn't, I couldn't..."

"I know," Juana says, hoarse.

Gloria leans over Bette, smoothing her eyebrows, a tuneless hum weaving from her throat.

The light and the laughter fades from Flynn. He's quiet, even as I reach across the space that divides us up front and grab his hand. He tears his eyes off the road just for a second, and when they hit mine, I see the truth there.

Same as fog twirled around him in the bookstore, I can see flashes of clouds circling the Earth. I can hear the engines.

The Metronomes are here. We're too late.

* * *

We march slowly up the entry stairs as we lug Bette into the freight elevator—Patrick limping at the rear—and drift through the sheet maze to the front loft. Shadows wrap the place, still hours from dawn. Late Sunday night. Really, early Monday morning in LA. *Tick, tick, tick. Too late.* On the dancefloor, the Lovers look like corpses, crumpled in piles and trippy angles, all tangled up together. Ricky's laid out on top of some boy's chest. Both breathing. All of them, breathing. I try to pull a Flynn and tell myself they're just sleeping off a hangover.

Flower crowns from the dolls are trampled on the floor.

When the Metronome ships shiver down from the clouds, we'll see fighter jets racing out to meet them. And fire in the sky, and blood and bodies on the ground. And no more music.

Fun to think we had a chance. To stay on the dancefloor, and kick up Tempo, and forget that it was eight of us against the world outside, and the World-Ship blasting here on the way.

Lainey rustles to her knees when we walk through to the couch by the kitchen. She blinks her big eyes at how crazy we must look. Her black braids unravel when she sweeps her hands through her hair.

"The disco biscuits musta got me good," she says, eyeing the piles of Lovers around her.

"Sleep, baby," Gloria tells her.

Rex rests Bette on the couch and Juana sweeps to the floor to kiss her girl's hands. All of us hold vigil, shifting on our feet, and wiping our faces. I accidentally kick over a stack of *Honcho* magazines I left by the couch. Stupid. Leaving a mess everywhere I go. Hot tears track down my cheeks. Flynn slicks back Bette's Elvis pompadour and I can feel him trying to trickle Tempo into her. I know his power doesn't work like that. He can only take and not give.

I kiss Bette's forehead hoping I can heal her, somehow. Wishing I could hear her sing out, *look alive, boys!*

Silver-beaded soundwaves tie me and Flynn together. Lovers at the forge, and streaking across the sky in our hotrods, and on the fire escape as kids. Gloria won't look my way. That hurts more than a smoke snake choking the life out of me.

In the breeze that slips through the sheets over the busted windows, the borrowed disco ball spins overhead, dropping glass fragments on the Army of Lovers sleeping on the floor.

THIRTY

METRONOME MEN

Downstairs in our sleeping bag pile, Flynn whispers that he's freezing even though his skin scalds. I wriggle us both out of our clothes and press my body to his. In his eyes I see blue crystal islets swirled over with yellow fog. I have to be strong for him. I have to lock the questions behind my teeth when I kiss his eyebrows and the back of his jaw. *Did this even work? And look, Flynn, at the others, and...* The same questions I saw on the faces of the others. Patrick's bruised face. Blood in the salt-and-pepper hair on Rex's chest. Stetson whimpering, *I couldn't hold him back*, while Juana kissed Bette's hand on the couch. Gloria looking away.

"The—the Tempo from the engine core I pulled from the Vanguard." Flynn convulses with shivers. "Or... it's more than Tempo. Like it's alive." Another shiver curls his lips. "It's angry."

"Can you let it out?"

"I'm sure trying to. Or to heal it."

"I'm here. Take what you need from me."

He stiffens, gritting his teeth, and is quiet for so long that I think I've lost him. I almost break apart into mist, until he heaves in a breath.

"Once I'm out of this body I should be fine." His sigh is a sandpaper scrape. "We'll be home soon."

Home. We'll leave these Instruments behind. And the blue-swirled glass bodies, too, and turn to mist and slink into each other and all the others in the World-Ship's dancefloor. I know he means it to sound comforting, but right now home sounds like sleeping on a couch next to a stack of magazines and dirty laundry. With Gloria up early for church, and I can hear her in the bathroom, singing in the shower.

"And everyone here?" I peel myself off his sweaty chest to look down at him. "We leave them to get Silenced? Is stopping the Vanguard enough, or do we gotta go after Kern, too?"

"His c-cornbread's not done in the center." He stiffens and breathes through another avalanche against his lungs. "Crazy."

"We have to get the engine core away from him. Even if we have healed the Vanguard, he'll just make more."

"How?"

"Or—or we work out a deal with the Metronomes. Early intervention, same as on my planet. We evacuate Gloria and the others, as beings of Ascended Potential, and..."

He kisses my knuckles—though it's mostly a wince against my skin—and I know it's so he can look away from my eyes. How dare he. I saw the same look on Purple's face, a forever ago. *They're not ready.* How dare he think that when I want snap at him, *this is your fault.*

I hold my breath and let the heat move through me, trying to give it away.

"The Metronomes wouldn't Silence this whole world because of Kern," I tell him. "He's one asshole, sure. But the Metronomes have seen worse, yeah?"

He shivers. "Unholy. Unworthy."

"I *know* what they said. We still gotta try."

He pulls me back down to him. Even weak and shivering like this, he squeezes just a little too hard. He presses his chin to the top of my head.

"We'll try," he says.

The dark sky through the cracked window looks too much like when the volcano clouds blocked out the light over the black sand beach of my first home. I have to close my eyes and try not to get pulled under the green waves.

* * *

Flynn has either fallen asleep or passed out beneath me. At least he's breathing normally again. When the nightmares bowled me over before, I could always count on Gloria to wake me up. After my screams woke her up, first. Sleep's not finding me tonight, not with how I can still hear our screams through the magazine-whipping hurricanes. Not with Gloria avoiding my eyes.

I wait until the first pink light hits the windows, then slip out of the sleeping bag pile. I almost fish Flynn's keys out of his jeans and drive the van over to the disco to finish this myself. But I can't leave without making things right, first.

I climb the stairs to the top floor where Gloria is parked at her sewing machine in the corner. She changed out of her blood-spattered poncho into a loose white shirt dress knotted at the waist. She's pushing the pedal so gently that the machine barely makes a noise as the needle jabs in and out of red ruffled fabric. She looks up and knows. She always knows what I'm thinking.

She takes her sweet time loading up a Virginia Slim into her cigarette holder, lighting it up, and bringing it to her Cadillac Red-painted lips.

We patrol in silence past sleeping lovers in piles, and the sheet maze, to where the burnt, jagged black timbers are holding up the dawn sky in the back of the building. I don't know how this whole place doesn't fall to the ground.

Side by side, waiting. I light up, too, and we both blow out smoke for a while.

"Those things'll kill you," I sing out to her, my own cigarette sticking to the corner of my lips.

Her next breath sends a long blurry line of gray smoke into the perfect air. She lets it drift away before she turns.

"Check your tank," she says. "You're either choking or about to fill me up with hot air."

Oof. Right in the gut. Eyes, reading me like a star chart.

I try to laugh her off. "Go on, sister. Tell me what's what."

"You want to tell me what the hell happened? Between us getting pummeled, and Flynn getting possessed by a fog demon and—what—almost killing Hernandez and the others? Even if they were real so-and-so's to us—"

"Kern pumped poison into the Vanguard, and Flynn sucked it out."

"Flynn can suck on an egg. He gave me his whole honest word he'd heal them."

She plucks her cigarette out of the holder and tosses it over the side of the building. To hell if the rest of this place burns.

"He did. And it almost killed him. The Disharmony—"

"You want to talk Disharmony? Who gets to decide what's

Disharmony or not? The Metronomes? What makes them so special?"

"They—"

"*Don't.*" Bam. I get the full lean of her voice—echoing to the burnt beams, scattering birds. She draws in a long, shaky breath. "The Metronome machine that did that to those boys. What was it?"

"The engine of Flynn's ship."

"A ship that's runnin' on something that causes that much pain seems straight-up like the devil's work, Mitchell. I know who I serve. If you're some battery you oughta be real careful of who you give power to."

"You want to jive-talk power? You seem to dig floating jam glasses, and using your magic voice up there on stage."

My breath is a forge-blast. I regret the words the second they leave my mouth.

"I ain't your ma. I can share the spotlight."

Her eyes soften into something like a *sorry*. But she can't take her words back, same as I can't take back mine.

"You know every time I hit that stage at Circus Disco it was never about me," she continues. "I wanted to... *want* to take all of us outta here. Even for a night. Even for a couple of hours. That ain't a fix for everything. But that's something. And something's not nothing."

"I know."

"What do you even know about what Flynn really wants? Who he really is?"

I have to turn away so she doesn't see the thoughts flying outta my eyes. *What do you even know about who I really am, Glor?*

If she knew all I've seen, and been a part of—the judging,

the flying off before the Silencing because I was too scared to stay and see what I had a hand in making happen—she'd never look at me the same. Let the word burn instead. Her hating me would be worse.

"More than you think," I say. "And... and me and Flynn are fixing this. I promise."

"You two are making decisions for us—*all* of us—and you're keeping us in the dark. It's ain't right. This ain't about being jealous, or thinking Flynn is taking you away from me, or—"

"I know it's not."

"And goddamnit, Mitchell. Goddamnit!"

I have to look away before the tears in her eyes and in her voice tip me over the edge.

"I can hear that same stubborn song," she says. "You shoving me out. The Mitch thing. I'm a part of this. A big part of it. And. And, there's something here." Her loose-balled fist knocks against her chest, over her heart. "Something big and bright. And gold. Something I gotta do, or something I gotta say, and..."

Please, my eyes beg her, though I'm not sure for what. *Please.*

I can see her eyes playing our old game of either or. *Either or. Who do you trust more, Flynn, or me?* She knows the answer in my eyes isn't for her.

"I promise, I'll make this right," I tell her. "I promise."

She turns away from me, back to the burned timbers and the hole in the roof. All the better, so she doesn't see me crack. Angry. Sad. I've never been good about knowing which feelings are which, and now the tracks are even more tangled up. I pretend I'm wiping my nose and brush away the tear before Gloria can see it. A tear is more I've given to anyone else with how I keep the airlock door of my chest clamped shut. Flynn scolded me for being too soft, when we judged other worlds. The same tune that Watkins sang when he told me, *then you man up, and when the heat starts rising in you, you lock those feelings behind an airlock door.*

"That's it, then?" she asks softly, her eyes on the sky.

"I don't know."

"Promise me you're not going to do something stupid."

"Not sure I could keep that promise if I made it."

My fingers tap on my jeans. I should get back to Flynn. I'm about to go when she half-turns back to me.

"We never did talk about what we heard in the mist that day on the moon," she whispers.

"No."

"You first."

"I didn't hear so much as I saw. I didn't know it at first, but I know now that I got a vision of Flynn's ship crashing on the moon. Then a voice telling me not to be afraid. And that I was joining in the dance."

"That would've been nice."

Thank God for the cat smile she lays on me.

"You?" I ask.

"I heard a voice telling me some racket. 'Unsuitable Instrument, lacking the power for the Song. They will not hear her.'" She puffs air. "I know who I am. Ain't nobody got to tell me."

"Maybe they were right." I can't stop the words. "I mean, just that—that Flynn is supposed to be the one with enough power to save us, and..."

She stays quiet, looking away. The hurt in her cranks up the hurt in me, and we're just dancing circles around each other. So I leave without saying another word. She'll forgive me for shutting her out when I save her. She'll have to understand.

I let Flynn sleep a while longer—*good glory in the morning*—until I know we have to move. We might've knocked Kern's pieces off the board, but he'll just make more. And I can't let more pain happen to more people if I can help it.

Flynn is a gray ghost, shaking and shivering as he buttons my flannel down his muscled chest. His face is smudged with yellow. He doesn't let me help him into his Space Guard coat. Once it's around his shoulders, he straightens up. My starman. He's not running from duty, now.

I don't say goodbye to the others. My family up there must feel me, same as I feel them. Out on the sidewalk with Flynn, I look up at the top windows of Founding Mothers. I swear I see pale-faced Bette pulling the sheet away from the window, and pressing her fingertips on the glass. *Go get 'em, Junior.*

And look at that perfect blue sky. All the Mayflower artists couldn't have painted a prettier backdrop if they tried.

* * *

Flynn is shaking too hard to drive. I help him buckle himself into the passenger seat until he pushes away my hands, cracking about how he's not a cripple. He's a starman. He can shake this off with an easy jog.

The van's engine rumbles under me—*ignition, we have liftoff.*

We putter onto Santa Monica, headed to Circus Disco, and the standstill Monday morning traffic makes the endless line of cars look like oiled-up bodies tanning in the sun. We're going to lie to Kern about bargaining with the Metronomes on his behalf to spare America. And if he doesn't believe us, we somehow get the engine core out of there with my anger-fueled Tempo and the five Vanguard poisoned smoke storms spinning inside of Flynn. Assuming Kern and his army don't point tanks at us on sight.

Our plan is half desperation, half bananas, and half suicide. Flynn gets on me about the math, but I flunked all my subjects and besides, I tell him, he's half-delirious. What does he know?

If we can't stop the Metronomes from Silencing the whole world, me and Flynn will save Gloria, at least, and the other Tempo jockeys. And however many people in the family the Metronomes will let us bring to the music. Pop and Anita. The seamstresses. Watkins. There will be room enough for them all. *I have served you*, I'll scream at the featureless blue faces of the Metronomes. *Give me this Clemency.*

Well. One thing at a time. First we have to get there, and the traffic is making that just about impossible. Jesus H. You'd think everyone would have the good sense to just stay home and just dance and bonk each other like crazy like us Divine Deviants are doing. I refuse to let it stink up my mood, though, as I crank up the tunes and sing along to 'I'm Your Boogie Man' by KC and the Sunshine Band. Screech along, more like, Flynn says.

"You wanna scare the Metronomes off?" He winces as my wail bounces off the dash, into his face.

The hell of a party we'll throw when this is over, all of us dancing through the streets of the whole city, with Patrick pumping tunes out to the moon. That's what I gotta keep in a bright ball in my chest. We'll save them because we have to. There's no other choice.

I can almost hear the music.

The sounds start as a deep thrumming in my chest that spreads warm goop up my neck and into my ears. Starry wind chimes trickle across my cheeks and prick tears into my eyes.

Glass shatters.

Metal crashes and screeches and someone screams—and I tear my eyes up from the radio to see a car in the opposite lane careen across the painted yellow line and crash into a City Rover. I slam the brakes and the tires squeal as I just miss smashing into the stopped car ahead of us. Every car on both sides of the road stops just to rubberneck at the idiot who slammed into the Rover.

No. Wait.

The music isn't just in my head. Thick bass beats bowl over the boogie trumpets on the radio and replace them with shivering star-song. Tempo engines drown out the rattle of Flynn's shaggin' wagon.

Tick, tick, tick.

We look up. The Metronome's World-Ship breaks through the clouds, devouring the sky.

THIRTY-ONE

WELCOME TO THE STAGE

The side of Flynn's van scalds my palm. Me and him are standing in the street, just like everyone else, and staring up into the sky at the disco ball of a moon floating a mile over the whole city. The sun scorches off the glimmering globe of the ship, blinding me.

Tick, tick, tick. The clock hands moving are the music of the panels on the World-Ship that pop off, swirl, and click back into new formations.

Sirens squeal in the distance. I know I should panic. But the music washes over me in a sea of rhinestones and I'm grinning something fierce, same as everyone else. The car radios around us play the same star-song, and the music is threaded with deep-space blips and galaxy pulses and sighs from the mid-dance Metronomes. *Ooooo it's so good.*

Brothers.

The hot, sticky strawberry breeze carries the mind-flicker and hip sway of their words, only to me and Flynn, I know.

We have missed you
and though this world will
be Silenced, we—

have come to ease your duty. To lift you
back to the dance
where you
belong

Flynn's cough smashes me out of the song. I rip my eyes from the sky to him on the other side of the van, bracing against the hood, while his body rattles with hacks. He spits a toxic yellow wad of phlegm on the windshield.

"We're too late," he wheezes. "We—"

A guitar chord that sounds like galaxies colliding cuts him off. Panels on the side of the World-Ship snap open and drop rhinestones into the air. In a blink, one of the rhinestones whirls a few hundred feet above the city. The thing is a giant disco ball at the center of two rotating rings. A caravan, I know, thanks to the chord knocking loose some Metronome memories. In hotrods, me, Flynn, and the other Adjudicators duty scouted alone. The caravans are packed with Metronomes ready to party.

Blue flash, flicker, brain-boogie. In another world, in another time, I can see Metronomes floating down from caravans in their temporary blue swirled-glass bodies. Even after we Adjudicate, some of the Metronomes like to explore. Like cruise ships chugging into port to gawk at the strange landscape of a new country. Some of them save people on worlds, before Silencing, I know. They're not totally without mercy. Look at Flynn, and how he and Purple saved me and offered the chance to the others.

But what will they see here? Executive Orders, and burned buildings across this whole city. I'm surprised we haven't blown each other up, yet. Honestly.

The Metronomes have their own Dodge rules. *Rule one: We will be humane. These poor creatures deserve our Mercy even if their world at large does not.*

I'll save the others before the song ends.

Flynn reads this between my eyes.

"We get to my ship and get them to call off the Silencing," he rasps.

"We gotta run."

My track star can barely stand, but I'm running on rocket fuel, so I fling his arm over my shoulder, wrap one of my arms around his waist, and pound the pavement, weaving through frozen forms all around us.

* * *

As I half-run and half-carry Flynn down Santa Monica, the last mile to Circus Disco, people drift out of apartments and bodegas and freeze once their eyes hit the ships above, the music washing over them. Commdef officers step out of their cruisers, mouths falling open. The hoop skirt on a drag queen dressed like Scarlet O'Hara outside of the Hollywood Forever cemetery blows in the wind. Sunlight glints off the fake sword of three men in gladiator costumes frozen outside a bus that must've been on its way to their job at the Paramount. All of them with dreamy smiles on their faces, lulled by the music.

Gloria will protect the others. The thought of them frozen on the sidewalk has me stumbling into Flynn.

Tick, tick, tick. The clock hands of my heart crank up, out of time. My pounding footfalls drum out two words. *Too. Late. Too. Late.*

Flynn nudges me off him once we see the black tarps

surrounding the disco, and he can run on his own. Together, we dodge the platoon of starmen in the street. Paralyzed men in green camo—Kern must've called in the National Guard, either for more test subjects or protection from us—gaze at the sky, their hands frozen as they reached for their rifles. Their necks craned up so they can stare straight up at the caravan ship hovering over the disco. Drawn here by the music, same as Flynn the night we met again.

The cannons from the tanks guarding Kern's blockade point up at the sky. We bolt past them, into the black tarp maze.

Someone threw a blanket over the music from the ships, here in the maze, with how muffled the star-song sounds. Record-player static and the crunch of tires over gravel fight with the honey of the music. Dizzying, cotton stuffed in my ears. Soldiers in hazmat suits, frozen just as they pulled off their face shields. We trip over forgotten soldering irons and rifles and camo helmets, our ragged breath adding to the snaps of black plastic in the wind. Flynn's the one to move faster than me, now. He got his wind back and he's vaulting over prone bodies with smiling faces pointed at the sky.

We bang around a tight maze corner and Flynn knocks into a statue of a starman and careens into a black tarp wall. The poles holding the tarps up knock over, and he skids onto his ass over the pavement. A fighter jet hulks in the center of the black tarp maze. Except mad scientist hands welded disco ball panels, and pipes, and swirled metal bits to the gunmetal gray. The ship glints with its own strange light under the blue sky. Wires snake from the underside of the jet to the closed bank vault with *Bolt*'s engine core, that Kern must've dragged here from inside the disco. He stands by the core tank. The vault door is still closed, but I can feel the song like frozen waves.

They promised they would save us.

They will do the same to you.

I can feel the core sending out spikes of panic and power, wanting to explode. Deafening me with the bitter sound of 'Taps' played at a starman's funeral.

By the nose of the jet, Kern's face is tipped up to the caravan ship in the sky, frozen. I follow his eyes, aching, to the spinning rings around the disco ball. *Save us,* I beg the ship. I could scream the words and I'd still get drowned out by the sour music from *Bolt*'s engine core

I look back down and Flynn flows from the pavement up to his feet, like slow smoke. Following the tip of Kern's head up to the ship.

"Did the song call you here, same as me?"

Echoes edge Kern's voice. Standing this close to *Bolt*'s engine must be canceling out the Metronome music for him. But then I see the yellow smoke misting out of his eyes when he turns his head from the ship to look at us, and I know he's something different than human, now. I smell sulfur and burnt skin and the stink of gushing blood. And on the breeze, maybe—maybe?—rose perfume.

I can't move.

"We can hear it, now," Flynn says, dreamy-voiced like he's on stage again. "We can hear what it asks."

"Yes. To right the balance," Kern echoes. One of his hands—I see burns across it, and up his neck—waves at the jet. The flicker of yellow in his eyes is his tell. *No one but me was ever truly worthy of this power. I will be its bearer.* "We tried to repair the ship. The beings of this planet are children, with their combustion engines."

"There's another ship," Flynn says, the tremors in his voice from in the car long gone. "Down below."

"Too deep for us to reach." Kern's sigh slices my skin. He stalks closer to us. "We were preparing to dig, if not for the presence of the invaders."

"We will raise it," Flynn says.

When Flynn—no, not Flynn and not a Metronome either—turns to me, yellow smoke hides his eyes. Not-Flynn's beautiful face twists into a sad smile. So, so sad because the ones who hiss in the yellow fog know what Metronomes mean by sacrifice. The engine core in that bank vault is what's left of their world. Their voices called out to Flynn and to Kern, and begged and begged.

We must put a stop to the Score, once and for all.

They just need a little more juice.

The few must serve for the sake of the many.

Smoke snakes curl out of Not-Flynn's back, flicking and tasting the strange air of this broken world before it knocks me onto my back. A deepwhale blast shudders from the caravan ship above us, and I have to cram my hands over my ears—screaming, eyes closed, skittering over the black-tarped pavement—to try to keep the sound and the smoke out.

Another blast and I'm lost in the beautiful pain of their music.

THIRTY-TWO
REFRAIN

I've got company with me on the blue-tinted stage in the Calypso Room when I open my eyes. Flynn is here to meet my Ma, I think. I think? His eyes are dancing, and sweat plasters his wavy hair to his forehead. He looks around. The seats behind us are empty. The chairs and tables of the audience stretch out into forever.

He snares me by the waist with a few fingers in my belt loops.

Wait. I push him back gently with one hand on his chest. Yeah—he feels it, too, by the way the pink tip of his tongue locks between his lips. Something's not right, here. The cornbread's not done in the middle.

The fog machine on stage must be on the fritz because the smoke is all greenish-yellow and wrong.

Oh. Right. The same yellow smoke that's choking the life out of me is poisoning Flynn from the inside out.

We're dying.

"What's that?" Flynn asks, pointing to the Moonboom on the stage floor.

I pick it up, pop out the tape, and look at the label.

METRONOME/FLYNN – HOME WORLD – FOREVER AGO DEMO.

He sees the label and looks at me with sad blue glass eyes. I hold up the Moonboom for him to replace the tape. He hits play, takes my hand, and leads me through the dusty red curtain into what's beyond.

* * *

Me and Flynn glide like mist all around each other. Me into him, him into me. I can see his whole song.

Flynn was born under an iron sky on a jagged mountain-peak-speared world of red rocks and bleach seas. By the time he took his first breath, quakes had ground countless empires to gravel and scattered the remains. What the planet didn't kill, the sun did—just a little too close—with solar flares that flambéed the atmosphere. On their world, the sun didn't give a shit about them. So after the latest solar flare, not long after Flynn and his brood-mates wiggled their spiny arms to the sky, his people moved underground.

They lived deep in the scarred soil and out in space, both in blackness.

It took a long time for Flynn's tiny eyes—bright blue, a good omen—to adjust. He missed the light like it was air.

In the torches that lined their underground caverns, his exoskeleton flashed bronze like everyone else's. Almost like. His outsides were too soft, one of his allmothers or allfathers spotted, he didn't know who. Soft was weak, and they figured his insides were even squishier than his other broodmates'. Conundrum: do they protect him or bring him to the surface and drop him in the ammonia air by one of the bleachy shores to let nature do its thing? They all twitched their spiny arms, arguing, while he tried to puff up and hide with the others, playing rock-ball.

He must serve, they decided. *They all have to.*

Since their planet wouldn't give them much, they took from others.

Flynn and the others got to be kids, sort of, while their exoskeletons hardened enough to survive the shuttle-launch up to the spiked disc of their harvest ship in orbit. The allfathers shoved the spear and the plasma gun at him, same as every other kid. They played rock-ball between training sessions that almost seemed like a game. Stab the Six-Arm, the allfathers called the game. They showed Flynn and the others how to snoop out the soft spots from the joints in the exoskeletons of their neighbor-world dwellers, then stab their spine-arms through to suck out the juice, or pump them with paralyzing venom, and lug them back to the harvest ship. The ones on the neighbor-world were the enemy, the allfathers said. Those freaks weren't even people. What kind of abomination has six arms instead of seven, like the All-Being planned? And, besides, there was only so much juice to go around this hell-hole of a solar system, and Flynn's people had to eat.

Flynn's clumsy spine-arms couldn't quite hold the weapons like the others. Maybe the grownups were right, and he really was too soft.

Chin high, shoulders back. Don't be a pansy. This is just how it's always been. Service or the bleach-beach.

The tank ships that dropped from the harvest ship and bombed through the skies of the six-arm world looked like thorns. Flynn shivered and ached when his feet touched the alien world, which, he reckoned, didn't look all that alien. Funny, the way the allfathers never mentioned during the training games the way the six-arms screamed, and how their eyes looked just the same as the seven-arms' eyes. The allfathers told Flynn and the others that they'd get used to the screams.

They lied.

His sixth tour of harvest duty—the screams still found the seams in his exoskeleton, same as the first—the Metronome World-Ship blinked into space beside the harvest ship.

We saw your island of life in the sea of blackness, the Metronomes sang out. *May we share our knowledge and joy, joining as fellow sacred lifeforms in this dance of boundless love.*

Flynn heard their music from the red dirt of the six-arm world on that last raid, cutting through plasma-gun sizzles.

We are good on the boundless love front, Flynn's people answered. *The last group of tree-huggers who rolled in here led with that, too, before the invasion. This ain't our first rodeo.*

His people answered, too, with antimatter bombs and gravity arrays.

Holy fuckcannons, the Metronome tune changed. *Who knew these cats had antimatter bombs? If you're going to harsh our vibe, we are going to boot you off the dancefloor.*

Thorn-swarms of tank ships strafed the World-Ship. The Metronomes barely escaped and left that iron-sky hellscape and its seven-armed assholes alone. They told Flynn, later, how close the seven-arms came to cracking the disco-ball eggshell of the ship and ending the whole dance party for good. Which is why, from then on, whenever they passed a world that might develop guns big enough to blast them out of the sky, the Metronomes had to Silence them first. How's that for a dance lesson?

Then the Metronomes dropped by the six-arm planet. They sent a delegation in clumsy space suits—long before the Tempo taught them how to shift to mist, and my no-name world showed them the blue-swirled glass—to the red world, singing about celestial harmony. And when they spotted Flynn and his fellow soldiers and the way their spiny arms could stab out paralyzing venom and suck up life-force, even the Metronomes chirped, *Well, hold on now. That could be useful.*

Because with all of their dancing and spreading messages of joy and love throughout the universe, the Metronomes were gonna run out of fuel, one day. Unless they found a new power source for the World-Ship. Like, say, Tempo, which they couldn't generate. But they could find worlds and civilizations that did, and bring them to the dancefloor to spark and spread the beautiful nonstop dance party of the Manifold. And worlds that posed a threat? Well, Flynn and the others could teach the Metronomes how to reach out with spiny arms and drain the juice out of them and their worlds, turning them into fuel. Flynn and the other survivors of his world were the first Adjudicators, the scouts traveling and judging. No spears and plasma guns, but soldiers just the same.

Consider this your cover charge for being at our dance party, boy-o, the Metronomes sang, *or we can drop you at the nearest ammonia ocean.*

Safeguard and protect, and his exoskeleton hardened until one Tempo-rich planet taught them all how to slip to mist. On a no-name planet, he met a shining blue-skinned boy—*Hey, hey! That's me!*—and he recognized the softness in the blue-skinned boy and loved it in the ways that his allmothers and allfathers couldn't.

How do you be yourself? a soft boy asks another soft boy on a fire escape, in a billion years, give or take. The other boy answers, *Who else am I gonna be?*

My eyes filled him with some of the light he missed, buried in the caverns of his home world.

And then the postings pummeled him. Screams on every planet we visited sounded the same, and in time even the bliss of the dancefloor doesn't sweep the screams away.

He started flying in *Bolt*, alone between postings, and the screams turned to whispers from the damaged engine. They found the soft spots between his exoskeleton joints and wiggled through. And he was so tired. He tried to tell the voices *I was just doing my duty.* But so, so tired of the postings, even if visiting a new planet with me felt like a little slice of heaven, when the light hit just right.

He wanted to serve, but there's only so much he can give.

Because Camp Puller. Jesus Christ, Camp Puller. The top brass tried to tell the starmen, *Don't be a pansy. This is just how it's always been.* But the locals looked just like them.

* * *

Click. The demo tape reaches the end.

My hands solidify back into skin and bone from mist. I flip the tape, and when I look up we're back on stage in the Calypso Room, facing the empty tables and chairs.

Way off in the distance, I can see glints of light. I can smell rose perfume over the dust and old cigarettes of this place. And hear Gloria's voice coming up through the Moonboom. *Hold on. We're coming. You're not alone.*

At my side, Flynn squeezes my hand. All the memories

he showed me are his way of saying he's sorry, I know. And I know that with the World-Ship hanging over the Earth, it's stupid for my heart to be breaking about just one boy that one world failed. But here we are.

"I'm sorry I'm soft," he says over the music. "Maybe the others were right and I'm too weak."

I read the secret code in his eyes. *I can't fight what the screams and the smoke are getting me to do anymore. I'm trying to fight it. I'm so, so scared.*

That goddamned fog machine billows smoke all around the stage. I bend over, coughing with my hands on my bent knees. When I look up at Flynn, yellow smoke-snakes coil and hiss out of him. And what a time for a martini glass to shatter at my feet. I look out at the audience, where Ma is wrapped in shadow and swirling yellow. I ruined her Hollywood movies, and ruined her big-stage dreams, and now she lifts her arms and martini glasses and rocks glasses—I should've cleaned them up like I was supposed to and *goddamnit Mitchell you ruin everything*—whip off the tables and all around her.

She throws the whole glass storm at me and my arms fly over my face against the shards that rip me up.

* * *

Huffing, screaming against shards of glass. No. That wasn't real. When I open my eyes, I'm on my back on the concrete. Fog, everywhere. A yellow windstorm whips black tarps and metal into the air above the disco. Flynn is up ahead in the swirling yellow, and Kern is near the vault with *Bolt*'s engine core. He grips the vault wheel just to stay on his feet. I see the tell in the wicked curve of his smile. *Yes. More.*

I'm trying to fight it, Flynn's eyes told me in my vision. I'm not dead, so some part of the real Flynn must've taken control back from his body and pulled the smoke snakes from my neck before I bit it.

Move. Open your eyes. Every breath brings an ache. Ribs creak, lungs gurgle, joints groan as I crawl to my knees against the storm. I hack up every cigarette I've ever smoked. But I can move.

Up ahead, Flynn stands in the middle of the cyclone, blurred by yellow-streaked storm winds, his arms outstretched like he's conducting an orchestra. Smoke blasts around him, flapping his Guard jacket. The air tastes like pain. Voices hiss and cackle and groan in the wind. *They must pay. They must pay.* The mangled jet by me screeches on its landing gear. Steel tables and tools and dropped rifles kick up into the air. I raise my arms just before a Guard helmet slams me in the face.

"Bring us the ship," Kern shouts.

Flynn slices his hands down and a thunderclap blasts my ears. A crack races from him and right into the clown mouth of the disco that I can barely see through the storm. Slice. Crunch. The crack widens, and chunks of concrete tumble into the air and join the cyclone and slam against the jet and vault. He sweeps his arms, swaying to the music of screaming metal and shuddering earth.

"Keep going!" Kern snarls.

Slice. Crack. The hole he's digging in the ground with smoke and yellow jets of lightning widens. Rumbles and groans, deep below. Snarling, I try to stand but the wind keeps knocking me down.

Almost there, the wind howls. *They were right to fear us.*

The walls of Circus Disco crumble when *Rush* blasts out of the roof. Lights flash along the swirled metal. The fried-egg ship wobbles in the air, tugged by invisible hands closer to us. Closer, closer—metal legs from the underside of my ship unfolding. And then *Rush* zips to the ground, bouncing on its landing gear on the concrete right in front of Flynn.

The second it lands, he crumples to his knees, then falls back.

I crawl over chunks of concrete and twisted metal, grunting and splitting my forearms on my way to Flynn. His chest heaves. Yes—he's breathing. Closer. Almost to him. Every muscle is screaming at me to lay down and let myself turn to mist.

Somewhere near us, Kern slowly circles the ship.

Finally, I get to Flynn and pull him onto my lap. And he's Flynn, yeah. Shivering and shaking with the yellow smoke burned out of his eyes. Flynn on my fire escape as a kid, scared about his dad coming home. Blood trails out of his nose. His window-cleaner blue eyes are cracked with red veins. I lug him tighter into my lap. One of his weak hands trembles in mine.

"I'm sorry," he wheezes.

"Hey. Heyheyhey. You're fine. Stay with me." I grab his hand and press it to my chest. My hot tears turn him into swirled colors. "Take whatever you need from me to heal. Take it all."

"It's alright, Mitch." He coughs and blood spatters his lips. "We've been here before. We..."

My blue swirled-glass travel Instrument lands on the ground a foot away from me and Flynn, its eyeless face watching us. I tear my eyes from Flynn and see the disco ball hatch of my hotrod popped open, and Kern in the driver's seat. He's already fiddling with the controls. I don't care. Let him ride it out of here.

I look back down at Flynn. The edges of him seem to waver and soften. I can see him leading me onto the crystal dancefloor of the Metronome ship for the first time. The millions of years with us flowing into each other as fog seem to blink by in a flash. All leading up to seeing him as a kid sitting on the floor of the empty hallway outside the principal's office, hitting me with those big blue eyes. *You have to play the game.*

I'll play this game with him, again and again. Please. Please.

"Thank you for your service, starmen," Kern calls out from my ship. "You're dismissed."

Over the whir of *Rush*'s engines, I can hear the glass of my Instrument ring like someone hit it with a mallet, just from the heat in me. The engine blast of anger starts in my lungs, but I'm not strong enough to keep it in. I'll burn out same as Flynn. His blue crystal islet eyes glow from within. Light—so, so light in my lap. A shuddering deep breath brings a smile to his face.

His body fades to glittering mist and slides out of my lap.

I don't have time to crumple because my hotrod bobbles into the air. Kern is leaving us all to face the Metronome music, when this is his fault. No. I'll rip him out of the sky even if it burns me out, and hand him over to the Metronomes. I just have to make it to the bank vault with Flynn's damaged engine core, and suck enough juice out of it.

Kern points my hotrod right at the disco ball of a caravan ship floating right above us.

Wait. Wait—

My hotrod's engines shred the air.

Tick, tick, tick. Boom.

My ship crashes into the caravan and the whole sky explodes into a red flower of fire.

THIRTY-THREE

THE MITCH THING

Oh God, the music.

I'm suffocating and trapped on the ground in total darkness—screaming and pounding—but I hear everything. Metal screeches and shreds must be the rotating wheels of the caravan ship flying off their tracks. *Shoooooom.* A synthesizer blast of hot air. Rumbles rock the earth. Concrete splits and explodes. I wait and I wait, and still, the music. The *ping, ping, ping* must be searing metal rain. Booms and shrieks must be other caravans dropping down from the World-Ship. No more hypnotic Metronome silk sounds, just screams. Me at the mic the loudest, howling like a bloodhound. Sirens, and sizzles, and more screams, and thrashing against the weight until it slips away.

Gasping and dazed from my head knocking the ground, I sit up.

Flynn—if I can call him that—slinks back from me in the blue swirled-glass body of my traveling Instrument that he slipped into when he burned out to mist. His face is a blank curve. No eyes to beam secret codes to me. No lips to scrape across my neck. He's human shaped, just a little too tall and too big, with long limbs sticking out of a wide chest. A space suit with a swirling glitter ghost inside. Blue glass that protected me from getting squashed by the rain of wreckage.

The boy I knew is gone.

No—he's there, somewhere in the mist beyond the glass. He doesn't have eyes, but I can still feel them move over me, and up into the sky, where other Metronomes in blue swirled-glass bodies whirl in bird formations down from the caravan ships. Smoldering ship pieces have knocked down the whole black tarp maze, and the air stinks of smoke and melting plastic.

Our posting wasn't supposed to go down like this. His voice is mostly trumpet rattles, though I know what he means.

"You think?"

That wasn't me. One long-fingered blue-glass hand reaches for me, then stops. He shrinks back. *The fog from the engine core was all hollering for revenge, and my weak human head couldn't block them out.*

"I know."

I'd never hurt you.

We've been on duty too long, and it's breaking us both apart. A charred mirror shard from the caravan ship splits the pavement nearby. In its reflection, we're both smeared blobs of color.

"You think they'll spare the world? Kern is kablooey. All that's left of the Disharmony is the engine core." I heave a shaky breath. God, I miss my inhaler. "They can take it and leave."

Not after this act of war. They'll blow the whole planet.

"But what about the rules of the Score? They wouldn't hurt Ascended beings, right?"

They'd wait until they get us back on the World-Ship.

Me and him aren't the Ascended beings I mean. My sweet soldier has always been a little slow when it comes to Tempo.

"Unless we give them a reason not to."

You got a miracle in your back pocket you're not telling me about?

I keep my mouth shut. The air stinks of smoke and spilled gasoline from shrapnel-speared cars. Sirens whoop and screech against the backing track of car horns, screams, and shattering windows. Above us, black smoke drifts against the blue sky.

"We could've fought harder for those other worlds," I whisper.

Maybe.

"We can start with this one."

His eyeless face peers up into the swarms of blue-glass bodies flying from the ships overhead. *Clemency. We could still have time. I'll go to the others.*

"Yeah."

If things get hairy, you split, you hear? Let one of the others take you back to the World-Ship. And then we rest. And then leave we the service, and the Metronomes. Off to wherever the dance takes us. Together.

"That sure sounds sweet."

Another trumpet trill from his mouthless face, and he jumps into the air after the others.

My knees almost buckle as I haul myself up, spitting blood. See, the time for arguing for mercy from people who ain't likely to dole it out is done. That's not the kind of fight I was talking about. I just need a little pick-me-up, and luckily there's a nice big battery in a bank vault waiting for me. Telling me about all the power it can give me. *They will end you. Let us show you how to stop them.*

And honestly. Those cats are on to something.

I stumble over mangled metal. The roofs of the old factories that ring the alleys around the club belch smoke. I hobble to the bank vault and collapse against the crank wheel on the side. Just by grabbing the wheel and sinking to the ground I open the vault just enough for a yellow line of light to seep out.

We will show them, the twining voices whisper and hiss.

Yes, we will.

This first contact shit is not where it's at. We don't need Adjudicators touching down, planting a flag, and informing us *you have hereby been contacted by a superior species, hoorah.* We need an exchange. We need to cruise, and cruising I know. We need a slow walk-by, eyes to lips to eyes again, deciding if we're going to take this meetup somewhere. *Hey handsome, how's your day going? What can we do for each other?* The Metronomes showed us theirs. It's time to show them ours. I just need a little help getting the job done.

Finish the job. The voices scrape over my skin.

They promise me power. I promise them release.

Somewhere over the sirens, I hear the shimmering synths and star heartbeats of Hat-Trick's music, and the church bell call of Gloria's voice. The music builds and soars, but the noise of the war all around us will drown out the music, soon. It always does.

I grab the wheel and yank hard. One turn. One more. Each wheel-crank cranks up the heat in me as it opens the blazing, burnt-yellow glittering globe to the sun.

Yes. We will show them.

I kneel and press my forehead to the glass. A whole well of Tempo from a dead world invites me to take a dip. I lay my hand flat against the warmth. Then ball it into a fist. *Bam. Bam.* Flaming-hot Tempo from my fists crack the glass.

Let the others be the smoke, and the fog, and the light. I can be the fire.

Yellow fog slips through the cracks and into me. The yellow orb of the core ripples and spins as I pound harder. *Tick, tick, tick.* The sound is hairline cracks spreading over the containment tank of the engine core.

Yes, the voices rasp. *Should the containment field rupture, so goes the Metronomes.*

I scream over the cracking tank. Blue-tinted visions of dying worlds blur in my eyes as Tempo blasts into me. The fire cranks up and up. And if I got a chance to take out some of them with me? Watch me burn. Last Mitch Effort, and all.

The few must sacrifice for the many.

Through the fog, I can see blue glass bodies dip down from the sky towards me. Reaching out and vibrating—until they freeze. I can taste the fear. Dozens of them stop and turn to me. The closest Metronome hovering in the air ten feet away drifts back a little.

They should be scared.

Let us dance. Or else.

I look at the containment tank and can see light and dancing shapes glittering across the glass. Laughter like caramel washes all over me. I turn from the tank and try to shield my eyes, but when I tug, my hands are stuck to the glass.

"Mitchell Moses on Mountain Sinai, what in God's holy Name do you think you're doing?"

Even from across the concrete lot, as she's laughing and swaying in the glittering fog, Gloria clocks me with that church girl glare. She's wearing a silver sequined caftan and the biggest goddamn afro wig out there, with Hat-Trick leaning against her with his cans over his ears and his Moog strapped to his back, pumping tunes even if the thing's not plugged in. Juana holds up Bette. Rex, gritting through the pain, leans into Stetson, who flicks his hands, dismissing his bubble shield. And of course the ones who were bloodied and broken would be carried by the others. Everyone's coming to our dance party. A whole squad of leather-daddies rev their motorcycles behind Gloria and the Tempo jockeys. They must've given my brothers and sisters at the front the lift.

Stolen Commdef cars and Studio rovers stretch out into the streets. All of the Divine Deviants wave tambourines and scarves in the air, sequins and rhinestones flashing. The shards of broken glass in their hair are just more glitter. Blood streaked on their faces is just makeup from a compact that they use to touch-up before the show. More and more of them round the corner, dancing while roofs burn, while every radio in every car in the city plays Hat-Trick's beats, even as more Metronomes swirl and scatter in the sky.

Gloria steps away from the pack. I don't deserve the hand that she rests on my shoulder. The Metronomes drift further from her, now. Hesitating.

"Now," she says with a huff. "I certainly hope I'm on time for the big bad court-martial."

I see my twisted face reflected back at me in the glass tank. I look up into Gloria's bright eyes and crumble, at her seeing me like this.

I'm just as awful as the Thems.

A thorn-swarm of Metronomes crowds the sky over the

disco. Hundreds of eyeless faces look down at us as deepwhale-horn minor-chord symphonies blast out from their glass bodies. An invisible foot hits the kick-drum over and over again until I look up and realize. Shit. Sonic booms.

Airforce jets blast through the blue-painted backdrop skies towards the Metronome caravans.

* * *

A Metronome whose voice I don't recognize reaches out a blue hand and seals the cracks I pounded into the tank with a glimmer of light. Maybe there's some mercy in the Metronome's music. I don't know. A few of them float closer and make vibrating electric guitar clangs with each other at the sight of Gloria. One of them is Flynn. I know the trumpet of his voice when he talks about his fault. His error. How the ones here hear the music, and the chorus must weigh the grace of Clemency.

I can almost pick up the tune of what the others are saying. *A pause in the Silence is the correct Pitch, given this unprecedented Improvisation from the Score. We must call the Chorus.*

Flynn buzzes, turning his blue-glass face to the burning city. *And maybe we can meet somewhere a little more quiet? As equals.*

Blue heads turn and chatter in electric rainstorms. Something about the word *equals* sparks an annoyed bee-buzz in their voices.

Yes. We will find the appropriate house in the in-between place of the Music and the Dance. We will listen.

"I got a suggestion," Gloria tells them.

I mean, of course she understands their music. Music is what she's made of.

The Metronomes turn to each other and start buzzing. Arms outstretched—buzzing, vibrating, so loud it shakes the sky—until a bubble of blue light explodes from the swarm, blinding me.

* * *

The place we are in, once the blue light clears, is Circus Disco, and not really Circus Disco. It's Founding Mothers, and the Calypso Room, and every gay bar I've ever hit up all at once, packed for the Silencing Showcase. Not so much a place as a moment. The instant you drop the needle on the record, before the music starts up.

Gloria knows how to handle an audience, thank you very much. I've seen her turn sweetly to hecklers, and by the end of her number they were handing her crumpled dollar bills. I've seen her get the crowd to break up a fist fight between two coked-out queens with just a couple shimmies of her shoulders and an eyelash flick. She's laughing from the center of the stage, where she belongs, with the silver crescent moon painted on her face flashing in the lights. I'm in the lighting catwalk above the stage, keeping the follow-spot on her. I know I'm up here since the folks in charge don't know what to do with me, yet. And that's fine. When I lit Ma, I was trapped up in the dark. Somehow, Gloria connects to me through the beam of the spotlight, and makes me feel like I'm on stage with her.

For some reason, my palms on the handles of the spotlight are burning up. My hands and arms are covered in searing mirrored scales.

She is a blaze of light in her giant afro wig and a red

rhinestone choir robe with slits up to you-know-where. I helped her glue red rhinestones to the sleeve of the microphone and door-knocker hoop earrings because she's all about details. In the dark of the endless audience, claws reach out to her from yellow smoke. Metronome bodies ring out with trumpet blasts as jet-plane engines pump through the speakers. Her laughter sounds like a viola trill, somehow louder than them all.

The queen at her side—pale as the bright sun, wrapped up in blue, with glass bracelets stacked up her arms—isn't really one of us. Her skin doesn't fit right around the eyes. She brushes a stray tendril of her blonde up-do from her face.

"As an Ascended Being in the presence of Adjudicators," Blue says, "you have been granted the Clemency of leaving this dying world and joining us in the Dance."

"Lady Moondust has never missed one of her shows, sugar," Gloria purrs. "And I don't do duets, so how about you leave the stage to me?"

Blue pouts. She's the kind of girl that's used to everyone falling over themselves and shoving bills at her because of her Miss Moonie pinup vibe, I know. With a theatrical sigh, she glides off the stage, into the dark.

Gloria jerks her head and I swing the spotlight back over to just her.

"Now, I see a whole lot of beautiful new faces in the crowd," Gloria sing-songs. "Welcome! If you have a good time tonight, my name is Lady Moondust. And if you don't have a good time? Well—my name ain't none of your business."

The crowd cackles, already. They're a live one tonight. That's a good sign.

"Remember to tip the girls. Remember to drink up.

Remember to shake your cans, and let's get it started, my sweet chickens."

She nods in the darkness to the DJ booth, and when the shimmery beats rain down on us, she starts to twirl.

The music, though. Holy shit. Liquid kaleidoscope tunes spill into the air—I can practically see the shards of a million different dancefloors like this spinning from the disco ball—and I let it wash over me. Gloria sways and coos, cranking up the heat in her voice. Her vocal run has so many pivots that my legs ache. Spirituals, church bells, gospel hymns, rhythm-and-blues melodies flow from her. Her voice sizzles across the backs of my eyelids. Makes me want to drift apart into fog, and all I can do to hold on is to look on stage with a gasp, where she's twirling and glowing in red rhinestone sparks.

I've never been good at understanding my feelings and now a bright ball is working around in my chest, spinning between joy and sadness. I can feel her voice weaving around us all in a building tapestry of light. I can feel her trying to gather and shape. I can feel her asking. Praying to make us all whole again.

And this is all just the vamp. Everyone's eyes are on Gloria, wondering what song she'll kick off the night with. I sure am. *There's something here,* she told me by the burned roof of Founding Mothers, her hand over her heart. *Something big and bright. And gold. Something I gotta do, or something I gotta say...*

I know what I would do and say. I know what song. *Burn, baby, burn.*

She stops swaying and reaches out with arms that look so small in her billowy choir robe, laughing with us and up to the spotlight. Each of the rhinestones on her choir robe sparks and reflect a million shards of light. No, that light is coming from her. Definitely not from me up here in the catwalk.

"We feel love." Her Cadillac Red lips glisten as she sings. "Love multiplies."

Light from her washes over the whole crowd. I move the spotlight from her—she's so bright, anyway—and into the audience. Beings from another world dressed up in Space Guard jumpsuits and Commdef uniforms sway in the yellow fog, closing their eyes. They just wanted to be left alone, I can read in their sad sways, how their curled claws drift down to their sides. They never wanted the Metronome's help—there's always a price from the ones who say they're above you—and the pain is too much. The anger's been eating them up inside forever and forever and—

The tracks fade and mix together, too. I can feel other things through the music. This is mostly about the feel of the music anyway.

And it's alright, her sway and her voice tells the crowd. *The judgment they put on you, and the things they made you do, and the people they made you be to survive. You don't have to hold it in.*

She's saying this to me, of course, same as when we were in the Boom Boom Room together.

That hurt doesn't belong to you. What if it was just a song you heard, and you let it move through you and then fly off to wherever else it needed to go?

I sag against the spotlight. I still can't let it go.

The ones in the fog sigh and sway, drifting to mist.

Old ladies at church used to sneak Gloria candies, she told me in the Boom Boom Room. She said she heard them whispering to each other about how *that child's voice is going to deliver souls to the Lord.*

I can see us both in the shuttle that brought us back to Earth for the last time. The vibrations of the ship warp through me, grinding my bones. The high note she hits now is the same one that washed over the whole ship, glowing with silver light, and kept it from flying apart. I know that, now. I always knew she was a walking miracle. Now others will, too.

In the wings off-stage, Blue is gabbing with the others in her swirled blue-glass bodied chorus. I don't envy her having to follow up Gloria's number.

Honestly, if we have to show them more proof than this that we're divine—that we're deserving, that we're worthy—fuck 'em all anyway. Because we're all we need.

THIRTY-FOUR
HIGH NOTE

Long after the audience drifts away to mist, I'm still holding onto the spotlight up in the catwalk. I can't let it go. I want to let it go. Well—I want to want to let it go. But somehow the way my legs and back are all cramped up here in the catwalk is familiar, even as much as it hurts. Like it feels good to let that hurt knock around all in me because it's so big and bright, even if it's eating me up.

Gloria's high-heels on the catwalk sound almost like the Metronome clock. She scoots down next to me.

The fire in my hands worked up my body and turned my throat to spent firewood.

"It's so tiring, huh?"

Gloria smirks at my hands on the spotlight. "Well, you could let go. Easy-peasy, lemon-squeezy."

"Not working the spotlight."

"Then what?"

My lips harden into a line. "Just living through all the shit everyone shoves on us, and... and not burning down a world that doesn't want us in it, and..."

I know I don't have to explain this, least of all to her. The

Only Girl on the Moon.

Her laugh weaves around the black metal of the catwalk. "A real hoot, ain't it?"

I tug at my stuck hands. "Hilarious."

"Mercy and forgiveness are gifts, you know."

"Even if they don't deserve it?"

Sounds a lot like the compassion stuff she tried to tell me back on the moon. I really am slow on the uptake.

She shakes her head. "That's the rub. That's the Grace stuff. The mercy and forgiveness ain't for them. It's for you, so you don't turn into something you don't wanna be."

"That sounds nice. And easier said."

"Can I let you in on a little secret?" She presses one finger to her Cadillac Red lips. "You gotta promise not to say a word."

"Cross my heart."

She's so close her afro tickles the side of my face.

"When you looked out for me, and made me a home on Founding Fathers with you, well..." She looks away, back down to the stage. A quick fingers swipes at the corner of one eye so she doesn't smudge her crescent moon. "Knowing someone loved the real me made it a lot easier to do the same."

Unsuitable Instrument, lacking the power for the Song, she told me the Metronomes said of her, in the mist on the moon. *They will not hear her.*

"I'm sorry I pushed you away, and made you think I didn't believe in you. Or trust you, or..."

"You saw Lady Moondust before Lady Moondust did." Her shining eyes loosen my grip just a little bit. "I will forgive you for getting all dumb and macho if you promise not to blow up the world."

I manage a laugh through the tears in my eyes.

"And what if I don't deserve that forgiving-and-letting-go rub?"

"I see who you are. I know you're more than this."

Yeah. Makes sense. She sees all of me—more Mitch than Mitchronome—my sister. We protect each other.

"And you're not alone, you blockhead." She shoulder-checks me. "You can let the hurt—all of it—go if you want. There's still time. But..." She looks around. "Not a lot. They're waiting on you."

Right. I still got a job to do. Even with how far we strayed from the right notes of the Score, I'm still supposed to Adjudicate, and I'm such a good soldier. Flynn said he'd ask the others for Clemency. If I vote for Silencing, the whole Chorus of Metronomes will be the one to break the tie. And I got a feeling Kern pushed them over to the wrong side.

The tears in my eyes blur everything around me, and when they drip down my face, my vision clears. We're out of the in-between place, back on the concrete outside Circus Disco, and I'm kneeling in front of the engine core tank. The world is frozen in blue light. Fighter jets and smoke and the dancing Deviants in the glass reflection, all stilled. The light races back down into the Metronomes, and an invisible hand presses play on the track. Smoke swirls, metal shards skitter in the wind.

My arms are turning to crackled mirror ball pieces, my whole body on fire. A yellow smoke cyclone beats around in my chest.

The Metronomes around us drift farther away, watching and waiting. Screams, glass-cracks, big drumbeats in the sky. Yellow fog whips all around me.

Finish the job, the voices in the cyclone wail and whisper. *You can clear the ones that hate you right off the dancefloor with just a double-clap and a couple of hip-hustles. They'd do it to you.*

Except the engine core tank is empty, now that Gloria healed it and delivered all those trapped souls to higher heavens than the Metronomes ever dreamed of.

Oh. The voices are coming from me.

I don't want to carry them around anymore. I don't want to carry around all that fire. At the Metronomes for saving me, then making me do their dirty work. At Ma for loving me and leaving, and Flynn for doing the same, and the starmen who fucked with me and Gloria's tanks, Reagan for ripping the music outta the world, and Commdef for trying to make us hate ourselves and each other. And me. I got a lot of hurt for keeping all this inside and letting it burn me up for this long. I could've asked for help. I could've—

"Let go of the tank, Mitch," Gloria says.

She's so gentle. The tears sizzle off my face as I howl. As her soft hands lay on mine and pull them off the glass of the core. But I'm still burning up. I sucked too much Tempo out of the engine, and it has to go someplace or I'll burn away. Already, bright embers spark off my skin and die in the air.

It takes a higher being to hold that much Tempo without burning out, Flynn said, fresh off me jacking him up with juice from the Manifold.

You're not alone, you blockhead. Gloria slips her hand into mine and we turn to the whole parade of Divine Deviants and motorcycles and stolen Commdef cars, arms out.

I'll be the light switch if she'll be the light, beaming power and love and her goddamned—oops, sorry Gloria—her gee-dee grace onto everyone. We've always had our hands on crackling power lines—dancing power, creating power, fucking power—and it was just Mayflower Studios movie tricks that made us forget.

Tempo and power and light moves through me, and—finally, finally—I let it go where it needs to go.

This whole shrapnel-studded battleground, this whole world is our dancefloor. I can see others like us in queer bars I've only ever read about in my magazines. Atlantic House. Julius's. Resurrection. Playland Café. Parliament House. I blink and, holy shit, all those places are packed like Easter Sunday, with the Rapture scheduled for first thing Monday morning. Everyone I've ever seen on every dancefloor. Every lover from every bus stop and park cruise, every queen I've ever shoved a crumpled dollar bill to, every doll who walked through me and Gloria's apartment, every man I've ever taped pictures of to the walls. All of them and a million, million others. We're an Army of Lovers boogieing, all connected now by sizzling powerlines of silver-beaded fringe.

Welcome to the Disco at the End of the World. Tonight is everybody's night. Me and Gloria whipped up a mean Tempo Punch and drinks are on the house.

Gloria heals the fire and the hurt in me, and sings that pure core juice right into everyone else. Silver-beaded fringe dazzles out everywhere. This fuel isn't going to last forever, but we can work a helluva lot of big mojo while it does.

Love multiplies, she told us.

Our love is our power. Our love is boundless. Just for today, our mercy is, too. Today we fight and heal and protect. Tonight we dance it off. And if tomorrow or the days after—once the ships are gone from the sky and the shrapnel and fires cleared from the cities—if anyone tries to come toe-to-toe with the higher beings that we are, whipping out Executive Orders, or raids, or rocks? Honestly, I want them to try.

Let's see what happens.

"Go," Gloria voice echoes out.

The silver-beaded fringe knocks into Rex first, then sizzles through everyone else in our family. I can feel bones and bruises patched up with song. The end of his cigar flares. He's the first one to gasp as the juice fills him up. He sways from Stetson, strong enough now to stand on his own. Patrick slips off his headphones. Bette twirls Juana. Stetson wiggles his fingers and bullet-proof bubbles snap off him and float into the air.

I know they'll freeze jets in the sky and wrap them in bubbles and bring them back down to Earth before those dumb shits get us killed. I know they'll haul broken ship pieces off cars and wrestle people out of the flames, healing them up. I know they'll chase off soldiers that Reagan is probably sending all over the city.

I don't need mind-flashes to know what the others will do, because I know my family. And let this whole goddamned world see it was an army of queers who saved them.

How we protected them, even if they wouldn't do the same for us.

A real hoot, ain't it?

Rex steps forward, laughing, and then jumps up into the sky with a roar. Other Divine Deviants streak after him on fog clouds, and dance right into the fires and screams of the city. The Metronomes closest to us vibrate and echo. In the mind-flash that hits once I see their eyeless faces turning to each other, I know they're afraid of us. Good. They wave their hands and the blue-glass thorn-swarms retreat into their ships.

Metronomes buzz and zip all around us, ringing like church bells. *Sister!* They sing out. *Sister! We dance and celebrate your radiance as an Ascended One and a protector of this world. And what joy you bring to the Manifold.*

Gloria lets go of my hand and tips her head back, letting the blue light wash over her face.

And this is but the first note in the great Score that maps the universe, they continue, holding out their arms. *Already, we long to see how far you will go and what wonders you will sing to life. And how we may collaborate in Song and aid each other in this Universal Dance.*

There it is. I'd laugh if I wasn't trying to keep from flying apart.

Metronome Flynn bobbles closer to us.

I echo my co-Adjudicator's ruling of Clemency, he says. *The Disharmony has been healed, and under the guidance of an Ascended Being, this planet is well on its way through the Score.*

"And the madness that starmen have been bringing down from the moon for years 'n' years, that caused all..." I cough, looking around. Gloria has to steady me on my feet. I don't have the energy to ramble about raids and Studio Zones. They must catch my drift. "This."

Blue faces turn down to me.

"You'll get rid of it all?"

Gloria turns to me with smirking cat eyes. *Oh, honey.* Metronomes buzz and confer with each other.

The madness here is of your making.

Fair. Sure.

And then I drop to my knees now that the airlock doors of my chest are wide open. Now that all the hard armor around me softens and falls away. Funny. I don't know why I was fighting that softness this whole time. Now I can actually breathe.

* * *

Gloria won't leave with the Metronomes when they offer again. *The Lower Frequencies of the music here will be unkind to you*, they say. *We have seen this many times.* She's not bailing on the party, she tells them. They could load her and the others into one of the caravan ships and they'd be on the crystal dancefloor as mist in no time. And to that she answers a sweet, *I'm good.* She's got work to do.

She won't leave the planet, never mind my side, as I try to push her away and tell her I can get out of here myself. For Christ's sake, half of Hollywood is buried under caravan ships and people are rioting in the streets, so she has bigger fish to fry while that big wallop of Tempo is still working through her. She finally lets up once I stop shaking. And I only stop shaking because I soften, and breathe, and let the edges of my body turn just a little bit to mist, anyhow. I don't think she sees.

I don't have much longer.

"This 'protecting me' gig is startling to feel an awful lot like control," I quote herself at her.

With a glare that tells me *we're going to talk about this later*, she dusts herself off, pops into the air on a puff of fog, and twirls away.

We really got to get her a cape.

I joined the Metronomes because my world was dying, and they took pity on me since I could see Tempo a little and build up the strength of others. Flynn vouched for me. Gloria is Ascending to higher levels all on her own, and she'll bring others up with her. I can almost hear the music she'll make.

Maybe the Metronomes will be worthy of her by then.

The Metronome caravan ships are already bobbing up through the sky towards the waiting World-Ship. All except one. A single ship floats down from the blue, its disco-ball egg yolk shimmering in the sunlight. The hatch pops open and a blue glass body hovers out to me. Another empty body—my escape Instrument—waits inside. I'll have to come up with a name for my new ship. *Glory* sounds real nice.

When you're ready to come home, Flynn's hesitant arms tell me.

I'll miss his crystal islet eyes and the hard and hairy muscles of his body on this beautiful dancefloor. The waves of his hair that looked like frozen waves crashing on the black volcanic beach. Maybe some of the sad song he picked up here is fading away, already.

I'll tell him what Gloria told me, when I see him again. *That hurt doesn't belong to you. What if it was just a song you heard, and you let it move through you and then fly off to wherever else it needed to go?* I'll remind him as often as I need to. Dancing in circles and circles, again. And then we can start to heal.

Watching him dart into the air towards the World-Ship has got me aching all over again. Until I soften, and try to turn the pain into music, and let it flow away. Broken glass on the concrete looks like glitter.

This world isn't a spiked ball in a glass tank right now because a power greater than fear and hate saved us. I wish I could say it was love and joy. My time in the Guard and on

Adjudicator duty and roaming the outskirts of the Studio Zones is hollering otherwise. I know the Score. The only thing stronger than the thirst for power is the thirst for even more power.

I bet Flynn helped with some closing arguments. I can hear his trumpet voice, now. *This backwater planet colonized its moon and discovered nuclear energy all without Tempo. And now that they've discovered it, and now that an Ascended Being manifested here all on her own, I reckon they're going to work up wonders. Why settle for one engine core out of this place when we can come back in couple thousand years—what, one track in the setlist?—and see what else they cooked up?*

And then the Metronomes telling Gloria about *how we may collaborate in Song and aid each other in this universal dance.*

Maybe Kern was right about the whole deterrent thing. I'll give him that. His body is also confetti all over the city, so maybe he's not all that smart.

Anyway. I should get walking.

Goddamnit, I'm beat-up and don't even have my smokes on me. I trip over a charred curved bit of metal and almost flop onto my face. Maybe I should've gotten that lift from Gloria after all.

THIRTY-FIVE

PLAY THE NEXT TRACK

The sunset and the lights from the fire engines still streaking through the neighborhood are painting stained glass light across the windows of Founding Mothers, now that we pulled the sheets down and stopped hiding. Holy smokes. The lights catch on the disco ball hanging in the center of the front loft, and maybe this whole world-ender of a day was worth the sight of shards of light beaming down on all of us. Divine Deviants are napping in pillow piles all over the floor, and necking, and passing peanut butter sandwiches, joints, and magazines from my stash.

Gloria is working magic with some red sequined fabric at the sewing machine, by Patrick at his DJ pulpit in the corner. Stetson and Ricky round up drinks in the kitchen. Mostly we've just got Dr. Pepper left. Someone has to make a beer run, and it's not going to be me, you dig? Rex is parked at my side on the couch. He keeps draping the blanket around my shoulders when it falls. Good. I don't want him to see the burns all up my arms. Bette and Juana are the last of us Tempo jockeys to pound up the stairs. Ash streaks Juana's face and Bette shakes broken glass out of her pompadour. They're up next for a shower. The creaky water pipes of this place have been working overtime all day.

I spot trouble in Bette's eyes from my perch on the couch. She hollers about how those Metronome fucks left without waving their hands and rebuilding Circus Disco, so now we all gotta fly back over there and get to work. Rex sighs for her to cool it. They rescued kids from burning school buses, chased down jets, and stopped the president from launching a nuke at the World-Ship, so maybe, you know, they could get some R&R. Besides, the best part of the Circus Disco is under this half-burned roof.

Bette locks her arms over her chest, considering. "I suppose I can punch through a few more Commdef cars instead."

Juana arches an eyebrow. "Baby?"

"Freeing the pigs trapped inside, or something," Bette offers.

"Or something," Juana agrees with a wink, then grabs Bette by the hand, and off they go into the sheet maze.

Someone makes the mistake of asking Patrick to tune his radio to the news. Reagan is letting loose some barf about alien invaders scared off by the combined might of all the branches of America's military. And how God is watching over the greatest nation on Earth. And through Faith and Patriotism and Strength may we face this bold new chapter of history Together as True Americans.

Except, on my way over here I passed an electronics store on Santa Monica Boulevard. Every TV in the row in the window was playing footage from a traffic helicopter of a squad of leather daddies floating trapped civilians across the gap of the half-collapsed Sixth Street Bridge on their bikes. Funny how Reagan left that part out of his address to the Nation.

And I know we still got the Studio Zones, and the Moral Codes, and all that bullshit to deal with. But come on. I'm pausing the panic track in my head and just giving myself a break. We just chased the Metronomes out of here and saved the city from crumbling, so it's gonna take a little time to boot out the goons that were already here, too.

"I'd like to thank law enforcement—"

"Booooo," Ricky hisses. "Turn that shit off." Then he looks at Stetson, smiling all goofy. "No offence."

The tips of Stetson's ears turn pink. "Copacetic. I'm not going back to the force."

"Heard, daddy-o," Patrick says. He shimmies to the music only he can hear as he loads up a record. Soon enough, the sizzling high-hats and jangly fuck-me-good guitars of Donna Summer's 'Love To Love You Baby' wrap me up something warmer than the blanket. He always knows what tunes to play.

The Bureau of General Wellness has got another thing coming if they think they're going to keep Patrick from playing our tunes, or any of us from telling the story that the Reels won't. They'll sing it out through every radio from here to Founding Fathers if they have to.

"The bodega down the street was playing KPTLA when I dropped in for smokes," Lainey says from the pillow piles. She nudges Daisy in her lap. "The news cameras caught us kicking open that hydrant and floating water right up onto the fires in the Beatty Bungalows. The cat at the cash register gave me a whole carton of Virginia Slims for free."

Gloria quits hammering away at her sewing machine to look up like a proud mama. "Superdolls to the rescue."

She pulls a pin out of the fabric she's sewing, and holds

it at side of her mouth. She's loving sitting in her corner and pretending like whipping up a new dress is the most important thing on her mind. I caught her, a couple of times, turning away and smirking when other Divine Deviants hit me with sentences they can't finish. *Thank you for... We couldn't have... How did you...*

That glass of brandy by her sewing machine ain't even got a Lipton bag in it. She more than deserves it.

They've got it all wrong, as much as I try to tell them, and Gloria isn't helping with how she's church-giggling in the background. The others have this idea that I'm the one that saved them. That Flynn sacrificed himself to stop Kern and it didn't work, and I grabbed onto the battery of the engine core and gave all the Divine Deviants the boost they needed. When really it was all Gloria. She saved me from the anger in the engine core and in my own heart, when I would've flown up to the Metronome ship and punched a hole through it. Even if that meant them Silencing the whole world.

She said the others can save the hero worship until her first album comes out. She'll thank us all in the liner notes. Besides, Laterian is doing enough worshipping for all of us—hovering, and asking her for the third time if she wants more brandy. Or maybe she's hungry? He could just run to the deli and be back, ten minutes, tops, and—

"Baby." She rests a hand on his arm. "I'm golden. Don't you worry."

Carla bee-lines for me on the couch and I can see in her eyes she's already loading up a *Mitch, I never thought that...* Rex interrupts her speech to ask her to get me a Dr. Pepper, which sends her running and knocking over cans in the kitchen.

Gloria hides her next giggle fit under the buzz-saw of her sewing machine.

* * *

Lainey brought a Polaroid and camera flashes spark against the growing dark as the evening glides from blue to black. Once the pictures she takes are done developing—portraits of the dolls, and the butches, and the leather daddies, and the rest of us—she tapes each one to the wall above the altar. By the posters of our goddesses. Donna, and Dolly, and Tina, and Marilyn, and Mary, and all the rest. I rip out a couple of centerfolds from my magazines and gather enough strength to tape them to the brick, too. More of us are wandering in off the streets. Whoever needs a place to stay can find one here while their homes are still smoldering outside. On the top floor, though, it's just us family.

Once Rex gets his film developed, we'll have enough pictures to cover the walls of this whole place if we want.

I say *we* when I should say *they*. My rotation is almost done. I can feel it. I wander back to the couch, carried off on the buzzing air, and my ass sinks into the familiar dent in the worn cushions.

When my Pop brought me to his construction site, he showed me building plans and half-built houses. I was as empty as those house frames. Nights building brick walls, and painting always made me feel better. Now I know why.

Even if you don't end up living in the house, it just feels good to build something.

Pop tried to tell me that. I'll have to ask Gloria to pass word along to him. Tell him I did some good. Tell him the city was on fire and I stopped to save some kitten stuck in a tree, and. And...

Thinking too much about that *and* part makes my edges start to blur. Not yet.

* * *

I mean, of course we're going to party tonight. What kind of people do you think we are?

Hat-Trick pumps his Endless Orgasmatronic Remixxx extended cut of 'Love To Love You Baby' and Donna moans while the floors creak under dirty high-tops and scuffed high-heels. The others sing, and scream, and laugh. Hips sway. Arms reach out. Lips brush lips. I push off the couch, order up a rum punch from Ricky, and boogie by the bar for a bit. What the hell. One drink's not going to kill me.

Not all of us came back to Founding Mothers laughing today. The darkness of the disco hides bruises, burns, and tired eyes. Deviants showed up streaked with blood that wasn't their own, after they pulled bodies from the caravan ship wreckage, or pressed their hands over gunshot wounds from riots. The Metronomes blue-swirled bodies deflected bullets, but some of those bullets found another body to call home. They worked miracles—fucking beautiful miracles—until the Tempo boost in them drifted away into mist, and they had to save the rest of the rescue work for the fire trucks and the ambulances.

They know how to séance now, though, how to call up Tempo and let it build. They'll need it.

I'm gonna miss me and Gloria's game of either or. Either or, if someone tries to bury the Army of Lovers, what'll the Lovers decide to be? Seeds, or landmines? These cats can multitask. Why not be both.

My favorite blue flannel hides the engine core burns on my arms, but not my hands. Ricky doesn't care. He gives me my cup and when he holds my hand, it feels like a kiss. I linger by the bar and lean against the kitchen counter for the show. Rex follows because now I've got a shadow that trails cigar smoke and laughs like Santa Claus.

Gloria is taking a break from hosting duties tonight. Soon, Lainey takes to the mic and hops onstage to fill Gloria's heels. She's in full Conda Sending naughty librarian drag, giving us her best *and who do you think you are* smirk. Smart for her to let Gloria be everyone's big sister. A queen needs her own gimmick.

I don't quite get the storyline of the opening number, just that a queen in a red jumpsuit with a big curly black wig is high-kicking and splitting around backup dancers in camo underwear while lights flash. I can't tell if this is supposed to be a big fight scene or foreplay before they all get it on in the sheet maze. At the end of the song, she tears open her jumpsuit and shoots glitter confetti from her bra.

Rex leans in close to me, "I think that's supposed to be you?"

This close, I can feel his moustache on my neck. His gray eyes dance to mine and soon we're both laughing so hard we can't breathe. Until he looks away and I can see his eyes misting over, and—goddamn it. The way he's been watching me, of course he knows something's up.

I poke him in the chest. "I expected better from you."

He nods, crams his cigar back in his mouth, and hooks an arm around my shoulder. I borrow his warmth, closing my eyes, and letting it press me back down again from mist. His chest shakes, just once. Until he kisses the top of my head and wriggles off into the crowd.

Two dancing divas later, and it's almost time for me to head out. The other Tempo jockeys are off doing their things. Gloria swore she wasn't performing tonight and—whoopsie!—here she is, gliding to the stage in a new red sequined choir robe. Hat-Trick fiddles with some knobs and it's like he pours molten glass in the air with how the light moves. Light shards from the disco ball, and laser lights that we borrowed from other clubs, and lights in our eyes. Gloria coos wordlessly and I can feel her trying to pull. Trying to pour enough music into me so my edges will harden again, and keep me sealed in. Even though I know the softness is where my heart lives.

Soft, not weak. Soft enough to let in the light, now, and let what I don't need just blow away.

I wipe away the tears just in time for her to meet my eyes from the stage. I wag a finger while my eyes do the talking. *No ma'am. I know what you're trying to do. These cats don't have the juice in them for big mojo. They need to save their strength for what's coming.*

Her eyes sing back, *you can't blame me for trying.*

I blow her a kiss and think, yeah. Yeah. It's time to go. You should leave a party when you're still having fun. So that you remember just how good the night was.

* * *

I thought I had it in me to not fall apart until I was alone. I'm just outside the front door and on the sidewalk when Gloria's hand on my arm stops me in my tracks. I took the elevator down, and she must've beaten me by bolting down the stairs when she saw me leave, even in her heels. That girl works miracles. I can barely hear Hat-Trick's electric rain. That must be what hits my cheeks in this bubble of shadows, away from the others.

"You turning in early?" About a million colors dance over her brown eyes.

"Helluva song." That's all I can manage to say, trying to smile. I wish my lips didn't shake so much.

"Just a little something I tried to improvise."

We hold each other so tight that I don't know who's keeping who on their feet.

"Love you, Gloria." Some things you can't just say with your eyes. Worth letting her know, finally, even with how my voice quakes. "Thanks for showing me how."

"Love you, Mitchell Terrence."

"And when the next Vanguard rolls in here? What about..."

She just squeezes more air out of me. "You did your part. We got things from here on out."

Tonight the news stations that we're not watching must be playing footage of queers flying on fog clouds and lifting things with their minds, same as footage of the Metronome ships. Tomorrow will come the questions. Then the cops and the government suits with more questions. Then the soldiers, if they don't like the answers. And if they're stupid.

"I almost feel bad for anyone who tries to rush the disco when there's an Ascended Being on stage, spitting jive talk about cosmic love."

I lean back from her and she hip-checks me. "Shh." She winks. "That last part's our secret."

* * *

Maybe I got it wrong before when I thought heaven is a dancefloor. Maybe it's an empty street where you can look up and see the lights of the party, and hear the music. The night's almost over, but not yet. Not yet. All your friends are dancing and singing along to the track and they have one last chance for love. You, meanwhile, can finally kick off your sneakers and rest easy.

My new hotrod is waiting for me by the rubble of Circus Disco, where Flynn left it. I don't know how I'm going to stop the Metronomes just yet, just that Last Mitch Effort will. I'll empty all the dead worlds from their gas tanks and get them to stop their big Tempo harvest across the universe, or die trying. Heaven's not worth it if the door fee is dragging someone else down into hell.

I hope Flynn will help, once I get back to him. I can hear the Pensacola in his voice. *I reckon we might have to make up a thing or two about our time in the service.*

Up above, whoever is in the catwalk in the sky is pointing the spotlight of the moon right on me. Already, I can feel myself drifting. Like I could fly apart and wrap the whole moon in a gauze of mist that everyone can see from the windows of Founding Mothers.

We got things from here on out.

I really do love how disco tracks seem to never end, they just fade away, or into the next song in the set list. Feels right.

Moonlight slides through my skin. The knot in my chest unravels and opens. Softens and spreads. I'm not leaving the dancefloor so much as circling around, breathing in and bopping my head, getting ready for one more lap.

ACKNOWLEDGEMENTS

Thanks to many, especially the Massachusetts Cultural Council for a grant that in no small way helped me take the time to finish the novel. I'm so proud to live in a city and a state that supports artists and culture when arts funding is being cut all over America.

COVID was, among many scary and sad things, a weird time warp. Maybe it was wanting to escape the present, but I started researching gay culture in the 1970s, first for editorial work. I became kind of obsessed with the time—watching movies, reading men's magazines, talking to people who lived through those years and saw obvious parallels between COVID and the early days of the HIV/AIDS crisis. I'm usually drawn to writing about the future, so I was surprised that I couldn't quite shake this feeling about wanting to set something in the past.

Then, Boston ended its COVID State of Emergency on June 15, 2021, which just happened to be Pride weekend. After over a year of lockdown, going to the gay bar down the road and hugging friends and just being able to laugh and dance after everything we'd all been through ignited the first sparks of what would become *The Disco at the End of the World.* I've been back to that bar and others a lot since then, both to celebrate and to shake off that *I just want to be alone in a dark room* feeling that hits when something awful is going on. Because queer spaces are little pocket dimensions of joy where we can find strength in being together. So, thank you to the people who keep these spaces alive.

Thank you to Frederick Woodruff, John Calendo, Sam Staggs, Tim Wilbur, and Mark Krone and the folks at the community-driven nonprofit Queer History Boston for the 1970s conversations. Enormous thanks to Patrick Batt, accidental activist and historian, who runs the time capsule of a store named AutoErotica in San Francisco. I scheduled a 2024 book tour stop in San Francisco just to talk to him. Those life-changing conversations turned into a profile on him and his work for *Esquire.*

Thanks to the artists for being touchpoints. Thanks to musician and performer Todd Alsup for his one-man show, *Donna, Disco & Us,* about the role of disco music in queer liberation and Donna Summer's sometimes complicated relationship with the queer community. Thanks of course to Donna Summer, Giorgio Moroder, and Pete Bellotte for giving the world "I Feel Love" and changing music forever. Thanks to Bowie, Cass Elliot, and Sylvester. I can't thank musician and DJ Patrick Cowley enough for his riotous mix of "I Feel Love" that transports me to deep space with every listen and inspired a complete overhaul of this novel. The character of Patrick/DJ Hat-Trick is named in his honor. Whenever the enormity of what the world lost due to the HIV/AIDS crisis feels like a big black hole, I put on his tracks and dance, thankful to feel more alive through his music. Thanks to Dark Entries for publishing his journal, *Mechanical Fantasy Box*, and for keeping his music alive.

Endless thanks to my amazing agent Naomi Davis for encouraging me to move forward with this concept when doubt hit. Huge, huge thanks to my wonderful editor at Titan Books, George Sandison, for letting me go on this ride. And for patience and guidance when the novel had to change in 2025 because the world changed. Who encouraged me to go big, weird, and lean hard into the "alternate" in "alternate history," and whose edits turned this into the book I hoped it would be. Thanks to Titan folks: Julia Lloyd for the absolutely beautiful cover, Richard Mason for typesetting and design, publicity pros Kabriya Coghlan and Katharine Carroll, editorial assistant Rachel Vincent, copyeditor Kevin Eddy, and proofreader Saxon Bullock.

Thanks to my friends for the laughter. Thanks to my family for the constant support. Thanks to Ruby for the reminders to move and play. Thanks to Eamonn for the love and adventures. And especially for dancing and singing with me every time Donna Summer's "Last Dance" closes a night out.

And thank you for reading.

ABOUT THE AUTHOR

Nathan Tavares is a writer from Boston, Massachusetts (USA) and the author of *A Fractured Infinity* and *Welcome to Forever.* He grew up in the Portuguese-American community of southeastern Massachusetts and developed a love for fantastical stories at an early age, from superheroes to mythology. His editorial work celebrates queer culture and historically excluded communities, with pieces appearing in *Esquire*, *GQ*, *The Boston Globe* and elsewhere.